Skeleton Women

Skeleton Women

Mingmei Yip

KENSINGTON BOOKS
www.kensingtonbooks.com

KENSINGTON BOOKS are published by

Kensington Publishing Corp.
119 West 40th Street
New York, NY 10018

All Kensington titles, imprints, and distributed lines are available at special quantity discounts for bulk purchases for sales promotion, premiums, fund-raising, educational, or institutional use.

Special book excerpts or customized printings can also be created to fit specific needs. For details, write or phone the office of the Kensington Special Sales Manager: Attn. Special Sales Department. Kensington Publishing Corp., 119 West 40th Street, New York, NY 10018. Phone: 1-800-221-2647.

Kensington and the K logo Reg. U.S. Pat. & TM Off.

ISBN-13: 978-0-7582-7353-6
ISBN-10: 0-7582-7353-3

First Kensington Trade Paperback Printing: June 2012

10 9 8 7 6 5 4 3 2 1

Printed in the United States of America

To Geoffrey, who makes the whole world beautiful

ACKNOWLEDGMENTS

I would like to thank my husband, Geoffrey Redmond, who, like a magician, turns every experience into a pleasure. Without Geoffrey's encouragement, I never would have enjoyed the colorful, creative life of a writer, a profession I aspired to since I was seven.

Besides being a caring, compassionate, and extremely knowledgeable endocrinologist, Geoffrey is also an excellent writer who has penned six books, the most recent being a medical text for laypeople, *It's Your Hormones,* and one on Asian religion and philosophy, *Science and Asian Spiritual Tradition.*

Before and since I became a published author, I benefited by attending numerous writers' conferences. I would like to especially thank Lewis Frumkes for the annual conference at Hunter College, where I shared experiences with enthusiastic readers and writers. Through RT Book Review and RWA I meet wonderful writers, readers, and dedicated staff who are always helpful and make me feel at home.

I would also like to thank: my agent Susan Crawford, at Crawford Literary Agency. Professor Jiayan Mi, who invited me to the College of New Jersey for a lecture on my novel *Song of the Silk Road,* and Ellen Scordato and her husband, Mark Rifkin, who have greatly aided my writing career.

Special thanks to some of the writers who have helped me along my writer's journey: Kitty Griffin, Kate Douglas, Mary Jo Putney, Shobhan Bantwal, Marilyn Brant, Lisa Dale.

And, of course, thanks to those at Kensington Books who gave me tremendous help: my wonderful editor, Audrey LaFehr, and her associate, Martin Biro, publicists Karen Auerbach and Vida Engstrand, and Kristine Mills-Noble, who designed beautiful covers for all my books.

I would also like to thank my friends Teryle Ciacica, who always warms my heart with her cheerful voice and smile, and Eugenia Oi Yan Yau and her husband, Jose Santos, who are always ready to lend a helping hand.

Never give up working to defeat your enemy.
Master his fate. Exploit his unpreparedness
and attack him when he is unaware.

—*Art of War,* Sunzi (ca. 544–496 BC)

Stir the water to catch the fish—benefit by creating chaos

—*Thirty-Six Stratagems,* collection of popular ancient
Chinese proverbs on outwitting your enemies. First
mentioned in Southern Qi dynasties (847–537 AD)

So long as my body is still here, so will be my love for you.

—Li Shangyin (ca 813–858 AD), Tang dynasty poet

PART ONE

PART ONE

Prologue

It all happened because I was considered perfect material to be a spy—beautiful, smart, and, most important, an orphan.

I am well aware of what people call me behind my back: *Skeleton Woman!*

Actually, this does not bother me a bit. Let others feel spite, jealousy, hatred for me. At times I feel a secretive, ticklish glee.

I am a woman who can turn men into skeletons under my touch, though it is as light as a petal and as tender as silk.

My name is Camilla. At nineteen, I'd already become the lead singer at Shanghai's most popular and elegant Bright Moon Nightclub. It was through powerful connections that I got this position at my young age, with the bonus of being the object of desire of many men and the jealousy and hatred of countless women. And then there were Shadow and Rainbow Chang.

They were the *other* skeleton women.

But unlike me, Rainbow and Shadow were not nightclub singers. Rainbow, Shanghai's most popular gossip columnist, made her fortune by digging up secrets and dirt for the *Leisure News*. Though she had a woman's name, she exuded the charm of both sexes as she rode the waves of in-between. Short haircut, silk tie, and outrageously expensive and impeccably tailored suits contrasted with white-powdered face, rouged cheeks, pink lips, silvery-pink eye shadow, and long, lush, artificial lashes. Rainbow neither dressed like a woman nor looked like a man. Exposing everyone else's secrets in her column, for herself she chose camouflage, in sex as well as in life. But why? It was yet to be found out.

If Rainbow Chang presented herself as mysterious, then Shadow was absolutely unfathomable. Everything about her was staged like a magician's stunning feats—jumping into thin air; escaping from locked chains under water; cutting a volunteer into multiple pieces, then restoring her in seconds. Carried out in a skimpy dress, enhanced by snake-slick movements, with an expressionless, stunningly beautiful face. Who was she? I was dying to find out.

We used artists' names; no one knew our real ones. With our own agendas, we were the three most pungent ingredients in this boiling cauldron called Shanghai. Men went crazy for a taste of us, while women sought our elusive recipe.

People admired or hated me as the ultimate femme fatale. But I myself had no idea who I was. I was a nobody, literally. An orphan, I was adopted by a man and his gang for their own purposes. Later I learned that the man was Big Brother Wang, his gang, the Red Demons. Under their constant watching and fussing over me and their strict discipline, by fourteen I'd grown up to be a watermelon-seed-faced, full-bosomed, slim-waisted, long-legged beauty, possessing everything desired by men and envied by women.

Of course I had not been raised and disciplined just to be a refined, well-mannered lady to be married off to the son of a rich family. Instead I was groomed to lure Master Lung, head of the Flying Dragons gang, to his doom. I had quickly figured out that I'd been given a roof over my head, fancy clothes to wear, and gourmet food to consume for a reason.

I was raised and trained to be a spy.

I was to be the Red Demons' secret weapon in a meticulous plan to topple its bitterest rival, the Flying Dragons. For nineteen-thirties Shanghai was the battleground for relentless wars among the triads, wars in which I was to be merely a pawn.

And what a life that was.

Having schemed for most of my nineteen years in this dusty world, I'd already turned a few men and women into skeletons dangling in hell—literally or otherwise. I didn't feel any guilt. This was the only job, the only life, I knew.

This was how they had trained me—to have no attachment, no feelings, no conscience. I was the woman who would, when needed, reduce any man or woman to a skeleton at the blink of my mascaraed eye.

Until the day I met Master Lung's son, Jinying, and Lung's bodyguard, Gao. But that was not part of the Red Demons' plan for me. . . .

The Naked Girl Jumping
Toward Eternity

Against the sapphire-blue night sky, a young woman was pacing along a ledge atop the Shanghai Customs House tower like a circus girl treading a tightrope.

Except she was stark naked.

The Shanghainese say that nothing will surprise them, that they've seen it all. But now they were surprised. No one watching had ever seen anything like this.

Not even my new lover, Master Lung, head of the most powerful black society in Shanghai, the Flying Dragons, nor his slew of bodyguards scattered among the crowd, alert for danger and shoving anyone who seemed about to get too close to their boss.

Lung's and my eyes had stopped staring licentiously into each other's and were directed skyward—to the clock tower of the Customs House with its fake European style, far above the Bund and the Huangpu River.

The crowd held its collective breath. Their probing, lascivious eyes were glued to the muscular, round-bosomed, naked body above, expecting at any moment that she would jump to her death. I imagined the onlookers' agitated thoughts:

Is she really going to jump?
Why doesn't she want to live?

Jump! I want splashing blood, crashing flesh, crackling bones!
What a pity, a beautiful girl soon to turn into a puddle of vomit.

Tonight the air was balmy, but the naked girl playing the tug-of-war with death hundreds of feet above chilled us all, both those appalled by someone about to plunge to her death and those perverts who secretly thirsted for the morbid sights of splattered blood and scattered human pieces. I bit my lip, my hand tightly clutching Master Lung's arm while my heart pounded like a tribal drum trying to scare away demons.

Not that a smashed face and broken limbs would have bothered me much. For I had been trained since my teens to wipe away all human emotions. I had been molded for one purpose and one purpose only: to be a spy. Though, ironically, I earned my living singing sentimental songs in a nightclub.

As I continued to watch, the two hands of the clock merged into a single one pointing north, setting off the imitation Westminster Chimes to suddenly flood us with an eerily cheerful melody. But then, in the midst of the clear sky, thunder cracked, and lightning flashed. . . .

And the naked figure jumped!

The onlookers gasped collectively, their expressions ranging from horror, to sorrow, to unabashed thrill. . . .

All heads dropped down to gape, some of the women through cracks between their many-ringed, red-nailed fingers. A pause, then another shock. There was no body. Only a pair of red high heels in the middle of a pool of blood!

"What happened?! Where is she?!" A collective question burst into the night air.

A group of policemen arrived to inspect the scene, accompanied by a few reporters snapping pictures and asking dazed onlookers questions no one could answer.

Nothing was happening now, except for an excited buzz from the crowd. Master Lung gave my elbow a tug. "Let's go, Camilla."

"You don't want to find out where she's gone?"

"She's probably dead."

"Then where's the body?"

"Maybe you'll find out in tomorrow's *Leisure News*. Their gossip columnist, Rainbow Chang, knows everything." He shrugged. "Anyway, I've seen it all."

Of course. Master Lung had seen it all. He headed *the* most powerful black society in Shanghai. Not only had he seen it all, he'd also performed it all: shooting, stabbing, strangling, poisoning, decapitating, and other acts I'd rather not imagine. And that was only ways to kill. Before the final moment there were often tortures: beating, electric shocks, finger-crushing, eye-gouging, flesh-slicing, tiger-feeding, stuffing inside a snake-filled cage, nailing inside a coffin in a ghost-infested cemetery. . . .

As the onlookers began to disperse, a young couple ogled us, probably recognizing me as the famous singer and Lung as the famous gangster head. Immediately one of Lung's bodyguards approached them and lifted his jacket to show his gun. The two ran off as if they'd been accosted by the ghost of the naked girl who'd just jumped. Just then Master Lung's driver pulled up. We climbed into the huge black car and went back to his mansion on Junfu Lane.

Soon I was sipping his wine next to him on the sofa, the question still swirling in my mind: Who was this beautiful but mysterious jump-and-disappear girl? My spy's training to dig out secrets just wouldn't leave me alone.

Lung cast me a stern look. "Camilla, what's going on inside your head now?"

I stared at the scar that divided his right eyebrow into two lizardlike halves. "Master Lung, the girl who jumped—what happened?"

"You're still thinking of her?" He smirked. "Why are you so curious?" Lung stuck his fat cigar inside his thin mouth and puffed, making a heavy, asthmatic sound.

"Master Lung, you're not?"

He studied me with his protruding eyes set into his monkey face. "I have much more serious matters on my mind, not trivialities like that."

Those "serious matters" were what I, the spy from his rival gang, the Red Demons, was trying to find out.

But I asked, "A girl jumping off a tower is trivial to you?"

"Yes!" He took a big gulp of his expensive whiskey, then slammed the glass down with an intimidating thud. "Unless that girl is you, my little pretty. So, will you stop your silly thinking and come to bed now?"

Early the next morning, I left Master Lung's house and snatched up a copy of *Leisure News* from a street urchin. Standing on the sidewalk, I impatiently flipped through the pages until I saw the big headline:

Naked Girl Jumping to Her Disappearance

Last night at the Customs House on the Bund, the crowd was startled to see a young, naked woman pace on the ledge of the clock tower and then jump. But, strangely, no body was found, only splattered blood and a pair of red high heels. The police are investigating this mysterious, inexplicable incident.

Some say this was an attempted kidnapping but that the young woman escaped. No one can explain where she went. Others say she killed herself—but no body.

But now more and more are saying that the girl was, in fact, a ghost. They say that before the Customs House was built, that same spot was a cemetery where the bodies of women raped and murdered were dumped by black-society members.

The police claim they are working hard to solve this case to appease people's fear of a ghost's vengeance.

Meanwhile, girls from my Pink Skeleton Empire and I have our own sources.

More to follow. . . .
Rainbow Chang

After I finished the article, I almost burst out laughing. It was certainly strange. But a ghost?

The naked girl was definitely not a spirit but a spirited human.

That was worse than if she'd been a ghost, because now there was a woman who could outdo me in getting headlines from Rainbow Chang. I was used to being the center of attention as the most celebrated singer in Shanghai's most famous Bright Moon Nightclub. Yet none of my patrons or customers knew anything about me besides my singing, my body, and my name, Camilla, which was fake, anyway. For since my early teens, I'd been trained to be in the public eye but to keep my real intentions secret.

Now my place in society was under challenge. Someone had stepped into my well-guarded territory. For I didn't buy that Naked Girl was dead. She was somewhere, and I had to find out where and how she'd pulled off her stunt. Even though I had no idea who this girl was, I knew she was my enemy.

Thus thinking in the chilly air, I knew it was time to hurry back to Lung's house to warm his bed.

❧ 2 ❧

Bright Moon Nightclub

Four times a week at six in the evening, a limo would take me to the Bright Moon Nightclub. This was Shanghai's most fashionable—and expensive—entertainment establishment. It was located in the International Concession between Yuyuan Road—the Fool's Garden—and Fanhuangdu Road—the Emperor's Crossing. These roads were fittingly named, because, although there were no more emperors, there were still plenty of fools.

The nightclub had a gaudily lit circular façade topped with a torchlike, cylindrical tower. If you were allowed in, you would see a huge hall with many tables surrounding a polished dance floor. Above was a mezzanine from which the VIPs could watch those equally rich but less important. On its all-glass dance floor, powerful men became addicted to pirouetting with their seductive, hired partners in rhythm to waltzes, fox-trots, rumbas, sambas, tangos, even marches played by the impeccable Filipino band. Under the chandeliers, diamonds and pearls glittered as young bodies swayed beside their tuxedoed partners, fueling the clients' urge to splurge yet more on an evening's decadence.

But Bright Moon was not always a paradise; in seconds it could descend into hell. Shots were often heard, and stabbings might spray blood onto an expensive gown. Even the private rooms and restrooms were not safe havens from scores being settled. Targets of assassination could be almost anyone, from celebrities to politicians, black-society members, even suspected *hanjian*, traitors who spied for the Japanese.

The most talked-about assassination was of a gangster head a few years back. Late one evening as he was gleefully swirling, lifting, and dipping his girl on the dance floor, four men approached. Sensing trouble, he shoved his girl hard against them and tried to run. Their long knives were quickly stained with the freshly minced flesh of the poor girl as they flung her back at him.

But he was a gangster head, after all, not a sniveling coward. So he pulled out his gun, shot down two of his assailants, then collapsed only after both of his arms had been chopped off. Under the astonished scrutiny of the other customers, he bled quickly and heroically to death. His lifeless body had found its final rest on his favorite glass floor, this time flooded not with his rivals' but with his own precious blood.

People saw only the glamour in my job, but few thought of how the money I made had been recycled in blood. Anyway, only the rich and powerful in Shanghai could afford to come to Bright Moon to be entertained—or murdered.

I was proud to say that, together with seeing and being seen, I was the nightclub's biggest attraction, but that had not happened overnight. Though only nineteen, I'd already come a long way.

I lost my parents at four and had been sent to the Compassionate Grace Orphanage. Unfortunately I didn't have much memory of my parents except for a few blurry images of their faces. Worse, I had no siblings, relatives, or friends I could ask about them.

At the orphanage, outside volunteers would come to teach the children to sing and dance so they could perform on holidays like the Mid-Autumn Festival, Dragon Boat Races, and Chinese New Year. Even before I became the most popular songstress in Shanghai, I'd already had to learn to charm audiences.

However, these free lessons were not given out of compassion but to discover beauty and talent so that the gifted children could be sold to work as cheap labor at nightclubs, dance halls, and, of course, prostitution houses. While hard work—most of the time forced—was abundant inside the orphanage, talent was unusual and beauty, rare. Since visitors seemed to find me attractive, I always wondered why had I not been adopted much earlier. I'd heard from the girls who came back to visit that it was a better life than inside the orphanage. Many times I would watch with bitterness as other girls—less pretty and talented than I—were led away to waiting rickshaws and cars.

Then Mr. Ho, owner of the Bright Moon Nightclub, began his visits to the orphanage, bringing the children toys, candies, food, and clothes. When I was fourteen, Ho decided to rescue me from this institution notorious for cruelty and neglect. He immediately put me to work with the other singing and dancing girls at the nightclub. Though living and training together, we were not allowed to be friends, nor even talk to one another too much. If we did so, we'd be sent to a closet to reflect on our misbehavior on an empty stomach.

The other girls were either orphans like me or had parents so poor that they were forced to sell their daughters to the nightclub, so that they would have a roof over their heads and soup to warm their stomachs.

But sometimes fate was in a good mood, and a girl would become famous and, like a hurricane, lift her whole family out of poverty. The rest of us, who were not famous, lived together in one big room and were not paid.

My sense of freedom from escaping the orphanage hadn't lasted long. One day Ho took me aside and informed me that my real boss was not he but Big Brother Wang, head of the Red Demons Gang. He introduced me to Wang, who told me he was an old friend of my parents. They had been killed in a car accident, and he and his underling Ho had been trying to find me for years. Smiling, he told me that in rescuing me from the orphanage he had fulfilled his duty to his deceased best friend. But next, his smile gone, he told me that finding me had been expensive and how I had to repay him. I was to continue being a singer, but now it was a cover for my real job—to spy on Master Lung of the Flying Dragons.

Before I even had time to think or protest, my training with Big

Brother Wang had begun. I realized once again that beggars cannot be choosers, and that to continue to keep a roof over my head, rice soup in my stomach, and, most important, my head on my shoulders, I had to do what I was told.

Much of my training was concerned with perfecting my ability to charm men. I was taught ballroom dancing, which was now all the rage in Shanghai. Dancing with a patron, I would put my arms around his neck and exhale my fragranced breath onto his face. And I would press my equally fragranced body against him and feel the heat shooting out from his groin. He might wrap his arms around my much-coveted twenty-one-inch waist, move his hand between my neck and bottom like an elevator, or lift me up toward heaven, then dip me back toward hell. I learned early on that I should cling only to the important ones, such as Master Lung, and steer clear of the insignificant losers. Did I enjoy doing this? I can only say that it kept me alive while I watched other people's lives.

I knew well that I was but a shadow of someone else's existence.

I took singing lessons from a fiftyish Russian woman, Madame Lewinsky. Mr. Ho picked her because she was a famous teacher who'd turned a few nobodies into somebodies. And she was too busy to be nosy. Also, as a foreigner, she was safe because too ignorant to perceive the complexities of Chinese society, especially the black ones.

Madame Lewinsky put a lot of effort and time into teaching me. But I heeded Big Brother Wang's warnings and so told her nothing about myself. She probably assumed that I came from a rich family or had a wealthy patron, since I could afford her exorbitant fees.

Lewinsky had come from Russia with her husband to escape the revolution. But he'd died in a freak construction accident before they had a chance to have children. So now she was all by herself in this dusty world. Perhaps because of her loneliness, she often tried to act like she was my mother, which, of course, she was not.

Her face was distinctively Russian, with high cheekbones and a strong jaw, but her figure was voluptuous, like that of a Greek goddess. When she opened her mouth to sing, it was like a lark spreading its wings to soar above the clouds.

Was I fond of her? No. But I did appreciate the way she taught.

She also taught me how to feel—something absolutely forbidden in my training to be a spy.

However, all the songs Lewinsky chose for me had sad overtones. She told me that my voice—high-pitched, tender, innocent—was perfect for this bittersweet sentiment. And, contrary to my training, sometimes I just couldn't help but feel the music tugging at my heart. Whether my emotions were genuine or pretended, the audience at Bright Moon was crazy about the "feelings" in my voice.

It was not exactly right to say that I had no feelings, although it had been my training to stifle them. However, as I was not supposed to have feelings for people, I'd secretly developed feelings for my singing. I wondered if my boss, Big Brother Wang, understood the irony that, if I was trained not to feel, how could I become a great singer? Maybe he didn't think that far, or maybe he thought this was just life's inevitable dilemma. Or maybe my vigorous training had enabled me to perform anything, like a magician, from putting great feelings into my singing to hurting people without a twinge of guilt.

For four years I worked as a singer at Bright Moon Nightclub while secretly being trained to be a spy. Then, the summer when I turned eighteen, I won the coveted title of Heavenly Songbird from the Recording Songstress Contest organized by the *Big Evening News,* a newspaper secretly sponsored by the Red Demons gang. Madame Lewinsky had thrown me a big celebration party and flooded me with gifts—candies, cake, clothes, small jewelry, sweet little somethings.

Privileges soon followed. I was assigned to sing solo and given my own apartment. I had more good luck in that Lung, though an extremely mistrustful person, never suspected my real standing. My background as an orphan was just too plain to arouse any doubt.

Then one night I was sitting inside my private dressing room, scrutinizing my illusory self in the big gilded mirror. Standing beside me was Old Aunt, whose job was to do my makeup and hair.

Old Aunt was now putting her finishing touches on my melon-seed-shaped face. "Miss Camilla, if you were not a performer, you would not need makeup. You must have heard the saying, 'I lament using makeup that only mars my natural beauty.'"

"I never thought about it one way or the other. I only do what I'm supposed to."

She nodded at me knowingly, then pinned a flower above my right ear to complete my Heavenly Songbird look. "Miss Camilla, you look perfect. Now go out to charm Shanghai."

"Thank you, Old Aunt."

I stood up and cast a last glance at the mirror. Tonight I was dressed in a turquoise body-hugging *cheongsam* with high slits up the sides. On the front were embroidered pale golden camellias, enhanced by matching elbow-length gloves and dangling gold earrings. During my training, I was constantly told, "People respect your clothes before they respect you." And, "Women need beautiful clothes like the Buddha needs golden robes." The message is obvious: If you want to be accepted into the high society, dress like a high-society lady. If you want respect, dress elegantly. If you want to lure a huge following, dress in gold.

But the main reason I dressed my best was to lure Master Lung to keep visiting my bed so I could fulfill my mission: learning all his secrets, then eliminating him.

I took a deep breath, smoothed my facial muscles, thrust out my chest, and pranced onto the stage in my shredded-golden-lotus steps. The sensuous silk rubbed against my thighs as the cool air caressed my alternately hidden and exposed legs.

As soon as the audience spotted me, thunderous cheers flooded the packed hall. I took my place at center stage, under a banner emblazoned with big gold characters against a crimson background: *Bright Moon Celebrates Heavenly Songbird Camilla's Performance.*

My eyes scanned the audience until they landed on a scrawny man in front with a crew-cut head and a monkey face—Master Lung. For the last few weeks, Lung had been coming here regularly to watch my performances, always accompanied by his underlings and a slew of bodyguards. Because of his famously infamous reputation, he and his entourage were constantly fussed over by nervous waiters and the fawning manager.

Lung alternated between chugging down his expensive wine and twiddling his fat cigar in his bony fingers as he stuck it between his thin lips. While his fingers and lips were engaged in these suicidal activities, his eyes molested me unrelentingly. To my satisfaction, I saw him rhythmically strike his fist against his thigh, showing how excited he was by me.

But something was different tonight, and at first I could not place what it was.

I decided to make this audience wait while I took time to study them. The usual crew: successful businessmen, influential politicians, high government officials, black-society members. Also poets, artists, writers, a few professors, all no doubt the indulged sons of rich families. And the women with them: older ones who were obviously wives, younger ones who were just as obviously concubines, mistresses, courtesans, or just prostitutes hired for the evening. But not everyone was what he or she seemed. A bomb-carrying revolutionary or two might be concealed in the crowd of revelers.

High-end nightclubs were miniatures of the greater Shanghai. I knew well that the expensive attire, polite speech, and elegant manners were but tools to hide the itch for blood and money. As if oblivious of the tension in the air, white-shirted and black-suited waiters busied themselves topping off wineglasses, warming teapots, proffering hot towels, extending trays laden with cigarettes, and depositing a variety of respect dishes—complimentary snacks.

Every evening I began with "Nighttime Shanghai," a syrupy tune favored by the rich and decadent. The small orchestra—consisting of a pianist, violinist, drummer, and trumpet, trombone and double bass players—watched me, ready to strike the first note.

I always held a prop—an embroidered handkerchief, a painted fan, or simply my long, red-nailed fingers imitating an orchid swaying in a gentle breeze. Tonight the prop was a golden fan adorned by a red camellia, a gift from Master Lung. Holding the fan to hide my lips, I meditated a bit more, then dropped the fan to breathe out my first note, trying to make it as tender as a baby's breath.

Nighttime Shanghai, nighttime Shanghai,
A city of sleepless nights,
Lights dazzling, cars hustling,
Crooning songs and flirtatious dances filling up the night. . . .

I half closed my eyes to let the tune, the dreamy air, and the audience's hushed attention wrap me like a silk cocoon. I didn't know what I was thinking, if anything. But I did feel, maybe a little nostalgic, even melancholy. About what, I had no notion.

I continued to croon as I swayed my waist in synchronicity with my fan, on which the painted flower seemed to be shyly nodding in approval.

They only see my smiling face
But will never guess my heart's pain.
Singing for my living,
Intoxicated not by wine but by this lush nightlife.
My years are spent in dissipation.
When someday I finally awaken,
I will still love Shanghai at night.

I could identify with the sentiments of the song. But had I been spending my life in debauchery? Did I still love Shanghai at night? Thinking, I let the last note end its decadent incarnation in the air.

The audience, as if awakened from a dormant past life, burst into thunderous applause.

"Wonderful!"

"What a heavenly voice!"

"Wah, melts my ear wax!"

Again, my eyes made my obligatory rounds, right, left, middle, back. But then they stopped at a new face among a group of richly attired, refined-looking young men. He looked shy, seemingly ill at ease, as if he had been raised in a different environment and was thrust into a nightclub for the first time. Since the people with whom I had grown up all lived by cunning and cruelty, innocence always surprised me.

I threw this youth a nonchalant glance, bowed deeply, then threw the fan in his direction before I sashayed backstage in my golden stiletto heels.

Ten minutes later, after the crowd had quieted down, I left my dressing room and headed straight to Lung's table under the audience's intense scrutiny. Because of my popularity, I was usually expected to make my rounds, stopping at different tables and pleasing the patrons by making sexy small talk. But for the past few weeks, I could sit only with Lung. Once the other men realized I was Lung's favorite and might be his concubine someday, they quietly backed away. Because Lung or his thugs would not hesitate to strangle anyone—not only men but even a crippled oldster, a pregnant woman, or a newborn baby.

Behind his back Lung was nicknamed "Half-Brow," because, it was said, years ago his right eyebrow had been slashed into two by a would-be assassin using a sharp razor. The assassin had probably meant to slash his carotid artery, but during the struggle Lung must have dipped his head to protect his neck, so his brow was slashed instead. While a non-Chinese might have borne this as a sign of bravery, for Lung it was a mark of shame, to the point that no one would risk asking him how he had gotten it.

For the Chinese, to "shave off the eyebrow" is to inflict the most extreme insult, even worse than calling his mother a dog-fucked whore or his father a shit-chomping tortoise head. Splitting a person's eyebrow is believed to cut off his vital energy, life breath, and good fortune.

Like all Chinese gangsters, Lung was terrified of bad luck, so after his eyebrow was split, he had become extremely superstitious. Now he would never take off his amulets, not even when he bathed. From his thick golden neck chain were suspended Guan Yin, the Goddess of Compassion; General Guan, both loyal protector and relentless killer; the ubiquitous money god; and a new addition—a soaring dragon, his zodiac animal carved from translucent jade. A gift from me for his recent fifty-fifth birthday.

In less than twenty years, Lung had risen from a spat-upon shoe-shine boy to being respected and feared by Shanghai's most powerful people, even the police chief. The gangster head had begun his ascent shining shoes for celebrities, wealthy business-men, powerful gangsters, influential politicians. His shoe-shining was rumored to be so painstaking and immaculate that with it he softened the hearts of some of his influential customers. He'd rub harder, longer, and use more cream than the others. He ran errands faster than anyone else and somehow knew whom to ingratiate himself with by not charging them for his services. If the right situation arose, he would chat briefly with these dignitaries but always remain respectful, never crossing boundaries.

Soon he was invited into the Flying Dragons. Though he was no more than a gofer, rumor had it that once he took a bullet for a powerful gang member. The gangster he saved was an important politician, and so Lung was catapulted to fame, fortune, and power. His generosity also greased his way to the top. Unlike many warlords, Lung was free in passing out red envelopes stuffed with lucky money. His beneficiaries were not only his underlings and his favorite women of the moment but also police and politicians. Whether to ease his conscience or simply to ease his way into Shanghai society, he held lavish banquets and donated millions to charities, especially if they were run by influential people. On his way up, he somehow managed to shed most of his shoe-shine boy speech and mannerisms. Though his speech was still not refined, his money and violent reputation more than compensated for that.

Of course, most of what I knew about Lung was based on rumor. He never told me anything about himself, and asking a too-personal question was possible suicide.

Looking at Lung as I approached his table, I was, as usual, re-minded of a monkey. Not only his face but also his limbs that seemed always to be moving like those a monkey leaping be-tween branches. During his shoe-shining days, he could steal al-most anything from anyone without them noticing. Usually he sold his booty, but if the victim might benefit him in some way, he would return the item, pretending that he had found it.

All the other gentlemen—or gangsters—stood up to greet me, except Master Lung and his right hand man, Mr. Zhu.

The boss stared at me with his big, protruding eyes, rumored to be the result of a near-strangling by a rival.

"Camilla, you smell really good. Your singing is also getting better. Do you drink special herb soup for your body and your throat?" Lung's own voice was hoarse from years of smoking, drinking, and screaming.

I smiled, sitting down in a chair automatically pushed under my bottom. Crossing my legs and feeling the squeeze between them, I said in my innocently sexy voice, "Master Lung, what else is so 'special' besides you?"

I had been trained to say whatever was beneficial to a situation. As the Chinese saying goes, "When you run into a human, speak the human language; when you run into a ghost, speak a ghost's."

He laughed, his belly making waves. "Ha-ha! My Camilla, your tongue is getting more glib, too."

Of course I never told him, or anyone, how hard I'd been working to improve my voice. I'd rather that they thought it was all natural talent. Nobody wants to hear about the painful years of tedious, bitter practice, only their pleasurable result.

What no one knew was that when my act finished, I would sleep for a while if I was allowed to evade Master Lung's clammy hands, then walk to the Bund and sing to the sun as it rose, then to its reflection on the Huangpu River. This way my voice would absorb the powerful *yang* energy from the rising sun and the *yin* from the softly flowing river. I hoped to expand my range up to heaven and down to earth, so that when it reached the highest register, instead of cracking it would be as soothing as the morning light. And when it reached the lowest register, it wouldn't disappear but would be as deep and fathomless as the sea.

I knew the truth of the Chinese sayings: "One minute onstage is worth ten years' cultivation offstage," and, "You plant a melon, you harvest a melon; you plant a bean, you harvest a bean." Success will not arrive at your doorstep if you just mope around the house instead of getting out and taking action.

But I doubted anyone in the audience tonight cared about the long, arduous hours I'd spent to perfect my four minutes of singing "Nighttime Shanghai." However, that innocent but intelligent-looking youth I'd noticed earlier at the adjacent table, maybe he could understand.

"Thank you, Master Lung." I smiled, taking a delicate sip of his whiskey as if swallowing all the bitterness that came with my practice. As I felt my tongue pricked by the rough-tasting liquid, in my peripheral vision I spied a pair of eyes fixed on me like a mistress's on her patron. Just then Lung signaled to the next table, and the shy, fresh-faced young man hurried over. His tall, slim frame was covered in a gray pin-striped suit set off by a silver tie with a pearl stickpin.

I wondered, what did this refined-looking young man have to do with the uncouth Lung?

Gao, Master Lung's most trusted bodyguard, stood up to pull a seat out next to Lung. "Young Master, please."

Lung smiled till his eyes became two slits. "Camilla, meet my son, Jinying."

Could he really be Lung's son? Maybe he was adopted, or a *guoji,* a child given to a childless man by a male relative—a gift to maintain the family tree.

The young man and I shook hands. Wrapped around mine, his palm felt warm and cozy, like a cocoon. If I was a *yin* type of person—remote, cool, calculating, meticulous—then he definitely was a *yang* type—warm, straightforward, impetuous.

Now Lung smiled a proud, open-mouthed smile, revealing a few sparkling gold teeth. It was the first time I had detected anything like tenderness or kindness in the underworld boss. "My son just came back a few days ago from studying in the US."

I smiled. "That's very impressive. May I know what subject the boss's son studies?"

The young man smiled, blushing slightly. "Law—"

Lung interrupted. "At Ha Fuk."

The son corrected his father. "Father, it's Har*vard* University, not Ha Fuk."

The father laughed, watching his son admiringly, as if now he were his son's underling. "Yes, Harr . . . Fud."

"Father, you're embarrassing me!"

"So-ri, so-ri, son," Lung apologized in pidgin English. The most powerful gangster in Shanghai, who never hesitated to eliminate fools, now looked like a fool himself.

I suppressed a smile. Even this ruthless gangster chief had his soft spot. No one is invincible; it's just a matter of finding his weakness and waiting for the right time to attack it.

The young master ignored his father and turned to me. "Miss Camilla, you have the most beautiful and intriguing voice I've ever heard."

"Thank you," I said, not really meaning it. I'd been taught not to fall for flattery, because to be distracted would ruin my mission. I never forgot that even though people might praise me, it was unlikely they cared for me beyond my beauty, celebrity, and talent to entertain.

Oblivious of my bitterness, Lung again cast his son an appreciative look. "I want Jinying to help me in my business, but maybe he won't do a good job, because he only cares about music." He paused to pinch the sleeve of his son's suit. "See? I even have this suit made for him at Gray to suit his Hardfud- lawyer status."

Gray was the most expensive tailor in Shanghai, even more outrageous than the famous Paramount. I heard that each suit would cost nearly three times what it would at the expensive Paramount, which meant a tael of gold.

The young man, red-faced, turned away from his father and said to me, "Miss Camilla, my father told me about you and your legendary voice, and it's such a pleasure and honor to finally have the chance to hear you sing and then meet you tonight."

I was astonished that the son of the most feared gangster in China would act and talk in such an elegant and courteous way. But with such a powerful father, no one would imagine that he spoke that way from weakness. However, his father might have taken it that way, because he cast his son a disapproving look.

Abruptly Lung stood up and held out his hand to me. I let him lead me to the glass dance floor amid the scraping of patent leather shoes and stiletto heels. Lung put his arm around my waist, and we began gliding to the dreamy tune of the "Blue Danube" waltz.

Some of the men, when they waltzed near us with their partners, bowed their heads respectfully as they said, "Good Evening, Master Lung." The boss returned these greetings with a simple nod.

As we swirled in circles, my eyes glanced alternately at the orchestra and the audience. I peeked toward the young master Jinying, who was intensely watching us. I found myself tightening my arm around Lung. I'd only just met this young man; I wondered, why should I want to arouse jealousy in him?

Finally, when we had made enough dents on the dance floor, Lung and I returned to our seats. But Jinying's friends kept calling him back to his own table, so he quickly apologized to us and left. Then Mr. Zhu, Lung's right-hand man, picked up a newspaper and handed it to me, pointing to an article. It was the latest gossip column by Rainbow Chang.

A Naked Shadow

We can now reveal the identity of the girl who plunged to her disappearance three days ago. This stunning escapade was staged by a magician, Miss Shadow.

The incident was a prelude to promote her show opening on Thursday at the Ciro Nightclub, the upcoming rival of the older and more classy Bright Moon Nightclub. With this fanfare Miss Shadow has instantly become the talk of the town. So I believe that the Ciro Nightclub will steal many customers away from Bright Moon.

We were also told that the night she jumped, Miss Shadow was not really naked but wearing a flesh-toned tunic. The blood, of course, was fake, probably from a slaughtered chicken or pig or dog.

Like me, many of my readers must wonder what will happen now to Camilla, our beloved

Heavenly Songbird. Will she still dominate the Shanghai nightclub scene, or will she soon be pushed into the turbulent sea? Who will be our supreme entertainment queen? Who will be Shanghai's ultimate skeleton woman?

Well, we will soon find out.

One question to Miss Camilla: How will you feel when you finally meet your worthy rival?

More to follow. . . .
Rainbow Chang

I bit my lip, then quickly regained my focus and conjured up my most flirtatious smile. "Master Lung, have you read this?"

"Do you think I'd waste my time on gossip?"

Good. "Will you be here Thursday night?"

He cast me an amused look. "Depends. Why?"

My heart suddenly turned cold, like the ice floating in my drink. I couldn't bring myself to ask if he would go to Ciro to see the naked magician and her show.

Back in my apartment, I couldn't shut my eyes. Sipping wine, I could only think of this new rival, her inconceivable trick and her genius in getting attention. Why did she call herself Shadow; did she not have a real existence? Was she a ghost? The name was fake, of course, just like mine. Not that this Shadow, having already bewitched Shanghai, would need a response from me. Did she want to replace me as the number one nightclub attraction? Or maybe Rainbow Chang had guessed wrong. Maybe Shadow's target was not me but someone else. My heart rose in alarm. Could that someone else be . . . Master Lung?

Of course I was smart enough to realize that this Shadow had not jumped to her death and was not a ghost but a human rival.

So of course I was smart enough to deal with her. I remembered the lines from Sunzi's *Art of War*:

Know when to attack and when to wait.
The essence of warfare is not attack but strategy.
Know yourself, and know your enemy even better.

Yes! That's it. Know yourself, but know your enemy even better.
Knowing her would be the next step toward clearing this weed on
my path to completing my mission of eliminating Lung.

Thus resolved, I reached to turn on the radio. As if on cue, a
recording of my singing "Nighttime Shanghai" began to flood the
room.

They only see my smiling face
But never guess my heart's pain. . . .

I sighed, then downed the whole glass of wine.

3

Madame Lewinsky

As a spy, I had to study strategies about scheming. My favorite was the *Art of War* by the most famous military strategist, Sunzi, who lived twenty-five hundred years ago.

Everything I learned from this book can be summarized in one sentence:

Build your presence, and use your cunning.

Sunzi says that on a battlefield, there are only two realities: win or lose. So there is no room for virtue, unless being virtuous or being a gentleman is your strategy. To win, every position has to be thoroughly known, every plan meticulously studied, and every act carefully worked out. As there is no room for virtue, there is no such thing as "a glorious failure." On the battlefield, "honor" is just an empty comfort for losers.

Losers don't get sympathy; they get killed.

History is written by the victors. So no matter how heartless and dishonest you are, after it is written, if you win, you'll be remembered as a paragon of virtue and honor. The Chinese say, "Those who win become kings, those who fail, thieves." Steal a nail, you're a thief, steal a nation, a king.

You must show no weakness, no human feeling. Like King Liu Bang, who lived over two thousand years ago.

When they were battling for the kingdom, Xiang Yu kidnapped Liu's father and threatened to cook him alive. Expecting his rival to surrender, Xiang Yu was shocked when Liu Bang exclaimed, "No problem. After you've cooked my father, don't forget to save me a piece for dinner!"

In war, you have to be that ruthless.

Having studied the *Art of War,* the *Thirty-Six Stratagems,* and all other major works on strategy, I believed no one, trusted no one. So I'd already guessed that little naked Miss Shadow had not plunged to her death—and was probably not really naked, either. I didn't trust my own shadow, so why would I trust anyone else's?

To decide how to deal with Shadow, I needed to talk to my real boss, Big Brother Wang.

A bodyguard let me into Wang's spacious study filled with antiques, polished redwood furniture, and string-bound books. My boss sat at a massive desk, where smoke curled up from a cone of incense nestled on a celadon disk. He was reading a book cradled in his jade-ringed, long-nailed fingers. Above him on the wall was a calligraphic scroll:

Befriend all scholars under heaven; study all books written by sages.

So I worked for a scholar-gangster. Maybe that was why he had never been able to beat the cunning, streetwise Master Lung.

The door closed as quietly as a drop of water in a bucket. Staring at the bald spot on Wang's lowered head, I could see that he would not look up at me until he finished the page. I was curious to know what he was reading but kept my lips tight to prevent questions from popping out of my itchy mouth. Instead I glanced at his many books on the shelves.

Trained to be aware of everything in my surroundings, I wanted to know what these books were about and why, as a gangster, Wang liked to read. In addition to his more active pursuits of cheating, scheming, gambling, threatening, kidnapping, torturing, killing, and, of course, womanizing.

Despite this last proclivity, Big Brother Wang had never tried to seduce me or even force me to have sex with him. This was not because he respected me but because I was the queen on his chessboard. If the pieces on the chessboard of the gangster world shifted, I would have to shift in response, even at the risk of sacrificing my life. But not my happiness, because I'd never known that sort of emotion.

Wang put down his book. His eyes searched mine, gazing intensely above the gold-rimmed reading glasses perched on his square-jawed face.

I straightened myself, cleared my throat, and spoke in my most respectful tone. "Big Brother Wang . . ."

"This is my study time. Do you have a good reason for interrupting me?"

As I told him about Shadow, he closed the book. I saw that it was the *Romance of the Three Kingdoms,* the story of endless battles among feudal lords during the most chaotic time in Chinese history.

"So, do you think this Shadow will be an obstacle?" he asked.

"She will be if Lung stops coming to my show and goes to hers instead."

"You think that will happen?"

"It must not happen, Big Brother Wang."

"You can prevent it?"

"Yes, but I need to get to know her first."

"You think she's working for someone else?" he asked.

"You mean as a spy for another warlord?"

"Yes. But I can't see who at this point." He knit his brows in thought. "I can make her disappear."

Fearing he would give this order right away, I said urgently, "Big Brother Wang, if I may give my opinion . . ."

"I'm listening."

"She is a woman and hasn't made any trouble for us, so if you—"

Wang cut me off. "All right, I understand. You've got a point there. I have to protect my gang's reputation."

Even a gangster had his reputation and honor to protect! But the real reason I didn't want Shadow killed was not because I had any sympathy for her, but because of my own excruciating curiosity. I wanted to find out just how clever and scheming she was in comparison to me. Besides, I was dying to put more of my secret training and abilities to use.

So I said, "Big Brother Wang, I will handle her."

"Good." Wang spoke in his gravelly voice. "We spent a lot of time and money training you. So don't disappoint. You understand? You must not let Lung fall for this girl. Report to me soon."

Though my boss for the past four years, Wang remained an enigma to me. He talked only about what was necessary for business. I only knew what he did, not why he did it or how he felt when doing it—if he felt anything at all. If I tried to probe, my questions, like bullets hitting a metal wall, just bounced right back.

I thanked him, bowed, then started to walk to the door.

Wang spoke to my back, the temperature of his voice dropping. "Camilla, do not come here again. You may telephone me when absolutely necessary. You got it?"

I understood. Since Master Lung was getting serious about me, his men might be watching me closely. Though a little disappointed not to be able to visit this gangster with literary tastes, I was pretty sure he did not want to stop seeing me, either, for he often looked at me like a cat does a fish. However, I was just a woman, and what he wanted was something much bigger—to topple the invincible Lung and replace him as Shanghai's number one boss. To achieve this, my boss was more than willing to send me into the tiger's mouth.

Of course Big Brother Wang might have more personal plans for what to do with me after I'd eliminated Lung. But by then I'd be a different woman, not the innocent little girl he'd rescued from the orphanage. I would be the poisonous skeleton woman, the ultimate nemesis.

After I left Wang's place, I decided to go to my singing teacher, Madame Lewinsky, whose apartment was situated in a quiet spot inside the French Concession. I needed to relax after my meeting with the gangster. Wang's presence seemed to deplete the very air around him. Since I had no friends or relatives, Lewinsky was the only person I could go to. Moreover, she'd always pamper me with her delicious home-cooked soup and gooey, oven-baked cookies dipped in warm milk. Best, unlike my boss, she never scolded, only praised me.

When my teacher opened the door, a big smile bloomed on her heavily made-up face. Her distinctive perfume snaked its way into my nostrils, soothing my nerves.

"My darling Camilla, what a surprise! Come on in. I've been practicing on my own." Her big-boned figure was encased in a flowered dress topped with a black-tasseled shawl.

The neat, cozy apartment smelled of delicious food. Of all the houses and apartments I'd visited, I liked Lewinsky's the best. The sun filtering through the lace curtains boosted my energy and lifted my mood. I imagined that the velvety chocolate sofa was having a pleasant conversation with its matching floral pillows. Plants crawled leisurely down from the tall bookcases stuffed with books and music scores. Atop her grand piano were arrayed miniature busts of famous composers and knickknacks she'd collected over the years, all seeming to have interesting stories to tell. A vase was filled with fresh cut flowers. Were they from an admirer? I wondered.

Entering her apartment was like entering another world, softer and more human. Perhaps like being back in my mother's womb— if I had known who my mother was.

I sat on the sofa, my teacher studying me closely.

Then she told me, "You look too thin, Camilla. Let me get you something to eat and drink."

Madame Lewinsky then disappeared into the kitchen, only to reappear moments later with two steaming bowls atop a lacquered tray. Setting the tray down, she seated herself in a rocking chair across from me. "This is authentic Russian soup from my mother's recipe. Very nutritious."

After I commended the recipe with smacking lips and abandoned slurping, she asked, "Why this surprise visit? Are you okay, Camilla? You look worried."

Damn. I was not supposed to let people see my emotions. "Everything's fine, Madame Lewinsky. I'm just having some difficulty singing *Carmen* right." I hoped my lie sounded convincing.

Lewinsky took another big helping of her soup, then said, "Oh, don't worry about that. Just be patient, and you'll get there, talented as you are."

My main repertory was Chinese and Western pop songs, for these were what the nightclub-goers liked. However, once in a while I'd also sing an opera aria or art song in Italian or French to entertain the foreigners and impress the Chinese.

My teacher cast me an affectionate look. "Let's finish our soup; then we'll go through *Carmen*'s "Habanera"—how's that?"

So after I helped her put away the dishes, we walked to the piano. She sat down, her thick, round-tipped fingers immediately plunging into the keyboard. I closed my eyes to savor her powerful voice massaging my ears.

> Love is a gypsy's child,
> It has never, ever, recognized the law.
> If I love you, you'd best beware!
> The bird you hope to catch
> Will beat its wings and fly away. . . .
> Love stays away, making you wait and wait.
> Then, when least expected, there it is!

I might have burst out clapping and exclaiming how beautiful her singing was, but I never forgot my training to conceal any emotion.

Madame Lewinsky spoke. "Camilla, don't you find this music wonderful?"

I nodded, feeling a little confused.

Silence.

She smiled mischievously, her crimson-painted lips like two leaves curling in the spring breeze. "Perhaps I shouldn't ask you, but I want to know: Are you in love?"

"No." I always kept my answers short and simple. I feared if we engaged in a long conversation, I might tell this motherly woman more about myself than was safe.

She cast me a curious look. "Have you ever been?"

I shook my head.

"But that's not possible, a beautiful, talented girl like you! So many men admire you. What about all the rich customers at the nightclub and their rich sons? Or those successful young businessmen? The erudite young professors? Don't tell me none of them ever chases after you."

"I want to concentrate on my singing."

She took my hand and rubbed it lovingly. "Oh, my little Camilla, don't work *too* hard. It's time for you to fall in love. Trust me, it's a wonderful feeling."

Wonderful or not, I was not going to fall in love and ruin my mission—and possibly my life. Look at how Carmen had ended up! I wanted this beautiful Gypsy's freedom, her nonchalance, her power over men, but definitely not her pointless, tragic end. But as long as I was careful, I hoped I wouldn't end up like her. If I failed in my mission, it would not be carelessness but fate, like my bad karma of being an orphan. But not the foolishness of love, not for a trained spy like me!

My teacher's soothing voice awakened me from my pondering. "Maybe the next time I go to Bright Moon to hear you sing, I can pick out a suitable young man for you."

I didn't respond, silently discouraging her suggestion.

She was smart enough to stop insisting and change the conversation. "*Hai,* since my Sergi's death twenty years ago, I thought someday I might fall in love again, but the chances, as if they had wings, have flown away. And now I'm too old—"

"No, you're not."

"That's very kind of you to say, Camilla, but I know the ways of the world."

Then all of a sudden she began to sing the famous Xinjiang melody, "The Waltz of Youth."

> After the sun goes down, tomorrow it will climb
>   back up in the sky.
> Flowers wither, then bloom again next year.
> But the beautiful bird of youth flies away and disappears,
> The bird of my youth will never return. . . .

I closed my eyes to feel her voice's penetrating sadness. I thought about the two birds—the rebellious one of love that knows no law and the one of youth that flies away and never returns. I sighed silently as Lewinsky's last note, like the disappearing bird of youth, faded into the unforgiving air.

Her eyes looked as if they were dipped in sweet wine. "My Sergi, we were so young, so much in love, and so filled with hope and dreams for our future. Just as we thought that the world existed only for us, in a minute, he was gone." She wiped away a tear with her lacy white handkerchief. "All of a sudden the world decided to turn against me full force. Had I not learned to sing and won awards back in Russia, I'd be starving on the street and wouldn't be here talking to you, my dear."

I blurted out before I could stop myself, "Why do people fall in love?"

She laughed, her eyes glistening. "You're so naive, Camilla. Love only *is*—there's no reason. Of course I could tell you that Sergi was handsome and kind, ambitious and talented and very nice to me. But I didn't analyze all those qualities before I fell in love with him. I just did."

Now her eyes drifted like two dreams. "You know, when I used to perform, just before I started, I'd look for someone in the audience, pretending he or she was the only person in the hall, and then I'd just sing for that special one.

"So on that evening—I will always remember, it was on September twelve, nineteen twenty-five—even though the hall was packed, my eyes, with a will of their own, landed on this young man in the back row. I couldn't move them away. So for the entire hour I was singing, heart, body, and soul, just for him. From then on, like the telepathy between identical twins, we were deeply connected. Even now, sometimes I can still feel his presence."

I'd heard these sorts of sentiments before.

"But he died. . . ." she breathed.

"How?" I had heard the story many times, but I would not stop my teacher from reliving her tragic love once again.

"Sergi was a very talented, aspiring composer. However, unable to make a living by composing, he had to take up odd jobs to bring in money. The only work he could find was at a construction site. Then one day, a beam fell on his head. He literally dropped dead on the spot."

"I'm so sorry," I said, as a courtesy. Why should I feel anything for this man I didn't even know?

Some silence passed, then Lewinsky dabbed her eyes as she changed the topic. "Camilla, why don't you sing *Carmen,* and let me hear your beautiful voice?"

I nodded, and she struck a key on the piano. Before I began, I tasted that starting note as if I were sucking on my favorite chocolate truffle. To help me sing better, I sensed each note with its own color and personality. Middle C is yellow and virtuous, because it takes the imperial position—in the middle of the keyboard. The D next to middle C is orange and honest, for it has royalty as a neighbor. E is Chinese red and expansive. And the rest: F is blue, G is green, A is gold, and B is purple. I gave the sharps and flats variations, so F-sharp is turquoise, A-flat becomes a brownish gold, B-flat bluish purple.

I straightened my back, inhaled deeply, then blurted out the first note, singing in French at first, but then reincarnating Carmen as Chinese. I used all my skill to imitate my teacher's style and emotional nuances. But I especially liked, "Love is a Gypsy's child; it has never, ever, recognized the law." Because I had lived my whole life controlled by others, even when outside the law.

When I finished, Madame Lewinsky nodded appreciatively. "Very good. But, Camilla, sooner or later, you've got to develop your own style."

Lewinsky stood up and went to put a record on her gramophone. Besides her piano, this was her most treasured possession. Even in affluent Shanghai, few could afford this amazing machine from the West. She set the needle down on the record, and a beautiful voice singing "La Habanera" perfumed the room like fine old wine being poured. We half closed our eyes and let the music kidnap our minds for a few moments.

"It's Maria Gay. You feel her subtlety and sensitivity?"

I nodded.

"That's what I want you to focus on, my dear. Camilla, you're gifted with an innocent, sweet voice that is like a pacifier in this ruthless, chaotic world. Those people at Bright Moon, they're wicked and scheming, but deep down they crave purity."

I chuckled inside. Did she really believe I was innocent? If I ever had been, my training as a spy had long since ended it.

My teacher spoke again. "Maybe those politicians and business-men at your nightclub can't tell, but I can."

"Sorry. What can you tell?"

"Let me be blunt with you, Camilla. Your singing doesn't have real feelings, only the imitation of feelings."

I didn't respond.

"Don't worry, once you fall in love. . . ."

"But I won't."

My teacher cast me a curious glance. "What makes you so sure?"

Of course I knew why, but the "why" was not something to be shared.

Lewinsky winked, smiling. "Hmm . . . you're sure you're not in love already?"

"No way."

"I can tell your mind has been wandering."

I meant to ask how could she tell, but she was already speaking. "With my experiences of focusing on one person during my con-certs, I can spot any musician's wandering mind."

"Hmm . . . Madame Lewinsky, unfortunately I don't have your kind of sensitivity."

"Next time when you sing at Bright Moon, find someone to focus on."

"I will."

Just then the bell rang, and Lewinsky went to open the door to let in a student. It was time for me to leave. This was the first time I'd visited except to have a lesson.

Was there a genuine bond developing between us? I both hoped and feared that.

At the door, my teacher winked at me and hummed the tune from *Carmen,* her eyes twinkling with mischief. *"The bird you hope to catch will beat its wings and fly away. . . . Love stays away, making you wait and wait. Then, when least expected, there it is!"*

When finished, she reached to pat my cheek. "Beware, my little sweetie. Karma happens. So be prepared." She winked again, then closed the door with a very tender click, like the sigh on a lover's lips.

4

The Red Shoes

Visiting Lewinsky was an all-too-brief intermission from my tension-filled, murder-oriented existence. But I couldn't do it often, because being relaxed was dangerous. Tension is like spice on food; without some, the dish would be tasteless, if not inedible.

After having had the right dose of tranquility, now I needed to plan for my next move: to discover Shadow's intentions and prevent her from stealing Lung from me. And, if there was any chance that she was smarter and more talented than I, plot how to get rid of her.

After some hard thought, I decided to cancel my Thursday night performance and take the risk of inviting Master Lung to see Shadow's debut magic show with me. In the subtle Chinese art of calligraphy, this is called *pianfeng,* an unorthodox brush movement for the sake of a startling aesthetic effect. In military strategy it is called *bingxing xianzhe*—send the soldiers to advance into danger. An illogical move is applied to win an impossible battle.

So now I was using a *bingxing xianzhe* in asking Lung to Shadow's show. My real purpose was to prevent them from having any contact with each other without my knowing. In old China, this strategy had been adopted by many first wives. They would rather handpick the woman to be their husband's concubine than let him pick himself. That way they would have some control over the interloper who was to share their house and their husband's bed. The shrewd first wife would pick a concubine who, though younger and prettier, was respectful and submissive and, most important, a little stupid.

Know yourself as well as your enemy; then out of one hundred battles you will win one hundred. Sunzi's advice was as useful now as when he'd written it twenty-five hundred years ago.

Having Lung escort me to Shadow's show would let her know that the gangster head was my not-to-be-trespassed-upon property. Of course that didn't mean she wouldn't try to cross the line. But at least she'd get my message. Best would be if Lung had no interest in her big, muscular physique.

But I had learned never to rely on hope. Anyway, the first step is like a house's foundation; if it's not cemented right, the whole house will sooner or later collapse. Actually, each step is critical; as the sage Laozi said, "Things are more likely be spoiled at the end than at the beginning."

But as I contemplated this more, I felt as if I were hanging on a cliff above sharp rocks surrounded by starving tigers. Then I told myself, if it was easy, where was the thrill?

Shadow's debut show was held at the Ciro Nightclub, a competing establishment with Bright Moon. The manager greeted Master Lung and his entourage with a smile as gleeful as if his wife had just given birth to his first son, then led us to the table in the middle of the front row.

Lung, his right-hand man, Mr. Zhu, and I all sat down at a table already set with bottles of expensive wine and plates of snacks—watermelon seeds, dried plums, olives, sugared lotus root. As usual, Master Lung's head bodyguard, Gao, and his team took the neighboring table. Nightclub-goers threw us curious, envious stares. Among them I noticed a flamboyantly dressed, striking young man four tables from ours. Five or six tall, beautiful girls in matching pink dresses surrounded him like stars about a bright moon. The only strange thing about this figure, at least from the distance, was that he had makeup on.

When our eyes met, he smiled, then raised his wineglass and made a toast. I smiled back, then quickly averted his scrutiny as an uneasy feeling rose inside me that Lung might notice. Or even Gao, because the quiet but physically intimidating man was watching me intently. I feared, not that he had any inkling of my secret mission, but that he had a crush on me, which could be dangerous for us both. He might not survive trying to seduce his boss's woman.

Once in a while I admit I did flirt with him, though indirectly, by twirling my hair as if deep in thought, or wriggling slightly when he was watching. I sensed that he was the kind of man who'd risk death to protect a helpless, beautiful woman in danger.

Even though my present status was above his, I always treated the bodyguard with respect. It's smart to accumulate good karma by acknowledging, and even doing small favors for, those beneath you. You never know when you might need their help or when they might decide to mess up your life, no matter how small a cog they were in the big machine.

Although tonight Lung was physically present, I could tell his mind was somewhere else.

My patron took a long sip of his whiskey, then asked, "Camilla, how come you're so curious about this magician—what's her name—Shadow?" Then he turned to Zhu, scoffing. "Why would someone in their right mind name their girl Shadow? What did they call their other children, Ghost, Apparition, Phantom? And the parents, Specter and Silhouette? Eh?"

Lung laughed his full-toothed laugh with his thin lips stretching downward. The Chinese call this the capsized-boat expression. In physiognomy it is deemed an unlucky trait. But so far Lung's luck, like his bodyguards, was always there for him.

Except for Gao, who was always serious, everyone else burst into hilarious laughter. Not that the joke was that funny but because it had come from the mouth of the most relentless man in Shanghai.

"Maybe her other siblings are called Smoke and Mirror?" I

quipped, a risky move, in case Lung might think I was trying to outsmart him. However, judging from his past mistresses, he could be fascinated by a woman's brain, not just her breasts.

Now it was Lung's turn to laugh, followed by even more hilarious laughter from the group. Not because my joke was so funny but because I was the number one gangster's number one woman.

This was the satisfaction of being at the top. But as the great sage Laozi said, "When things reach their zenith, they have nowhere else to go but down." So there is always the dread of the possible downward journey or, especially the fate of many gangsters, assassination.

When the laughter subsided, Zhu leaned over to his boss. "This Shadow must be an illegitimate child or an orphan to have a name like that."

Was Zhu subtly deriding my orphan status?

Lung scoffed. "Maybe you're right. Ha-ha! But who cares about a shadow, right?" Then he said to me, "Camilla, this had better be a good show. I don't want to waste my time being bored. How come you wanted me here tonight?"

I smiled my heart-softening, man-hardening smile. "Master Lung, what a question. You want to embarrass me by having me declare my love for you in public?"

He squeezed my narrow waist with the same hand that had inexorably squeezed out many rivals' last breaths. "Besides your singing, your speech is also getting more clever. Whom did you learn this from?"

"You of course, Master Lung. Who else?"

"Ha-ha! Ha-ha! I like smart, beautiful women, just like you." He pulled my head to him and planted a kiss on my cheek.

I caught a jealous glance from Gao, followed by an ambiguous one from that young person four tables away.

Just then the orchestra struck up an animated tune, a signal that the show was about to begin. I'd already guessed that the first act on the program wouldn't be Shadow's. As the star, her act would come last.

The opening act was a songstress, mediocre in looks, talent, and dress. Following her was another mediocre singer, better dressed but with a screechy voice.

Master Lung, looking bored, raised his rough voice amid the loud music. "I really don't understand why Ciro Nightclub hired two homeless cats to *meow*."

I giggled. "Master Lung, you're so funny! Because these two mediocrities are only here to make us appreciate the following show."

He hit his fist on the table, causing a small earthquake. "You're damn right, Camilla. What do you eat to get so smart?"

"All the meals granted by you, Master Lung."

He laughed, and the earthquake shifted to his belly. "Good, Camilla! That's why you're my favorite!"

I could only hope that would last—until my mission was completed.

"Thank you, Master Lung." Though I feared his impatience if he were bored, I silently prayed that Shadow would not be my match in beauty or intelligence.

But Master Lung would be the one to judge. And unfortunately men's opinion about women is unpredictable and subject to change, like a child's in a toy store, or a woman wandering the aisles of the expensive department stores on Nanking Road.

Still smiling, Lung playfully pinched my hip. I pretended to fend off his ambush by hitting his arm flirtatiously with my hand.

He cast me a curious look. "Where's the painted fan I gave you?"

That was the fan I'd thrown toward his son the other night. To be courteous, I should have invited the young master tonight. But I hadn't because I didn't want him here to further complicate things or to be another distraction to my goal.

I responded. "Didn't you see that I threw it to the audience? I guess someone must have caught it."

"Next time, don't throw my fans away."

"Of course not, Master Lung."

As if on cue to save me from more chiding, a burst of loud drumming rolled out as multicolored lights crisscrossed the stage.

A quiet fell over the hall as people anticipated the long-awaited act. Soon a black-tuxedoed man entered from the right side of the stage.

"We want Shadow and her magic!" someone shouted.

I smiled inside. Any performance is a form of seduction. Playing hard to get is always a winning strategy.

With his white-gloved hand, the master of ceremonies tapped lightly on the microphone, then cleared his throat. "Ladies and gentlemen, welcome to Ciro Nightclub!"

A round of applause burst in the packed hall.

"Are you ready for our mysterious guest tonight?"

Another burst of applause as the audience shouted a collective, "Yes!"

"Are your eyeballs ready to be astounded?"

An even louder "Yes!"

"All right, so now be prepared for Miss Shadow's impossible show. If you saw her daring stunt last week at the Customs House, I can assure you that tonight's show will be even more astonishing." He paused for a moment.

"Okay, everybody, let's hear a loud welcome for the incredible Miss Shadow!"

The MC strode off the stage as another fusillade of drumming burst from the orchestra. All the lights dimmed in the hall except those onstage. An unworldly silence seemed to stretch into infinity. Then, to everyone's surprise, instead of the much anticipated appearance of Shadow herself, there was only a pair of red shoes floating in the air!

My heart sank. If she could think of this, she might actually be able to outshine me.

I cast Lung a secretive glance and found that his eyes were protruding more than usual. He must have found her intriguing, if not downright attractive.

More gasps and exclamations sprinkled the hall. Now we only saw one bare foot, toenails painted bright red, like drops of blood from a slaughtered chicken.

I could see that, like me, the magician knew how to create a presence. I wondered, was she also well-versed in Sunzi's *The Art of War* and the *Thirty-Six Stratagems?*

Then she materialized on stage, and immediately a collective gasp exploded in the hall. Just as at the Customs House, she had not a stitch on her entire body! The men laughed and cheered, and the women gasped.

My hear sank another notch.

Shadow had a voluptuous figure, her full breasts jiggling like tofu, with a firm, if generous, bottom atop muscular legs. Her face was rounder than mine, with a high forehead and two painted-on, crescent-moon-shaped eyebrows. Her hair was pulled back tightly like a ballerina's but slithered down her back. Sizing her up, I had to admit to myself that I could not compete with her athletic physique. But so far I had been able to rely on my narrow waist, long legs, slim, girlish figure, and innocent eyes. "Like a beautiful maiden walking out from an album of exquisite paintings"—that was how the entertainment newspapers in Shanghai described me.

A few seconds passed as the audience—at least those who sat close to the stage in the first three rows—realized that the magician was not naked but wearing a tight, flesh-colored tunic. Some men emitted a disappointed, "Huh!" and a few women, "Thank old heaven!"

Shadow began slow dance movements to the dreamy music from the orchestra as the red shoes floated teasingly in front of her. Then she paused, hands on hips.

She made a face, chiding the shoes, "Oh, you terrible little twins. Now come back to Mommy!"

The shoes shook but came no closer. Looking annoyed, she reached to snatch them, but they playfully bounced away.

"Come back, good girls, come back to Mommy. . . ." Shadow cooed as the shoes kept backing away like playful toddlers, advancing and retreating until Shadow suddenly slapped them down onto the floor.

Then a gasp of shock came from the audience as a pool of blood appeared around them—just as had happened in front of the Customs House. She shook her fist at the shoes, then put them on and exited the stage, leaving a trail of blood in the shape of a zigzagging snake.

There was an explosion of laughter and applause.

My heart was now groveling on the floor. Damn this Shadow who was trying to steal away my mystery, my show, my life!

When Shadow reappeared, she was wearing a traditional magician's outfit: black tuxedo, white gloves, and tall hat. She did some usual tricks, like pulling rabbits out of her hat, but with great flair. For her finale, a large glass bowl filled with black ink was wheeled onto the stage, and a scroll was hung up next to it. With a graceful movement, Shadow dipped a huge brush into the bowl, then splashed the Chinese character for *fish* onto the scroll. She took down the scroll, wrapped it around the bowl, then whisked it away, to reveal the bowl now filled with fish swimming in clear water.

Spectacular as this was, I knew she must have even more spectacular illusions yet to come.

She would be the talk of Shanghai, stealing the limelight from my show. I had to put a stop to this.

Get close to yourself; get closer to your enemy. If Lung was going to fall for her, it'd better be under my eyes.

I turned to the gangster head. "Master Lung, why don't we invite Miss Shadow to our table for a drink?"

Lung nodded, looking excited. "This Shadow is pretty good, isn't she?"

Fifteen minutes later, a stunning Shadow floated to our table, trailed by flashing eyes and heated whispers. Her dress was light purple with swaying green willows, making me dizzy. For Chinese, the willow symbolizes rootlessness. Was that the impression she intended to give? A mysterious magician whom no one could pin down?

Gao immediately stood up and pulled out a chair for her.

Lung smiled, his eyes traversing her body like wild horses galloping in a meadow.

After Gao went back to his table, Zhu spoke to the magician for his boss. "Miss Shadow, what a show!" Then he introduced us.

"Thank you so much for coming and inviting me to your table,

Master Lung, Mr. Zhu, and Miss Camilla. Your names have long been thundering in my ears."

The moment Shadow's and my eyes met, I knew, and was sure she knew, that we would be rivals to the end.

It was a contest of feminine energies. I, slim and small-framed, was purer *yin,* and she, tall and robust, had some admixture of *yang.* I could only hope that the sage Laozi was right when he said, "The soft always overcomes the hard, the feminine, the masculine."

I was also sure that only one of us would emerge victorious.

Lung was about to say something, but the manager came to tell him he had a telephone call.

The gangster head said to his right-hand man, "Zhu, you'd better come with me, in case it's something important."

After the trio left, Shadow smiled generously. "Miss Camilla, what an honor to be invited to your table."

She was trying to please me, exactly the same strategy I intended to use on her.

I lifted the corners of my lips a little less than hers to show that my status was higher. "Thank you, Miss Shadow, but I'm sure you know that all eyes were upon you tonight, as they were the other night, too."

"You overpraise, Miss Camilla. I still have a long way to go, especially in Shanghai."

"You don't need to be so modest. Your magic is astonishing." I paused to sip my Champagne, then asked the question that had been burning in my mind, "Where did you learn your magic?"

Just then the evil duo, Lung and Zhu, came back.

I didn't ask Lung what was the phone call about, because as a woman and his mistress, I had no business knowing.

The two sat down. My patron looked happy. It must be that the phone call had brought good news, plus he was returning to sit with two dazzling women.

"All right, I'm hungry. Let's have something to eat."

Mr. Zhu waved for the manager and ordered dinner. In almost no time our table was covered with fresh drinks and plates of exotic gourmet food like drunken fish, fried quail, stewed rabbits' legs, spicy deer tails, and pigeon hearts with ginger.

While we ate, drank, and chatted, I tried to study Shadow without being too obvious.

"All right, what did you two girls talk about when I was away?" Lung asked, picking up a fish head and chewing out its eyes. Maybe to look at women better, because fish eyes are supposed to be good for your eyesight.

Hoping to force Shadow to respond, I told him, "I asked Miss Shadow where she learned her magic."

Lung turned to stare at the magician, chewing and waiting for an answer.

She dabbed her lips with a napkin, put it down, then said, "I consider myself extremely lucky, because my teacher taught me everything he knew before he passed away."

Since her answer was not a real answer, Lung pursued the point. "What's his name, then? And his school?"

"Mine is an esoteric tradition, not to be made public."

Probably seeing a fleeting shadow cross the gangster's face, the magician immediately made amends by smiling flirtatiously as she apologized. "I'm so sorry, Master Lung. I had to swear a blood-oath to my ancestors—"

Lung waved a bony hand. "No need to apologize." He turned his attention back to the fish.

But of course I knew full well that no magician would ever reveal his or her secrets but would carry them to the grave.

"Anyway, I learned it in Shandong, not here," Shadow added.

An unexpected revelation—we Shanghainese look down upon anyone from outside our city, because they are never as smart or as scheming or as sophisticated as we are. But perhaps she said she was from Shandong just to put me off guard.

Lung threw her a slanted glance, his cheeks masticating rhythmically to the nightclub's music. "Shandong? I have some business there."

Shadow's eyes brightened. "That's wonderful! What kind?"

Lung looked at her condescendingly. "I don't think a woman would be interested in men's business. You are too pretty to trouble yourself about such things. Anyway, you wouldn't understand even if I told you." He cast his right-hand man a conspiratorial glance. "Right?"

Zhu sneered. "Completely right, Master Lung. That's why I never talk to my old lady except to tell her what to cook for dinner."

We all laughed, except Shadow.

Her smile froze, and her body stiffened, but she was smart enough to immediately try to make amends. "Of course you are both right, Master Lung and Mr. Zhu."

Lung nodded, then gave her a once-over. "Hmm . . . Shandong. That's why you're so damn big and tall!"

I was not sure if this was supposed to be a compliment or a criticism. But judging from what I knew of Lung's previous conquests, or captives, he favored women with small frames and delicate features. Lung was a small man himself, about five feet four, with a narrow face on which sat a few crude features not unlike a monkey's. But although he was short, the gangster boss never failed to project an intimidating presence. Wherever he went, he splashed the air around him with menacing, don't-mess-with-me expressions, surrounded by bodyguards with fight-me-if-you-dare expressions.

Chinese opera actors cultivate the same kind of presence. Before going on stage they cross an imaginary line—the "tiger crossing gate" from the anonymity of the actor to the power of a mighty general or king. However short and puny, they miraculously transform themselves into heroes or villains. They meditate, thrust out their chests, relax their shoulders, hold their heads high. Only then do they cross the line into the illusory life of the drama, where they instantly become generals, warriors, or emperors, controlling the fate of millions.

"Build your presence." Big Brother Wang had repeated this over and over during my training.

Reflecting on these matters, I poured Lung a full cup of tea, then turned to my rival, hoping to smooth out the growing tension in the air. "Miss Shadow, I'm sure you learned from the best. I have never seen anything close to what you do."

"I believe my repertory is unique in Shanghai, if not all of China."

As I was about to ask more, Lung suddenly turned amicable, smiling at us appreciatively. "Are you two going to be like sisters, huh? That would be big news, two pretty, talented women joining forces to win over Shanghai. Why don't you two stop chattering for a while so we can eat more, eh?"

Mr. Zhu immediately poured more wine into our glasses and heaped more food onto our plates. Though I didn't know Zhu well, and he was the only man Lung trusted, I had never liked him. His small eyes were always darting inside the confinement of their two sockets, ready to spot any impending trouble. His nostrils were always enlarged, as if sniffing for anything fishy. Lung almost looked benign next to Zhu, whose face spewed evil and murderous thoughts wherever he went. Perhaps Lung face's was less warlike because the guns and knives had already been transferred from his hand to Zhu's.

I glanced back at Shadow, but her gaze was fixed on my patron.

"Master Lung, if you ever want to hold a party and need a magic show, please don't hesitate to ask me. It would be my greatest pleasure and honor."

Zhu answered bluntly for his boss. "Miss Shadow, Master Lung is a very busy man."

"Yes, of course." She split an embarrassed smile, then looked back at her rice bowl.

Just then, we were approached by the striking young man I'd noticed earlier. Before he reached us, Gao, the head bodyguard, sprang up, ready for action.

Zhu leaned toward Gao and spoke softly to him. Gao then waved the intruder on to our table. "It's okay, Master Lung," Gao said. "This is Miss Rainbow Chang, columnist at the *Leisure News*."

So this was the gossip columnist? I'd been reading her column for a while but never imagined she was of ambiguous gender.

Chang smiled an elegant smile. "Master Lung, Mr. Zhu, Miss Camilla, and Miss Shadow, what an honor to meet you all tonight after I've heard so much about you."

Zhu smiled stiffly. "Miss Chang, please take a seat."

The gossip columnist said, "Oh, please don't let me take up your precious time. I came over to propose a toast to Miss Shadow's brilliant show."

Shadow barely acknowledged her compliment with a slight nod. Didn't she know that this was the heartless reputation-killer Rainbow Chang? Or was she too distracted and eager to butter up Lung? However, her bad manners could only be to my advantage.

Then the columnist turned to the gangster head. "Master Lung, you have an excellent eye. Our Heavenly Songbird is beautiful as well as talented."

Lung patted my back affectionately. "I do have a good eye, especially for women. Ha-ha!"

Rainbow Chang smiled. "Ladies and gentlemen, enjoy the rest of the evening." After that, she went back to her table, where the group of pink-clad ladies awaited her.

I turned to my patron. "Master Lung, had you known that Rainbow Chang dresses as a man?"

Lung shook his head, while Zhu cast me a disapproving look and said, "Maybe you also don't know that she's calling you the skeleton woman, eh?"

Of course I knew. In the less than a year I'd been singing and dancing at Bright Moon, one man had killed himself over me, another had divorced his wife, and yet another had gone bankrupt after selling his apartment to buy me a flawless, eight-carat diamond ring.

If a skeleton woman had to destroy a family just for one night's shelter, she wouldn't hesitate for a moment. Words like *compassion, kindness, love,* or *generosity* did not exist in their dictionaries. For them, it was either win or lose, succeed or fail, destroy or be destroyed.

However, I was never sure, was being called a skeleton woman an insult, a curse, or a compliment?

5

The Young Master

As I'd feared, Shadow was dangerous, and something needed to be done about her. And soon. As the Chinese say, *suzhan sujue,* "Quick battle, quick victory."

So as soon as I arrived home, I took out all the books of strategy I'd collected over the years and flipped through them for possible solutions. Judging from how Shadow had orchestrated her debut on the Shanghai scene, she was talented and imaginative. Though she said she was not from Shanghai, she was as scheming as the best of us. However, her bold interaction with Lung and her casual negligence of Rainbow Chang showed she still had a lot to learn. So now was the best time to crush this poisonous weed, before it grew out of control.

But I needed to figure out what she was plotting: to usurp my fame, to steal Lung from me, or to supplant me as the ultimate skeleton woman.

Most likely, it was all of the above.

Most important, I had to look for her weaknesses. To achieve that, I would become her close friend, to control my space and invade hers. To become master of *her* fate.

So I invited the magician for a chat at the famous Chocolate

Shop located on Jingan Ci Road, in the International Concession. She accepted without hesitation.

I preferred the quieter, upper floor of the café and arrived fifteen minutes before we were to meet. The ambiance was elegant but relaxed, with young Russian waitresses in white and green striped uniforms silently serving the customers. A white-gloved waitress led me to sit at a round table next to a floor- length window framed by grass-green curtains. Here I watched life pass by outside on the busy Tranquil Peace Temple Road. From the street below, the tune of "I'm Always Chasing Rainbows," wafted up.

> I'm always chasing rainbows,
> Watching clouds drifting by.
> Some people look and find the sunshine.
> I'll always look and find the rain. . . .

Soon I spotted Shadow getting off a rickshaw and hurrying inside. A moment later, she made her magical appearance on the upper floor.

Precision, a trait necessary for both magician and spy. We smiled at each other as she was seated by the same Russian waitress. After our orders were taken, we politely complimented each other on our good taste in clothes—she was clad in a black-dotted pink dress with a rather plain gold pendant, and I in a beige, lacy *cheongsam* with matching pearl earrings and necklace. We chatted until the waitress arrived with a layered silver tray with our drinks—café crème for me and vodka for her—together with Russian bread accompanied by butter and jam. Sipping my coffee, more bitter than sweet, I studied her smooth, lightly made-up face, and smiled, hoping she would break the silence.

She smiled back, her face as inscrutable as her magic. "What an honor to be seen with Shanghai's Heavenly Songbird."

"Overpraise."

Her eyes penetrated mine. "Don't be modest, Camilla. You know you're way ahead of me."

And you're desperate to take my place.

She sipped her much stronger and more expensive vodka. Then she tilted her head, her waves of shoulder-length black hair glowing in the early- afternoon sunlight. "May I know the purpose of this invitation?"

What a blunt question! I'd better get used to her brusque style. In replying, I was careful not to sound too eager nor too cold, in order to maintain just the right distance. "Shadow, I am most impressed by your talent, and I still would like to know, how did you do it?"

Of course I didn't expect an honest answer, or any answer at all. My goal was to evoke a response, to get a sense of how she handled things.

This time she let out a soft laugh, revealing rows of smooth, pearly teeth. "This will be my secret, unless someday I encounter a worthy student to pass on my teacher's heritage. Or if I have a child."

"Do you have a father in mind?"

"Camilla, do you think women like us can find someone suitable?"

The idea of having a husband and a family was as alien to me as going to America someday in the future, but I asked, "Why not?" just to hear what she would say.

"How long do you think people like us will stay in our prime?"

"We're both still young."

"You know, time never waits for anyone, especially not for glamour-girls like us."

"You're right," I said, suddenly feeling older. "Just like the Huangpu River flowing on forever and, with it, our youth and beauty."

Would this be her weakness—fear of losing her beauty, her possible fame and fortune, her magic? But why was she so fearful when she was yet in her prime?

She cast me a curious glance. "Camilla, I'm sure you've been carefully planning out your whole life, and that's how you've gotten to where you are now."

She was wrong, of course. But how could she have guessed that my life was not my own and that it had been strategically mapped out by others?

"Shadow, I'm not as much in control as you think."

"I doubt that."

After a pause she blurted out, "Camilla, do beauty and talent give you the happiness you're looking for?"

Again, what a question. She must know that a pretty young girl like me would not really be in love with the old, puny, monkey-faced Lung.

But she'd never learn the truth from me. I threw her question back. "Shadow, how about you? Does your beauty and talent give you happiness—or trouble?"

We both laughed.

She raised her glass to tap my cup.

"Let's just hope that fate has a worthy purpose in granting us our beauty."

I had my agenda, but what was hers?

As we resumed sipping our drinks and munching the delicacies, she asked, "Camilla, what made you want to be a singer?"

Of course my training had well prepared me to cover up such matters. I never told anything but lies about myself. *The Art of War* says, "To guard yourself, hide your secrets below nine layers of earth." In other words, others should know as little about you as possible.

"It was my mother's dream to be a singer; that's why she sent me to take singing lessons."

"And your father?"

"Oh, he died when I was a baby. My mother never talked about him. I guess it was too painful."

"Are you living with your mother?"

"No, she's in an asylum."

"Oh, how terrible! What happened?"

"She became insane and can't take care of herself. She's much better now, being cared for by professionals. That's why I have to work hard, to pay for her care."

I had just made up another elaborate lie. I'd better remember to whom I told which story about my nonexistent parents—in case it mattered.

"I'm so sorry. It must be very difficult for you."

I changed the subject. "So, will you come to hear me sing at Bright Moon?"

"Of course. I've been wanting that for a long time. I just didn't have the connections to get in."

"Don't worry. Just come tomorrow at eight, and I'll tell the manager to let you in."

The meeting with Shadow wore me out. So the following morning I arrived early at the winged-goddess statue by the Huangpu River. As usual, I went behind the gigantic column so I'd be left alone to practice. The sun had already risen over the wide river that seemed blissfully oblivious of the troubles and miseries of the human world. Staring at the peacefully rippling water always calmed me. What I loved most was that, though I would whisper my secrets to the river, it would never betray me by spreading them.

After I finished my vocal gymnastics, I turned around to watch the bustling boulevard. Vendors screamed their breakfast offerings: *Wholesome soy milk! Tasty green bean soup! Sizzling scallion pancakes! Crispy fried dough! Extra juicy pork buns!* Competing to be heard, street urchins shouted at full throttle: *Leisure News! Heaven Daily! Flower Moon News! Pleasure Talk News! Idleness News!* Amid the din, fast-walking businessmen with serious expressions lugged bulging briefcases, maids followed housewives carrying their shopping bags, children in uniforms headed toward school, coolies staggered under heavy boxes as they headed toward the piers. . . .

The collective *qi,* or energy, of this city always fascinated me. Though pulling in every direction, the resulting cacophony created a strange harmony, chaotic yet orderly. As I watched the people and their intersecting lives in this dusty world, a song I'd written escaped from my lips:

> Everyone has parents, but I don't.
> Where are you hiding, dear Mama and Baba?
> When, if ever, will we meet?

Would we recognize each other,
Or merely rub shoulders as we pass?

Unexpectedly, a deep and mellow male voice rose beside me, singing the famous song "Looking for You."

You are the floating cloud in the clear sky,
The fleeting star at midnight.
My heart is caught in a pool of passion.
How can I hold myself back,
Hold myself back from looking for you. . . .

His voice sounded as if it could lure a lark down from a tall tree. When he finished, I could almost see the sad notes lingering above the rushing river, reluctant to end their melodious incarnation on earth. I felt strangely drawn by the singer's unseen presence behind me. When I turned, I found myself under the scrutiny of Master Lung's son.

"Hello, Young Master Lung." I quickly pulled myself up from the well of my dangerous sentimentality. "I never imagined . . . what a beautiful voice you have."

Did he blush, or did I imagine it?

"Good morning, Camilla. . . . May I call you Camilla?"

"Of course, Young Master."

"Camilla, my name is Jinying."

I smiled, glancing at the crowds along the Bund. "What are you doing here so early in the morning?"

"Listening to your singing."

We looked at each other in silence for a moment before he spoke again. "Camilla, when I was watching, I saw the sun's rays splashing all over you. I really thought I'd seen a goddess. Or an angel."

If only he knew. If I was an angel at all, it would be to his father—as the angel of death.

He went on. "When I saw you, I could only think of Botticelli's *Birth of Venus*."

So he was already visualizing me naked, my private parts covered only by long, flowing hair!

"And your voice, heavenly and golden like the sun . . ."

I was not going to let him change the air by the river from foggy to romantic, so I responded matter-of-factly, changing the subject. "Young Master, how did you know I was here?"

"I like to come here and watch the river. Last week I saw you practice. You were so absorbed that I was afraid to interrupt you."

"You don't have to work?"

"I just got my law degree and wanted to stay in America. But my father sent me a telegram saying that he was not feeling well and needed me to come home. So he lied to get me back here. At first I was furious at him, but now I'm happy."

"Happy, why?"

He blushed. "Anyway, it is the will of heaven. . . ."

Yes, it is also the will of heaven that your father will soon die through my efforts.

Oblivious of my secret thoughts, he spoke again. "But I don't want to be a lawyer. I only want to sing and play the piano. Camilla, I'm so glad that we share the same passion."

I didn't respond. So he went on. "May I take you for a morning coffee or tea?"

"I'm afraid not."

He made no effort to hide his disappointment. "You have something else to do this early in the morning?"

"Not really, but I just met you. Besides, I don't go out to cafés with men. . . . Someone will see us and set off gossip."

He protested. "You're friends with my father, so it's not like I am a stranger."

"Young Master, I am a very busy woman. I wish I had the luxury for chitchat or wind-and-moon talk over a cup of bitter Western coffee or sweet Chinese tea. Besides, gossip is the last thing I need in my life."

"But—"

"Sorry, I've got to go."

"Wait a minute," he said, then took something from his pocket. "Can you at least sign this for me?"

It was the fan I'd thrown into the audience the other night. "It was you who caught this? And you kept it?"

"Of course! How could I have thrown it away?"

I quickly signed the fan and turned away.

As I walked, I felt his eyes drilling small holes through the morning fog into my back.

The young master incident threw me off balance, and it was not until much later that I regained my composure. He wanted friendship, something I could not allow myself to have.

Or maybe more?

How complicated this could turn out to be. I was bedding the father, while the son wanted me in *his* bed? When father and son competed for the same woman, would they destroy each other? Or would one step aside? If so, which one? That would be interesting to know. If Lung found out about his son's advances, would he get rid of him? What if instead Lung thought I had seduced his innocent son—would this be the end of me?

Now my mission to eliminate Lung faced two obstacles instead of one: Shadow and now the young master. But was Jinying really an obstacle or just a nuisance? Perhaps he could be distracted . . . by Shadow?

Conveniently, Master Lung told me he'd be out of town with Mr. Zhu for a meeting. I grabbed the chance to invite both Shadow and young Master Lung to my show at Bright Moon. But I couldn't invite the son without the father's suspicion.

So I told Lung, "I'm very disappointed. I'm going to debut a few new songs, and I really want you to hear them!"

"But you can sing them for me when I'm back, right?"

"Of course, but that won't be the same."

"How come?"

"Because this is the premier, and your presence gives me lots of face!"

"All right, all right. . . ." He paused to think, then cooed, "What if I send my son to represent me?"

Wonderful.

* * *

That evening onstage, I followed Madame Lewinsky's advice to pick one person in the audience to focus on. To my alarm, my eyes, with wills of their own, went straight to meet Jinying's. Just then the pianist hit the first note for "Nighttime Shanghai." Throughout my whole performance, the gangster's son's eyes never left me. Not even to appreciate the sensuous Shadow sitting right next to him.

After finishing my act, I went to sit at their table. The young master poured me Champagne. I took a delicate sip, appreciating my two handsome guests.

"I hope you two have been getting to know each other?"

Shadow smiled. "We were too busy watching you and listening to your music."

Jinying nodded.

"Young Master—"

"Please call me Jinying."

"Jinying, have you been making conversation with our beautiful Miss Shadow?"

"Yes, we've been discussing your wonderful voice." He sipped his Champagne and went on. "Camilla, when you sing, you are so spontaneous, hitting those high notes so effortlessly." He eyes searched mine like a miner looking for gold. "I know how hard you must work to achieve this."

I sighed inside. The last thing I needed was for Lung's son, of all people, to have a crush on me. If only he would switch his infatuation to Shadow. But my idea of getting him and Shadow together looked to be a bust.

What to do? All I could think was to try one last time.

I raised my glass, and we all toasted to one another. After that, I said to the magician, "Shadow, when you have your next show, please let me know, and I'll definitely go." Then I turned to Lung's son. "Jinying, you will be stunned by Shadow's impossible magic."

He smiled politely at the magician, then turned to me. "Sure, Camilla. Let me know, and you and I can go together."

It was hopeless. Didn't he worry that his father would discover his feelings for me? Surely he did not imagine that his father would be willing to share his mistress. I really didn't need this; my life was complicated enough. But how could I get rid of him?

Just then I felt a pat on my shoulder. I turned and saw, to my surprise, Madame Lewinsky's kind face smiling down at me.

Before I had a chance to say anything, my teacher was already speaking. "My darling Camilla"—she winked at me, tilting her head toward Jinying—"congratulations. Your singing has improved so much!" She leaned toward me and whispered into my ear, "I can feel your genuine emotion now."

I asked, "You think so?"

She nodded. "Absolutely. I'm a woman, I can tell you're in love."

"No, I'm not. No, no." My voice rose.

She smiled tenderly, like a mother at her daughter. "Camilla, trust me. I know these things. You're fighting it, but you don't need to. Just relax, and give yourself some time, won't you, my darling? Love is the most wonderful thing that can happen to a woman. If you want to talk about it, I'm all ears. Just pay me a visit."

I paused before I said, changing the topic, "Madame Lewinsky, why didn't you tell me you'd be here, so I could have sent you a ticket in advance? Please sit down and chat with us for a while."

She shook her head. "I've got to go, but nice to meet you and your friends." Eyes sparkling with mischief, she again whispered into my ear, her head nodding toward Jinying, "He's a really nice young man, and I can tell he's madly in love with you. Remember, once your bird of youth has flown, it will never come back."

After that, she cast another appreciative look at Jinying, turned back to wink at me, and left.

Jinying poured more Champagne into my glass. "Who was that lady?"

"My singing teacher."

"Then you should have introduced her to us."

I explained that she was in a hurry, but the young master continued. "Maybe I should also take lessons from her."

Alarmed, I exclaimed, "Oh, no, I am sure she is all booked!"

PART TWO

6

Life Between the Two Gangs

Among the city's numerous black societies, the two most power-ful, headed respectively by the warlords Master Lung and Big Brother Wang, were the Flying Dragons and the Red Demons. However, the Flying Dragons were always a few steps ahead of the Red Demons in their various "business enterprises"—gambling, prostitution, opium, "protection," kidnapping, loan-sharking, as well as smuggling guns, gold, US dollars and medicines in, and na-tional treasures out. Ironically, as the two gangs competed in illegal dealings, they also vied in doing charitable works.

My boss, Big Brother Wang's, lifelong obsession was to destroy Lung so he could replace him not only as the richest and most feared boss of the Shanghai underworld but also as its most re-spected philanthropist.

That was how I came onto the scene—a minuscule screw wrig-gling between the city's two most powerful machines.

Wang's plan was to apply the famous *meiren ji,* beauty strategy, or honey trap, one of the *Thirty-Six Stratagems*. Simple in principle and timeless in effectiveness, it involved sending beautiful women to eliminate anyone from lord to emperor. Twenty-five hundred years ago, during the chaotic era known as the Warring States, King Goujian of Yue used it to defeat King Fuchai of the State of Wu.

King Wu won the first battle, and so King Yue sent him ten carts of priceless treasures as tribute. But cleverly he also included eight of the most beautiful women in his state as peace offerings. As intended, King Wu and his ministers became so immersed in dalliance that they neglected state affairs. Tipped off by his spies, King Yue sent his army and easily defeated King Wu. Though Wu offered Yue his country and all its treasures, the victor was merciless. Wu was ordered to commit suicide in front of the very women who had brought about his ruin.

Even the most cunning man becomes a fool for a beautiful woman. Friends' warnings fall on deaf ears. Men blind themselves to the schemes behind the pretty face and the poisons in the beloved heart. When clothes come off, thinking stops.

My job was simple in principle, though not in operation. It was to win Lung's complete love and trust, then lure him to a place where the Red Demons gang could assassinate him. Of course I'd been told to do the murdering myself should the right situation arise. But this was really *chiren shuomeng,* crazy dreaming—pure wishful thinking on their part.

Because every time before I was allowed inside Lung's bedroom or hotel room, I'd be stripped naked and searched thoroughly by Gao, his head bodyguard. I was even asked to jump up and down in case a weapon—small knife, razor, poisonous pill—had been hidden inside my vagina. Of course he'd also scrape my mouth for possible pills wedged between my teeth. Was I humiliated? No, because acquiring a thick skin was part of my training. I had learned not to be distracted by pointless feelings such as humiliation or embarrassment. These things were just part of the job, along with the singing and dancing, except that this part was in private, with only one admirer instead of a hall filled with them. But it was boring, not to mention tedious.

Whenever I came out of Lung's room, Gao would look flushed and embarrassed. His eyes would be filled with bitterness or sadness, depending on what he'd heard—cow-slaughtering cries or puppy-beating whimpers—from my fake orgasm. Like the young master, the head bodyguard seemed to have stepped onto a dangerous path by falling for a woman he'd be better off pretending not to notice.

Anyway, even a beggar on the street in Shanghai would know that to assassinate Lung would be as difficult as to get a virgin pregnant. Lung, Zhu, and all the bodyguards were extremely cautious. Gao, though, might be different, because of his crush on me. Sometimes I wondered, if I became his lover, would he kill Lung for me? But to imagine this was pointless; to seduce the bodyguard under Zhu's sharp eyes was as likely as a baby crawling out from a virgin's narrow gate.

Warlords, though powerful, were not invulnerable, since many ended up being assassinated. Some, however, managed to live to die in bed. But survival required constant vigilance. It was rumored that Lung had a double who would travel in his limousine, while the boss himself was going by another route. So to eliminate Lung was no simple matter. It was rumored that Lung wouldn't trust any Chinese tailor for fear that he might be an assassin in disguise. Scissors in the back during a fitting were not unknown in Shanghai.

I was Wang's means to discover his rival's defense tactics, his daily routine, where he entered and exited, his secret hiding places, who of his guards were the most formidable. And the grand prize: Lung's bank account.

Most of spying is not exciting but tedious, though still very dangerous. I was supposed to put together a complete list of Lung's contacts: his close friends, relatives, and all who worked for him or did business with him. Not only those in the underworld but those supposedly above it. This also included a list of the spies who worked for Lung and who, ironically, might turn out to be my boss, Big Brother Wang's, most trusted men!

Like Lung, Wang always had an ominous feeling that he was marked for assassination. Of course the most likely source would be the Flying Dragons. So I was to try to find out who was on Lung's assassination list and how high Wang was on it. Eliminating Lung had been Wang's goal from the moment he became a gang head. He just hadn't yet figured out a good plan—until his underling Mr. Ho had discovered me in the orphanage.

After winning the title of Heavenly Songbird last year, I was given a luxury apartment inside the French Concession. This included a maid and a driver, but I knew full well that their real jobs were to keep track of me for Wang. I made good money, but unfortunately Wang took half and most of the rest for "safekeeping." He knew that if I had my own money, his hold on me would be weakened. Though I was free to go places within Shanghai, I couldn't just disappear. Wang repeatedly warned me that his gang men were everywhere, so he would know everywhere I went and everything I did.

Yet life as a nightclub singer was incomparably better than in the orphanage. I now had a comfortable apartment, which was decorated in a mixture of Chinese and Western styles. The Chinese elements—calligraphy, landscape paintings, antique furniture and vases—were there to impress people, especially the refined ones, that I was not just a singer but one steeped in traditional culture and taste, perhaps from a prominent family. The Western décor—velvet curtains, soft sofas with silky coverings, a gilded and latticework clock, and oil paintings showing classical scenes—was to show that I was also cosmopolitan.

To others I was the beautiful, sophisticated woman who had it all. But I was well aware that Big Brother Wang didn't pay my rent because he liked my singing, but to keep me under his control. My amah and cook, Ah Fong, and driver, Ah Wen, who did almost everything for me, were also his spies. The best I could do about this was, from day one, to tip them generously, hoping they would avert their eyes or keep mum when I needed them to.

Unlike most gangsters, Lung favored talented women. With me it was singing; before it might have been speaking a foreign language, horseback-riding, or even flying a plane. For him, women like us were like a rare Ming vase, while others were but ordinary kitchenware. No doubt this was Lung's way to compensate for starting out as a shoe-shine boy.

Now that Lung had finally fallen for me, I had to work steadily to complete my mission, because the boss of the Flying Dragons gang would not stay long with any woman. No flower blooms all year long. No matter how enamored he was with her, Lung believed that any woman who'd warm his bed for too long would bring bad luck, polluting his bedchamber and harming his business. That was why the sudden appearance of Shadow worried me. I did not want him to be thinking of her as my successor.

But with or without Shadow, my situation would likely be lose-lose. Mission successfully completed, I'd have served my purpose. And as in the Chinese saying, "After the rabbits are caught, the hounds will be cooked."

That was the inevitable fate of spies. I had read that in China's Harbin province, one time the Japanese sent a prostitute-spy to seduce a Russian general so as to steal his map. On this map were marked the soldiers' positions, their planned route of attack, and their supply lines. Succeeding in stealing the map, she was able to send it to the Japanese embassy. But the Japanese never sent anyone to rescue her. Instead, they referred to her as "the sakura blossom without root" and abandoned her to die alone in a prison in Siberia.

If I did not begin to plan for my escape, I was sure to end up being another sakura blossom without root, if not in Siberia, then in my own homeland. Not in a prison but sprawled in a back alley, bobbing in the Huangpu River, or rotting in a well. Or, as the story was told of one of Lung's former mistresses, fed to tigers . . .

Someday, probably soon, I would need to escape. I would need a plan, and I would need money. So I tried my best to save. Although I didn't get to keep much from the nightclub, I got expensive gifts from admirers, most generously from Master Lung, who had been pampering me with American gold pieces, fur coats, and lavish jewelry. Of course my boss, Wang, knew about the gifts, but he could not take away those from Lung, who might notice that they were missing. Meanwhile, I tried to waste as little as possible on frivolities like the theater, movies, high tea, or amusement parks.

However, even if I had the money to escape, where would I go? I had neither relatives nor real friends. I knew great danger was approaching, but all I could do was wait for the right moment to act. As the sages tell us in the three-thousand-year-old *Yijing,* or *Book of Changes,* "If you step on the tail of a tiger but use extreme caution, you will be fortunate in the end."

* * *

When you first glimpsed him, Lung looked quite ordinary. This was in fact a gift from heaven that enabled him to conceal his astute mind and scheming heart. But, despite his small stature, Lung could inspire fear. His dealings were of extreme complexity, but, unfortunately for me, he seemed to keep everything in his head. No one had any idea of his many business dealings. His routes were untraceable, his hiding places unfindable, and even his facial expressions gave away nothing.

Lung's gang, the Flying Dragons, took its name from the *Book of Changes*. The name was appropriate because Lung himself was like a dragon, whose body is always half revealed and half hidden by clouds. Lung heeded well the advice of *The Art of War,* "See all, but stay hidden." According to the *Book of Changes,* there are three kinds of dragons. One soars to heaven and leads the world; one hides in the field and waits for the auspicious moment to act; one becomes arrogant and ends up in bitter failure. The first one is the leader, the second the sage, the third the loser.

Master Lung was already a leader, would never be a sage, and was certainly arrogant. So he was ripe for being overthrown. The moment would come when he would relax his vigilance, but I would not relax mine. The Chinese say, *congming yishi, benzai yishi*, "Smart for your whole life, stupid for a moment." All I needed was for Lung to be careless for one moment.

And that would be the moment when I would act. Because no matter how brilliantly cunning Lung was, he did have a weakness—his infatuation with beautiful, classy women. But most mistresses are enjoyed for a brief time, then cast away. Infatuation by itself is not enough. Most women did not understand that to bewitch a man, sex is only the beginning. After you have captured his heart, you must also capture his mind.

If Lung really had a heart—or even if I had one. But we both had minds—scheming ones.

～ 7 ～

Temple Celebration

One evening, in my living room, I was sipping tea and savoring its warmth slowly soothing my Heavenly Songbird throat. I enjoyed the warmth that I never received from human beings, except maybe Madame Lewinsky. My gaze wandered out the window at nighttime Shanghai glittering like an enormous multifaceted diamond. People must be enjoying their youth, beauty, and wealth out there, I mused. I knew I was getting sentimental, something I could not allow myself. Then, for no reason at all, the face of Jinying, Lung's son, flashed into my mind. As if on cue, the telephone beside me rang like a barking dog who'd just lost sight of its master.

I picked up the receiver. "Hello?"

"Camilla?"

I immediately recognized the voice that had sung "Looking for You" to me at the Bund. "Yes, Young Master?"

"Please, I beg you, Camilla, call me Jinying. I really don't like to be addressed as Young Master."

My voice switched to the teasing mode. "Do you have a choice?"

As the father was imprisoned by his own suspicion and superstition, the son was confined by his father's wealth and power.

"I . . . really don't want to go into this."

"Why don't you like the title of young master?"

"Because I don't like to be thought of as superior to you or other people."

I almost chuckled out loud. Of course. He had been educated in America, a country that supposedly advocated liberty and equality. So his mind was liberated, or poisoned, depending on how you looked at it, by this ridiculously unrealistic concept.

"But you are," I cooed into the receiver.

"Please, Camilla."

"All right, Jinying, what do you want?" Of course I knew exactly what he wanted, the same thing as his father—me. Did he think his father would share with him?

"May I come to visit you now?" The tone was plaintive, like that of an orphan desperate to be adopted.

That was an unexpected and daring request. But of course he was, after all, the indulged, privileged son of the most powerful gangster in Shanghai. At least he was courteous enough to ask before coming.

I inhaled deeply. "But why would you want to come here?"

"Camilla, since I heard you sing at Bright Moon and at the Bund, I just can't shake you from my mind. You sing like an angel."

If only I were one. "Don't you know that I am your father's woman?"

An uncomfortable silence passed before he spoke hesitantly. "Yes, of course."

"You're not afraid?"

"No."

"Maybe you're not, but I am."

"My father won't hurt you."

This time I laughed out loud. Was he that naive?

"Please don't make fun of me."

"I'm sorry. But do you know who your father is and what he is capable of?"

"Yes."

"Then what makes you think he won't harm me—or you?"

"Because he loves me the most, and he's superstitious."

My ear perked up at the word *superstitious.* Though it was not news to me that the gangster head was a believer in *fengshui, Yijing* divination, physiognomy, palmistry—the whole gamut of Chinese ways to attain good luck—his son could be a source of other useful information about his father.

So I immediately curtailed my sarcasm and replaced it with a warm, tender tone. "Jinying, yes, please do come up to my place so we can chat over a glass of wine."

In a mere five minutes, Jinying was at my doorstep.

I opened the door and asked, "Were you downstairs?"

He nodded, looking anxious.

"Please take a seat on the sofa, and I'll ask Ah Fong to fix you tea and snacks."

He looked around, his expression disappointed. "You have someone else living here with you?"

"She's my amah."

Moments later Ah Fong came out with a tray of tea, coffee, and sandwiches.

After she laid it on the table, I smiled. "You can leave now, Ah Fong." And I took some coins from my purse and pushed them into her hand.

She looked at me appreciatively. "Thank you so much, Miss Camilla." Then she cast the young master the same look and left.

Delicately sipping my fragrant tea, I asked the fine-featured, intense face across from me, "Jinying, what is the purpose of your visit?"

He looked surprised and pained. "Camilla, I . . . wanted to see you. I am hoping you will sing for me again."

I studied his eager eyes and their two brows. Unlike his father's, they were smooth and unscarred, like two distant mountains shrouded in the mist. "Jinying, you have the money for casinos, nightclubs, anything you want. So why are you so interested in music?"

His smile showed a trace of bitterness. "That's exactly what displeases my father about me. That I would waste my time on something so decadent and worthless."

This seemed ironic. Wasn't music the reason the old man came to Bright Moon?

Lung's son's face softened under the gentle light of my chandelier. "My passion began when I visited New York and a friend took me to see *Madame Butterfly* at the Metropolitan Opera. Since then I've been hooked. I used some of the money Father sent me for singing and piano lessons. At Harvard I even performed a few roles in musicals."

"When you were in America, you must have heard the most famous singers of the world." My curiosity was piqued.

"I did, but I like your voice the best. I've heard all the famous singers, and of course they're all first-rate, but in my opinion, they all have one basic flaw. . . ."

"What's that?"

"Too much training and not enough being."

"What do you mean?"

Maybe he thought I feigned not understanding, but it was true that I didn't. For "too much training, not enough being" was exactly what Madame Lewinsky seemed to criticize in my singing. But of course neither she nor the young master had any way to know that I'd been trained *not* to have feelings.

"They are so conscious of their fame and status that they gradually lose contact with their heart. In my opinion, they should strip away their mannerisms and let the audience in." He picked up his cup and took a long sip as he studied me intensely. "Camilla, I'm amazed that you don't need to use technique or posture to hide your vulnerability. You just let your goodness shine through."

I suppressed a smile of relief. He was completely fooled by me, or, to be exact, by my training! This showed that he was the one who was naive. *Wonderful.*

On the surface I stayed calm. "But you have only heard me twice. How do you—"

"I go to hear you sing almost every night. I sit in a corner seat in back so if my father's there, he won't see me."

He shook his head, then downed more coffee. "My father is getting old and wants me to start in his business so I can take over someday. But so far I've stayed away. I'm just not interested. Also, well, his business is just . . . not right. I wish I were someone else's son." He put down his coffee cup with a loud *clink.*

As I studied his anxious expression, I felt a perverse relief rising inside me. "I'm sorry that's how you feel, Jinying. Can't you explain to Master Lung how you feel?"

"That would not matter. He loves me, but I am his only son, and so there is no one else to take over. And he considers me his good-luck son."

"Oh, yes? How is that?"

"Because since the day I was born, his business has boomed, and it has lasted until today. The Red Demons have tried but failed to kill him many times. So he believes my lucky star shines on him to protect him."

Now I was glad for his interest in me. I was also getting an idea.

The Chinese say, "If you want to shoot the person, first shoot his horse; if you want to capture the bandits, first capture their chief."

What if I seduced Jinying—the boss behind the boss—and set father and son against each other? Of course it might end up that Lung would kill his son, but that sort of possibility was why I had been trained to have no feelings. If it ended up the other way around, then my mission would be successfully completed even without my having to get my hands dirty.

I looked admiringly at the young master's angelic face. To lie under the owner of this face would be a much better deal than being fucked by his monkey-faced, split-browed old man.

I tried to hide my smirk by downing more tea, but I burned my tongue and choked myself.

The angel dropped from heaven asked, "You all right, Camilla?"

"Couldn't be better." I smiled, still choking.

Two days after Jinying's visit, I got an invitation from the Eternal Luck Temple to participate in a celebration, but of what, it did not specify. Then Mr. Zhu, Master Lung's right-hand man, called.

"Miss Camilla, be prepared to accompany Master Lung to the Eternal Luck Temple."

"Mr. Zhu, may I know what is the purpose of this event?"

"To celebrate the opening of the temple's new wing. Gao will pick you up next Saturday at one in the afternoon. Dress your best, and be ready on time. We cannot miss the most auspicious moment meticulously calculated by the temple's *fengshui* master. You got it?"

"Of course, Mr. Zhu."

"Good," he huffed, then hung up.

For the temple event, instead of a *cheongsam,* this time I picked a white silk Western dress embroidered with pink camellias and light green leaves. The hem was slightly below my knees, revealing just enough of my high-heeled, hundred-dollar-silk-stockinged legs. A red camellia, pinned above my ear, echoed my matching pink high heels and purse.

To bring out the green, I put on a jade necklace and a matching bracelet. To set off the jade, my huge diamond ring was perched regally on my middle finger, demanding attention.

Whenever I was invited to an important occasion, jade and diamonds were always my favorite choices. Jade's cool nature conveys a reserved, Oriental sophistication, like a woman's silent declaration: "I am beautiful but coy, so please don't stare." On the other hand, a diamond is fiery and Occidental, like a tall, voluptuous woman strutting confidently and exclaiming, "Come, see how sexy I am!"

However, today my most exciting feature was neither the jade nor the diamond but my dress's heart-shaped neckline cutout, revealing my undulating two half-moons. I knew I succeeded in creating an intriguing presence. But disturbingly, as I felt happy looking at the beautiful face that stared back at me from the mirror, now, for the first time, I wanted to avoid looking deeper at what was within.

Gao arrived to pick me up in a black Cadillac. As we drove to the temple, I caught his eyes wandering off the road to look into the rearview mirror at me or, to be specific, my bulging half-moons.

Finally he blurted out, "Miss Camilla, you look gorgeous today."

I smiled sweetly. "Thank you, Gao. Glad you like my outfit."

"I don't mean only your outfit."

I could say, "Of course I know what you meant," but I was not going to chide him by telling him to keep his eyes on the road instead of on me. I didn't want to completely discourage his interest.

One never knew; someday I might find him of use on my path to defeating Lung.

So I said, "Thank you, Gao, whatever else you mean."

I studied the bodyguard's face in the mirror and found myself liking it. He took his job seriously and was good at it. He was also a martial artist and Thai boxing expert, and I had heard that on a bet he had shot right into the red heart of an ace from forty steps away. I knew him to be alert, careful, and, unlike Zhu, gentle and courteous.

But Gao had his weakness: his huge crush on me.

I realized that because I often noticed his gaze traveling downward from my face to my chest, waist, and legs. Didn't he realize that even a split second of his distraction could cost his and his boss's lives? But of course he was a man, and he couldn't help it. That's why there are skeleton women. We use men's lust to turn them into skeletons.

With Mr. Zhu, the situation was entirely different. He was impatient, ferocious, and even more bossy to me than his boss was. However, this was, in fact, a good thing. Because the less attention I received from this ruthless man, the better, lest he see through my pretense and detect my true intentions.

A few minutes later, the car pulled to a stop in front of the Eternal Luck Temple and awoke me from my reveries. Gao opened the car door for me, and my ears were instantly filled with the buzzing conversations of the important-looking guests. He helped me out and led me into the temple's front yard. I enjoyed the envious glances of the women, beautiful and otherwise, as I was escorted by the handsome, muscular man ready to serve my minutest need.

Monkey Face was waiting for me, surrounded by his usual entourage. As Gao brought me over to the gangster head, he gave me a licentious once-over, looking happy and proud. "Camilla, you sure are easy on the eyes. And your fragrance is intoxicating!"

The abbot and his entourage of Daoist monks hurried to greet us. Soon Lung and Zhu were the center of attention, not only for the monks but also for a circle of obsequious businessmen and politicians.

I got a drink and walked around. Recognizing me as the Heavenly Songbird, some guests nodded in my direction; others cupped their mouths and whispered to their partners. My attention was drawn to a tall woman dressed in a man's white suit, a golden tie, and a white fedora. She easily could have been mistaken for a man were it not for her exaggerated makeup. Her stark white powder, bright red rouge, and scarlet lipstick formed the background for long, artificial lashes fluttering in front of golden eye shadow. A weird, even haunting combination. Flanking her was a small group of tall, strikingly beautiful girls in matching pink dresses.

Of course this time I recognized this cross-dressed woman as the famous, or notorious, gossip columnist Rainbow Chang, with her enigmatic clique of pink-clad followers. Were they her confidantes? Bodyguards? Lovers? Anybody could be anyone in Shanghai. Watching her poise and ease working her way through the crowd, I could only hope that she was not yet another obstacle on my path. Dealing with a Shadow, a gangster, and his son was already more than enough for a nineteen-year-old songstress-spy.

When she was in front of me, the columnist reached out her hand. "It's such a pleasure to meet you here again, Miss Camilla. I am Rainbow Chang, remember? We met at Bright Moon."

On the surface, I stayed calm. "Yes, of course. What a lucky encounter!" I said, feeling her fleshy palm tightly squeezing mine. "I've been a fan of your column."

"Really? The most famous Heavenly Songbird, my fan? I'm flattered."

Underneath our polite words, we were scrutinizing each other like two unneutered cats under the full moon.

She gave me a meaningful once-over. "Wah. Look at you, Camilla. May I call you Camilla?"

"Of course."

"No other singer in Shanghai has your kind of presence."

Of course she was referring to my expensive clothes and even more expensive jewelry, and on top of that, my much-envied position beside Shanghai's number one gangster head.

I decided to play modest. "I owe it to the help of your column."

"Hmm . . . is that true? You're not offended by my writing? You know, sometimes I can be pretty straightforward."

Now I'd play the flatterer. "If you never mentioned me in your column, I would not be so famous today."

Her expression turned mischievously delightful. "Then maybe we should be friends, or at least business partners?"

What did that mean?

"You know, Camilla, we could build a long-term, mutually beneficial relationship."

Oh, heavens. This was exactly what I didn't need: one more complication! I knew I had better tread this path with utmost caution. While Lung could kill with a knife or gun, this Rainbow could do the same with her pen, without even having to waste a bullet!

I asked, feeling a little nervous, "But how?"

She looked at me deeply, as if I were her lover. "I'll tell you if you let me take you to dinner. I'm sure we'll enjoy each other's company. What about next week?"

I sighed inside. I was sure many people wanted to meet this famous gossip columnist and her pink entourage, but I couldn't wait to get rid of her.

"Thank you for the invitation. I would love to have dinner with you. But I hope you will be free some other time?" I gestured to Lung's back in the distance. "Right now my schedule won't even afford me the luxury to breathe—"

Before I finished my sentence, I felt a large hand on my shoulder. I turned and saw Gao's concerned face. He leaned down to whisper into my ear. "Miss Camilla, the ceremony is to begin in fifteen minutes. Master Lung's good friend the police chief has arrived, and Master Lung would like to introduce you."

I turned to smile at Rainbow Chang. "Sorry, Miss Chang, but I have to excuse myself."

"No problem." She winked. "Go ahead. *Lairi fangchang.*" Time is aplenty in the future.

I stared at her retreating back and felt a chill. Would she prove yet another rival in my life?

With this new worry, I let Gao steer me back to Lung, who was now standing beside a stout, uniformed man. Gao stepped back to join another bodyguard, both men watching us closely.

Master Lung turned to grab my waist. "Please meet my beautiful Camilla."

Although I'd never met the police chief in person, I'd seen pictures of him in the newspapers. I also heard rumors about his proclivities, most infamous being that once, when he and Lung were drunk, they threw their respective ex-mistresses to Lung's pet tigers, whom they kept starving for just such occasions.

Chief Li cast me a licentious glance and shook my hand hard, as if he were tormenting a helpless kitten.

"Miss Camilla, I have heard your name for a long time, but you are much more beautiful in person than in your pictures."

I returned him a demure smile. "Thank you for your praise, Chief Li. Likewise I've also heard your name like thunder in my ears."

Together we walked into the newly built wing. A crimson signboard with four big gold characters, *huakai fugui,* "Flowers bloom and fortune looms," hung above the portal. *Fortune* really meant *making money.* Many Chinese believe that donating to temples will bring them good fortune, so perhaps the temple wanted to be sure they would not forget that. Monks, of course, have no desire for riches, but donations to their temple in the form of checks, jewelry, gold bars, antiques, and land are always welcome.

Inside, the hall décor resembled a Western casino, with red and gold as the main colors, for double luck. Male staff in black tuxedos and female staff in pink and green *cheongsams* flanked the entrance, nodding and exclaiming, "Welcome, our honorable guests!"

We nodded and smiled back. Inside, scrolls of calligraphy adorned the walls, proclaiming auspicious sentiments: "Invite money; welcome treasures;" "Gold bars fill the house;" and "Money flows in like rushing water."

As I was wondering what these phrases were doing in a temple, my eyes spotted men throwing dice and playing mahjong in the distance. In one corner, a uniformed man was shaking a cylindrical tube and exclaiming, "Big! Big! Big!" followed by another man's louder, "Small! Small! Small!" After that, the first man threw the contents of the tube onto the table as the customer yelled, "Big!"

The uniformed man smiled cunningly at the anxious customer. "Sorry, sir, but it's small."

After that, the pile of money immediately shifted from in front of the client to that of the uniformed man.

I realized that this was none other than a casino! But inside a temple?

Then my eyes landed on red lanterns hanging low from the ceiling above the gaming tables. Could cameras be hidden inside to catch cheaters?

"Master Lung, so this is a . . ."

"Yes, my new gambling den."

"But in a temple?"

He laughed, his belly trembling. "Ha-ha-ha! For the gods' protection and blessings, what else?"

Thinking about that, I realized that a temple was, in fact, a perfect place to operate a gambling den. If a gambler won, part of his winnings would be donated to the temple as a token of gratitude. If he lost, he'd also donate as a bribe to the money gods so that next time they would direct the propitious winds to blow in his direction.

What other kind of business could be win-win like this? I smiled, toying with this "win-win" idea. Wouldn't it be wonderful if I could also put myself into a win-win situation—successfully completing my mission and escaping from both the Flying Dragons and Red Demons?

As soon as we finished touring this sacred casino, we were all ushered back outside to the courtyard, ready for the auspicious opening ceremony.

8

The Lion Dancers

It was three minutes to two o'clock. Our mandatory early arrival had been to make sure the ceremony would start exactly at the time calculated by the fortune-tellers, not a minute early nor a minute late. Otherwise the auspicious moment would be missed, possibly ruining Lung's gambling business even before it started.

According to these fortune-telling savants, the first moment of an event determines everything. Unfortunately mothers couldn't choose the time of their babies' birth; otherwise they'd all grow up to be kings and queens, dragons and phoenixes. Perhaps my parents hadn't believed in fate calculation, and that was why I'd ended up having this horrible life. But I hoped someday to undo my inauspicious beginning. After all, as the ancient *Yijing* tells us, "Everything changes."

Lung, Zhu, Chief Li, me, and a few other honorable guests were led to stand at the front of the newly opened temple wing. Two girls placed red ribbons with a wreath at each end into our hands. Photographers and reporters streamed in, snapping pictures and taking notes. I spotted Rainbow Chang furiously scribbling in her notebook. Scattered around were Gao and his team of bodyguards, all dressed in black and eyes continuously scanning the crowd.

"Eyes never leave people, gun never leaves hand," is the body-

guards' motto. But it seemed that Gao was not paying close attention to this principle. For his eyes tended to come back to linger on
me a tad longer than they should have. An opening for mishap. But
that was his problem, not mine.

I continued to look at the crowd and realized that Lung's son,
Jinying, was not there for the occasion.

I turned to my patron. "Master Lung, how come your son's not
here? Didn't you invite him?"

Lung made a face. "Of course I did. But he said he doesn't believe in gambling. Must have learned that at HarFud."

I knew I was not supposed to further inquire, so I changed the
subject. "Hmm . . . then what about Shadow? I don't see her either."

"Ha! What a thought, Camilla. I know you two are becoming
like sisters. But you think any gambling house would invite a magician so she can trick all the money into her pockets and disappear?" He playfully patted my cheek. "Huh?"

"Of course you're right, Master Lung."

Just then the abbot, an emaciated, ancient figure, lifted a hand
to signal the arrival of the auspicious moment—two o'clock sharp.
We cut the ribbon as onlookers applauded, shutters snapped, and
firecrackers popped, followed by the beating of drums, blasting of
trumpets, and clanging of cymbals—all to scare away evil spirits
and welcome the gods to protect the business.

When the noise subsided, we were all invited to sit on a row of
chairs under the temple roof and offered fragrant tea. We started to
sip as a red-maned yellow "lion" pushed aside the excited crowd
and danced toward us, followed by renewed beating, banging, and
clanging. Seemingly encouraged, the three-man team covered by
the lion costume pranced around, leaping up, then kowtowing to
all the guests, particularly Master Lung. We all laughed and applauded at their blinking, long-lashed eyes and trembling, flowing
manes.

Next, each of the two men in front mounted the shoulders of
the one behind him. Then the "lion" reared up to be ready to
"grasp the green"—snatch the lettuce hanging from the roof for
everyone's good luck. I was excited to watch the "lion," or the

three men, perform all kinds of *kungfu* gymnastics—fists thrusting, legs kicking, making imaginary offerings to heaven and earth, kowtowing in the four auspicious directions. Finally, after all the contorting, the top man made a vigorous sweep of his *kungfu* hand and snatched the green vegetable hung high from the temple's roof.

I peeked at Lung. He looked extremely happy, even relaxed, a rare moment for him. Of course with all these bodyguards around him and the audience having been meticulously screened, what could possibly go wrong?

But the dance wasn't over. The two men on top jumped down, and the lion began to cavort again, playing with the vegetable, tearing it up, chewing it, and scattering its pieces all over the ground.

Lung, Mr. Zhu, the abbot, and Chief Li yelled, "Excellent! Money will flow in endlessly like the Huangpu River!"

As I watched, the lion approached Lung and opened its mouth. Lung's hand plunged into his pocket. My heart skipped a beat. Was Lung pulling a gun? But then I realized that it was time for the lion to receive its fat red lucky-money envelope.

Just then a thunderous sound racked the air. All looked up and saw the smoke from huge strings of firecrackers exploding right above the gambling den. Red confetti showered down upon the crowd, another symbol of good luck.

But from the corner of my eye I spotted the opposite.

The man inside the lion's-head mask, his face still hidden, took out a gun and fired at Master Lung. Because the firecrackers were still thundering out good luck, nobody noticed the assassination attempt except me.

A loud "Help! Master Lung is shot!" involuntarily shot out from my mouth as I saw Lung fall to the ground, followed by his even louder *"Aiya!"*

Then I bit the inside of my lips until I tasted blood.

How stupid!

What was wrong with me? Why couldn't I just keep my mouth shut and let Lung bleed to death?! Had Lung died right here and now, I would be done with my near-impossible mission!

It took a few seconds for Lung's gang to realize what had happened. Gao was the first to react, leaning over his boss to shield him against any more bullets. But all that was to be seen of the lion was the costume lying deflated on the grass. Gao tore off Lung's bloodstained silk gown and, after a brief examination, declared that his boss was fine, since the bullet had missed his heart.

"Are you sure?" Zhu, the abbot, Chief Li, and a few other dignitaries barked simultaneously.

"Honorable guests"—Gao looked relieved and shaken up at the same time—"Master Lung is fine. The bullet hit his dragon amulet and bounced off. The bleeding was nothing serious, just from his skin being grazed."

Right after Gao finished, Zhu pushed him aside, probably to resume his right-hand man status. As he put his handkerchief on his boss's chest to soak up the blood, he screamed, "Call an ambulance!"

Lung suddenly sprang up, yelling, "Go chase the lion dancers!"

Immediately Chief Li and his team, together with Gao and his bodyguards, pushed aside the onlookers and dashed away.

Seeing that the gangster head was indeed very much alive, everybody clapped. The abbot leaned toward Lung, smiling. "Master Lung, anyone who impossibly survives such a calamity will be blessed by many generations of good luck and longevity!"

Danan Busi, biyou houfu.

Then I noticed Rainbow Chang trying to approach us but being stopped by Zhu. It was obvious that the right-hand man didn't like the columnist. Did he have reason to be suspicious of her?

A few moments later, the group that had set out to chase the lion dancers came back. But to Lung and Zhu's bitter disappointment, they were empty-handed. Chief Li announced that they had found three dead bodies just behind the temple. To everyone's disappointment, the bodies were not those of the would-be assassins but those of the real lion dancers.

This is what the Chinese call *fang bu sheng fang:* Being careful is no guarantee for success.

Lung struggled to stand up, then slapped Gao and the other bodyguards. Obscenities, including cutting off their father's turtle head and fornicating their collective mothers' vaginas, spewed from his mouth like lava from a volcano. I was taken aback to hear

Lung speak with such vulgarity. But then I realized that this was the former shoe-shine boy revealing himself in public.

Then another surprise followed. He slapped the abbot.

"Damn you and your mother's cunt! You told me you'd screened the lion dancers!"

The abbot lowered his head, looking humiliated and terrified. "I . . . I . . ." he stuttered. "I did, many . . . times, very thoroughly. But . . . how was I supposed to know that the assassins would murder them and take over the performance?"

Zhu shot the abbot his I-will-wipe-out-your-whole-family look. "Shut up! Don't you know the rule that no one talks back to the master?!"

The abbot's head dropped almost to his navel. "Yes, yes, of course. I'm . . . sorry, so sorry."

Besides Zhu, Police Chief Li was the only person who was spared by Lung, so he was happy to play the mediator. "Master Lung, everything is okay. Trust me, we will catch the assassins soon."

"You'd better, Chief," Lung said, then turned to me—to my surprise—with a big smile. "Camilla, your dragon amulet saved my life." He touched my cheek affectionately. "You're also the first one who screamed for help." Then he made a sweeping gesture to include everyone. "From now on I declare Miss Camilla my lucky star!"

Everyone clapped.

"Master Lung, thank you." I smiled demurely. "Of course I'll do anything to protect you, always."

I bit my inner lip. Lucky star or not, now I had to think of another way to have him killed. Damn my unintended benevolence!

Lung yelled to no one in particular, "Now take me back home!"

Zhu leaned toward him and said gently, "Master, the ambulance will be here any minute. It's better to be checked by a doctor to make sure everything is all right."

In no time an ambulance pulled to a stop in front of the temple. Two uniformed attendants jumped down and dashed over to lift Lung onto a stretcher. Zhu, Gao, and I hopped in to accompany our boss to the hospital.

* * *

With Lung safely under the care of doctors and nurses, I was finally able to return home at nine in the evening. I sprawled on the sofa and poured myself a whiskey. After a few sips alternated with sighs, I called Big Brother Wang to report today's happenings—except, of course, my stupid screaming.

From miles away, his voice rushed to attack my eardrum. "Damn! I wonder who was behind this. You're sure he's okay?"

"Yes."

His response surprised me. "Good."

"Why's that, Big Brother Wang?"

"Because once he's dead, I'm afraid it'll be much harder to get his secret bank account and other information. So be nice to him and nurture him back to health so he'll trust and love you more."

"I will certainly do that."

"Report back to me any further news about his condition."

"I will."

"That's a good girl."

"Thank you, Big Brother Wang."

I discovered that with my boss, I was beginning to sound more and more like a parrot.

Then he said, "One more thing."

"Yes?"

"Next time, if you have a once-in-a-lifetime chance to kill him, just do it. I will figure out how to get his list later. Understand?"

I felt a chill crawling up and down my spine. Today's near-assassination made it all the more real to me. Did he really want me, a nineteen-year-old girl, to commit murder myself? I'd practiced singing, ballroom dancing, knife-throwing, contortionism, but kill a man? How was I supposed to practice that?

But I would never forget the rule of not talking back or saying no to my boss. I uttered a submissive, "Of course, Big Brother Wang."

Though feeling extremely exhausted and anxious, that night I could hardly close my eyes as the assassination scene kept spinning in my mind, along with the question: Who had sent those lion dancers?

Of course, besides my boss, Big Brother Wang, there were many other warlords in Shanghai eager to get rid of Lung. The one who succeeded might then be able to take over all his lucrative businesses: prostitution, gambling, opium, smuggling . . . even the newly opened gambling den in Eternal Luck Temple.

The next morning, the first thing I did was to pour myself a glass of milk and flip through the *Leisure News* to read Rainbow Chang's column.

Attempted Assassination

Yesterday, during the Eternal Luck Temple's opening ceremony for its good-luck den, three lion dancers attempted to gun down the Flying Dragons' boss, Master Lung.

Fortunately, due to Lung's frequent visits to consult a mysterious fortune-teller, he was wearing a highly efficacious amulet. It was this amulet, in the shape of a soaring dragon, that stopped the bullet and saved his life. It is rumored that Lung has now hired this fortune-teller to serve him exclusively, because there's no way the Flying Dragons' boss will let others share this kind of luck.

Anyway, who are these assassins? No, my question should be: who is behind these assassins?

On a lighter note, at the ceremony, I also had the pleasure to encounter two beautiful skeleton women, Camilla, the Heavenly Songbird, and Lung's new flame, the magician Shadow. Both graced the ceremony with their stunning beauty and charm.

More to follow. . . .
Rainbow Chang

I put down the newspaper and cursed.

Damn! Where did she get the idea that the amulet was given by Lung's *fengshui* master? It was *my* gift! But wait . . . maybe she thought I'd snubbed her, and she had gotten her revenge by mixing up the information?

I sighed, because one can be destroyed not only by a bullet but also by a few words.

It was no secret that Rainbow Chang's most powerful weapon was to spread rumors, a strategy also favored by the "rumor creation" departments of several political parties. Spies would be disguised as students, businessmen, office or factory workers, then sent to parks, teahouses, movie theaters, restaurants, and other public places to spread tales about their enemies. Once a powerful rumor starts, even if it is later proved wrong, the damage has been done, and the stain is permanent.

I picked up the glass of milk and took a meditative sip as another question arose. What if Shadow *was* at the ceremony, and I didn't see her? Had the columnist also lied about this, or could the magician really make herself invisible?

Feeling uneasy, I went into my bedroom to get dressed to visit Lung at the hospital.

9

Hospital Visit

Once I got out of the car in front of the hospital, I saw many reporters crowding the entrance, trying to push through the staff and guards to get inside. Two of Lung's bodyguards pushed them back to let me in. I hurried through the lobby before any patients or staff milling around could catch sight of me.

On the third floor, I saw Gao standing guard right outside Lung's private room. We exchanged greetings, and he assured me that Master Lung was doing well.

I looked around. "Where's your partner?'

"He just went to get something to eat. We've been here since yesterday."

"So, are you feeling all right?"

He nodded. "Just doing my job."

"Gao, you really take your job seriously."

He lowered his big torso so his head was at the same level with mine. "Miss Camilla, I'll also do anything for you. Just tell me."

I leaned back and whispered, "Even dash out into the street and be hit by a car?"

His expression turned intense and serious. "Only if you're not joking and it serves a purpose. But do you really mean it?"

Shocked by his reaction, I giggled. "Of course not, Gao! Just joking!"

"Then please don't joke with me, Miss Camilla, ever. Because I'll always take your word seriously."

Staring at his rugged face, I wondered, could I lure and bribe him to kill Lung?

"Please go in, Miss Camilla, I'm sure Master Lung has been waiting for you."

Gao knocked, then opened the door. When I moved past him into the room, I felt his body heat gently wrapping around me like a blanket.

The door closed behind me with a soft click. Inside the spacious, medicinal-smelling room, Zhu was watching his boss slurp a bowl of steaming rice soup.

I smiled and nodded to Zhu, then went to peck Lung's cheek. Sitting down next to my patron, I reached to smooth his hair as if he were my little boy. Only after Lung had proclaimed me his lucky star would I have the nerve to make this daring move in front of his right-hand man.

"Master Lung, it is said that heaven favors the lucky," I cooed. "You are indeed the luckiest man in China."

He put down his soup and grabbed my hand. "Is that so, my little pretty?"

"Of course. Even the bullet was afraid of you, so it made a last-minute detour."

He turned to Zhu. "Ha-ha-ha! That's why Camilla is my favorite. I just love beautiful women with a sugared tongue and a brain stuffed with clever phrases!"

In the orphanage, I had never been considered a sweet child; otherwise I might have been adopted by a family much sooner. In that comfortless institution, I never smiled, didn't make friends, and withdrew into my own world of reading and thinking. Though the orphanage had a decent library, it was rarely visited, so most of the time I'd be left alone there to enter a happier and more orderly world merely by flipping pages.

The reason I'd finally been taken out of the orphanage by Mr. Ho, boss of the Bright Moon Nightclub, was not only that he found me pretty but because he deemed me the most intelligent of the lot. Most of the girls there couldn't write their own name properly or even tell the difference between a book and a box. Because I like to read, I was able to educate myself. But the last thing I'd ever imagined was that liking to read would lead me to warm the bed of Shanghai's most powerful gangster head.

I picked up Lung's bowl of rice soup and said, "Master Lung, why don't you let me feed you so you can save your energy for more important things? Shanghai is praying for your speedy recovery."

Lung smiled. "Ha-ha! Of course, but give me a kiss first."

I leaned to press my lips to his soggy ones.

Zhu lowered his head to read his newspaper, pretending not to see our flirtation. Lung was as happy to see me today as a sick child his mother. But an old saying is that being with the emperor is like walking beside a tiger; at any moment he might turn mean and devour you. So at every moment I was watching Lung's expressions and gestures, trying to guess his thoughts, always apprehensive I would make a wrong move.

After I finished feeding him, I asked, "Master Lung, do you need anything? Snacks, magazines, newspaper?"

He touched my cheek with his bony fingers. "My men will get me whatever I need." Then he thought for a moment. "But, Camilla, you can sing a song for me."

As I hesitated, Zhu lowered his newspaper to cast me a stern look. "Just pick a song to entertain your boss."

I decided to sing "I Can't Stop Thinking of You." I cleared my throat, half closed my eyes, and began:

> As the breeze moves my hair, I can't stop
>   thinking of you.
> The moon is in love with the sea,
> The sea falls in love with the moon,
> During this silvery, honeyed evening,
> How can I not think of you? . . .

Unexpectedly, as I sang, the face that appeared in my mind's eye was not the old man's but his son's. While I was trying to blink away this disturbing image, the door opened, and in walked the same man who had just intruded upon my vision. Startled, I abruptly stopped singing.

When our eyes met, the young master said, "Please don't stop your lovely song, Miss Camilla."

Zhu waved a dismissive hand at his boss's son. "It's all right. Camilla had a long day yesterday and must be tired. Let her take a break."

"Of course," Jinying said. Then he went to sit on the bed next to Lung, asking, "Father, how are you feeling today?"

Lung smiled, the corners of his lips soaring as high as a crane. "Jinying, I'm fine. What a luxury that I'm forced to rest, don't you think, huh?"

Surrounded by his *fengshui* son, his lucky-star mistress, and his most trusted man, no wonder Lung looked relaxed and genuinely happy. That was the best moment to kill a person—when his guard was down. Too bad I was not ready.

The son cast me a quick look, then said to his old man, "Glad to hear Father's having a good rest."

"That's why I've asked you so many times to help me run the business. But you don't care to help your old father. Don't you know many men in Shanghai would run over their own mother to grab this chance? A son should follow his father's wishes for him. But you won't. Why is that? I don't understand." He tapped his temple to emphasize his point. "Was your mind poisoned by those nonsense lectures at HarFud?"

"Father, I've told you many times that it's pronounced Har-*vard*," Jinying exclaimed as he quickly glanced at me.

Today was only the second time I had seen Lung and his son to-gether. I found it amusing that this powerful, ruthless man actually showed another side to his nature. *Good.* This could be his major weakness, his son. He was a loving, indulgent father—the same man who had thrown his mistress to feed pet tigers.

Then I wondered, why was I so keen to find out other people's weaknesses? True, I had to seek Lung's. But did others figure out mine? I knew I had to hide from others my detachment, my emotional void, my scheming heart. . . . But were these weaknesses or strengths? Breathing the hospital's unpleasant air, I felt confused and didn't like the feeling.

Just then I noticed that Zhu was staring at me. From his look, I had a feeling that he might sense something between Jinying and me. But the fact was, there was nothing between us. Or was there? I felt confused again, and this time I liked it even less.

But Zhu smiled at Jinying. "Young Master, don't you agree that a son should fulfill his father's wish?"

Seemingly not knowing what to say, Jinying remained silent, looking discomfited. Finally he muttered a weak, "I'll try."

"Good," both Lung and Zhu said as they exchanged glances.

Then the boss grabbed my hand and said to his son, "Jinying, you know that Camilla saved my life?"

The son nodded.

"Good, then be nice to her. She's now your father's lucky star!"

The son nodded again, his eyes almost as hopeless as an abandoned puppy's.

The father glanced at Zhu, then turned to me. "Camilla, how come you were the first person who noticed I was shot?"

"Master Lung, what a question! Because I care about you so much, I watch you always."

Zhu cast me an angry look. Suddenly I realized he might be thinking I had just made him look bad in front of his boss.

I immediately tried to smooth things over. "Master Lung, everyone was paying attention. It's only that as a woman, I was the first one to scream, because I was so scared."

I was relieved to see a smile emerging on Zhu's face.

Lung exclaimed, "Yes, all my men are first-rate. How could they not be, since I was the one who handpicked every single one? Ha! After my release, I'll have a big banquet to celebrate my cheating death. How's that?"

We all responded, "Excellent idea!"

Zhu smiled obsequiously. "Boss, I'll make preparations for that. How about a Manchurian Han banquet?"

"Excellent! How come I never thought of that?" He made a fist, striking the stale hospital air. "And I'll toast to the King of Hell and see how he'll respond! Ha!"

∽✺ 10 ✺∽

Manchurian Han Banquet and a Private Magic Show

A week later, Lung hosted the Manchurian Han imperial banquet at a famous high-end restaurant in the French Concession. I had heard about this kind of elaborate banquet but had never had the chance to see, let alone taste, one. It was based on the one that was served to celebrate Emperor Kangxi's sixty-sixth birthday.

That evening, I put on a purple *cheongsam* embroidered with a soaring golden dragon, a gift from Lung. This exquisite piece had been made in the Xiang province, where the embroiderers are renowned for the variety of their patterns, stitches, and color gradations. Thus the saying, "On a piece of *xiang* embroidery, you can see the birds fly and hear the tigers roar."

The golden dragon was enhanced by my gold earrings, necklace, and high heels. My other "props" included a silk golden flower pinned above my right ear, an Hermès handbag, a gold fan painted with blossoming camellias, and my fragrance, which scampered around me alluringly like a cat with a spool.

After Lung and I entered the restaurant's spacious VIP banquet room, we saw preparations fit for an emperor. On the stage, a small ensemble with *erhu,* a *zheng,* and percussion instruments was playing the lively tune *gongxi facai,* "Wishing You Good Fortune and Happiness." Twelve tables were set with embroidered tablecloths, napkins folded in the shape of a flower, enameled plates, and glasses with gilded borders. One tablecloth was yellow, a color once reserved for emperors; all the rest were red, the color of good luck. I immediately knew that Lung, Jinying, Zhu, Gao, and I, were to sit at the yellow one. Gao was included because his status had been upgraded since he had dashed to take a bullet for Lung.

The owner of the restaurant, its manager, and a group of waiters and waitresses flanked the entrance. The waitresses were dressed in the Qing dynasty imperial costume—a long, loose, yellow gown and a black vest embroidered with pink flowers. Another embroidered flower, also pink but much larger, perched on the girls' elaborate, beaded headgear. Two pearl tassels swayed from the sides like miniature waterfalls. The girls, the flowers, and the tassels all seemed to have entered a smiling competition. As I looked down, I noticed that the waitresses' shoes were five inches high on tiny platforms.

Lung nodded to the group as Zhu handed each a red lucky money envelope. The owner, a plump, middle-aged man, and the equally plump manager greeted us and told us that each table would be served by three imperial maids. The number was picked for good luck—*three* is a synonym of *birth, life.*

Upon seeing us, the other guests who'd arrived earlier stood and kowtowed. After that, we took our seats at the golden table. This evening the king, of course, was Master Lung—the triad king who had even beaten the King of Hell!

I noticed that the imperial-yellow tablecloth and its matching seat covers were embroidered with colorful clouds and dragons, as if to honor the Flying Dragons gang. The gilded silverware glittered regally under the intricately carved imitation palace lamps.

Three Qing dynasty "princesses," actually waitresses, came to fuss over us: holding out hot towels, pouring tea, serving respect dishes, lighting cigarettes. Of course there was no need for us to order, because the dishes for such an extraordinary banquet had to be selected well ahead.

As one of the "princesses" poured tea into Lung's three-legged cup, an imitation of the ancient, wine-offering tripod, the manager said, "Master Lung, this is the most expensive Big Red Robe tea. It costs more than my whole month's salary."

Another waitress presented wine, and the owner gushed, "Not only do we offer Master Lung the best wine, we also serve it to you in these ceramic bowls from the famous Jingde province."

The manager continued to babble while keeping his face pasted with a dog-shit-eating grin. His unctuous flow of words amazed and amused me.

"Master Lung, we would like you to know that it normally takes our chefs three months' of traveling to different provinces to gather all the ingredients for this feast, then three weeks with twelve assistant chefs to prepare, and finally three days to try and test all the one hundred and three dishes. But since you are our most honorable guest, we speeded up the whole process by having the ingredients specially shipped here. Only our restaurant with our personal connections could achieve this. So I hope you and your guests will enjoy what we serve tonight."

Lung laughed happily. "Of course I will. Especially after I cheated death, everything will taste heavenly, let alone the famous Manchurian Han banquet!" Then he turned to introduce me. "Meet Miss Camilla, my lucky star. She's the one who gave me the dragon amulet that fended off the evil spirit and saved my life."

"Welcome, Miss Camilla!" both the owner and the manager exclaimed.

Finally the manager finished his harangue and passed around the menu printed in golden characters against a crimson background: HEAVENLY DRAGON MANCHURIAN HAN IMPERIAL BANQUET. Then the manager pointed to the dishes on a small round table next to ours. "See? Honorable guests, these are the eighty-eight small dishes with their eighty-eight different condiments. And the eighty-eighty medium dishes with their eighty-eight different *pe-icai*."

Peicai is matching food, such as celery to go with Peking duck, dried vegetables with marinated pork, black fungus with fish fillet, chives with pig's liver.

I had been to lavish banquets before but had not imagined that there could be so many condiments and *peicai* to match the main dishes. The serving array was extraordinary, on plates arranged in concentric circles in matching colors. All the condiments in the innermost circle were in different shades of yellow, the next in shades of orange, then shades of brown, and finally black. From a distance, the whole thing looked like a huge blossoming flower, matching those on the waitresses' vests and headgear.

Soon chopsticks began clicking, lips smacking, glasses clinking, and flattering words pouring out.

Guests from the other tables came over to greet Lung, proposing toasts.

"Master Lung, that's why you're the number one boss—you even beat the King of Hell!"

"Congratulations, Master Lung! May your fortune be as infinite as the Eastern Sea and your longevity as immeasurable as the Southern Mountains!"

When everybody had fulfilled their obligatory rounds, we resumed eating. Soon the manager advised that we should taste only a small portion of each dish, saving room for more yet more to come. As best I could remember, the dishes we'd already tasted included: four-delicacies soup, gold-thread porridge, lotus prawns, sweet-scented osmanthus and dry scallops, Mandarin-duck thin milk, panda-tasting bamboo, phoenix spreading the wings, braised shark-fin phoenix tails, tiger skin and rabbit meat, dragon and phoenix heartthrob, French bean goldfish, pearl and white jelly fungus, osmanthus and pigeon eggs. . . .

The dish that really overwhelmed me was Immortals Pointing the Way, which, the owner told us, was made from the roots of green sprouts hollowed with a thin wire, then stuffed with shredded, newborn baby chicken. Almost as amazing was the One Hundred

Happiness, consisting of one hundred carps' whiskers meticulously collected, cooked, and arranged in the shape of one hundred different writing styles of the character *shou,* longevity.

Yet another one was Mandarin duck legs. This time the manager hastened to explain, "Ladies and gentleman, don't let this ordinary-looking dish fool you—"

Jinying blurted out, sounding like a spoiled child, "But we eat duck leg all the time."

"Young Master, but we only serve drumsticks from the left side of the duck."

Jinying widened his eyes. "Why eat the left and waste the right?"

A few guests smiled at his naivety.

"Because a duck always urinates by lifting its left leg. The results are, first, the left drumstick tastes much better because of the constant exercise. And second, the urine always flows to the right leg, resulting in an unpleasant, acidic taste."

An expression of amazement appeared on Jinying's face.

Lung looked at his son admiringly as he said to the manager, "My son is Western educated, a lawyer from HarFud. He knows much about the West but is still a beginner in Chinese culture."

Jinying pointed to the plate. "Is this considered Chinese culture?"

This time Zhu chimed in, "Of course. This is our five-thousand-year-old culinary culture."

The boss's son made a face. "Then I'd rather not learn about it." He paused before muttering softly, "It's disgusting."

No one seemed to, or pretended not to, hear what he'd said. The son looked in my direction, and I returned an understanding smile. Just then I noticed that Gao was studying us curiously. So I smiled again, making sure the one I aimed at him was a tad more flirtatious than the one I'd just sent to his possible rival. But he turned away, refusing to acknowledge my good intention. Nor did the bodyguard make any conversation with anyone else; he knew well his place in the black-society's hierarchy. He was lucky enough to have been invited to this table. So why push his luck further?

Tonight the only thing appropriate for him to do was to eat. And I was glad to see he'd been doing it with abandon.

More dishes, wine, and tea were consumed, and more congratulatory remarks poured out until at last the final dish arrived. Flanked by the owner and manager, two waitresses, between them balancing a huge golden plate, walked with delicate steps to our table. After they set down their burden, what we saw was a painting.

Jinying was the first to exclaim, "Wah! What a beautiful painting!"

Zhu added jokingly. "So now, after all the food, it's time for art appreciation?"

His boss scoffed. "Ha! Everyone knows I'm not interested in appreciating art, only making money."

The restaurant owner proudly announced, "Exquisite, isn't it? This painting is called *ruyi shanshui*, Good Luck Landscape. But don't let appearances fool you. Because this painting is edible!"

Jinying spoke again. "So this is food?"

"Of course!" Both the owner and the manager laughed at the young master's naivety.

On the "painting's" top left-hand corner shone a red sun with golden rays. Under it soared white cranes above luscious trees and colorful houses.

"This dish is vegetarian." This time the manager spoke, pointing. "See? The sun was made of carrot, its rays pickled radish, the flying cranes, tofu cut into different shapes. Take a close look, and you will see that the trees are seaweed and the houses different kinds of mushrooms."

Everyone *oohed* and *aahed* over this stunning culinary art.

I asked, "How can we have the heart to eat something so beautiful?"

Lung leaned close to me. "Do you also think that I shouldn't have the heart to eat you?"

I flung my fan playfully at him as I conjured up a matching smile, hiding my distress at his ominous words. "Master Lung, if I were a dish, do you think it would also have a boosting effect?" Of course the "boosting effect" I meant was sexual.

Lung patted his chest emphatically. "Huh! What do you think? I even cheated death!"

Now everyone focused on studying the "painting" and pretended that they didn't hear any of our conversation nor see the old man's dirty little hands taking tasty trips on my body. Everyone except the young master and the head bodyguard. The former's face was turning red and the latter's pale.

Finally, when we were all complaining about our bulging bellies, Zhu stood up, tapped his glass with his spoon, and announced, "Thank you, everyone, for coming here tonight to celebrate Master Lung's cheating death! Now that our bellies are satisfied, what about our eyes and ears?"

People clapped. "Yes, let's hear Miss Camilla's heavenly voice!"

Zhu waved a dismissive hand. "Wait, not so fast. Miss Camilla should always be the last, since she's the best, right? So we'll have a surprise show first!"

Just then, the orchestra played something loud and boisterous as a woman walked briskly onto the stage and deeply bowed. To my utter shock, it was Shadow!

My heart beat wildly. Lung had never told me about inviting Shadow to the banquet for entertainment. Was this simply a pleasant surprise, or a sign of danger ahead?

The magician appeared half-naked, wearing flesh-colored tights with sequins covering her breasts and the valley between her legs. People looked shocked and amazed that she appeared naked but was in fact not, part of her constant, seductive navigation between illusion and reality.

Shadow thanked Zhu for the introduction, then smiled to the audience. Finally her eyes landed on Lung.

She picked up a glass of wine. "May I suggest that we all toast to Master Lung's health and longevity?"

After everyone upended their glass, the magician continued. "I know you're all waiting eagerly for Miss Camilla to round out this wonderful evening with her heavenly singing. So my show will just be a warm-up." Then she looked toward me. "Will Miss Camilla come up onstage?"

Now what trick was stored inside her sleeve?

I cast a questioning glance at Lung. He responded by looking extremely happy. "Camilla, at the temple's opening ceremony, you said that I forgot to invite Shadow. So here she is tonight!"

But that was not what I'd meant—or wanted!

I asked, "Then why didn't I see her earlier, during the dinner?"

Zhu answered for his boss. "The Manchurian Han Imperial Banquet is not for everyone."

Hearing this, I felt a little better.

As I stood up, Lung pinched my bottom. "No more talk. Let's see what you two pretty sisters are going to do to entertain us."

Onstage, Shadow made a gesture for me to sit in a chair.

"All right, Shadow, what are you going to do to me?" I asked, faking fear. Or was I really scared?

The audience laughed, eyes Ping-Ponging between us, waiting for something exciting to happen.

She smiled, sitting down across from me. "Nothing. Why don't we just chitchat and get to know each other better?"

"What do you want to chat about?" I asked, wondering, *What kind of trick is she pulling?*

"Hmm . . . can you tell us about your family?"

Even as a magician, did she think she could trick me into revealing my secrets—as an orphan and a spy—in front of an audience?

"Miss Shadow"—I smiled—"I believe people are much more interested in a beautiful magician who can plunge to her disappearance than a songstress's humble background. So why don't you tell us the secrets of your magic?"

This strategy is called *yitui weijin,* retreat in order to advance. I feigned being modest as I threw the ball back to her.

She stayed calm. "Miss Camilla, we Chinese believe that the highest form of success is symbolized by a dragon soaring in the sky. And what contributes to this success is secrecy, as a dragon never completely reveals itself but is always partly hidden by clouds. Therefore the saying, 'When the heavenly dragon's head is seen, its tail will be hidden; if its tail is seen, its head will be hidden.'"

She turned to smile at Lung. "Just like our Master Lung. And who would reveal our boss's secrets?"

The audience yelled, "Well said!"

Master Lung burst out laughing, hitting his fist on the table.

I tried my best to conceal my anger, even fear. *Very clever.* As she was humiliating me, she was also flattering Lung, because not only was Lung being referred to as a dragon, but his gang was called the Flying Dragons. In addition, she had also subtly equated her own success to Lung's!

I thought for a few seconds before I replied, quoting the ancient strategist Han Feizi's famous words, " 'The bright master observes but is not to be observed.' So, if you won't tell us your secrets, are you saying that you're just like our venerable Master Lung?"

This time she looked upset. If she said yes, Lung would be greatly offended, but if she said no, she was refuting her own statement.

As I was wondering how long would this go on until we'd both gotten ourselves into trouble, a voice from the audience exclaimed, "Thank you for your repartee! We greatly enjoyed it!"

It was Jinying. He went on. "Now, why don't we hear Miss Camilla's singing?"

Obviously he was trying to relieve the tension onstage. And no one dared object to the young master's suggestion.

Shadow stood up and bowed to me, then to the audience. As she was about to walk away, someone asked, "What about some magic? We haven't yet seen you perform!"

"You'll see." After that, she walked off the stage.

Though people looked puzzled by the ambiguous statement, no one inquired further.

I spoke through the microphone. "Master Lung and honorable guests, tonight I'll sing *"Huahao Yueyuan"* to celebrate this auspicious occasion."

All Chinese love this song, "The Flowers Are Blooming, and the

Moon Is Round," because the two images symbolize happy reunion and a full, blessed life.

Every time I sang, I'd use my fan to make pretty gestures. But this time, when I tried to pull my prop from my lapel, I was shocked to find it was not there. Distracted, I emitted a wrong note. Fortunately I was an experienced singer, so I immediately dragged that off-tune note back to its right position. Since I did it so calmly and naturally, the audience didn't seem to notice. Even if someone did, he or she might think it just an odd, decorative note that I'd thrown in to liven up the song.

But when I tried to pull the handkerchief out from my sleeve, like the fan, it was nowhere to be found. Suddenly I realized Shadow had stolen all the props from me during our chat! But I was not going to make any more wrong moves and a fool of myself. So I continued to sing, about to use my fingers to gesture instead. But when I lifted my hand, I discovered that my sparkling diamond ring had walked away from my finger as well!

I felt my blood boil inside my arteries, but I was not going to let a mere shadow ruin me. I decided I would upstage her by showing off my combined, ultimate skill of singing and contorting. The tune was already slipping from my mouth.

> The clouds disperse, and the moon shines.
> Tonight is for reunions.
> In the pond, a pair of Mandarin ducks frolic.
> The lotus flowers bloom,
> Always in pairs . . .
> The world is full of love and tender sentiments. . . .

As the notes continued to spill from my throat, my body and limbs began to twist. Now and then my Chinese dress would slide up to offer a glimpse of my underwear. I was sure the audience, especially Lung, his son, Gao, and even Zhu were all turned on by my perverse act. One time my head was resting between the valley of my legs, another time my head was on the floor with my legs above, and yet another time my body was twisted into an S shape like a mischievous snake.

The audience looked shocked by this perplexing, surrealistic spectacle. Their jaws dropped, eyes widened, and mouths gaped, emitting no words, only gasps. As the surprise subsided, the applause began.

I saw that Jinying had his head lowered, only occasionally lifting it to peek. He must be too embarrassed or too titillated to see his innocent dream woman displaying herself like this. But I didn't care. My fame and *presence,* which I'd spent years to build, was not going to be eclipsed by a mere shadow.

The evening finally ended, and we were waiting outside the restaurant for our cars.

Lung said to Zhu and his son, "Why don't you two leave first? Gao will drive Camilla and me back to my place."

This took me a bit by surprise. Lung rarely let me travel in the same car alone with him but perhaps now gave me this honor because my status had been elevated to that of lucky star. Jinying cast me a resentful look, then crawled into a waiting car with Zhu, not saying good-bye to either his father or me.

Inside Lung's car, as usual, Gao peeked at me from the rearview mirror, but this time his stare, like his boss's son's, had an element of sadness and anger.

The moment Lung and I stepped into his house, he dismissed Gao. To my surprise, he even forgot to ask the bodyguard to search me. But it didn't matter, because I didn't carry any weapon, nor could I use his phone to call my boss to send assassins. Besides, Gao and his men would be on duty all night as usual.

Once we were inside his bedroom, Lung tore off my clothes, then went to sit on the bed. He poured himself a brandy as he studied me like a teenage boy ogling a prostitute for the first time.

"Camilla, don't you know you're a woman full of surprises? I like that!" He was already drunk from the banquet, but now he took another big gulp of the liquor. "How come you didn't let me know about your contortionist skill, huh, you little fox spirit?" He molested my whole body with his fuzzy eyes. "All right, now give me a private performance. You know what I want."

So I began to perform again, adding some new twists. This time the only difference was that there was not a single stitch on my body. Then, when my head was on the floor and the valley between my legs above, Lung approached me, flung off his bathrobe, and came into me as if entering his bathroom to answer nature's call. . . .

≈ 11 ≈

The Bund and the Amusement Park

Early the next morning, still feeling stung by Shadow's tricks and Lung's perversity, I headed straight to the Bund. Whenever I went there, I never put on makeup. Instead, I wore big sunglasses to hide most of my face and tied my hair into two pigtails so I would look like a student.

Today, as usual, I stood behind the winged-goddess statue facing the river. This daily ritual of meditating on the river had become the only real comfort in my solitary, fearful life. As I watched the waves, Confucius's saying again emerged in my mind. "The river flows on endlessly day and night. . . ." Though having lived only nineteen years in this world, I understood perfectly what the sage meant: Life moves on, no matter what we do. Indifferent to my schemes, my ups and my downs, whether I live or die, the river flows on. One day all of us will be dust scattering in the thin air above its ripples.

Feeling the *yin* power of the water enveloping me, I imagined I could remember being inside my mother's womb, the mother I had never known in this dusty world.

A wave captured a ray of sunlight, giving out a hopeful sparkle as I contemplated my big question: Who was this woman? She had given me life, but a dreadful one. Did she and my father really die in a car accident as Big Brother Wang had told me? I imagined that he was a rich village chief's son, and she a poor farmer's daughter. But then I would think, maybe my father was a gangster like Wang and my mother his mistress? And he'd killed her because she knew too much about his secrets, then left me at the orphanage's door as a worthless girl. . . .

Or had my mother abandoned me? If yes, was there a poignant story behind? Did she have me because she was really in love with my father, or was I just a moment's impulse? I sighed. I needed to set aside these meanderings to stay focused on my mission, not waste time feeling sorry for myself. So I imagined these worries floating away on the flowing river. But one returned: Even if I was able to carry out my mission, after that, what would I do next? Would Big Brother Wang take me as his concubine, or kill me?

I had no answer, so I resumed practicing my singing, beginning with "It's Rare We Can Be Together."

> Can there be a time we will meet each other?
> On the path of love, there will be wind and rain,
> Let them keep you company.
> There will be laughter and tears,
> Let them be part of you. . . .

Absorbed in my singing, I suddenly felt a hand warming my shoulder. I turned and found a tender, heartbreaking face. For no reason, I felt an urge to smooth its knotted brow.

"Camilla," Jinying said, wiping my face with a handkerchief. It was then that I realized my eyes had been raining tears.

But that was not possible. I could not allow myself this.

Just as I was about to say something, my mouth was sealed by his.

When the young master finally released me, he said, stroking my face, "Camilla, please tell me why you were crying."

I tried to put on a false smile, which I hoped would look as genuine as the pain I was really feeling. "Don't worry, Jinying, everything is fine. I'm very happy."

"How can you be?"

"What makes you think I'm not?"

"Because you're with my father. Anyone around him is cursed."

"How can you say that? You're his son."

"Then I am the most cursed."

"But he brings everyone lots of money and . . ." I trailed off. My voice now sounded not heavenly but dejected.

"Camilla." The young master looked hard at me with his penetrating eyes."Please don't say things to me that you don't mean."

I hardened my heart. "Young Master, what makes you think you know who I am? Please stop following me here!"

He didn't respond but took my hand and led me toward the street.

A few passersby cast us curious glances.

"What are you doing?"

He hailed a tricycle-rickshaw. "Relax, Camilla, and let me take you to a place where you can be yourself. This time I won't take no for an answer."

"But your father . . ."

"Forget my father for now. Let me bring you a taste of happiness, won't you?"

Actually, I had no idea what real happiness felt like.

Or did I? Because the little space under the rickshaw cover suddenly seemed like a bit of heaven on earth. I was not looking at Jinying, but my hand was tightly held in his as we idly observed the bustling traffic. Bicycles, tricycles, rickshaws, cars, trams, double-decker buses, people on foot, all rushing to their various destinations. People of all sorts. A young woman held a child by one hand, and in the other hand was a bamboo basket filled with food wrapped in newspapers and tied with sea reeds. An open-air street stall was filled with workers munching scallion pancakes and gulping down bowls of steaming congee. Inside the park, people relaxed on benches, reading newspapers or staring at the river. Among them, two well-dressed white women were chattering intensely with matching hand gestures. In front of the post office, gray-uniformed letter carriers leaned on their bicycles, ready to set out.

When our rickshaw was passing a big signboard, its English

words caught my eye: *Where friends meet . . .* But when I looked closer, it was an ad for cigarettes. I sighed.

Finally the rickshaw pulled to a stop in front of a huge walled compound.

I turned to my "kidnapper." "Jinying, where are we?"

He smiled mischievously. "I'm sure you've never been here before. We're between Astoria Road and Mintiniyin Road. This is the famous Big World Amusement Park."

Of course I'd heard about this most popular entertainment center in Shanghai, but I'd never had the chance to come here. Waiting while Jinying went to the counter to get tickets, I read the huge signboard next to its entrance.

> Welcome to Shanghai Big World Amusement Park, the first modern amusement center in Shanghai, built in 1917. We have more than thirty attractions: restaurants, shops, concert halls, movie theaters, opera houses, bowling alleys, skating rink, and a circus. All day you will be thrilled by our dancers, singers, musicians, gymnasts, figure skaters, and magicians. Here, it's festival and carnival every day!

Just as I finished reading, Jinying came back, grinning and waving two tickets in his hand. "Let's go."

"Jinying, this place is for kids!" I pointed to the many children holding toys or licking candy as they skipped around under their parents' proud eyes.

He winked. "At nineteen, aren't you still a child yourself?"

I protested, playfully hitting his shoulder. "Look at me. Do I look like a child?"

"But can't we go back to our childhoods just for a little while?"

I bit my lip hard so I wouldn't burst into tears. I would not want to go back to my childhood for even one minute. Unlike the children here, I had never had proud parents, nor toys, nor candies! Perversely, sometimes I even wished that Lung were my father, so he would love me the way he loved his son.

Probably sensing my mood, Lung's son wrapped his arm around my shoulders and said very gently, "Please, Camilla, if you're suffering, let me know, and I will make you happy again."

"Young Master, with your privileged life, I don't think you know what suffering is."

He sighed, shaking his head. "Camilla, don't you see I'm a prisoner of my father's power, even his love? That's why I tried to be a student in America as long as I could."

"Then why did you come back?"

"My father told me he was sick. And I was worried about my mother."

"Your mother?"

"It's a long, sad story. My mother scolded my father all the time. Then one day she was gone, and he told me that he'd had to send her to a mental institution. Even now I have no idea if this was the only way my father could shut her up permanently or if she was really crazy. Or maybe she just feigned madness so she could get away from him." He shook his head, looking very sad. "I was never allowed to see her."

What a coincidence. I'd told Shadow at the Chocolate Shop that my mother was in a mental institution. Maybe in a strange way the young master and I did have something in common.

"Not even now?"

"When I got back, my father told me she had died when I was in America."

"Oh, how terrible for you!"

"He said he didn't tell me because he didn't want to interrupt my studies. Sometimes I suspect she may be still alive, but I have no way to find out. Or maybe she has been dead for a long time."

"Did he ever take you to visit her grave?"

"No. He said she was cremated and her ashes scattered into the Huangpu River."

Despite my curiosity, I willed myself to stop asking more questions. I feared I'd feel so sorry for him that I'd end up showing my feelings.

Seeing that I didn't respond, Jinying said, "So let's forget about all this and have some fun, okay?"

I nodded. He took my hand, and we began to walk. Maybe because it was Monday and most people had to work, the park was far from being packed. Mostly there were young couples and families with children, all looking happy and relaxed under the warm, soothing sun.

What a beautiful life, only it wasn't really mine.

Jinying led us past the movie theater, the opera stage, the shooting gallery, and the skating rink. Then we stopped in front of the carousel. A dreamy tune spilled from the merry-go-round to envelop the air in bittersweet nostalgia. On the colorful wooden horses sat little brave riders, laughing and waving. Parents were busy smiling, taking pictures, and waving back as their little ones swirled by. On other horses, babies and toddlers were held tightly on their parents' laps, some chuckling, some fussing, yet others looked completely oblivious of their good luck.

As a little girl on a wooden horse swung past us, a young woman, probably her mother, reached to hand her a candy. The girl shrieked with happiness. Surrounded by these elated faces and the cheery tunes, instead of happiness, I felt a tremendous sadness lodge in my heart, unwilling to leave. To my frustration, my tears ignored my training and found their way to freedom. But since I was with Jinying, I decided I might as well indulge my true feelings for once. But just this once. He was not going to hurt me or tell anyone about my loss of control, was he?

The music and the revolving platform came to a stop.

Jinying pulled me close to him as a sigh escaped from his mouth. "Camilla, you can trust me."

I shuddered inside. If he only knew where I was coming from, what I'd been trained to do, and what I was really going to do!

I didn't respond, couldn't.

"Come ride the horses with me," he said, then dashed away to get tickets.

In no time he rushed back, and before I could say anything, he dragged me onto the round platform and lifted me up onto a pink horse. After that, he hopped on behind me, grabbing my waist. Soon the carousel began to revolve as another dreamy tune spilled out. Around us were mostly children, some riding alone, the smaller ones held by their parents. The one next to us was a small boy of four or five riding by himself.

He was dressed all in yellow, his outfit a perfect match to his yellow horse with its green saddle. He looked so cute and serious, as if he were riding a real horse.

I asked, "Little friend, what's your name?"

To my surprise, not only did he not answer me, but he cast me a suspicious look and turned away. Could I blame him? I'd been trained to be suspicious my whole life! At least he could be honest, instead of having to feign friendliness like I did.

As we sailed past a young couple on the ground, they waved to the little boy, and he shrieked with happiness, yelling, "Baba! Mama!"

The man cheerfully waved to his son, yelling, "Baobao, hold tight!"

The nostalgic atmosphere, the happy children, and their doting parents jolted something in me, as if I had a vague memory of riding a carousel like this when I was very little. . . .

Sometimes I would dream of outings with my parents, but whenever I woke up, no matter how clear their images had been, I couldn't recall how they actually looked in real life. No matter how hard I tried to fix their images in my mind, they faded just as I awoke. Eventually I gave up. What good would it do me to remember how they looked? I would never see them in this world.

Just then Jinying's voice startled me. "Camilla, I hope you're enjoying this."

Damn it. His interruption cut off the faint memory.

I snapped, "Yes, until you interrupted!"

"I'm sorry, Camilla. I just want you to enjoy yourself."

"I was happy at least once in the past."

Despite my outburst, he rested his head on mine. "Then can't you give me a chance to make you happy now?"

Just then the music stopped, and we all began to descend from the horses. Some children were scooped up by their parents; others plunged into their embrace.

The yellow-attired boy, now being lifted to sit on his father's shoulders, turned to me and made a face.

His mother spotted this and scolded him gently. "Baobao, don't act rude to the nice lady. Can you say sorry?"

To my surprise, the little boy suddenly smiled sunnily and blew me an air kiss just like the one he'd sent to his parents.

Jinying's tenor voice rose next to my ear. "Camilla, wouldn't it be lovely if we had a boy like that someday? And that we loved him with all our heart and soul?"

"Sure," I snapped again, at Jinying and also at my own secret sentimentality.

The little boy and his parents waved to us and walked away toward the ice cream stand.

Seemingly oblivious of, or deliberately ignoring, my rudeness, Jinying took my hand and kissed it. "Camilla, let's go to my place."

"Okay," I said, surprising myself. My reasoning self argued that this might actually be a good thing; maybe I could find out something important about Lung from his son.

I liked Jinying's apartment immediately. The furniture—a plain sofa, wooden coffee table, redwood dining table and matching chairs—was clean and simple. The walls were lined with bookcases overflowing with books, music scores, and decorative objects. Serene landscape paintings opened unexpected vistas through the white walls. Small busts of musicians and composers graced his upright piano and windowsills.

The young master smiled, then led me to sit on the sofa. After that, he went to put a 78 on his gramophone. What flowed out from the disk was me singing "A Wandering Songstress." As I was about to say something, he disappeared into the kitchen. Soon he reappeared with two glasses and a bottle of red wine. He sat down by me, filled the two glasses, and handed me one.

"To our meeting!" He tapped my glass with his, emitting a pleasant *clink*.

I took a few meditative sips, then quietly put down the glass. The young master took my hand and lifted it to his lips.

"Camilla . . . I'm sure you know that I fell in love with you the first time I saw you at Bright Moon." He pointed to the stack of 78s next to the gramophone. "I have all your records and listen to them every day."

"But, Jinying, you know I can't love you back."

"It is because of my father?"

I didn't respond. If only life were that simple. I gulped some more wine.

"Let me deal with him."

I chuckled. "How? You think anyone can just get away from your father's grasp, or slip through the cracks of his callous fingers?"

He shook his head like a stubborn child. "He loves me. . . ."

I said, "You think love solves everything?"

He pulled me to him and kissed me passionately on my mouth. Despite all my training at suppressing emotions, I found myself kissing him back with equal vehemence. His tongue eagerly searched mine. Then his hand reached inside my blouse. After more kissing and caressing, he lifted me up and carried me to his bedroom.

Soon I was lying on his spacious bed, naked and half-drunk, nervous as if it were my first time. His lips and hands, hot and feverish, explored my body like an adventurer seeking buried treasure. I responded by clinging tightly to him like a child fearing being abandoned by his mother. My nipples hardened, and the wet valley between my legs trembled, as I felt *qi* shooting right up my directing meridian, from my golden gate all the way to my mouth. I moaned and squirmed and pleaded for him to stop, but his hands and tongue, seemingly deaf, kept ambushing me from all sides.

He stared at me with his sad, penetrating eyes as his other self slipped inside me. His thrusts were deep and fervent, buoyant but hopeless. Our eyes locked with each other's as we felt our rise to orgasmic heaven, then our plunge to fiery hell. I squirmed and screamed in abandon, venting a lifetime's bottled-up emotions. My fingernails dug furrows in his back, leaving my marks of unbearable pleasure and insufferable miseries. . . .

After making love, we cuddled on the bed, feeling the sensuousness of the silky sheets.

I didn't know if what I felt for this good-looking, refined-acting, Harvard-educated lawyer was love. I did know that I enjoyed the fiery sensations produced by his hands and lips. It was certainly much better than being with his old father and having to force myself to moan and groan while wearing a "becoming an immortal" expression. . . .

I was afraid of letting myself feel too comfortable, so I turned to Jinying and told him I had to go.

"Please, just stay here with me."

"I can't."

"Camilla . . ."

"Yes?"

"Let's go away together."

Although I acted calm on the surface, my heart was beating hard against my ribs. "What do you mean?"

"We can elope to Hong Kong, or even the US."

"Are you out of your mind?"

"That's our only way out."

"Your father will kill us."

"We're already on a path of no return. Camilla, I don't want a life without you."

"Young Master, are you serious?"

"Yes! If not, let me be struck down by lightning or run over by a car the second I step out of this building."

I put a finger across his lips. "Shh. . . . please don't say something unlucky like that, ever." If I did have a chance to run away with him, I certainly wouldn't want him killed. "What if your father and his men track us down?"

"They won't. I can carry you in my suitcase and take the ship back to America. You're such a good contortionist, you definitely can hide in a suitcase, right?"

I smiled. *What a silly thought.* But right now I could not think of any more realistic way to escape.

"Please come with me, Camilla."

"I need time to think."

"Of course."

Some silence passed before I said, "Jinying, I'm your father's mistress, so what makes think you can trust me?"

"Your voice."

"My voice?" I was suddenly alert. "How?"

"No one sings like you. When I first saw you at Bright Moon, it was as if everyone else simply disappeared, and there was only you and me and your heartbreaking voice. Camilla, I love you, and I want to spent the rest of my life with you."

"The rest of your life?" I smiled. "I'm sure you'd get bored quickly."

He shook his head, looking very serious. "Never."

Another pause followed, and then I asked, "If you leave your father, will you have enough money to live on?"

"I can always find a job at a law firm. Although I don't like being a lawyer, I'm good at it. And you can still perform, or you can teach singing. But I'll support you if you don't want to."

This was his naïveté coming out. The idea of teaching singing had never even once crossed my mind. But if I performed, I would be recognized, and Lung's men would find me. I was sure he had no idea what we would be up against.

I looked at his innocent expression and wondered how a rough old man like Lung could sire and raise a clean, refined son like Jinying. Still staring, I felt heat shoot from my vagina to my head. I pulled him to me and kissed him fervently on his lips while my hand reached to grab his sex.

"Gentle, Camilla. Please be gentle with me. . . ."

Back home, I kept thinking of Jinying's proposal to elope with him and the idea of teaching singing. Somehow my encounter with him seemed to open a window—even if just a crack—in my life. It made me realize that life might offer me more possibilities than I had realized. Wouldn't it be nice to be a singing teacher like Madame Lewinsky, making a good income, being respected by students with their friendly visits and thoughtful gifts?

Just when I felt the corners of my lips lifting, my maid, Ah Fong, came into the living room. She carefully placed a cup of ginseng honey tea on the coffee table and said respectfully, "Miss Camilla, please drink this—very good for your voice. Big Brother Wang always say that I should cook you nutritious dishes to boost your energy and nurture your voice."

As she walked away, I felt I was being slapped awake from a dangerous dream—back to an even more dangerous reality.

❦ 12 ❦

The Castle

Two days later, I was still thinking of the afternoon at Big World Amusement Park—and what came after—when Shadow called to invite me to her next show, "The Castle."

I feigned excitement. "Congratulations, Shadow! So this time you're going to perform magic in a castle?"

"The name 'castle' is but a gimmick; it really is just a dilapidated old mansion. You know, Camilla," she laughed, "for a magician, everything in life is a prop."

Or an illusion, like a spy's life. I smiled into the phone. "That's an interesting way to look at things."

I was probably also a prop in her life. So, how was she going to use, then discard, me? I'd better get rid of her first. As the Chinese say, "He who strikes first gains the upper hand; he who strikes second gets killed."

During our conversation, she never mentioned my handkerchief, fan, and diamond ring she'd taken during the banquet, nor did she apologize. But I was not going to say anything about it, not now. I'd wait and see.

Two weeks later, on a Friday evening, my driver, Ah Wen, took me a long way to an unfamiliar suburb outside Shanghai. We turned off the main road and continued for another ten minutes until we reached level ground some twenty yards from the "castle" on a hill. A group of about fifty people was milling around, looking excited. A signboard erected on the ground read: WAIT HERE FOR THE BUS TO TAKE YOU TO THE CASTLE. I was sure everyone was wondering why we couldn't just have our cars leave us off right at our destination.

Soon a bus arrived to take us up the hill to the old mansion. Another signboard in front of the building read: PLEASE WAIT HERE FOR THE INVITATION TO ENTER. THANK YOU FOR YOUR PATIENCE.

The mansion, a grandiose, Western-style structure with pillars along the façade, looked old and forlorn under the full moon streaked with wisps of wandering clouds. Was it lamenting its inevitable fate of outliving its owner or, like a beautiful woman, its inevitable decline? In front of the mansion was a small pond covered with moss, withered petals, and debris, giving off a bittersweet smell. Under the moonlight, the architecture reminded me of a sleeping beauty waiting for her prince to wake her with his kiss. Had Shadow picked this mansion to perform her magic with some sort of symbolism in mind? If so, what was it?

Then I turned and was struck by the magnificent view of nighttime Shanghai below. Colorful neon lights blinked incessantly, as if beckoning us to indulge in all sorts of decadence in this Ten Thousand Miles of Red Dust. Calling us to have our fun before it was too late, before the bird of our youth flew away, never to return.

I looked around me at the small group of elegant guests. The men wore long Chinese silk gowns or Western suits, and the women high-collared *cheongsam* or cocktail dresses, with matching accessories like hats, walking sticks, gloves, fans, jewelry. Although it was September and not even chilly, several dignified-looking *tai tai,* society ladies, had donned their thousand-dollar furs. There was an air of excitement and anticipation as the group waited for the event to begin.

While I was looking for Lung, I saw Jinying walk past an old couple toward me.

He planted a kiss on my cheek.

I complained in a heated whisper, "Young Master, are you out of your mind? What if people see us and tell your father?"

"Relax, nobody's watching. I already looked around."

"But not again. I'm serious."

"All right, all right, I'm sorry." He sighed, looking as forlorn as the abandoned castle.

I asked, "Where's your father?"

"Camilla," he scoffed, "you know he's not interested in magic. He has much more important business to handle."

"How come you're here?"

"I knew he'd be away and you'd be here tonight. So I took his invitation."

"What's he up to now? He never tells me."

"He's buying up rickshaw licenses so that the pullers work for him."

"Why does he want the pullers?"

"So they can serve as his informants."

"Really?"

"Sure. Rickshaws are allowed to move freely everywhere, even the foreign concessions, so the pullers hear everything that's going on in Shanghai. And some of them are strong and fierce enough to act as his hatchet men."

I remained silent, absorbing the information.

The young master shook his head, obviously disapproving of his old man's shifty deeds, apparently not conscious that what he was wearing tonight—a perfectly cut bespoke suit, shiny black Italian leather shoes, and gold Rolex watch, even his expensive cologne— had all been paid for from his old man's perennially bulging pocket, the contents of which derived from his evil-karmic acts.

He went on, lowering his voice. "My father is also trying to buy ammunition."

I made my voice lower than his. "Someone's going to start a war soon?"

"My father says that a war is always starting somewhere. He's just trying to sip the first drop of any nutritious soup, as the saying goes."

Of course, some of the wars were the black societies themselves fighting one another for ever bigger helpings of the lucrative shark-fin soup that is Shanghai. Loyalties and alliances changed almost daily to the sound of gunfire, making juicy copy for Shanghai's newspapers.

Jinying cast me a bitter smile. "Camilla, let's not talk about this anymore. Let's just enjoy the evening, okay?" He paused, then added, "By the way, you look gorgeous tonight." He had finally noticed my lacy white dress with matching gloves, shawl, and pearl necklace.

The boss's son took my elbow and steered me through the crowd. A few people gestured toward me and whispered to one another. I was always careful to smile back at anyone who acknowledged my presence. After all, some of these people were my meal tickets. But, as sometimes happened, a richly attired woman cast me a condescending glance, then turned away. That was fine with me, too. Since childhood, I'd had to learn to ignore snubs. Like a cold, they would sooner or later go away. My goal was to complete my mission. Distractions were to be ignored or eliminated.

Jinying's voice woke me from my thinking. "What's on your mind, Camilla?"

"Oh, I'm wondering what the show is about."

Just then, to everyone's surprise, a small dog came out from the mansion and barked at us playfully. People burst out laughing. The dog barked more, furiously wagging its tail and tilting its head, seeming to beckon us to enter the building. People threw one another questioning looks, but no one moved. Finally, a fiftyish man in a long coat, fedora hat, and carrying a walking stick took a tentative step across the threshold with his lady friend.

Once someone had broken the spell, the crowd relaxed and started to stream in. Inside, the first thing that caught my attention was that everything was red: the chandelier with its many faceted crystals giving out mysterious sparks on the walls and floor like blood drops, as well as sofas, vases, draperies, and abstract oil paintings.

The guests cast curious glances here and there, their expression a mixture of delight, surprise, and puzzlement. Why hold a magic show inside this strange old crimson castle? And where was the magician?

Then all of a sudden, the lights went out. A mere ten seconds later, they went back on, but something had changed. It took a moment for everyone to realize what it was: All the paintings on the walls were gone!

People exclaimed, asking one another if they had also seen the paintings when they had come in. Maybe this was a collective hallucination. Amid the questions and heated whispers, something stirred at the top of the long flight of steps. All eyes looked up and beheld the magician, who had transformed herself into a stunning goddess. Her face, powdered geisha white, contrasted strikingly with her purplish-pink eye shadow, bright red lipstick, and shiny black hair cascading over one shoulder. A bright light silhouetted her concave-waisted, big-hipped body encased in a tight, sequined, crimson evening gown, reminding me of a paper cutout. Rubies—I was sure they were costume jewelry—winked from her red-gloved wrists and fingers, as if beckoning us to enter her world of mystery and intrigue. I noticed several men studying her like connoisseurs appreciating an exquisite artwork.

I wondered whether Jinying shared the audience's admiration, so I remarked to him, "Jinying, she's stunning, isn't she?"

"Sorry, Camilla, too big for my taste, too threatening and oppressive."

I felt relieved at hearing this. Could I actually be jealous, fearing that the magician would be trying to lure the son as well as the father?

Shadow began to slowly descend the long staircase. The dog suddenly yapped, dashing up the stairs to greet its master. With an elegant sweep of her hand, the magician scooped up her canine prop. However, Shadow didn't descend all the way to meet us mortals but halted midstairs, smiling and studying us with the dog nestled happily in her arms, its eager red tongue matching its mistress's gown.

"Ladies and gentleman, tonight I and my Baobao welcome you all to my special show!"

The dog responded by yelping as if exclaiming, "Yes! Yes!"

Shadow affectionately stroked her prop. "Shh! Be quiet, and let Mommy talk."

People laughed. She was off to a good start.

"I hope you like what you've seen so far, and of course there's much more coming. Now please let's all proceed outside, where a reception is waiting for you inside a tent."

A gentleman in a gray suit and tie said, "I thought the magic was about the castle. Am I not right?"

Shadow smiled teasingly. "Of course it is."

As if on cue, the dog suddenly jumped from Shadow's arms and ran outside. We followed the dog like a herd of obedient sheep.

I asked Jinying, feeling his hand steering my elbow, "You like the show so far?"

"Only if you do."

"It's not exciting to you?"

"Why would people pay to be fooled?"

"Because they want to believe in the impossible."

"Me, too. But not fake magic." He stooped to whisper into my ear. "The magic I want, Camilla, is for you to truly love me and for us somehow to escape from my father's grasp. Life is mostly illusions—or disillusionment. I don't like being fooled. I like honesty, like you and your voice."

Before I had a chance to respond, we arrived at the tent.

As we followed the dog inside, someone hissed, "I swear the tent was not here when we came!"

Another one responded. "Don't you remember? This is magic."

"But how could she have set it up so fast?"

I said to Jinying, "It's not 'fast,' considering her years of hard work behind all this."

I remembered that Madame Lewinsky had once told me, "Genius, this word we use so casually, is mostly determination and perseverance." Then I remembered my favorite proverb: "The sharp blade of a sword is the result of constant polishing. The fragrance of plum blossom comes only from the bitterest cold."

Jinying said, "You're right."

Inside the big tent, rows of chairs faced the entrance and were flanked by tables covered with bottles of Champagne and plates of food. Tall red candles burned brightly, casting shadows on the food and turning the golden liquid into bubbly blood. The dog yapped toward the tables, as if beckoning us to take the food. Soon people were happily munching, sipping, and waiting for their hostess to cast a few magical sparks into their rich, boring lives.

Jinying got us Champagne and a plate of small dishes—mini ham sandwiches, fried shrimp, beef cakes, pate. He tapped his glass against mine and spoke in a near whisper. "Camilla, to our future."

I smiled prettily, as if I was actually foreseeing one.

We sat down. While Jinying was busy eating, I sipped my drink and looked around. Nothing seemed peculiar about this tent except that it had a high ceiling. Through the open entrance we could see the castle, its lights flickering as if winking to us.

Soon the view of the mansion was blocked by Shadow, who had made her entrance and seated herself on a high-backed chair, really a throne, facing us. "Ladies and gentlemen, please continue to enjoy the food and drink. Now, do you want to learn the history of this castle?"

"Of course!"

"All right, be very quiet, and listen closely." She gestured in the general direction of the grand architecture outside the tent. "It was built a hundred years ago by a banker as a vacation house. But rumor says it was not for his family but his beautiful mistress, a nightclub singer."

Shadow seemed to cast a fleeting glimpse at me. I jolted at that as I caught Jinying's questioning glance.

The magician went on. "The banker gave his mistress everything—expensive jewelry, fancy clothes, and a beautiful mansion on a hill filled with antiques and a slew of maids, drivers, chefs, gardeners, and pedigreed dogs." She took a conspicuous sip of the Champagne, leaving a moist red lipstick mark on the flute.

As our eyes were pulled to the bloody-vagina-shaped impression, she continued. "But she was allowed no freedom outside the mansion except to shop at the annual Paris, London, and Rome fashion shows. Ironically, though she amassed a huge, exquisite wardrobe that a queen might envy, she had no friends and no parties to show them off at. Just like the chess master who waits and waits for his most worthy rival, whom he never meets, or who perhaps does not even exist, this woman realized she was on a path of no return and descended into despair."

A collective question burst in the air. "Then what happened?"

"Unable to escape her imprisonment in a ghostly building, constantly spied on by her patron's staff, she ended her young, miserable life."

A sentimental sigh arose from the audience, but I felt only a sense of alarm. A nightclub-singer mistress, the imprisonment in a big house by spying servants—that sounded a lot like me. Did that mean she'd found out my true identity as a pawn of Big Brother Wang? But how? And what message was she trying to send to me tonight? Did she hope I would end up a suicide?

A middle-aged, bespectacled man asked, "Did she do it in this mansion?"

"Which room?" another asked rather eagerly.

The shadowy witch replied, "Not inside, but outside in a tree facing west."

"She hanged herself?"

"Yes, with her long-stranded pearl necklace and in a matching white dress."

That was exactly what I was wearing tonight! What was the purpose of this mind game?

Another male voice asked, "Why west?"

"Because that's where the Western Paradise is located, so that Amida Buddha would take her to a life without suffering." Shadow paused, an enigmatic smile hovering on her face. "She left a suicide note that said, 'I'm a free spirit now.' "

People whispered, probably discussing what the word *spirit* meant in this context.

"There was more than just her body and the suicide note." She paused, then blurted out, "There were also the corpses of her two bodyguards."

A man's voice asked, "What had happened?"

"She had seduced them, had a ménage à trois, then strangled them with her long, many-stranded pearl necklace during their sleep. After that, she chopped off their heads with a samurai sword from her patron's antiques collection."

A long silence was followed by heated discussion among the audience.

Finally, when the noise died down, a middle-aged man asked, "Who owns this castle now?"

Our magician smiled. "I'm afraid I can't tell you that. But this person, a wealthy friend of mine, generously let me use it."

When no one asked any more questions, Shadow announced, "Now let's take a break and—"

Just then the dog, who had been quietly sitting by her side, looked up at her and barked.

"Sorry, how come I forgot to introduce you?" Shadow chuckled, scooping up the dog. "Honorable guests, this is Baobao, the fifth generation of the mistress's original dog, named Runrun."

Before the amazed-looking audience had a chance to react, the magician went on. "Now that you've learned the story of the castle, do you want to take another look at it?"

"Of course!"

"All right." With an elegant sweep of her gloved hand, Shadow pulled aside the curtain that had been draped over the tent's entrance. I did not remember the curtain being there when we'd come in.

But there was no mansion! All we could see outside the entrance was a grassy slope.

"Oh, heaven! What happened?"

"Is something wrong with my eyes?"

The excited chatter died down as we all suddenly realized that *this* was tonight's magic show! The audience clapped enthusiastically and looked at Shadow as if she were a real goddess.

A triumphant smile bloomed on her face. "Thank you, honorable guests, for coming to my show. I hope you all have a wonderful evening. Now please proceed to the bus waiting for you right outside. It will bring you back to your cars."

One gentleman in an expensive Western suit asked, "Miss Shadow, can you tell us, where has the castle gone, or did it really exist?"

Shadow's silky black hair rippled under the candlelight like dark waves pulled by a full moon. "Sir, if I tell you that, then I'm not a magician but a university professor or his research assistant."

The audience burst out laughing.

Still under the spell of her magic, we all submissively walked out of the tent and got onto the waiting bus.

On the way to our cars, the question "How did she do it?" just wouldn't leave me alone. I determined to go out of my way to find the truth. Or the illusion.

I peeked at the other guests and saw that they wore the same puzzled, agonized expression, except the one right next to me.

"Jinying, why are you not curious about Shadow's magic?"

"She's an expert in fooling people, distracting them and stealing from them. I have no interest in a woman like that."

I sighed inside. He could not know that I was far more expert than Shadow in fooling people. And not for entertainment but for matters of life and death.

"I'll bet that story she told us was totally made up," he added.

"Oh . . ." I didn't know what to say. Smart as I thought I was, how come I'd never thought of that?

"It's just a deserted house nobody even knows about. A wealthy friend lent it to her for free? Just a clever lie!" Jinying hissed softly.

"Then what about the furniture and—"

"Those are her cheap props, probably picked up from the street. She creates an atmosphere to lure you in, so you'll believe whatever she wants. People want to believe, and that's why they're fooled."

I was stunned. Maybe Shadow was really my most worthy rival. Despite my training, I'd fallen so easily for her trick!

I asked, "But then how do you explain the house's disappearance?"

"That I don't know. I'm not a magician."

The young master leaned down to whisper into my ear. "Camilla, I love you. I am so glad you're not at all like her. You're so innocent, sincere, and honest."

∽ 13 ∽

An Invitation to a
Private Show

After Shadow's castle show, it was pretty clear to me that she was someone I had to watch out for. The tale of the pampered beauty who was a prisoner of her rich patron was just too much like me. Suicide was certainly not in my plans, but, I wondered, was this meant as a curse on me?

So I immediately drummed up a plan. I would send both the magician and the gossip columnist an invitation to dinner at my place. The pretext would be to celebrate the success of Shadow's show, but I would also show off the skills I had so far kept secret from the public—knife-throwing and my ability to contort my body.

This invitation would serve several purposes. First, Shadow would think that I did not hold grudge against her, even though she'd humiliated me at Lung's banquet. By inviting Rainbow, I'd let her know that it was really not my intention to snub her during the temple celebration. In fact, I liked her and wanted to know her more. But, most important, I would get Shadow out of the way to quickly search her apartment. I needed to learn how she did her acts, and also I might be able to find my ring, fan, and handkerchief in case she refused to return them. In addition, I wanted to find out whatever I could about her—her family, friends, business associations. I learned during my training that, to know how powerful a person is, know his rivals; to learn about a person's background, know his friends.

The strategy I would use is known as *yide baoyuan,* repaying one's enemy's meanness with kindness. This was the basis of a famous stratagem referred to as "Insult Under the Pants" more than two thousand years ago.

Han Shun was remembered as a famous general and military strategist. But when he was young, he was puny and poor. One time on his way home, he ran into several hooligans who made fun of his ragged clothes and small stature. The tallest and strongest further insulted Han Shun by ordering him to crawl between his legs. Knowing that he couldn't possibly get out of the situation, Han swallowed his bitterness and did what he'd been told.

Many years later, after Han had become a famous general, he again ran into the same hooligan who had insulted him. But instead of getting back at the man, Han appointed him as his *zhong-wei,* lieutenant. The general repaying the hooligan's cruelty with kindness gained him a lasting reputation and many die-hard followers.

Like Han, I had to swallow humiliation to get myself out of any life-threatening situations, but unlike him, I had no intention of helping or benefiting my enemy. For I had not been trained to be generous, or stupid. However, I could fake being generous. That was why I invited Shadow—so I could bond with her, gain her trust, then get rid of her. If I conducted myself right, she would not find out until too late that my kindness was cruelty in disguise.

As for Rainbow Chang, I already knew from reading her columns that she could be relied on only to be treacherous. The best I could do was to befriend her, hoping she would then show good faith. I also hoped she would write about the "friendship" between me and Shadow. That way, any harm done to the magician was less likely to be blamed on me.

* * *

My guests had been invited for eight o'clock in the evening. An hour before, Ah Wen drove me to Shadow's apartment building and let me off in the back. I hid behind a wall and waited. Twenty minutes later, I saw the magician walk out of her building and hail a rickshaw.

As soon as her rickshaw disappeared into the dense Shanghai traffic, I slid inside her building and dashed up to her apartment. Pausing in front of her door, I took out the special key Wang had made for me by Shanghai's best locksmith. Known as the Open-One-Hundred-Doors key, it would unlock anything, except perhaps the Hong Kong and Shanghai banks' vaults. Wang had only given it to me so I could open Lung's safe—once I was able to find it, of course—to get to his important documents. But for Shadow's modest apartment, a much more ordinary skeleton key would have sufficed. Unlocking her door was as easy as a man entering the gate between a prostitute's legs.

I flipped on the light to reveal a small living room with scanty furniture and a few bookshelves. My goal was clear, so my action was fast. I closed the door, then made a quick round of the small apartment to look for safes or secret hiding places. Seeing none, I flipped through the books on the shelves, looking especially for a notebook or journal. But nothing caught my eye. Then, when I turned my special key to open the desk drawer, I knew I'd found what I'd come for. It was a thick, faded notebook with a black leather cover. As I lifted the book, I felt a surge of excitement.

When I scanned through the pages, I had to remind myself to stay calm and focused. My eyes beheld handwritten explanations, some highlighted in red, blue, or green, and footnotes, diagrams, pasted-in photographs, even mathematical calculations. It was exactly what I was looking for to satisfy my curiosity—an esoteric manual for magic. There were altogether thirty-odd recipes for magic acts, ranging from the elementary to the grandiose. Forcing my hands to hold steady, I took out my lipstick camera and snapped furiously. There was not enough time to photograph the whole book, so I was only able to take pictures of those acts I'd seen her perform and others I found intriguing. When I finished, I quickly took photographs of what appeared to be a personal journal and then put everything back in its original place. Now I quickly went through drawers looking for my handkerchief, fan, and ring, being as careful as I could to leave everything in place. But no luck, and my time had run out. So I left.

When I was back at my apartment, I quickly put my camera into my safe. It was seven minutes before eight, and Shadow hadn't yet arrived. Perfect. I'd known that my car would be much faster than her rickshaw. The power of Wang's money.

At eight o'clock sharp, the bell rang, and Ah Fong opened the door to welcome Shadow. The invitation for Rainbow was for half an hour later, so I'd have some time to chat privately with the magician.

Shadow wore a blue chiffon dress with ruffles around the neck and some matching but cheap jewelry.

After we sat down in the living room, she sipped her—or my— red wine with pleasure. "Camilla, I really envy you—such a luxurious home with an amah and a driver and surrounded by beautiful art and antiques. Most of us girls are just barely getting by, but look at you. . . ."

"Shadow, as your friend, I wish that someday you'll live the same life," I said, while thinking just the opposite.

She stared at me. "Are we friends, really? You're not angry at my trick with your possessions at Master Lung's banquet?"

As I was thinking how to respond, she took out the stolen handkerchief, fan, and diamond ring and handed them to me. But I still wondered, had she exchanged my expensive rock with a fake one?

I stared at the retrieved items, then the magician. "I'm amazed, Shadow. Thank you."

"So, are we friends now?"

"What do you think?"

"I don't have friends."

"Me, neither."

We burst out laughing. "That's why we need each other!" I said.

Shadow spoke. "Good, at least we're honest. But, may I ask, what do we need each other for?"

"Shadow, as you know, I'm now the most popular singer in Shanghai, and you are an up-and-coming, attention-grabbing magician. So if we can co-operate . . ."

"You mean do a show together?"

I took a delicate sip of my wine, nodding. "What do you think?"

"Excellent idea!" She thought for a while. "But why are you willing to help me, especially since I stole from you?"

"We'll be helping each other. Haven't you heard it said that 'if two work with one mind and one heart, the profit can only be measured by gold'? To be honest, I am greedy. I believe if we combine our forces, the money will pour in like the Huangpu River."

She sipped her wine, her eyes widening as if she were now actually seeing the river turning into gold liquid.

"So, Shadow, do you want this or not?"

She chuckled. "You think anyone can afford to turn down such an offer?"

We clinked our glasses together, toasting our future continuously flowing river of money, but hers fell and broke into shards.

"Ah . . ."

Was this a bad omen, or a good one for me? For another Chinese proverb says, "Blossoming flowers bring wealth; shards on the floor fetch prosperity."

Just then the doorbell rang, and this time Ah Fong brought in Rainbow Chang. The columnist was in her usual man's outfit, this time a striped three-piece gray suit with a pink tie and matching pocket handkerchief peeping out as if investigating the outside world.

After the obligatory greetings were exchanged, I led my guests into the dining room, where we settled into comfort for the evening.

Rainbow's smile was stretched taut on her face like an elastic band. "Camilla, Shadow, tonight I'm really honored to be in your glorious presence. I'm sure you two will take over Shanghai in no time."

She might have intended this as a compliment, but the effect was the opposite. I thought I had already taken over Shanghai, and I definitely didn't want to see Shadow doing the same. Yes, she was getting a lot of attention lately, but she was still many steps behind me in terms of fame and fortune, and I wanted it to stay that way.

Shadow threw Rainbow a flirtatious glance. "Thank you, Miss Chang, I certainly hope so. But what about yourself?"

"What about me?" The androgynous columnist raised one perfectly painted eyebrow. "I believe I've already attained my little bit of fame and fortune, so lately what I've sought is love." She cast me a meaningful stare, giving me a chill.

"So, have you found what you've been looking for?" I asked, feigning innocence.

"Yes and no. As you know, like friends or the wind, love comes and goes."

I was not sure what she was suggesting but did not want to get into a discussion about it, so I contented myself with returning her meaningful stare. "Maybe. Now, why don't we enjoy our friendship, food, and the evening while they last?"

After a very satisfactory meal complete with copious wine to soothe our dry throats from all the talking, I invited Shadow and Rainbow to the spare room that I used to rehearse.

I signaled them to sit, then announced, "Shadow and Rainbow, Shanghai people know me as a singer, but I am more than that. . . ." I paused, staring at Shadow for a response.

"Of course," she said, "you're also a contortionist."

Rainbow smiled. "I heard about that but regretfully had not been invited to Master Lung's Manchurian Banquet to be stunned by your performance."

"But you'll see it and more tonight."

Shadow asked, sounding a little upset, "More? What is it?"

Rainbow raised another painted eyebrow to ask the same question in silence.

"You'll see." I smiled mysteriously. "Please have some more wine, and I'll be right back."

After that, I went into the bathroom to take off my *cheongsam* and change into a black tunic. Then I kicked off my high heels and put on a pair of soft, flat shoes. When I returned, Rainbow was studying me like a teenage boy a woman's nude picture.

She smiled. "My eyes are ready to be stunned."

Shadow also smiled but didn't say anything. Of course she already knew how good I was. But tonight she was yet to witness my other stunt—knife-throwing.

Even though my audience consisted of only two people, I bowed as deeply as I did to my fans at the Bright Moon. "Ladies, I am now going to expose my inadequacy."

The two clapped enthusiastically. Of course they well understood that "expose my inadequacy" was but a euphemism for "show off my ultimate skill." Arrogance wrapped in modesty.

Holding six knives, I faced the target hanging on the wall ten feet away. I meditated, focusing my energy on the red dot in the middle, imagining it as Shadow's blood. Then, *Swish! Swish! Swish! Swish! Swish! Swish!* Even before my audience had time to blink, the six knives had flown from my hand like bullets from a gun, now protruding from the target in a perfect circle around the red dot.

Shadow and Rainbow's jaws dropped, but no words came from their mouths.

Rainbow exclaimed, "What can I say?"

Shadow asked, a little sarcastically, "Is this some kind of magic I never knew existed?"

I smiled inside; they had no idea that my ultimate skill was yet to be revealed.

"Thank you." I bowed, pulled the knives from the target board, then went to the gramophone to put on a record. As an eerie jazz tune began to fill the room, I walked to the carpet placed in the middle of the room. Slowly I began to raise myself on one hand, my other hand holding the six knives. Soon I was upside down with my legs in a straight line, forming the English letter T. Again, the knives flew from my hand to form a perfect circle surrounding the red dot.

Before they had a chance to applaud, I had already changed into another posture—feet and one hand on the floor like a spider's, torso facing upward and face inverted. Again, *Swish! Swish! Swish! Swish! Swish! Swish!* This time a heart-shaped form appeared on the target board.

When I finally returned my limbs to their normal positions, the two looked at me as if I had just come from another realm.

As she clapped, Rainbow's eyes were rounded like two soy sauce dishes. "Camilla, you took my breath away, literally. I feared that even my slightest exhalation might blow this magic moment away. Are you also a magician like Shadow? Surely what I just saw could not have happened."

Shadow's brow knit briefly upon hearing the word *magician,* but she quickly regained her calm and put on a forced smile. "Camilla, if you open a class to teach, I'll be the first to enroll."

"It is you who should be my teacher, Shadow. If you are ever willing to pass on your magic, I'll be your first student."

"So, should we trade lessons?"

Of course she was not going to let me know her magic in exchange for my knife-throwing and contortionist skill. My skill could be attained by anyone with the right talent and years of relentless practice, but her repertory used secrets that would likely accompany her to her grave, unless she could be persuaded to part with them for an astronomical sum.

The three of us continued to throw compliments back and forth like Ping-Pong balls.

Finally Rainbow peeked at her watch. "Camilla, thank you for inviting me to your beautiful home and treating me with such delicious food, exquisite wine, and a stunning show. As much as I'd love to stay, I am on deadline for my article for tomorrow's *Leisure News.*"

"Of course, Rainbow, don't let me hold you up. Thank you for coming and spending your precious time with us."

"Maybe I should leave, too," Shadow said, about to stand up. "You must be tired; we should not keep you up."

I made a gesture for her to sit. "No, Shadow, please stay and have one more glass of wine with me. You don't have articles to write, do you?"

"No, I can stay a little longer."

That was exactly what I wanted.

After Rainbow left, I took Shadow to my study. As we sat and chatted, I refilled her glass again—hoping to get her as drunk as possible.

I could see that she tried to hold back, but she couldn't resist the expensive, rare—and free—wine. As I saw the struggle on her face, a saying in *The Art of War* emerged in my mind: *By waiting for your enemy's moment of vulnerability, you'll surely triumph.*

I asked, "Shadow, would you like to see my art collection?"

Her eyes were glazed with alcohol. "You collect art?"

"Yes, but only recently. I didn't have much money in the past."

"I love art but can't possibly afford even a small piece."

"But your magic shows were packed. . . ." I was hoping to get some idea of her finances. Her home was modest, but that did not mean she wasn't hiding money away somewhere.

"Oh, Camilla. You know, my kind of shows are expensive to put on, and most of the ticket sales at the Ciro Nightclub don't go to me. Besides, the disappearing act was free, and so was Lung's. I'm still struggling. . . ." She looked at me intently. "How did you become so rich?"

What a foolish question. Of course I was not going to tell her how I did it—nor that I was not nearly as rich as she thought. "Oh, my story is not very interesting. Maybe I'll bore you with it some other day. Now let's look at my collection."

I brought out and let her touch some of my—actually Wang's— most expensive pieces. First was a Ming ivory statue of Guan Yin, the Goddess of Compassion, then a pair of Qing dynasty celadon vases, and finally a jade lotus pod. Then I opened one of my jewelry boxes, revealing to her envious eyes a gold filigree necklace, translucent jade earrings, and a dragonfly brooch encrusted with diamonds and emeralds.

When I placed the dragonfly brooch in her hand, she caressed it like Lung stroking my breasts. By now she must be dying to have my rich, pampered life.

"Camilla, if you don't mind my asking again, how did you become so famous and so rich so fast?"

"It was not as fast as you think. I worked very hard, just like you, Shadow. But of course it's also dumb luck. I happen to have a voice that people love, so they are willing to pay anything to hear it."

In her drunken state, Shadow threw me an unexpected question. "Does Master Lung pay . . ." Then she stopped.

Of course she wanted to know if Lung paid for my luxuries. She must be thinking that if she could steal him from me, she could live my life. But since Lung had shown no interest in her, I could safely enjoy inflaming her envy.

Ignoring her question I decided to further test Shadow's greed by slipping a small, inexpensive jade ring onto her pinky.

Finally, deciding that that was enough, I said, "Shadow, thank you for coming tonight; I've had such a wonderful time. Now it's almost midnight, and you must be tired. So let me ask my driver, Ah Wen, to take you home."

When we were at the door, as if by impulse I snatched another bottle of wine from the console table in the foyer. "Please take this."

She smiled. "Sure, why not?"

As we walked to the car, a saying in *The Art of War* flashed into my mind:

> Preventing defeat depends upon oneself;
> To achieve defeat depends on the enemy.

So I smiled at my enemy. "Shadow, let me ride with you. I could use some fresh air after all the wine."

"You're so kind, Camilla."

Inside the vehicle, we continued to chat about this and that, nothing of significance, just idle conversation.

A little later, a car behind us suddenly speeded up and was trying to pass.

"Ah Wen, pull to the side so this car won't hit us!"

But after passing us, the other car also stopped—right in front of us. A muscular man wearing a mask jumped from the vehicle and dashed toward us..

Shadow exclaimed, her voice filled with fear, "Is he going to rob or kidnap us? Oh, heaven, please, I don't want to die!"

I took her hand. "Shadow, calm down. If he wants money, I'll give it to him."

Then the muscular man flung open the back door and pulled Shadow out.

"No, don't hurt my friend!" I kicked at the muscular man's balls. He leaped back and let go of her.

Then he pulled a knife and lunged at me. Instinctively I raised my hands to protect myself, but just then another car came driving up from behind us. Probably wondering if that driver might see something and stop, Muscular dashed back to his own car and sped away. However, the third car just drove by without stopping. Either its driver didn't see anything or didn't care.

I got out of the car to check on Shadow. Dead drunk and scared to death, she was now an alcohol-sodden mess, slumped on the ground, sobbing uncontrollably.

I touched her arm. "Shadow, it's all right now. The robber is gone."

She couldn't be comforted.

"Shadow, we'd better get out of here in case he comes back!"

I helped her get to her feet and back into the car. It was then that I saw the stain on her dress and realized that she'd soiled herself. Worse, my driver, Ah Wen, had disappeared. Instead of fighting the attacker and protecting us, he had abandoned us to save his own meatless ass!

"Coward!" I spat.

Suddenly Shadow cried, "Oh, my heaven, you've been stabbed!"

I looked at my forearm and was relieved that the cut was not deep, only a surface scratch. The blood made it look much worse. I used my handkerchief to press on the wound.

Shadow looked at my arm with an expression of horror. "You'd better go to the hospital."

I looked more carefully at my wound. "I don't think so. The cut is not deep, so I won't need stitches. You don't want our names to be all over the newspapers tomorrow as victims of a botched robbery, do you?"

∾ 14 ∾

Shadowy Recipes

After dropping off Shadow and heading home, I laughed to my-self all the way back, pleased by my own ingenuity. The rob-bery had been my doing. The muscular man who'd attacked us was none other than Gao. At first, when I'd asked him to do it, he'd adamantly refused. Not that he was breaking his promise to do any-thing for me but because he couldn't bear to see me threatened, even though it would be fake. However, after a little flirting, he had agreed. Of course he wouldn't do anything to hurt me, so I deliber-ately hit my forearm against his knife to draw blood.

In the *Thirty-Six Stratagems,* this is called *kurouji,* literally "painful flesh strategy." You intentionally injure yourself to get the trust of your enemy. Now not only had I gained Shadow's trust, I had also discovered her weaknesses—greed and fear. She'd left with my jade ring on her pinky. She'd peed in her dress.

However, if I were in the same situation, would I stay as calm as the Buddha? I believed so. Because I was a spy. During my vigor-ous training, my boss had always quoted the Chinese saying:

Even when Mount Tai is collapsing in front of
you, your expression will be unchanged.

As soon as I arrived home, I took out my lipstick camera and went to my bathroom to develop the negatives, a skill I'd learned as part of my training to be a spy. As soon as they were dry, I printed them, then took the glossy images to my study.

The first one was from Shadow's notebook, a short article on "Teasing the Bloody Shoes."

> Tie the shoes with dark strings and manipulate them from the ceiling above. Use a black wall with a wavy pattern as background so neither the black strings nor their movements will be seen from ten feet away.

I laughed out loud. Was it really that simple? How easily we humans can be fooled!

I went on to read the next one: "Jumping to Disappearance."

> A basic technique in magic is to distract. You can do this in many ways: setting off fireworks, releasing smoke, playing loud music, even casual motions like scratching your head, blinking your eyes, adjusting your glasses, dropping a pen, or just chattering nonstop. This is called *shengdong jixi,* making noise in the east while attacking in the west.
>
> In this trick, a dummy, dressed to look like the magician and tied to a wire, will be thrown to the ground, then quickly pulled back up. At the same time, lightning, thunder, and smoke will blur the audience's vision so they cannot tell the object is a dummy or that it is being pulled up. Blood and shoes are thrown down a few seconds after the dummy plunges.

Next my eyes landed on the account of her recent grandiose act: "The Disappearing Mansion."

Make a Big Object Disappear—A house, a plane, a monument.

This is sure to stun your audience. You need a revolving tent with only one entrance. The spectators will be ushered inside the tent, facing the entrance so they can see the building outside, which is best if it is upon a hill. After the magician puts a curtain over the entrance, he'll distract the audience by talking to them nonstop, cracking jokes, mesmerizing them with a strange story, asking questions.

When finished, the magician will lift the curtain and the audience will be shocked to see that the building is gone. This is because the tent's entrance has, unbeknownst to them, slowly revolved to face another direction, so that the building is no longer to be seen.

The audience will be directed to a bus right outside the opening to take them back where they came from. This is to prevent anyone from noticing that the building is still there, albeit on the other side.

As for the disappearing paintings inside the mansion, they were but images from a magic lantern.

As is usually the case with these stage tricks, once explained, the magic seems as obvious as a reflection in a mirror. Then I realized that Shadow couldn't possibly do this all by herself, yet no assistant ever appeared. Who was she or he? A lover, a brother, a twin sister, or just hired help?

Since no answer was forthcoming, I picked up another photograph and read:

Seeing Is Deceiving—It Is a Mistake to Believe What You See.

People always believe what they see with their eyes. That's why we say "seeing is believing." But in magic, it is the opposite: "believing is seeing." When people see something with their own eyes—from a rabbit appearing out of thin air to a huge mansion disappearing in front of them—they have to believe it.

That's why seeing is also deceiving. This is what magic is about—creating illusions to fool the eyes and trick the mind.

Magic is a game of manipulation and distraction. When you pay intense attention to one thing, your mind will ignore everything else. Therefore, the magician directs the audience's attention to something irrelevant as he carries out his routine. They won't notice how the trick is done because their eyes are fixed on the magician's misleading maneuvers, like constant prattling, releasing pigeons, tossing a hat or waving a wand.

I sipped my tea, then was suddenly wide awake despite the late hour and the wine, as my eyes encountered a section entitled, "The Art of Stealing."

To distract your audience, lure their attention away from your real intention. This includes:

1. Keep talking to prevent the audience from noticing your stealing hand.

2. Touch your victim in different places—a pat on the shoulder, a squeeze of the arm, a palm on the back; when he is conscious of the hand that is touching, he won't notice your other one.

3. When you steal, let's say a wristwatch, first press your hand on your victim's wrist. This sensation will linger, so he will still "feel" his watch on his skin even though it's already gone.

4. Focus your victim's attention on another place: Tell him his hair is mussed or flick an imaginary bit of lint off his jacket.

To sum up: your hands should be like magnets pulling a compass needle in all directions so as to cause total confusion.

Then the manual took a philosophical turn:

People like to be manipulated, although they may not know it. They need to be guided and told what to do. Most of us are not born leaders and are inclined to be lazy.

That's why everyone wants to believe in miracles. And who doesn't hope for a little magic in their unsatisfactory, obligation-filled existence? That's why people are so easily led by those who promise them magic, not just stage magicians but politicians, priests, monks, even gangster-heroes.

Is there real magic in the world? Everyone looks for it, but in reality, "magic" is nothing other than the possession of a dazzling appearance, a clever mind, perfect timing, and infallible skill that has been developed with relentless practice!

If you have these qualities, people will believe in your miracles. If you don't have them, don't bore your audience and humiliate yourself onstage. Stay home instead to play with your children or dogs.

So magic is entertainment, but it is also poetry, myth, philosophy, even wisdom and an excellent way of life.

Wow. So magic is philosophy and wisdom. And a magician is not much different from a spy, since both need to possess "a dazzling appearance, a clever mind, perfect timing, and infallible skill developed with relentless practice"!

I smiled, thinking of my extreme skills of knife-throwing and contortion with which I had yet to stun the Shanghainese. So, when I performed, everyone would believe my knives had eyes, for they'd always go where they should, always just missing my assistant as they landed around her with soft thuds.

That was the real reason I'd invited Shadow to perform with me. I wanted her to believe that my knives had eyes, yet later painfully learn that in fact they were sometimes nearsighted.

Shadow was a master of manipulation, but so was I. In a perfect world we could be friends—even sisters, as Lung teased. We could share our insights, experiences, stunts, and schemes. But in this dusty world, it was more likely that one of us would end up destroying the other.

I sipped more tea, absorbing what I had read. After that, I picked up the photographs of what had looked like her diary. The characters were much smaller than those in the instruction manual, so I guessed the latter must have been written by her teacher. I strained my eyes to read:

> To be Master Lung's number one mistress has been my goal; unfortunately the place is already taken by Camilla. How to pluck her from Lung's side? I'm sure that would be even more challenging than jumping off the Shanghai Customs House.
>
> The first time we met at Bright Moon, Camilla asked me about my training and my teacher. Smart as she is, she should've known better. Will I just tell anyone about my past? She certainly won't. I never get anything from those lips except her singing, which everyone seems to think is so wonderful. Makes me wonder if her pretty little lips perform other naughty and dirty deeds. Maybe that's why Lung fell for her.

I'll never tell her or anyone else about my past. Why should anybody know that my magician stepfather would only teach me his craft if I let him fondle my breasts and sometimes, when I could no longer resist, even have sex with him? At least he's dead now, the cut-by-a-thousand-knives piece of dog-fucked corpse! If I ever visited his grave, I would spit, pee, and shit on it, so that his stinking, rotten cadaver would stink even more!

Fortunately, before I killed him, I took all his notes and repertoires that he thought no one could find inside our house's hollow wooden door. Ha-ha! He forgot how fine a magician I'd become under his coaching and molesting hands!

Nobody in Shandong knows about what had happened. One day both of us simply disappeared from this province. I, to Shanghai, friendless, he, to his grave, childless. I will laugh if his ghost thinks I am a daughter who will someday make offerings at his grave.

I never met my real father; I only learned from my mother that he was a half-breed—half foreign devil and half Chinese. That's why I have this big-boned physique with high nose, deep-set eyes, muscular body, pale skin, and hair with some brown in it, so I have to dye it black. My mother said that no one should know about this, absolutely no one. For I would be spat upon and my life would be ruined even before it began. But I was ruined, anyway, by her new husband.

I wanted so badly to be a magician that I let him touch my breasts when he taught me how to make rabbits disappear and reappear. Then when I let him touch me between my legs, he'd teach me how to make a house disappear. Eventually he'd touched my body everywhere and entered me more times than I want to remember. Finally, the day came when I had learned all that he had to teach about magic. But despite my numerous pleadings, he would never let me see his written manual.

Then my mother died. Followed by him, with his blood on my hands.

Actually, I didn't exactly murder him, only let him fall to his death without lending a daughterly hand. As I deserved his magic, he deserved my callousness. It happened one morning as he practiced tightrope-walking two stories above ground, with me treading behind him. When he was approaching the finishing line, I made a wrong move. The rope wobbled, and he lost his balance. Could I have prevented his fall? I'm not sure. Maybe. But I didn't, and then I never had to see his face again. Ever.

Before anyone knew, I gathered up everything valuable in the house—cash, my mother's jewelry, the gold chain from his neck, the watch from his wrist, the pen inside his pocket, and, most important, all the props that I could carry—and left for Shanghai. I changed my name to Shadow, so no one would know who I was or am. So if today I die, there won't be anyone to cry, burn offerings, or kowtow to my portrait.

There is no fairness in life. Look at Camilla. Yes, she's beautiful, talented, hardworking, smart. But so are many other girls, including myself. Then how come only she is Lung's number one mistress with an easy life, when mine is a constant struggle? If I want to be a huge success, I'll have to steal Lung from her, not waste my nights with the cut-by-a-thousand-knives manager at Ciro Nightclub, nor the Shanghai Customs House's dog-fucked tower guard.

Camilla has her heavenly voice, but I have my

magic. And I am particularly well-trained in stealing.

My heart sank. My suspicions were correct. My guess had been
right all along: Shadow hoped to take my place with Lung. Then I
shook my head. My situation was not nearly as good as she thought,
since most of the money I made did not go inside my pocket but
Wang's.

So she was wrong. Actually life is quite fair—no one gets what
they want.

I continued to read:

> I was the only one who knew my stepfather's
> background. He even kept it secret from my stu-
> pid mother.
>
> All magicians dream of living in big cities like
> Beijing or Shanghai, but we were stuck in the
> countryside in Shandong. This is because my step-
> father's father—that was my step-grandfather—
> had made his escape from the Empress Dowager's
> palace. A talented magician and a handsome man,
> he was the Empress's imperial illusionist and secret
> lover. But during one performance, he'd made dis-
> appear her most treasured pet parrot but failed to
> bring it back. The pet suffocated inside his long
> sleeve. He tried to fool the Empress with an identi-
> cal one, but the trick was discovered; the real one
> had a large pearl stitched inside its feathers for
> good luck.
>
> Before the court had decided on the most ap-
> propriately horrific way to slowly execute him, he
> had already fled to Shangdong with his son. In this
> desolate western province, he changed his name
> and worked as a farmer. However, unwilling to let
> his imperial court magic silently die out, he se-
> cretly taught it to his son.
>
> I am sure many would be stunned if they knew

my acts were originally for the entertainment of the Empress. But there are no more emperors; China is supposedly a republic. So I keep this to myself.

As the Chinese say, "It takes one hero to recognize another." After I finished reading Shadow's diary, I really thought we were evenly matched. Time would tell which of us would come out ahead in our great game of magic, schemes, and manipulation.

Our situation was like that of Zhou Yu and Zhuge Liang, two of the greatest generals in Chinese history. Zhou Yu once lamented "Why was I born at the same time with Zhuge Liang?" Zhou believed that if it were not for Zhuge Liang, he would be able to conquer all under heaven.

Now I asked myself a similar question: Why had fate thrust Shadow and me onto the same path? I thought Big Brother Wang asked himself the same question about his situation with Lung.

But there was no time to lose. As the proverb states, "Kill your enemy before he has time to even make a fist."

The next morning, I picked up the *Leisure News* and opened it to Rainbow Chang's column. I smiled; as I'd wished, she did write about our small party. Of course she didn't know about the little incident after; otherwise I was sure she'd have made that her headline.

A Stunning Private Show

I must have done something good recently that I had the lucky karma to be invited by our Heavenly Songbird, Miss Camilla, to be her guest.

Her home is beautiful, the food exquisite, and the wine divine. But the most amazing thing was the private show she put on for me and her other guest, the magician Shadow.

Camilla threw knives with deadly accuracy while contorting her supple body. I kept rubbing my eyes; was this beautiful woman in front of me real or just a figment of my imagination? Shadow must have been asking herself, "I am a magician; how come I've never seen anything like this before?"

The article went on to praise me and my stunts. Snobbish as she was, it was expected that Rainbow Chang would not write much about Shadow, who was still only a newcomer on the Shanghai scene. I had succeeded in getting the columnist to show that I, not Shadow—despite the fact that she was starting to get attention—was still the one on top and in control.

In *The Art of War,* this strategy is called "superior positioning." Always place yourself in an undefeatable position even before the battle begins. Then wait patiently for your enemy to fall into your trap.

I hoped to get Rainbow to continue to make me more prominent in her columns than Shadow.

PART THREE

∽❧ 15 ❧∽

Life as a Spy

All this began not by any choice on my part but because powerful men considered me perfect material to be a spy—beautiful, smart, and, most important, an orphan. My plate was so empty that Big Brother Wang could put anything in it, and I would lap it up like a stray dog during a famine. Or so he thought. Yes, he had trained me to be the perfect spy, but had he considered that I could someday use the same training to fool him?

Did I like being an informer? I really had no answer for that—it was the only life I knew, except of course, the one in the orphanage. As for my fame at the nightclub, it was not what it seemed but was just a cover-up for my true mission. However, in most ways my current existence was far better than life in the orphanage with all the other miserable, parentless, whining little people. At least I enjoyed beautiful clothes, designer handbags and shoes, and a luxury apartment with an amah and a driver.

Other than these perks, there was nothing desirable in being Wang's spy. I considered myself lucky, though, because my target was only a single gangster instead of a whole country. So I didn't have to deal with politicians, high government officials, ministers, or the president. And I didn't need to decipher codes, analyze data, or steal boring state secrets like military maps, battle strategies, designs of tanks, and the like. Nor did I have to sleep with officers to coax secrets out of them when their guard was down. However, though my mission was relatively less daunting and my training less complicated, it was still dangerous. Despite his seeming affection for me, I could not let myself forget that being close to Lung was like, as Chinese say, "walking beside a starving tiger," or "a sheep being put inside a tiger's mouth."

Any spy will have more than one name, one address, one disguise. Moreover, a spy must never cherish ideas such as love, money, fame, or comfort. To be distracted by such thoughts increases the risk of failure or, worse, being caught. For the same reason, neither should a spy develop a conscience. However, after a while I realized that having no conscience is, in fact, not something unique to a spy. Behind the heavy gates of ancient palaces, princes or princesses would not hesitate to kill their most loyal ministers, brothers, sisters, parents, or friends if these people were obstacles on their path to the throne. For the same reasons, queen mothers would poison their own sons. Compassion and kindness were talked about but seldom heeded.

What a spy needs is the perseverance to complete a mission, the courage and cunning to get out of a dangerous situation, and absolute loyalty to the boss. As for the rest, nobody cares.

That's why spies are also called the "four nothingness": no relatives, no friends, no identity, no morality. The advantages to being a "nothingness" is that no one can find out who you really are, and, having no attachments in the world, you will be unconstrained in your actions. If you're caught and have no attachments to anyone, your secrets are unlikely to be revealed. Your enemy cannot threaten you by kidnapping or torturing your wife, husband, parents, children, not even your cat or dog.

That's why a spy is supposed to think of himself as a "dead" person, or, since alive and active, at least consider himself fatally diseased so he'll be fearless under any threat or torture. However, in case the torture becomes humanly impossible to bear, there is also a way out. He can crunch the poison pill wedged between the teeth, choosing death over betrayal.

A good spy might tell you nothing but lies, but he'll never lie to his boss. An ideal spy is loyal, never questions his mission, will not hesitate to sacrifice his life, and will never reveal secrets under any circumstances. Therefore, any evidence a spy gives you, even under torture, will certainly be false.

Unfortunately, the Chinese are rightly famous for their tortures. In my training I was warned about all of these, though I sometimes wondered if some were made up just to scare me so I'd be careful never to be captured alive. Once having heard about these, it is impossible to forget them. Sometimes I would close my eyes and see a list of them, like something from a torturer's manual:

Beating—by rod/chain/whip filled with nails.

Grilling—to make a victim walk on burning coal until he drops.

Finger-crushing—place fingers between wooden sticks connected by strings, then pull the strings to crush the fingers.

Toe-hammering—smash all ten toes, one by one, with a hammer.

Pressing victim down—under a huge vat as it is gradually filled with water or stones.

Feeding victim excrement/urine—his own or that of others.

Feeding victim hair—The victim's hair is cut off and shredded into minuscule bits, then mixed with tea and poured into the victim's mouth. The hairs will stick to his internal organs, and there is no way to get them out.

Flower blooming in snow—Beating the victim in fallen snow so the torturer can appreciate the bright red blood spilling over a pristine white surface.

Lighting the kerosene lamp—Pour kerosene into victim's navel, then insert a wick and light it.

Slaughter-the-pigs bench—The victim is tied down on a bench and a four-inch thick book placed on his chest; then the book is struck repeatedly with a heavy hammer. This will cause internal bleeding and crush internal organs, but there will be no external wounds. For this reason, it is a favorite with police.

Flying a plane—The victim is on his feet and iron wire tied around his thumbs to lift him up onto tiptoe. When at last exhausted, he will lower his feet to the floor for support, causing the iron wires to tear away his two thumbs.

Flesh-slicing—Slow carving of the victim's flesh till he dies a lingering, painful death.

Sometimes I doubt if anyone, no matter how excellent his training, could withstand any of these tortures. That's why a spy will break any law or even kill a child to avoid being discovered—because he knows what tortures await him. Since no one wants to end up crippled or hideously murdered, if you are a spy, you don't, or try your best not to, make mistakes, period. Unfortunately, your enemy will probably adhere to the principle that, "It's better to torture or kill a thousand innocent people than to let a single one who did wrong go free."

A spy must learn endurance. As a test, the trainee is sometimes confined inside a very small cell for days on end, with only a small slot opened to deliver a miserable meal and, on occasion, to collect the bucket of excrement. A two-way mirror on the wall is used by the boss to observe every move and how well he can withstand the pressures of claustrophobia, malnutrition, and isolation. Even when trained at the same time and place, spies are absolutely forbidden to make friends with one another, sometimes even forced to wear masks during gatherings. To prevent revealing their true identity, spies will adopt code names such as Lark, Eagle, Red Hat, Black Coffee, Watermelon, a number like H21, C15, or even titles of children's songs such as Mama is the Best, My Little Sisters, Little Lamb Going Home, Mud Doll, Barking Dog, Ding-Dong.

There is a lot more to spying than just lying and deceiving. Spies must study the language—especially idioms and slang—of their target country. There are all sorts of technical skills to learn, such as writing in code or with invisible ink, eavesdropping on telephones, and using a hidden camera small enough to be disguised as a lipstick case.

I am sure that no one hearing me sing in a nightclub could imagine how cunning I had to be in order to survive. So I followed these teachings:

1. Practice the Dao of deception.

In *The Art of War,* one of the most famous lines is: "Warfare is deception." Not only does one have to lie, but the lies must change constantly.

2. Miss nothing.

Pay attention to details, from people's clothes, accessories, jewelry, to hiding places, exit locations, and numbers. Any numbers—on a door, a car, the date of a painting—may be clues to secret codes.

3. Keep everything a secret.

Never let your enemy guess what's on your mind.

4. Wear down your target.

A tired person is less alert, more likely to spill information and, if necessary, easier to kill.

5. Show no emotion.

When you ferret out information, no matter how precious, never show any emotion. Act as if you are receiving a store receipt or a grocery list.

6. Learn to read lips and understand gestures.

7. Pretend you don't know a language so that your targets speak freely in front of you.

8. Write in code.

Jot down information so that it reads like a grocery list or a family's to-do list. For example: two fishes, five tomatoes, three pieces of mutton could mean two women, five men, and three small children.

9. Never keep a diary, and burn your garbage every day.

Never leave anything in writing that might be found. Of

course you can write in code, but don't forget that another spy might decipher your code.

10. Only stay in places with more than one exit. The Chinese say, "A cunning rabbit always has three hiding places."

11. Develop a photographic memory.

12. Learn the art of manipulation.
The best way to destroy a person is to first destroy his mind. And to destroy his mind, you must build a daunting presence. That is why *The Art of War* says, "The best victory is won without fighting."

13. Blend in.
As a songstress, it might seem that I was doing the opposite—making myself as beautiful and talented as possible to attract attention. But as an entertainer I easily blended into the Shanghai social scene, and no one thought about me beyond my voice and my looks.

14. Stay calm in the midst of danger and chaos.

15. Wait for the right moment.
The ancient philosopher Laozi said, "In action, watch the timing." The even older *Book of Changes* teaches that the same strategy may work at one time but not at another. Or it might succeed for one person but not for someone else. Failure may just be bad timing.

16. Live in fear.
Fear motivates and concentrates the mind—for a spy it might be the fear of having to kill someone and, even more, the fear of being tortured or killed oneself.

Not only did I have to remember all these principles, I had to practice constantly—watching myself in the mirror as I put on different facial expressions, wiggled my body seductively, or struck elegant poses such as shredded-golden-lotus steps and orchid-in-the-breeze finger configurations. At the same time I had to appear mysterious yet innocent—not an easy task, since these traits are usually at odds with each other. Mystery piques a man's sexual curiosity and makes a woman more alluring, but innocence is useful, too, because it can arouse a man's protective instincts. On an even more subtle level, if a woman emits the right fragrance, a man might be intoxicated by her without knowing why.

Some girls might be born with a fragrance, but this is very rare. None of the girls at Bright Moon Nightclub possessed this gift of nature. Many used Chanel No. 5, but this meant that their scent was all Chanel's, and they all smelled boringly the same.

Therefore, though I received many costly perfumes as gifts, I only used them occasionally. To attain my special body fragrance, I had two procedures. Every morning I would bathe in a basin in which my amah, Ah Fong, had soaked fresh flowers—camellia, rose, lotus, lilac, water lily, and sometimes others. Every evening, she'd put flowers mixed with sweet-scented herbs underneath my pillow so the fragrance would permeate my hair, face, body, and even my dreams.

Even these efforts were not enough for my boss, Big Brother Wang, however. Still not completely certain of my charms, he had decided to do something unusual—and dangerous. He had long ago bought an esoteric, Qing-dynasty recipe from a one-hundred-year-old eunuch. This desexed, antique man had been the imperial herbalist who concocted perfumes for the emperors' favorite concubines. Wang had paid a huge amount for the recipe but had no one to experiment on until his underling Mr. Ho found me.

Of course I'd never been allowed to see this priceless recipe, but I had heard about its legendary origin. Consisting of thirty-eight different precious herbs, including the most expensive ginseng, ground pearl powder, fresh honey, and the morning dew gathered from lotus leaves in the West Lake during spring, it was said that the recipe was invented by a doctor in the Tang dynasty during the reign of Empress Wu. Supposedly when the notoriously lustful empress had heard about this cosmetic genius, she'd summoned him to court to serve her exclusively. Then, fearing that the doctor would try to profit by selling the feminine secret to other equally lustful and scheming women, the empress had him castrated and kept him like a pet in her inner palace. In the thousand years since then, the recipe had been buried, stolen, destroyed, rediscovered, and probably forged many times. The secret was always kept within the eunuchs' communities.

It is claimed that if a woman takes this concoction for a year, the herbs will saturate her entire body, from her skin to her internal organs. The result will be a natural body fragrance so enthralling an aphrodisiac that no perfume, no matter how rare and expensive, can compete with it. In addition, the concoction should render a woman's complexion taut, translucent, and glowing. Big Brother Wang was the only person who possessed this recipe, and I was the only girl "honored" to be used for this experiment.

I had earned the right to take on Master Lung only after my earlier successes in destroying lesser men as proofs of my training and ability. Hence my hard-earned "skeleton woman" status. I credited the natural beauty that fate had awarded me, and my Heavenly Songbird's voice, together with the cunning to skillfully deploy my feminine assets. However, my boss was convinced that his concoction played a significant part in my accomplishments and insisted that I drink it every day. But it was rumored that the longer a woman drank this bizarre cocktail, the shorter would be her life. This would not matter to Wang once I had served my purpose, but it certainly did matter to me!

So my longevity depended on making Lung's life as short as possible. Though I was frightened of the consequences if I botched Lung's final exit, delay was even more dangerous. For me, there was no way to escape the clutches of the Red Demons gang.

However, though afraid of taking this unsavory potion, I was equally afraid of stopping. Was Wang right that this was the secret of my heavenly scent, my beguiling voice, my power to bewitch? Deprived of the potion, would my face suddenly look like the ripples on Huangpu River? Without or without secret potions, the beauty of a face does not last forever, and that is why I kept working hard on my singing, knife-throwing, and contorting.

Knife-throwing had not been planned as a part of my original training. But one time Mr. Ho saw me throw a stone to kill a rat with such accuracy that he suggested to Wang that I had a talent that could be used for throwing things more lethal than rocks. And so I was trained in knife-throwing. To my surprise, I found that I really appreciated this art. From it I learned the importance not only of accuracy but also of speed. As the Chinese saying goes: "He who attacks first wins: he who attacks second is a corpse."

My training in contortion was inspired by the rumor that Master Lung was addicted to perverse sex and would keep a woman longer if she continued to provide new variations. But, Lung apart, I also enjoyed gymnastics. I liked the idea that my body had a life and will of its own but with intense practice could be brought under my mind's control. Watching my contorted self in the mirror was an eerie, out-of-body experience. My limbs could become a brood of snakes, an intricately composed sculpture, the snarled roots of an ancient tree, or complicated calligraphic strokes. It was liberating to feel such complete control over my body. While my limbs were twisted into impossible visual images, my head would seem to separate from my body, like a big crystal ball foreseeing future events. But it was nearly always others' futures I saw, not my own.

My control was such that I could feel my way into receptacles seemingly far too small for me—a box, a suitcase, an urn. However, one time after I successfully got inside an ornamental urn, I crawled right back out, because the story of Empress Lu forced its way into my mind.

Lu was King Liu Bang's wife during the Han dynasty. However, the king's favorite woman was not his wife but his concubine, Lady Che. Lu had been extremely jealous of the beautiful, flirtatious Che but failed to destroy her while the king was alive. So as soon as Liu Bang's demise was announced, Empress Lu ordered that the concubine's limbs be cut off. After that, Lady Che was stuffed into an urn with only her head sticking out so she could be fed and kept alive for more suffering.

Lady Che's life was exactly what is meant by "better dead than alive." Her sad story was also a warning of the dangers of depending on your beauty and attractiveness to men. Often I could not help imagining the anguished woman in her vase and wondering if I would end up like her. Her tale always made me fear that if I didn't get out of my present situation in time, I'd share the concubine's fate.

But how to escape and be master of my own fate?

I wished I had magic—not like Shadow's, but real magic, to actually disappear and leave my troubles behind. . . .

∽ 16 ∽

Peony Pavilion

Of course I knew well that my troubles were far from being over; indeed, they were about to multiply.

One day Jinying called and invited me to see the Chinese opera *Peony Pavilion* at the Xinguang Theater. Though I'd never been to the famous place located on Ningbo Road, I'd heard many interesting things about it. It was here where the first Shanghai film with sound, *The Sing-Song Girl*, had been shown. Here, too, the famous American comedian called Char-Lee Cha-Biling had attended a Kun opera performance and met Mei Lanfang, a female impersonator and China's most beloved opera singer.

So I shared Jinying's excitement when his voice rippled over my eardrum, telling me about the opera.

Of course I was eager to see this famous opera in the equally famous theater, but I tried to hide the excitement in my voice and asked instead, "Where's your father?"

"Don't worry. He'll be away in Peking for a week."

My ears perked up. "What's he doing there?"

"I have no idea. He left in a hurry."

"Does he know about this?"

"About what?"

"That you're taking me to see an opera while he's away, for heaven's sake, Young Master!"

"He likes me to go around and do things in Shanghai. And I don't have to tell him that I'll be going with you."

"Jinying, we might have already been seen together at Shadow's castle show. Don't you realize you're playing with fire, and you—and me, too—will be burned sooner or later?"

An uncomfortable silence hung in the air until his voice, deflated like a balloon, continued. "I don't care what the others say. I've been living my whole life under my father's control, and I'm really sick of it. I just want to be with you. . . ."

"It's not whether you care or not. It's that if we are not on our guard, the consequences will be dire."

"But how? Since my father is so powerful, no one would want to hurt him. I'll bet no one dares to tell him. Please Camilla . . ."

"Maybe not, but we can't count on that." I paused to think, then said, "If we go, we will have to be in disguise. Also, don't get those expensive box seats, just ordinary ones, so we can blend in."

So the following Monday, I put on an ordinary, deep blue Chinese cotton dress, wore no makeup, and braided my hair into two pigtails. I was sure no one would recognize me as the famous Heavenly Songbird, but if anyone noticed me, they would take me for a student, a factory worker, or a young housewife.

We met outside the redbrick theater. I was pleased to see the boss's son had replaced his expensive, tailor-made Western suit and Italian leather shoes with a gray cotton Chinese gown and cloth slippers. Instead of looking like a spoiled young man with a rich, powerful father, he looked refreshingly like a university student or a young professor.

I thought, how wonderful it would be if we could be what we were disguised as, an ordinary couple living a simple, happy life. Why had our fates made an ordinary life seem impossible to attain?

Jinying looked surprised. "Camilla, I never saw you dress like this. You look so fresh. I like that."

"You look very good yourself."

Silently we followed others into the theater's lobby. The walls were covered with movie posters, of which one was a Paramount Film, *Forty Winks*. Viola Dana, the star on the poster, looked like she was startled to see me, but in reality no one paid us any attention. People are so easily fooled by appearances!

Soon we settled into seats near an aisle. I immediately liked this cozy place with rows of plush red chairs sloping toward the stage, which was swathed in matching red curtains. Jinying looked around the packed hall, then waved to a boy vendor. He bought almond tea, hot towels, sesame cakes, sugared ginger, and roasted watermelon seeds, then handed me my share.

He squeezed my hand. "Camilla, I'm so happy. We should do this more often."

He looked so pleased that I didn't have the heart to say that this should be our last outing together; otherwise, sooner or later we would be spotted. So I did not reply but turned my attention to the program. The reason I'd never seen *Peony Pavilion* was because it was filled with sentimentality about love and its power, precisely the feelings that were absolutely forbidden to me as a coldhearted informer.

Jinying leaned to whisper in my ear. "Camilla, you have no idea how thrilled I am to watch this opera with you."

I snapped, "But this story is completely unrealistic. A fairy tale."

He looked upset. "But that's what we need in this cold, cruel world."

Just then the curtain rose amid the audience's enthusiastic clapping. Although I didn't care about the love story in *Peony Pavilion,* I found the acting elegant and the singing beautiful and intriguing. Chinese operatic singing is very different from what Madame Lewinsky taught me. The performers seem to sing from their throats, not their chests. To me, the effect is like squeezing lemons and tasting the tart drops. I like it because it is so different from the kind of singing I do and because the "strangled" style fits well the desperation of the star-crossed lovers.

My ears and eyes were both captivated by the actress in a long, flowing, white dress and veil, singing lyrics from the act "Strolling in the Garden":

Ah, the colorful flowers bloom everywhere.
Sadly, all end up withered in an abandoned well.
A pleasant evening, beautiful scenery . . .
What family so fortunate as to enjoy this?
Colorful clouds, silk like rain, and threadlike wind . . .

After more lemon-squeezing singing, accompanied by gesturing of delicate fingers and flowing sleeves, came the famous scene, "Interrupted Dream." A woman, Liniang, has a dream in which she meets a young scholar. He tells her how much he loves her, that he has been searching for a woman like her his entire life. Overcome by their passion, they consummate their love right where they are, inside the peony pavilion, where flower fairies provide them cover.

The dream was so real and the passion so deep that when Liniang awoke, she was filled with longing for her dream lover. However, he never returned to her dreams, and gradually she wasted away and died. Before she passed away, she painted a portrait of herself and buried it under a rock in her garden. She did this to leave a sign that she once lived in this world and that she'd had a handsome lover. In her portrait she would escape the ravages of time and remain beautiful forever.

Soon Liniang, as a ghost, appeared in the scholar's dream to charm him. Upon awakening he sought her but learned that she had long been deceased. But he was so infatuated that he decided to visit her grave, where the intensity of his love brought her back to life.

I found myself fascinated by this strange love story in which a man and a woman make love in each other's dreams. A love that crosses the boundary between life and death. I could not help but think of Lung's making love to me, for wasn't I about to make him a dead man? I felt a shiver rise up my spine, intensified by the scratchy, high-pitched music.

Then I felt my hand being squeezed by Jinying's. I turned and saw tears glisten in his eyes.

"Are you all right?" I asked.

He shook his head, dabbing his eyes with his white handkerchief.

As I was about to tease him for his sentimentality, his sad, piercing look touched something in me, and I suddenly looked at him in a different light. My hand involuntarily reached to take his.

"Jinying, please don't be sad. Everything will be all right."

"You think so?" He looked a little happier.

I nodded, not believing it.

When the play was finally over, we hurried out of the theater and hailed a rickshaw.

Inside the vehicle, Jinying asked me eagerly, his eyes curious, "You liked the play?"

"The music yes, but not the story; it's silly, making love in dreams and resurrecting a dead woman!"

His eyes told me that his feelings were hurt and that he thought just the opposite. "Camilla, I know you think I'm being sentimental, but I'm not ashamed to say that I'm very touched by it, even if you find it silly."

Before I could reply, he lifted my hand to his lips, then said, "Camilla, why can't we live in a dream for a while? You are always so serious about life."

If only he'd known why I was so serious. Did I have a choice? I didn't choose to be an orphan, nor to live the life of a spy!

Before I had a chance to respond, he went on. "What the playwright, Tang Xianzu, expresses through his opera touches me deeply."

"And what is that?"

He held up his program. "According to this, Tang said, 'No one knows where love arises, but it is so deep that it possesses the power to end life and resurrect the dead. If you are not willing to die for the one you love, or if the dead will not come back to life for you, it's because the love is not deep enough.' "

His eyes tried to search mine. Could he see deeply enough to discover that my loveless life was filled with cunning and scheming?

"I hope our love is also powerful enough to resurrect the dead," he whispered.

Feeling bad for him, I murmured, "I hope so, too." But I could not believe in what we said.

He sighed.

"What is it?"

He shook his head. "Nothing."

Of course I knew why he sighed. Deep down, neither did he believe any of this. Two lovers, two strangers, so close to each other and yet so far apart. Whose fault was this situation that was likely to end in hurt? Was it mine? No. Instead, blame my parents for leaving me an orphan, blame Big Brother Wang for taking me under his wing, and blame both Master Lung and his son for falling for me.

Blame fate!

Jinying pressed me. "You don't believe in the power of love, do you?"

I didn't answer. I didn't grow up with love but with hatred, scheming, and heartlessness. As a spy, I couldn't trust any person, let alone something as abstract as love. Yet I had read that some young girls were so touched by the power of love portrayed in *Peony Pavilion* that they even killed themselves. One girl wrote a poem after seeing the play:

> Ignoring the cold rain by my window's curtain,
> I am reading *Peony Pavilion* under the lamp.
> Is there anyone in this world more infatuated than I?
> Am I the only one who is so sad beyond words?

The young master suddenly threw me a request. "Camilla, run away with me."

I sighed in the shadowy confines of the rickshaw.

The young master in real life, like the young scholar in the play, sighed in response.

PART FOUR

❧ 17 ❧

A Luxury Cruise

As I was wondering if it would really be possible to run away with Jinying and leave my troubles behind, Lung returned from his business in Peking and called, wanting to see me.

Over the phone, his voice sounded rough and raspy, probably from a lot of smoking, drinking, and whoring on his trip. "Camilla, I need a vacation and want you to travel with me. What about Europe?"

The proposal came so suddenly that it took me a few seconds to think. Normally I would have said something like, "Ah, Master Lung, I'm sure I'll be happy wherever you take me as long as we're together." But this time I had to carefully weigh the options. I could almost hear my brain whirring like a fan inside my head. If I went abroad with him, would it be easier to have him killed? And easier for me to disappear? But would Big Brother Wang trust me so far out of his sight, and would he send men to follow us?

This could be a once-in-a-life-time chance—to eliminate Lung or even to run away without killing him. Though trained specifically to bring down Lung, I actually had no grudge of my own against him. Would luck smile on my path? If so, it would be for the first time.

So I projected a smile into the receiver. "Master Lung, can you tell me anyone who doesn't want to see Europe? And I know you love the culture there."

His happy laughter rolled loudly to my eardrum. "Camilla, how come you're always able to read my mind?"

It really was not hard. Rich and powerful now, Lung had never gotten rid of his inferiority complex from once being a shoe-shine boy. Visiting Europe, especially Paris and Rome, would add to his veneer of culture. Although he really only cared about making money, he loved to be complimented on his predilection for culture.

"Master Lung, I may not be able to read your subtle mind, but I definitely know your exquisite taste."

"Ha-ha-ha! That's why you're my favorite, Camilla. Good, I'll ask my men to arrange the trip."

After I hung up, I immediately called Wang and told him about Lung's travel plan.

My boss's tone had an edge of suppressed excitement. "It's good news. He will be off his usual turf and may let his guard down. But assassinating him still will not be easy, because I'm sure he will bring along some of his entourage."

I thought for a while, then asked, "Big Brother Wang, what about sending a couple disguised as Japanese tourists to ambush him?"

"Good thought, Camilla. I can see that your training wasn't wasted!"

"Thank you, Big Brother Wang. But you also want me to find Lung's secret accounts and documents, so if he is killed in Europe—"

"I thought about that. But I don't want to miss this rare chance to eliminate him. So we should go ahead with the plan and find a way to get at his accounts later."

"Yes, of course, Big Brother Wang."

I thought the long ship voyage to Europe might be a good place to trap Lung but wondered how the assassins—and I—could then make our escape. But I did not dare make any more suggestions, in case my boss might think I was trying to outsmart him.

Before we hung up, Wang went on to brief me on the people he'd send, the codes, gestures, and signals for possible communications, all mostly a rehash of what I'd learned during my training.

Preparation was hurried with the help of Ah Wen, who drove me around to shop at the four big department stores—Xin Xin, Da Xin, Sincere, and Wing On on Nanking Road. Since I'd be in Europe, it would be a chance to have Lung pay for a whole Western wardrobe—dresses and accessories like summer hats, straw purses, lace gloves, dainty parasols. Of course I'd also bring a few body-hugging *cheongsam* to show off my exotic Chineseness, my breasts as bulging as Lung's wallets, especially with their provocative contrast with my twenty-one-inch waist.

Only two weeks after Lung and I had talked over the phone, we were ready to go. Although I was well aware that this trip was not a vacation for me but a dangerous mission, I couldn't help but feel excited that I would be seeing Europe, especially Paris. Would Lung bring me to the shops along the famous, tree-lined Champs-Élysées? Or take me to see *Carmen, La Traviata,* or *Madame Butterfly* at L'Opera de Paris?

The morning of our departure, eight of us, Master Lung, Jinying, Mr. Zhu, Gao and his team of three bodyguards, and I arrived at the dock by the Huangpu River. I looked up at the towering ship, and, instead of feeling the corners of my lips curving up like the ship's lifeboat, I felt a headache coming on. We waved goodbye to Lung's underlings, who came to see us off, then followed other passengers to board the gigantic monster. Behind us, Gao and the other bodyguards carried our luggage—dispensable—together with their guns—indispensable. A few people, probably recognizing who we were, eyed us surreptitiously with intense interest. I looked around anxiously and finally spotted among the crowd boarding with us Big Brother Wang's assassins—a young couple wearing kimonos and talking to each other in fluent Japanese. The man wiped his hand across his forehead—the sign to me that he was Wang's man. My arm involuntarily tightened around Lung's as my heart beat like the bullets soon to be fired from all the guns.

Ten minutes later, everybody was aboard the luxury cruise ship. Over the odor of the salt air of the harbor could be smelled expensive perfume, nose-tearing cigars, and fishy money. Lung suggested that we rest, change, gamble for a while in the casino, and, after that, dine at the ship's fanciest restaurant. Jinying and Zhu acknowledged the master's order and left.

Lung turned to me. "Camilla, put on something really pretty and sexy. I want to show you off tonight—you got it?"

"Of course, Master Lung. Giving you face is my pleasure and honor."

He smacked my cheek. "You little witch. I'm sure you also know what I want after dinner."

This time I didn't answer but smiled coyly. What else besides sex? Would he suddenly want to discuss Chinese poetry or philosophy?

He turned to Gao and his men. "I'll be on the radio about some important business, then I'll take a nap. So do not disturb me unless someone is dying. You got that?"

"Yes, Master Lung." The four black-clad, muscular men answered in one voice.

I went to my room, which was situated one floor below Lung's. This was because those next to his deluxe suite were all booked, including the one two rooms away, which was now occupied by the "Japanese" couple, the would-be assassins. I took a shower, wrapped myself in the ship's bathrobe, and was about to get a drink when the doorbell rang. I dashed to open it, assuming it was Lung, but instead saw a nervous-looking Jinying.

"Jinying, are you crazy? The bodyguards might see us!"

"Don't worry. We're on a different floor. Besides, I just gave them money to get a drink in the bar."

"And they went, even Gao?"

"I insisted. I told them they looked tired and needed a break in order to stay alert. Please let me in."

"I can't. It's too dangerous."

"But now is our only chance. Tonight you'll be with my father!"

Ignoring my protest, the boss's son squeezed himself in, closed the door, and pressed his lips firmly onto mine. I could feel his nervousness, passion, and the thrill of the forbidden pleasure. Maybe sex was on his mind, but it was definitely not on mine, no matter how attractive he looked tonight. The romantic atmosphere of the great ship seemed to intensify his tormented infatuation. If the bodyguards were gone, it might be a perfect time—not for making love to a handsome man, but for the Japanese couple to kill Lung. But then I realized that the ship was still in the harbor, and once the murder was discovered, the ship would quickly be overrun with police.

I pushed him away and protested. "Jinying, please leave. The bodyguards will be back any time now."

He didn't respond but scrutinized me with his sad eyes.

I burst out in a heated whisper, "Aren't you afraid what will happen if your father finds out?"

"I hate him. If I continue to live in his evil world, I might as well be dead. You have no idea what my life is like."

Of course I knew; I couldn't share mine with him, either. So I said, "But he loves you."

"It's not real love, only that he believes I'm his *fengshui* son. If one day he doesn't think I bring him good luck anymore, I can imagine what will happen to me."

"I'm sorry, Jinying," I said, this time meaning it. Because I was also feeling sorry for myself for similar reasons.

"Camilla, let's—"

I put a finger across his lips. "Please go back to your room now."

He uttered a reluctant "All right," then quietly left.

A few seconds later, I dashed out of my room and ran to the upper floor where Lung and the Japanese couple resided two rooms apart. Running, I almost smacked right into a foreign devil.

He cast me a curious glance.

I smiled. "Sorry, mister."

"No problem." He smiled back happily, his eyes lingering on me for long moments before he disappeared into a room.

I inhaled deeply, then knocked tentatively on the Japanese couple's room. Just then, to my utter shock, Gao suddenly materialized in the corridor like a ghost snatched from thin air. It took a few seconds for him to recognize me, probably because I was not in my Heavenly Songbird outfit but in my bathrobe and with no makeup.

He gave me a curious, appreciative once-over. And, like the foreigner, he allowed his eyes to linger on me a tad too long. It was then that I noticed one of my breasts was showing through my loosened bathrobe. I felt my cheeks burning as I quickly tightened the robe across my chest.

Gao looked somewhat amused, then pointed to the other room. "Miss Camilla, *that* one is Master Lung's room."

"Oh, yes." I put on my best smile. "I got mixed up. Must be the wine."

My heart was beating fast. Oh, heaven, please don't let Gao suspect anything! Just then the door of the "wrong" room opened, and a head stuck out. But before the Japanese husband, code named Black Coffee, was about to say something, I was already speaking, in Mandarin.

"Oh, sir, so sorry to disturb you. I knocked on the wrong door. Maybe I should have some coffee to wake me up."

I was glad that he acted in perfect cooperation. "No problem," he answered in heavily accented Mandarin, then closed the door with a loud thud, like an emphatic nod.

To "have coffee to wake me up" was the code used when a mission was on hold and needed to be rescheduled.

Gao had been watching us, fortunately not with suspicion but with amusement. I doubted he was feigning. This man's emotions were written on his face like the inscription on a stele. An honest, loyal man. Good material for a bodyguard but worthless for a spy.

He said, "Master Lung is taking a nap now, so I'm afraid you have to wait for a while."

I put on a friendly smile. "So where are the others?"

"The young master bought them drinks at the bar."

"And why aren't you with them?"

He cast me a meaningful look. "You know me, Miss Camilla. I can't leave the master unprotected."

"Of course. You are a good man, Gao," I said, swallowing the remaining phrase—*but what a pity that your goodness is engulfed by evil*. Why did he work for Lung? I always wondered but never asked. There was a rumor that his father, a compulsive gambler, owed Lung's gambling den thousands of dollars so that the son was forced to work for the gangster to pay the debt.

He said, "If you don't mind, why don't you wait with me for a while? Master Lung asked me to wake him up at five-thirty, just ten minutes from now."

It was a daring request. But what could we talk about right in front of the tiger's lair?

My answer was a casual, "Oh, yes, why not? Hmm ..." I pointed to my bathrobe. "But what if someone sees me in this?"

"Then they will think what a fresh, naturally beautiful woman you are."

After some moments of silence, he took out a pack of cigarettes and shook one out. "Please have one."

"No, you know I rarely smoke."

"Please, just this one time?"

I rarely smoked because I feared it might ruin my voice. However, I always liked the wicked gestures that went with it, especially now that I was in a bathrobe in the company of a ruggedly handsome man.

"All right." I smiled, then took the offered cigarette. Gao slid out a lighter and, with a flick of his big, scarred hand, lit mine, then his. Soon smoke was puffing from our mouths. It was only after several more puffs that I realized, to my surprise, that he'd been blowing out heart-shaped smoke rings. I was touched by this ingenious way of expressing love from the tough bodyguard. But of course I was not going to accept it. So in response, I blew out smoke rings in the shape of a big zero, or emptiness.

In this lifetime nothing was possible for us.

Gao shook his crew-cut head and smiled. I didn't even try to guess what he was thinking.

Just then, like another ghost soundlessly approaching us, Jinying appeared.

"What are you two doing here?" the young master asked, giving us a bitter once-over.

I was the first to speak. "Young Master, I just came to see if Master Lung is awake. I have a question to ask him."

He cast a suspicious look at Gao, then me. "What question?"

"Nothing important. Master Lung told me to dress my best. So I want to ask if he wants me to look like a China doll or a Western one."

Gao chimed in. "Master Lung is about to wake up from a nap. That's why Miss Camilla is waiting here."

"Then I'll wait, too," Jinying said with a child's stubbornness.

With the boss's son's intrusion, the atmosphere had drastically changed. I could feel animosity Ping-Ponging between the two men who now engulfed me with their hopeless, suffocating love.

What a deliciously complicated moment.

At eight in the evening, my slender frame wrapped in a red, low-cut, Western dress, my feet in matching high heels, and my gloved arm around Lung's, I walked with the gangster to the ship's casino. Zhu, Gao, and the three other bodyguards trailed behind with bulging pants pockets—guns, knives, daggers, or other lethal devices.

Inside the gambling den, low-hanging chandeliers cast light on the numerous tables crowded with rich customers. Laughter, heated whispers, and lamenting exclamations were emitted here and there as one person won and others lost. Golden curtains and mirrored pillars reflected the light from the chandelier's many crystals, turning the whole place into one huge glittering diamond.

Despite my training not to become emotional under any circumstances, in this setting I felt an artificially induced excitement, even a fleeting moment of happiness.

Lung and I approached a table surrounded by a small group of richly attired couples, all clutching cards, chatting, drinking, and smoking.

Spotting us, the white-shirted and black-vested dealer asked the other guests to make room for us to sit down at the best *fengshui* place, facing the entrance. He smiled obsequiously as he held out the cards for Lung to cut. When the dealer's eyes met mine, his smile faded by half. For him, I, like the other beautiful women accompanying their important-looking men, was but decoration—like the big diamond ring on the hand of the lady next to me, or the gold and diamond Rolex watch sparkling on her patron's wrist. Women like us are commodities; we come and go like a merry-go-round. No reason for the dealer to waste any effort pleasing us, when next time it would be a different woman next to the high roller. That was just as well. So long as I seemed a mere adornment, no one would guess my deadly mission.

Over the next hour, Lung won two thousand dollars, a small sum for him, but gave a tip of fifty, a big sum for the dealer. The money meant nothing to Lung, but the good luck did—brought by me, since I was sitting next to him the whole time.

He pinched my bottom and whispered into my ear as a licentious smile bloomed on his broken-browed face. "Tonight, since I won all this good-luck money, I'll have a good-luck fuck."

His *good-luck fuck* meant to have sex with me in yet another odd position.

I didn't answer directly but instead asked, "Where's the young master? Isn't he your *fengshui* son?"

The old man spat a bitter chuckle. "Ha! You know my son. He disapproves of gambling and refused to come. 'To assist in doing evil?' he said. Ha! If he was not my son . . ."

He turned to Zhu, who had been content sitting at his boss's side, refilling drinks and lighting cigarettes. "Zhu, where's my son?"

His right-hand man said, "In the concert hall, listening to his favorite Western classical music."

Lung laughed out loud. "Ha! Classical? To me, it's absolutely nonsensical!"

A few guests at our gambling table smiled at Lung, then at me.

Lung burst out laughing in response. "Ha-ha! Let's forget about him and profit some more from my good luck!"

That night, Lung won close to five thousand dollars. After we left the casino, drunk and dizzy with excitement, he dragged me all the way to his bedroom for even more good luck. However, though half-drunk, the gangster hadn't lost any of his customary alertness. If I believed he would ever let his guard down, it was clear that I was wrong. Again, he asked Gao to search me. But of course I didn't carry any arms; the Japanese couple were carrying them for me.

The luxury suite had a living room, bedroom, and two bathrooms. Lung asked Gao to search me in one bathroom, while he took a bath in the one inside the bedroom.

I never felt anything when Gao searched me, because we both knew it was simply a security routine. Besides, he was never rough to me or tried to hurt me. But this time, inside the small confines of the scented bathroom, he looked and acted differently. His face was flushed, and his lips were trembling. In the past, he had always asked me to take off my own clothes, for he feared having any physical contact with his master's woman. I knew this was also to let me know he would not take advantage of me, even though we were "A single man and a solitary woman put in the same room," which could end up like "dry firewood ablaze with raging flames," Chinese sayings to describe the combustible situation when a man and woman are alone together.

Therefore, to my surprise, as I was about to unbutton my dress, Gao waved for me to stop. Then, with his trembling hands, he began to do my job for me. Slowly he peeled off my clothes, his gaze wandering over my gradually exposed body like a hungry wolf searching for prey. Then he unhooked my bra and let it slither to the floor like a mischievous animal. Abruptly, the bodyguard pulled me to him, buried his head between my breasts, and sobbed.

"Miss Camilla, excuse my imprudence. I can't help it anymore. I'm madly in love with you. Just tell me, and I'll do anything for you. . . ."

I touched his head, willing myself to keep my calm and focus, since he'd lost his. "Gao, please. You know you really shouldn't. . . ."

"Let Master Lung kill me for my sin. I don't care. I'd rather die a happy sinner than live without your love."

It took me a few seconds to absorb this unexpected, shocking declaration. Gently I pushed him away and wiped the tears streaking his square-jawed face. "Gao, sober up. You're drunk. You don't know what you're talking about."

"Miss Camilla, have you not heard of the saying, 'The truth comes out when a person is drunk'? Don't you believe that I love you?"

Feeling my heart almost jumping out from my throat, I said gently, "Gao, please, gather yourself up. We're right next to a tiger."

Oblivious of what I said, Gao cupped my breast, kissing it as tenderly as he would a newborn, then sucking on my nipple as if he were the baby. Then his hand, like a giant spider, pulled down my panties with as much urgency as if they had just caught fire. With the same eager hands, he tore off his tie, shirt, unleashed his gun holster, then pulled down his pants and underpants.

I was shocked to see that his naked, muscular torso was covered with scars from old knife wounds and even bullets. If I thought my sufferings were as deep as the Huangpu River, then his must be as unfathomable as the Pacific Ocean. How could one man's body withstand all these brutal assaults?

I felt an urge to give this man something, if not love, then at least warmth and affection. These feelings, unbeknownst to me before, surged inside me as my lips began to kiss his wounds.

The bodyguard touched my head and his manly voice rose in the air softly. "Don't worry about me, Camilla, I'm fine, really. My only worry is you."

Hearing this, the Chinese saying flashed in my mind: "Two forlorn people meet at the far corners of the earth."

In a time of peace, maybe we would be happy lovers.

But unfortunately fate had its own inscrutable plans for us mortals.

As my lips glided over his scars I noticed that his *yang* instrument, big, powerful, and hardened like a stone tablet, seemed to stare at me, pleading with such aching desire that my hand involuntarily reached to relieve its suffering. Now its master moaned as if inflicted by extreme tortures—burned by cigarettes, pressed by smoldering coals, slashed by a nail-filled whip.

Eyes closed, I let his hands roam all over my body like horses galloping on a meadow, his tongue slide into my mouth like a snake slithering in the bush, his *yang* instrument swelling inside my small hand like a big fish struggling for water. Our tongues and limbs became entangled, groans escaping our kissing and sucking mouths.

"Oh, Camilla, please just take my life away. . . ."

I didn't respond but focused on feeling the pleasure from this tough bodyguard's unquenchable desire and impossible love. I forgot all my training so I could relish this tough man's big hands and big chest, feeling so powerful yet vulnerable against my delicate body. Gently, he lifted me onto the sink, spread my legs like scissors, and slid his ballooning "fish" inside my watery gate.

Once inside, he engaged in a relentless game of digging until I felt my whole body on fire like a bomb about to explode. In "revenge," my long fingernails dug deeply into his thick, sweaty back as my teeth bit into his muscular shoulder. But that didn't stop the hammering, only encouraged it.

"Ahhhhh!" A loud scream shot out involuntarily from between my lips.

Gao immediately moved his hand to cover my mouth.

I couldn't decide, didn't care, if I was feeling pain, pleasure, or a mixture of the two. But then I heard, or at least I thought I heard, a sound from the master suite. Struck by a sudden rush of fear, I tried to push Gao away. But he must have thought the push was but a seduction in disguise, for he locked my arms with his and continued to thrust against me. From the mirror's reflection, I was alarmed to see that he was no longer the calm, alert head bodyguard I knew but a beast hungrily devouring his helpless prey. Finally, his body shook more violently, and the thrusting ceased. His eyes closed, and he seemed now far, far away. I used all my strength to slap him hard on his face. It worked. He lifted his head to stare at me with his sad, puzzling eyes.

"Why, Camilla?" Before I could reply, he added, "You . . . don't like this? Did I . . . hurt you?"

I said in a heated whisper, "Gao, I heard something. . . ."

Now he listened intently. "You mean . . ."

I nodded.

It was the first time I had ever seen fear in this tough man's face.

I already knew what he was going to say next, so I said it first. "Gao, don't worry. I'll never tell anyone about this."

"Miss Camilla . . . I . . . I . . ."

I put a finger across his lips. "Shh . . . just don't say anything."

Next, we began to pull on our clothes. I was surprised that after our devilish lovemaking, and his having seen my body more times that I could count, now the bodyguard looked away to let me put on my dress.

When we had our clothes back on, he said, "Forgive me, Miss Camilla. Please go to Master Lung now."

Of course he was not going to search me, for I had already bared myself to the last stitch. And if I'd hidden something inside my vagina, his little brother would have noticed or even been hurt.

Just then Lung's alcohol-slurred voice streamed from the bedroom. "Camilla, what's happening? You want me to wait till my balls drop off?!"

"Be right there, Master Lung!" I yelled back, smoothing my hair as I got out of the bathroom, leaving a completely crushed-looking Gao behind.

With a heavy heart and an exhausted body, I wiped as best I could between my sore legs and dragged myself into the master bedroom. Inside, I quickly took my clothes back off and crawled into bed and into the arms of my contortionist-sex-addicted patron.

The last thing I wanted right now was another man, especially Lung. But I was terrified lest he suspect something, and so when Lung was doing all sorts of gymnastics with my body, I screamed and moaned as loudly as I could. Aware that Gao was right outside in the same room, I could not help but imagine Gao's tortured expression and his heart breaking into a thousand pieces for a love he'd die for but that had no future.

I felt a little ashamed that I actually did feel perversely satisfied after my encounters with the two men. But when the excitement was over, I had to think again about why I was here. I was starting to worry there would not be any opportunity to kill Lung, that this vacation would soon be over, and Lung would still be alive. But in the meantime I might as well enjoy the trip—movies, massage, dancing, gourmet food—and the admiration of both Lung's body-guard and his son. I had to admit that I had enjoyed Gao's love-making even more than Jinying's. It was more thrilling to see a tough, big, muscular man breaking down in front of a fragile woman like myself. As the Chinese say, *tiehan rouqing,* an iron man with tender sentiments.

Thus thinking, I screamed and moaned more.

❧ 18 ❧

False Alarm

The next morning, while the gang members were still sleeping, I went up to the deck to gaze at the sea, hoping the deep blue waves would clear my mind and calm my spirit. Yet the scene with Gao kept coming back to me. As I was thus preoccupied with my thoughts, a man walked toward me, then bumped his elbow into my purse.

I was about to say something, when I noticed my purse was open with a slip of paper visible inside. Making sure that nobody was close enough to notice, I took it out and read:

> You've not been paying attention. From now on,
> stay alert, and try better to communicate with us.

My heart sank. Big Brother Wang had put another person on the ship whom he hadn't told me about. And this man was not happy with what I'd done so far or, to be exact, failed to do. Did my boss imagine I could just tell the assassin to break into Lung's room in the middle of the night? That was quite out of the question because Gao and his team, all armed, were always alternating their vigil outside Lung's door. Yes, Gao had been distracted by me briefly, but now I was sure he'd be extra alert.

Moments later, from the corner of my eye I saw the Japanese couple approaching the rail and, like me, looking out over the sea. They whispered into each other's ears and touched each other's faces and hands intimately. As expected, they acted like a newly-wed couple seemingly completely oblivious of those around them. Soon they were hugging each other, and a lipstick dropped from the woman's purse. Making sure that no one was watching me, I took out a small piece of paper, scribbled quickly on it, then walked toward the stairs leading back to the lower deck. As I passed the couple, I picked up the lipstick and handed it to the woman—with the small piece of paper. She pocketed both, then thanked me profusely in heavily accented Mandarin.

The third evening, inside the ship's packed ballroom, Lung and I were tapping our expensive shoes on the polished parquet floor. Jazz music from a Filipino band invigorated the passengers' feet so that they bounced energetically on the shiny floor. Lung looked very happy, swaying and twirling me this way and that and making me dizzy, not with happiness, but with anxiety. Mr. Zhu, Jinying, Gao, and one bodyguard sat at the front table, chatting casually, their eyes glued on us like snails on the ground. The two other bodyguards discreetly strolled, alert for anything suspicious. While Jinying and Gao's faces held sour expressions, Zhu and the body-guard next to him were happily drinking, snacking, visually molesting the beautiful women, and generally having a wonderful time, paid for by their boss.

The band played waltzes, fox trots, Charlestons, tangos, and jitterbugs. The more skillful their playing, the more Lung wanted to show off his skill and his mistress—me. Perhaps because of my patron's threatening, don't-try-to-beat-me look and his slick moves, couples began to drift back to their seats to watch us. *Oohs* and *aahs* shot from their mouths as they clapped fervently whenever Lung lifted me up to heaven, then eased me down to earth. Some of the Chinese probably recognized who we were, but I doubted the foreigners had any clue as to the identity of this small, powerful man and his fragile skeleton woman.

Looking extremely pleased with himself and his admirers, Lung let his shoes scratch the floor ever harder, as if it were suddenly festering with a rash. He twisted his small, lean body in all four directions so vigorously that sometimes he looked as if he were having a seizure or as if hundred of ants were crawling up his pants. Again, people laughed and clapped, but I wondered if they realized that this amusing man would slice them into pieces if it served his purposes.

As Lung was smiling on the outside, I did the same inside. Because I expected that soon our dancing would be complemented by another act, carried out, I hoped, with impeccable skill like Lung's dancing, though not likely to make him smile. In my peripheral vision, I saw the Japanese man whisper something to his "wife," plant a kiss on her cheek, then stand up and leave the ballroom. No one but me seemed to notice.

Besides the Japanese wife, I was the only one in the ballroom who knew what was going to happen. I prayed that my heart, beating like the drummer in the band, would not be heard by Lung. As I forced the smile to stay on my face and my feet on the floor, to my surprise, Jinying abruptly stood up from his chair and walked into the dancing area. Oh, heaven, I thought, let him not spoil my mission yet again!

When the young master was in front of us, he said, "Father, you two look so wonderful together. But you must be tired now, so why don't you let me dance with Camilla so you can take a break?"

Lung stopped and took out a handkerchief to wipe his perspiring forehead. "All right, I do feel tired. Here's my Camilla. Treat her well."

"I will, Father."

I cursed inside as I watched the gangster head walk back to his table to join his right-hand man and bodyguards.

"Jinying, I think your father is really enjoying this, so why didn't you let him continue?"

"Because I also want to dance with you. And I can't bear to see you dancing with him. Haven't you heard the expression 'a fresh flower stuck in a pile of dung'?"

Of course I knew the phrase. But what was I supposed to say? So I put on a faint smile and whispered softly, "Let's dance, Young Master."

Needless to say, the son was a much more pleasurable dance partner than his father. Not only because he was tall, lean, elegant, and young, but also because he was a gentleman. Lung was skillful only in a crude, clownish, showy way. Anyone could tell his partner was merely his rag doll, or puppet, so he could show off his absolute domination. But Jinying led me in a protective way, careful not to hurt my delicate frame and conscious to make sure I'd enjoy the swing, the twirl, the glide. I felt like I was dancing with a loving person, not a powerful machine running at full speed. Then there was Gao. I was sure he was dying to dance with me, but would he have the guts to cut in on his boss's son? I peeked at the bodyguard and met his sad eyes. *Good.* He looked too lost in his own troubles to sense anything between me and his boss's son.

But why was I analyzing all of this? I needed to prepare for what was going to happen, maybe in minutes, not ruminate on who was a better dancer, lover, or who looked sad.

Jinying's voice rose next to my ear, breaking up my thoughts. "Camilla, what are you thinking? Are you enjoying this?"

I looked up and found the young master's face forlorn and unbearably sad, just like Gao's, and equally poignant. From the corner of my eye I saw Gao help the staggering Lung toward the exit. Seconds later, the fire alarm sounded *Riiiing . . . Riiiing . . . Riiiing!* loud and clear in the packed ballroom like a newborn baby's life-entering cries. The orchestra abruptly stopped.

"What's that?" a male voice blurted out, followed by several other people asking similar questions. "What happened?" "Is something wrong?"

A tuxedoed man dashed to the small stage of the dancing area and grabbed the microphone. "Ladies and gentlemen, I'm the manager of this dance hall. Please stay calm. That is our fire alarm, and I believe it's a mistake. A mechanic has been sent to check, and everything should be okay. Sometimes we have false alarms. So please don't worry, and continue to enjoy yourselves." After that, he turned to signal the Filipino band to resume playing. But no sooner had he stepped down from the stage than someone yelled, "Fire! Fire!"

The players stopped again to stare at one another questioningly. The manager dashed back onstage, reiterating in his booming voice, "Ladies and gentlemen, trust me, it's a false alarm. Please stay calm, and don't cause chaos by rushing out of the ballroom."

Contrary to his advice, people began to head toward the exit as they whispered heatedly, "Fire! It's a fire! I can smell smoke!"

Jinying put his arm around my shoulders protectively. "Camilla, I think I smell smoke. Do you?"

My head nodded vigorously to match my pounding heart.

"Let's go."

He half pushed me onto the small stage, then led me through a back exit into a long, dim corridor. We groped in the dark for a while before we finally found our way to the main deck. People, some of whom I recognized from the ballroom, were milling around, looking frightened and helpless. Listlessly they either stared at the boundless sea or looked at one another, desperate for reassurance.

I was frightened as well, because I had no idea that starting a fire was part of the plan. I'd thought that the Japanese would just set off the alarm to create confusion and provide a chance to kill Lung, a strategy called *hunshui moyu,* stir the water to catch the fish. But the idea was certainly not to have ourselves killed to accompany the gangster head on his trip to hell!

Jinying and I squeezed our way through the other passengers till we reached the rail. As people pressed against my back, I stared at the dark sea and felt a sense of hopelessness.

"Jinying, if the whole ship is on fire, where can we go?"

"I don't see any other way out except the sea," he said, taking off his suit jacket and draping it over my shoulders. But this kind act hardly gave me any comfort.

Just then another mob of passengers, probably from the ballroom and its neighboring casino and restaurant, rushed onto the deck for fresh air. The adults looked alarmed and worried; the children had mixed expressions, some oblivious, others happy, probably thinking this was a much more exciting game than those played at home.

In the distance, a little girl cried hysterically for her parents. "Baba, Mama, where are you?"

"Jinying, where do you think your father is now?" I asked, secretly hoping that the old man's soul was already on its way to where it deserved to go.

He pointed to the milling, agonized mob around us. "Possibly in the front of the ship . . ."

"What makes you think he's in the front?"

He scoffed, "Because he has to be ahead in everything!"

I nodded, wondering what to do next.

"Anyway, I don't think we can get through this crowd to find him. But I'm sure he'll be safe as long as he's with Gao."

"I hope so," I said, hoping the opposite.

However, it seemed nobody was paying attention to anyone but themselves and their family.

Jinying said, his voice filled with worry, "I don't see any of the crew around. I hope they're downstairs extinguishing the fire. Camilla, can you swim?"

"But, Jinying, we'll freeze to death in the icy water!"

"I know. But sometimes in life we don't have a choice, do we?"

His sentence hit a chord in me so hard that tears rolled down my cheeks despite my effort to stop them.

Jinying pulled me to him and pressed my head against his chest. "Don't be sad, Camilla. If we die, at least we'll die together."

I was about to ask, "Why do you love me so much? Would you love me if you knew that I am your father's fateful star? That I am just using you for an evil purpose?"

But then a uniformed man climbed onto the ship's bridge and spoke through a megaphone. "Ladies and gentleman, I'm this ship's first mate. There's very good news—the fire has just been extinguished! Now everything's fine and under control. So please go back down to continue to enjoy our ship's many entertainments."

Thunderous clapping burst in the chilly night air.

A white-haired man asked, "What happened?"

"Somehow a fire started accidentally outside the ballroom. We have no idea how. My guess is that some children were playing with matches. Anyway, everything is fine now."

Not far from us, a gray-haired grandmother yelled in her alto voice, "Children who play with fire should be punished! And so should their parents, who fail to discipline them!"

The people around her echoed, "Yes, naughty children should be punished!"

Of course I knew this was not a child's game but an assassin's. I decided I should show some concern about Lung, so I said to the young master, "You think your father's okay?"

"Yes, as long as he's with Gao."

A man 's voice slashed the air. "You're sure nobody's hurt?"

"Absolutely—"

Just then a loud commotion burst forth near the bow, followed by a loud shout, "Someone fell overboard!"

Could that be Lung?

Jinying and I pushed forward to the front to have a better look. Not one but two heads were bobbing in the angry waves like two huge bugs. To my dismay, Lung was one of them, and the other was Gao. Lung was still alive. This meant that the mission had failed yet again. Now my only hope was that Lung would catch pneumonia and die. It should be so easy!

The first mate screamed to a uniformed man beside him. "Get the ship's doctor, quick!" Then he dashed to snatch two life preservers attached to long ropes and threw them into the sea. "Grab a hold! Hold on tight, and we will lower a lifeboat for you!"

As the two men bobbed in the sea, holding on to the life preservers, some sailors climbed into the lifeboat while others lowered it down. Soon both Lung and Gao were in the small boat, and it was being raised back up to the deck.

Jinying leaned over the railing. "Father! Hold on tight!"

I had no choice but to join in. "Master Lung, you'll be fine! A doctor's on his way right now!"

Other voices were heard in the chilly, tense air.

"Hang on there!"

"Don't be frightened—help is on the way!"

"Your lucky star is protecting you!"

Finally Gao, helping a soaking wet Lung, cautiously stepped onto the deck.

Cheers burst in the air from the crowd.

As if on cue, the ship's doctor arrived with his medicine box and two uniformed men. Immediately he pounded on Lung's, then Gao's, chest to clear the water from their lungs. There was much coughing and spitting, and soon color began to sneak back into their faces.

Blankets were draped over the two shivering bodies. Jinying and I knelt down beside them.

The young master asked, "How are you doing, Father?"

I chimed in, smiling faintly. "Master Lung, don't worry, you're safe now." I added, "Again, it proves your lucky star is shining high to protect you."

Gao, though a little pale, looked fine. But it took a few moments longer for Lung to completely regain his senses.

Then, to our surprise, he even regained his sense of humor, suddenly cracking a joke. "Hmm . . . then why did I fall into the sea in the first place, huh?"

I was relieved. Since he was in a good mood even after such a scary incident, he must not have realized his plunge into the ocean was not an accident. However, I was also regretful that he had escaped death yet again. Maybe Lung was right about *fengshui*. And maybe my boss, Big Brother Wang, had picked the wrong girl. For it seemed that I truly *was* his bitterest rival's lucky star!

People nodded approvingly and smiled, among them the Japanese couple, who cast me a disappointed look. Then suddenly, out of nowhere, Zhu and the other bodyguards pushed aside the crowd to get to their boss.

Zhu asked, "Master Lung—"

The doctor cut him off sharply. "Enough talking! These two gentlemen are chilled and need to be treated promptly." Then he turned to the onlookers. "Please go back. I'll take them to the dispensary for a thorough checkup. Make way! Move now!"

Reluctantly the crowd dispersed, heading toward the exit to go back downstairs. Four uniformed sailors helped Lung and Gao onto stretchers, then soon disappeared.

The doctor turned to Jinying. "Are you his son?"

Jinying nodded, and the doctor asked for his room number. After that, he said, "It's been a hectic evening. Go get some rest. When I have finished my examination, I'll send someone to tell you. It may take a while."

Zhu asked, "May we go with them?"

The doctor gave him a suspicious once-over and said sarcastically, "No, the exam room is too small for your gang here. You can all wait in the ballroom."

Had he known what kind of person Zhu was, the doctor wouldn't have spoken to him so flippantly!

As if hearing my thoughts, he softened his tone. "Anyway, don't worry too much; they'll be all right."

After the doctor left, Zhu said to his boss's son, "I think we all need a drink. You want to join us, Young Master?"

Jinying shook his head. "No, I'm tired. I'll stay in my room and wait for the doctor's news."

Zhu turned to me. "Miss Camilla?"

"I'm tired, too. I'll take a nap and wait for word."

"All right," Zhu said to his boss's son, "but when you get the news, come tell us in the bar."

Once Jinying and I were back to our floor, instead of letting me go inside my room, he pushed me inside his.

"Jinying! What do you think you are doing?"

"This is the perfect chance, Camilla. Everyone's away, so we have at least an hour together."

Ignoring my protests, he scooped me up, carried me straight to the bed, and impatiently pulled at my clothes. It must have been the release of tension, for instead of struggling to free myself from his grasp, I found myself helping him remove my dress, my bra, my panties. . . .

～19～

Plaza Athénée

The next morning, Lung held a small celebration in his luxury suite. Because Gao had saved Lung's life, he was invited, for the second time, to share his boss's table and meal. His three underlings stood guard outside the room.

Lung, still in his pajamas, looked fully recovered from last night's mishap. He ravenously gulped down his ham, eggs, potatoes, and toast and even cracked a few jokes. Unfortunately the chance that he'd catch pneumonia and die was vanishing as fast as the food disappearing into his mouth.

My heart was clicking like an abacus, but I tried my best to act calm and cheerful, so as not to arouse any suspicion.

I brought up last night's incident but only risked doing so in a humorous light. "Master Lung, were you trying to imitate our great poet Li Bai by scooping up the moon reflected on the sea?"

My patron thought for a while, then burst out, "You're damn right Camilla! Though I love money, once in a while I'd also like to be a poet—ha! I especially like Li Bai's 'Drinking under the Moon.' His broken eyebrow knit as he stumbled over the poem's famous lines. "I should take advantage of the moon's company to enjoy spring.... When I sing, the moon's shadow . . . when I . . . when I . . ."

I immediately came to his rescue.

I sang, and the moon danced with me.
I danced, and my shadow danced with me.
Sober, we talked together happily.
Drunk, we went our separate ways.
We met by accident, but someday,
We shall meet again along the Milky Way.

Lung smiled proudly at his son, his right-hand man, and his head bodyguard. "Wow! See how smart my Camilla is, huh? That's why she's my lucky star. Last night I cheated death again, ha!"

I smiled coyly. "Thank you, Master Lung. Like the moon, my light is but a reflection from you, the sun."

This time Lung laughed out loud, making his belly shiver like a small earthquake. "See how her tongue is washed in oil? I love that!"

Jinying cast me a disapproving stare, probably resenting my overly greased tongue. Then I noticed that Gao, looking upset, kept chomping down his bacon, eggs, potatoes, and whatnot. Maybe he was bitter that he had jumped in after Lung to save him yet I was the one who got the credit because I was supposedly the bringer of good luck. But that was life. You do your job, get paid, and the rest is up to your boss to decide. And the boss can be a gangster, a Buddha, God, karma, fate. Maybe Gao still feared that I'd tell Lung what had happened in the bathroom. Or maybe I had broken his heart, as I had broken Jinying's.

As I was feeling relieved that Lung had succumbed to my sweet talk, Zhu looked up from his plate and threw out a question. "Master Lung, we're all glad you're all right, but what happened?"

How came no one had thought of asking that question earlier? Of course he'd been pushed by the Japanese. My heart skipped a beat.

To my great relief, Lung replied, "I don't really remember. Maybe because of all the wine and the dancing, I was so exhausted that I fell overboard amid the crowd running from the fire. Anyway, the whole place was chaos." He turned to Gao. "Right?"

The bodyguard stopped chewing; his knife and fork were suspended in midair. "Master Lung, you said you were tired and wanted some fresh air, so I walked you up to the deck. Then you asked for a cigarette and another drink. As I was on my way down to the bar, the fire alarm went off. It took me a while to get back to you because everyone was rushing up to the deck. It was after I'd made my way through the crowd then I heard the splash. I pressed through another crowd, saw you, and plunged in."

Lung didn't respond but nodded approvingly, then went on eating with great relish.

With this new revelation, it was as if a heavy stone had been lifted from my chest. Now everyone resumed clinking their knives and forks and smacking their lips. Though Gao pretended that he was only interested in his food, his eyes were also devouring me.

Gao was a man of action and few words. I heard that he was single and didn't even have a girlfriend. Girls he met would fall for him, and friends proposed eligible brides. But a wedding banquet was nowhere in sight. Poor man, I thought, as I watched him sip bitter black coffee with an equally bitter expression. Too bad he loved me, since I could not possibly love him back. Nor any other man, for that matter.

I thought of the two men who were in love with me—and who had just made love to me. My eyes wandered to the young master, and I mentally compared the two. Gao was tall, muscular, loyal, cautious, responsible. Jinying was equally handsome but in an entirely different way—medium build, delicate features, refined manner. He was soft and naïve, the child of a privileged and protected life.

Gao, on the other hand, came from a poor family who used him to pay off a debt. Painfully, he had worked his way up to become Lung's most trusted bodyguard, by taking brutal knife wounds and excruciating bullets for his boss. Each knife and bullet hole, instead of turning women away, worked more powerfully on them than any aphrodisiac. Women, including myself, could not resist taking this damaged man into their arms to lick his wounds with their warm lips. Why had none of them been invited to stay?

Jinying's experience of life was luxury and privilege. However, rich or poor, privileged or impoverished, neither man, it seemed, had tasted much happiness, because they couldn't have what they most wanted.

Fate always has its own plan, in this case choosing me to be a spy, Jinying to be my patron's son, and Gao to work for my boss's bitterest rival. Had I not been thrown into this star-crossed configuration, I am not sure whom I would have picked to be my lover.

As my mind was imagining all kinds of possible or impossible scenarios with these two men, suddenly Lung spoke, his hoarse voice slashing the air like scissors ripping silk.

"I didn't drink all that much last night."

Our ears perked up like a dog's. We all stopped eating as we put down our silverware, cups, or glasses and listened.

A graveyard silence followed.

Zhu was the first to speak, his small eyes darting between his boss and us. "So?"

The boss replied. "So I don't think I was drunk."

"And?" Jinying was the second one who dared to pick up the conversation when his father's face was as dark as the mushrooms on his plate.

"So it's not possible that I simply fell," Lung huffed, his hand hitting hard on the table. Everything—knives, forks, spoons, plates, salt and pepper containers, as well as we—began to tremble.

"Then what happened, Father?" Jinying asked, dabbing his mouth and paying full attention.

"Now I remember—" Lung stopped in midsentence, his eyes scanning us for any response.

"Remember what?" his son implored innocently.

"I. Was. Pushed." One by one, the words spit from his mouth like mahjong tiles thrown onto the gaming table.

I bit my lip to will myself to stay calm. Then, with great effort, I put on a very tender smile and looked at my patron like a mother her firstborn. "Master Lung, last night on the deck, it was complete chaos. So maybe you were accidentally pushed by the panicky crowd, or even by children desperately looking for their parents."

"Maybe. But maybe not." As he stared at me, the gangster head's expression softened—to my great relief.

"Master Lung, last night everyone seemed to have lost their mind, screaming and pushing like crazy in all directions." I took the risk of painting an exaggerated picture.

He studied me, raising both his slashed eyebrow and his voice. "Then why was I the only one who ended up in the sea?"

Hearing that, Jinying immediately came to my rescue by asking his romantic rival, "Gao, you didn't see anyone suspicious, did you?"

Gao shook his crew-cut head. "I don't think so. Everything happened so quickly, and there were so many people."

The young master went on. "Father, maybe you leaned too close to the railing, and someone bumped into you from behind."

Lung said, "Could be. But I think this matter needs some investigation."

With an evil grin, Zhu volunteered, "I'll do that, Master Lung. And if I find out who did this, his brain will be like—" He concluded his sentence by poking the scrambled egg, then squirting a pool of ketchup onto it.

"Good! Find him soon!" his boss said, waving a dismissive hand. "Now let's finish our breakfast."

To distract the gangster head later that night, I had no choice but to offer yet another variation of my perverse, contortionist sex. Fortunately nothing came of Lung's well-founded suspicion that he had been pushed overboard. Perhaps he was so infatuated with me and addicted to my sexual bonanza that he never pursued the investigation. Although Zhu did ask the captain for the ship's passenger list, fortunately he couldn't find anything suspicious. So finally, to my tremendous relief, the matter was dropped.

After a month's imprisonment on the boundless sea, we finally arrived in *huadu,* the Flower Metropolis. Paris. When we stepped off the ship onto dry land, a stretch limousine was waiting to take us straight to our first destination, the Hotel Plaza Athénée in Paris's eighth arrondissement. Though my mind was burdened with a hundred shadowy thoughts, my eyes couldn't help but brighten beholding this famous city. Wide boulevards and cobblestone streets were lined with thick-foliaged trees casting dancing shadows on the fair-skinned, sharp-featured Parisians. Elegant, svelte ladies in body-hugging dresses with matching hats, gloves, and parasols were accompanied by dark-suited, straight-backed gentlemen. Green-roofed low buildings decorated with crawling vines and intricately patterned windows all beckoned me closer to explore what lay within.

I stuck my head out of the car and filled my lungs with the Parisian air, as the breeze caressed my face with an exotic massage.

Lung cast me a smug look as he squeezed my hand. "Like what you're seeing so far, Camilla?"

"Of course, Master Lung. Thank you so much for bringing me here!"

"I'll bring you anywhere as long as you behave" was the boss's teasing answer.

An hour later, our car pulled up in front of the famous Plaza Athénée. As we walked toward its grand entrance, the first thing I noticed was that its name had commas raining on the first two *e*'s. These "raindrops" made the hotel impossible for me to pronounce, even with my "heavenly" voice.

I'd been to a lot of high-class places in Shanghai, but nothing like this hotel, which was truly fit for a king or queen. In our case, the underground King Lung and me, as his queen of the moment. Outside, the grand building had balconies protruding like pregnant bellies. Pink blossoms crawled along the iron grillwork, unwilling to let go, like a baby's umbilical cord fastened to its mother's womb. On these outcroppings pretty women appeared and disappeared. One gazed meditatively onto the street below, a cigarette between her dainty fingers as smoke drifted up from her pouty lips. Another gazed deeply into a man's eyes as if they were engaged in a staring contest. I wondered, who were these women? Wives, mistresses, courtesans, and perhaps even a spy or two like me?

Uniformed doormen ushered us in with low bows. Inside, the grandiose Western décor dazzled me with its walls, pillars, and floor of polished marble, its golden velvet curtains, lush, reddish-gold carpets, and huge chandeliers shooting out sparks to further glorify the rich and powerful. Who could afford such lavishness? I assumed royalty, aristocrats, multimillionaire businessmen, and probably more than a few French gangsters.

The whole effect was of *shi,* overwhelming presence, the principle emphasized over and over in *The Art of War.* Had this hotel's architect, like me, been an avid reader of the famous military treatise?

In the lobby, we appreciated the décor before we were shown to our rooms. A few Western guests cast us curious glances, then nodded and smiled at me appreciatively.

Pausing at the door to his suite, Lung said to Zhu, his son, and me, "All of you come to my suite at six for a pre-dinner drink." Then he turned to Gao. "You and the others can take turns guarding my room. But don't be too obvious, you got it?"

"Of course, Master Lung," Gao replied.

For the visit to Lung's booked-months-ahead luxury suite, I put on an ankle-length plain purple dress with a plunging neckline. The minimal design was intentional, so people's eyes would be directed to my bulging breasts instead of silly frills, lace, or tassels created by some dressmaker. However, to add an interesting touch to the simple dress, I threw a pink feather boa across my shoulders at an artistic angle. This created a peek-a-boo effect with my pulsing half-moons. Finally, a camellia pinned behind my ear completed my carefully orchestrated songstress-seductress look.

Walking toward Lung's suite, I saw Gao and another bodyguard talking and smoking in a corner. Once he spotted me, Gao knocked lightly on the door and let me in.

This was my first time inside a luxury suite in a foreign country. The whole room was energized by its harmonious blend of orange, beige, and gold. Against one wall was a chaise longue, a piece of elongated heaven for the wealthy and spoiled to relax on this evil earth. In the middle of the room stood a low, gilded table on which were placed a big bowl of fruit, small plates of assorted chocolates, and a ceramic vase filled with pink orchids. Behind the table on a gold-bordered sofa sat Lung and his son. Zhu was nearby, smoking and looking restless.

Lung motioned me to sit beside him. Soundlessly, a white-gloved, black-tuxedoed waiter materialized and set down a silver ice bucket in which nestled a bottle of Dom Pérignon. I was sure Zhu had paid the young waiter a tip as generous as the glimpse of my breasts above my plunging neckline, for the latter bowed deeply as he backed out of the room.

After gulping down some Champagne, Lung leaned over toward me to inhale my special fragrance. "You smell nice, Camilla. Any special place you want to see in Paris tomorrow?"

"What about shopping along the Champs-Élysées?" I asked in an eager tone, trying to sound like a child asking to be taken to a candy store.

I caught Jinying's knit brow; perhaps he was disappointed that I did not ask for something more cultural, such as the opera or concert hall. But my real motive was not simply to be treated to expensive fashions but also to put Lung into an exposed position.

The boss laughed. "You girls never get tired of shopping, do you?"

"Just like Master Lung never gets tired of making money!"

He reached to touch my face. "Ha! I'm sure if there was a glib-tongue contest, even if you took second, no one would dare to claim first prize."

I laughed, not just to please Lung but to jiggle my exposed breasts. As expected, all three men's eyes fixated on my half-moons as they exercised their fox trot.

"Thank you Master Lung. If my tongue is washed in oil, then yours is soaked in Champagne."

Jinying's brow continued to knit. Finally he blurted out, "Father, maybe we should go to the opera one night."

I didn't like the idea, because there would be little chance in such a public place to finish my assignment of finishing off Lung. But I smiled anyway. "I'm sure Young Master is dying to have his ears greased by the heavenly voice of all the excellent singers in Paris. He has such exquisite taste."

Lung looked at his son appreciatively. "Of course he has. But as you know, I don't want to hear those slaughtering-the-chicken, scratching-the-pan, ghost-scraping-the-coffin, foreign voices. Camilla, since Jinying is an opera fan and you the Heavenly Songbird, why don't you do me a favor by accompanying my son to the opera for just one night?"

Jinying exclaimed, "Thank you, Father, I'd love to!"

Zhu immediately offered, "Then I'll book the best seats."

To my relief, after dinner Lung didn't demand sex but retired to his suite. Back in my own room, I sat on the sofa in my bathrobe with Champagne flute in hand and racked my brain. My trip to Paris was to complete a mission, not to be entertained. So far, befriending Jinying hadn't seemed to aid my cause, and I feared time was running out.

What to do? I looked out the window and silently prayed, "Please, heaven, help me!"

Then my eyes landed on the Eiffel Tower shimmering in the Parisian lights. Tonight, instead of going out to have fun in this beautiful, exotic city, I was sitting in a luxurious but lonely hotel room with nothing to think about but arranging a murder. What kind of life was this for a nineteen-year-old girl? Sadly I began to hum the song "Family Happiness":

> Everyone has a father, but not me.
> Everyone has a mother, but not me.
> White clouds leisurely float by, the river flows east,
> The fledgling bird returns to its nest to find it already
>   gone.
> When I long for home, there is no boat to take me there.
> I cry till all my tears dry.
> We all lose our parents. . . . So many tragedies in this
>   world!

Singing to myself, I fell asleep, only to be awakened by urgent knocking on my door. I rushed to open it and saw Jinying's flushed face.

Fearing that he might be seen, I had no choice but to pull him in.

"Jinying, again? What's wrong with you? You can't just keep coming to my room like this!"

Once the door was closed, he tried to kiss me, but I pushed him away. "Where are the others?" I asked.

"Don't worry, they're in my father's room discussing business they don't want me to know about. That's why I came."

"Please leave right away. You're playing with fire!"

"Calm down. Their meeting will take at least an hour."

He took my hand and led me to gaze out the window at the glittering Eiffel Tower. "Look, Camilla, and see the beautiful and romantic world out there. Why are we suffering instead of enjoying ourselves?"

"Because we were born in the wrong place and at the wrong time."

"Don't be so pessimistic." He turned to look me in the eye. "Camilla, a sweet girl like you, why are you willing to be my father's mistress?"

"I told you why. You think I can turn down Shanghai's most powerful gangster?"

He looked hurt and angry, then silently muttered, "I hate him."

I blurted out, "Me, too . . ." and immediately regretted it.

"Did he. . . ."

"Don't ask."

"Why don't we run away?"

I chuckled nervously. "Jinying, I haven't known anyone who could escape through the cracks of your father's fingers. So what makes you think we can?"

"I'll come up with a plan."

"All right," I said sarcastically, "then let me know when you have one, Young Master."

Some silence followed before he spoke again, a little breathlessly. "Camilla, you remember *Peony Pavilion*?"

"Of course."

"The scholar's love for Liniang was strong enough to resurrect her from the grave. So I know my love for you can find a way out for us."

I didn't respond, letting the rich young man drown in his own impossible dreams.

As Jinying was about to go on, to our alarm, we heard knocking at the door.

My heart skipped a beat. "Jinying, quick, hide—it must be your father!"

"How do you know? Did you order room service?"

I didn't have time for arguing, so I gave him a hard push. "Hide on the balcony, quick!"

He dashed over, and I pulled the curtains so he was hidden from sight.

I rushed to open the door and saw Lung and Gao. After I let them in, the boss sat down on the bed, then signaled his bodyguard to check the closet and bathroom.

"I'm too excited by all the business talk. So, Camilla, you know what I want."

Soon Gao came back to report, "Master Lung, the place is clean."

Lung waved a dismissive hand. "All right, then, you can go."

The bodyguard cast me a sad glance.

I bit my lip as my heart roared like thunder. Damn, I'd just lost another chance. Lung had asked Gao to search the room but not me! But even if I'd had a weapon on my person, how could I kill the father when the son was right in the same room? Even if I did, how could I escape? Fortunately neither Lung nor Gao had realized that there was a balcony behind the floor-length curtains.

Right after Gao closed the door behind him, I immediately went to sit on Lung's lap and conjured up my best smile. "Maser Lung, how come you still don't trust me? Look." I wriggled my water-snake waist. "Do you think someone like me could harm anyone? Especially you? "

He caressed my cheek with his murderous hand. "I know, I know. But, Camilla, a habit of thirty-odd years is hard to change. Besides, it's not that I don't trust you. I just don't trust any situation."

I could feel my heart beating like a hammer on an anvil. To distract Lung from noticing anything unusual, I pressed my lips urgently against his. My hand, like a poor child's, reached into his pants to play with his sex as if it were my only toy.

His face flushed, and his eyes burned as he pulled open my bathrobe. I immediately pulled it back, suddenly feeling modest.

Lung laughed. "Ha, Camilla, are you suddenly shy, or is this a new tactic to tease me? I like that!"

Yes, I did feel shy. But why? Lung was not a refined or handsome man but an old rogue who knew nothing about love or romance, only extorting money, cheating, killing, and, of course, fucking. But who was I to judge? Although I didn't know much about extorting money, did I really know anything about love and romance?

This time I felt disgusted by Lung's slobbering kisses and artless squeezing. And I suddenly realized I felt shy because Jinying might be watching us from the balcony. He might be witnessing the woman he loved dearly carrying on dirty business with the father he hated bitterly.

All right, since I had missed my chance to kill the father, what about playing the son against his father? Would he kill his old man for me? I didn't think so. He might warn his father instead, so doing anything to provoke him was out of the question.

I used all my willpower to seem to respond passionately to Lung's groping and pinching. I moaned and groaned as if I truly enjoyed his wrinkled lips and callous fingers. When we were completely naked, Lung, as expected, wanted contortion sex. Aware of Jinying's burning eyes, I couldn't do it.

But I needed an excuse.

I said, "Master Lung, I hurt my leg when I tripped earlier in the day, so I really can't do that tonight, but I promise I'll do whatever you want after my leg recovers."

He looked disappointed but grudgingly said, "All right. You need to see a doctor for that?"

I threw him a flirtatious smile. "I'll be okay; it just needs some rest." Then I repaid his "kindness" by again passionately kissing him on his lips as if he were my true and only love. My hands assisted by playing all sorts of naughty games with his swelling sex. Because I was imagining Jinying's burning eyes and eager ears on us, I didn't do as good a job as usual, but I trusted Lung to be too excited to notice.

Finally, after our artless war of sex, the gangster put on his clothes. "Camilla, get well soon. You know what I want."

"Of course, Master Lung."

After that, he gave my breast another squeeze, then left with a loud bang of the door, startling me.

Seconds after the old man left, Jinying's angry, jealousy-stricken face thrust itself in front of mine. Then he threw himself onto the bed where his father and I had just copulated. He didn't utter a word but buried his head between his hands, his face twisting in agony.

He blurted out, "I'll kill him!"

I almost exclaimed, "Good idea!" but stopped myself just in time. I said instead, "Shh . . . Jinying, lower your voice, just in case." I paused, then spoke again. "Jinying, don't even think of anything along that line. He's your father, after all." I said this just to test how far he might go for love.

He raised his head to look at me, his eyes tearing. "He does too many wrongs, kills too many people. He should be dead."

"You really think that?"

He hissed, "Yes! I love you, Camilla, and I can't bear what he does to you or the way you have to succumb to his evil power."

"Yes, you may want him dead, but I don't believe you have the heart to kill him." Testing him again, I felt myself slightly trembling. Persuading a son to kill his father—could there be any worse karma than that?

As expected, he shook his head. I wondered, was this cowardice or being filial?

Then he suddenly exclaimed, startling me, "If I can't strike him down, I wish that heaven will!"

"But if heaven chooses to be compassionate, what do you plan to do?" I asked.

"I'll drum up something."

Unfortunately so far it was only talk but no action.

"Jinying, you're tired and angry and can't think straight. Please go back to your room and get some sleep. We'll talk about this later. Go, quickly. Your father might come back at any time!"

"But—"

"Just leave!"

After the young master's departure, the question arose again in my mind.

Why couldn't I have contortionist sex with Lung when I knew Jinying was watching? Why should I care how he felt?

But it was very dangerous for me to even try to ponder this. Such thoughts shouldn't even exist in my head in the first place.

I reminded myself that I was a spy with no emotions, only a deadly mission.

I was a skeleton woman. And I was to turn Lung into my next skeleton.

∽◆ 20 ◆∽

Opera House and
a Deadly Thought

Two days later, Zhu told me that he had obtained two balcony
tickets to the Opera de Paris. Even better, he said that neither
his boss, Gao, nor the other bodyguards would be dining with Jinying or me. He didn't say where they would be, but I believed that
some especially secret business meeting was planned.

I knew Lung had dealings all over the world, so I was not surprised that this Paris trip involved more than just pleasure. In fact,
I had heard about his intention to open a bank in the French Concession, which was not under the Chinese government's control. So
maybe he was going to negotiate with French officials about this.
Would his travels to and from this meeting in rented limousines
offer a chance to attack him?

Of course the "Japanese couple," or assassins, were also staying
at Plaza Athénée. But in order not to arouse suspicion, they were
no longer Japanese nor a couple but now an old widower and his
nurse. Each morning, he'd have breakfast on the hotel's terrace
café, ready for my news, if any.

Early the next morning, while the others were still asleep, I went
to the café, where I had a coffee while pretending to read the newspaper. Ten minutes later, I put the newspaper back on the rack and

left. In my peripheral vision, I saw the widower go to pick up the newspaper I'd just left—with my note in it. How he would transact his business in Paris was not my concern; I just provided the information that Lung was having a meeting somewhere and suggested that he follow them. I hoped this time he would be able to get rid of Lung and end my troubles.

In the evening, only three of us, Jinying, a bodyguard, and me, had dinner at the hotel restaurant. After a full, satisfying meal, Jinying couldn't wait to dismiss the guard so we could go to the opera alone. Fortunately, the bodyguard was more than happy to have the rest of the evening to himself, so he could go to the red-light district, get drunk, then hire a woman's pleasurable treasure trough. Of course he wouldn't tell anyone about his private adventure. Especially since Jinying gave him a big tip. Besides, he would not be so stupid as to tell the others he'd had an evening off and left the boss's son unprotected.

The Chinese say, "There is always a mountain taller than the one you live on." So, when I had thought that the Plaza Athénée was the most grandiose building I'd ever seen, I was soon proved wrong. Now it seemed nothing could compare to this palatial opera house. The sumptuous interior was bathed in shimmering gold, orange, and ivory-white. Sculptures, candelabra, and paintings adorned ceiling and floor, corners and niches, archways and stairways.

As Jinying led me past a few elegantly dressed couples to mount a long flight of marble stairs, I felt like a goddess ascending to heaven. The corners of my lips, despite my effort to press them down, stubbornly refused to droop like a capsized boat but adamantly remained in the shape of a crescent moon.

Soon we settled in balcony seats that would no doubt cost an ordinary working person a full month's salary.

Jinying took my hand and put it to his lips. This time I let him, for Lung and his people were in a meeting elsewhere, and I hoped that this elsewhere would soon be their graveyard. However, I did not want Gao to accompany Lung and Zhu on their way to hell. Like the young master, he loved me and was good to me. At least for my vanity, if not my heart, I wanted him alive to keep loving and protecting me forever.

Jinying now looked a lot happier than he had in my room two days ago. "Are you enjoying this, Camilla?"

I nodded, then continued to look around. All around me was wealth and elegance but also pomposity and snobbishness. Did these rich and privileged people really love opera or merely love the idea of being opera buffs? I looked back at Jinying. He was equally rich and privileged, but his passion for opera was as genuine as his father's love for money and power.

Tonight's performance was *Madame Butterfly,* Puccini's famous work, which I knew because Madame Lewinsky sometimes sung arias from it for me. Unfortunately it was a tragedy, which I was not in the mood for. My life was unfortunate enough; I felt no need to be entertained by someone else's misfortune. Nevertheless, I still felt lucky to be watching a famous opera in the formidable Paris Opera House. So I decided to set aside my troubles for the next two hours to let myself enjoy some fleeting musical moments.

Before the performance started, I reflected on what I knew about the story.

Madame Butterfly, or Cio-Cio San, was a geisha procured to be the wife of B. F. Pinkerton, an American Navy Lieutenant. Although Pinkerton was at first infatuated with his beautiful, fragile Japanese lover, he never took the union seriously. She was but a romantic diversion to fill his lonely days in a foreign country. He always intended that someday he would go back to his country and marry a real American wife.

After Pinkerton's departure back to the United States, Madame Butterfly and their young son waited patiently and faithfully for his return. During her interminable wait, the devoted Cio-Cio San even turned down the marriage proposal of a wealthy prince. But Cio-Cio San's devotion was rewarded only by heartbreak. One day Pinkerton did return—with his American wife. Mortified, Cio-Cio San sent her son to play in the garden, then killed herself.

In the dreamy atmosphere of the grand hall, as we waited for the performance to begin, Jinying took my hand and stared at me with his dark, intense eyes. "Camilla, I'm so happy to see this opera with you."

I said nonchalantly, "Don't be."

He looked puzzled. "Why not?"

"Why are you so happy? This is a tragedy, and the world already has enough sorrow."

"Oh, Camilla, this is just a play."

I retorted, "You should know our situation better, Young Master."

He withdrew his hand as hurt spread over his face. "But can't we just enjoy ourselves for this moment, even though it's fleeting? Can't we dream and linger in the evanescence for a while, while we can?"

"As you wish," I said calmly.

My whole life, I'd been trained to live, or endure, each moment but never to enjoy it. I never forgot that I was a girl with no past or future, just the dangerous present. So how could I *not* grasp this fleeting moment? I remembered I read that Zen Buddhism says if you can truly live in the moment, you won't have any worries. Just look at me, and you'll believe the opposite!

Finally the curtain began to rise, and the orchestra struck its first note. This was the first time I'd seen a Western opera or even heard a full Western orchestra, and suddenly I couldn't help but feel elated. Although I didn't understand the strange-sounding language, I loved the music. The acting was quite exaggerated, especially that of the actress who played Cio-Cio San. Her makeup too; it was so heavy that I couldn't tell if she was a man or a woman or Asian or Western.

I turned to peek at Jinying and saw that he was totally immersed in the tragic illusion unfolding onstage. If he realized that my life offstage was equally elusive and tragic, would he still be as attracted to me as he was to the opera heroine? I sighed inside. Would I taste happiness someday? If happiness was the man now sitting right next to me, should I reach and grasp it tightly in my hand?

Pondering, I had been only intermittently following the story until the last act, when Cio-Cio San, her heart irretrievably broken by Pinkerton's unfeeling one, was about to end her tragic life. Although I already knew the story, I was still stunned when the actress onstage sent her son away, sang her last song, then plunged a knife into her already shattered heart. How sad that love could drive a woman, even one with a young, adorable son, onto this path of no return.

Why is love—and the falling in and out of it—such an overwhelming force? It brought Cio-Cio San to death but Liniang in the *Peony Pavilion* back to life. Which would be the outcome of Jinying's imprudent love for me? A happy life—or death?

The performance was a tremendous success. The thunderous clapping seemed to last a whole incarnation. The actors came out three times to bow and thank the audience. It was nice to see that "Cio-Cio San," who had been the personification of tragedy, was now as happy as a tickled baby.

Finally, when we made our way through the crowd to the outside, leaving the glory of the opera house behind, Jinying asked, "Did you like it?"

"It was sad," I said softly.

"Then let's take a walk along the Seine—its tranquility will pacify your mind. After that, we'll have a drink at a nice café. How's that?"

"Sounds good," I responded, not knowing what to feel anymore.

The leisurely flowing Seine, the luminous moonlight, the looming mystery of Notre Dame playing hide-and-seek in the fog were so beautiful that, strangely, instead of making me feel poetic or amorous, they made me sadder. I feared that if I allowed myself pleasure, or anything even agreeable, disaster would strike. After all, wasn't I a spy and a wicked person who didn't deserve happiness, nor even a beautiful evening accompanied by a kind, handsome man?

Jinying put his arm around me as we ambled along the quay. There were not many people about, only a few couples here and there. Some sat on the benches watching the occasional pleasure boats float by. Others, like us, strolled along, quietly accompanied by the soft sounds of the river. Under trees or behind the wall, couples kissed passionately, unperturbed by curious eyes or heated whispers.

My daily meditation on the Huangpu River always gave me a sense of calm that was much needed in my chaotic life. But this equally famous river in an exotic land did not give me the same calmness; instead it stirred something deep and dark inside me. But what that was I couldn't yet name.

We continued to walk. Suddenly, when we were passing a big boulder, Jinying pulled me behind it and pressed his mouth to mine. His searching, burning lips were so urgent that I could almost read what was on his mind: *Time is running out, so let's enjoy these exquisite moments before they vanish!* Instead of pushing him away, I surprised myself by responding passionately to his advances. I pressed my body hard against his until I felt his sex burgeoning. My hands, like a naughty beggar's, ambushed his body's forbidden places.

After we had kissed and caressed for a while, I pushed the young master away to take a good look at him. His face was glowing, his lips moist, and his breathing deep, as he savored the aftertaste of our illicit acts. I searched his eyes, trying to find something there to comfort me, to change my mind. To save me from sinking, and eventually drowning, in love, in life.

He spoke. "Camilla, I can't go on like this. I love you too much. You're killing me."

I remained silent. What else could be done?

He touched my cheek, his hand warm and gentle. "Camilla, let's elope."

A few seconds passed before I asked, "You've suggested this many times."

He nodded.

"Then where, and how?"

"I'll find a way. I have to. I can't live like this."

I didn't respond, fearing any words, or even an exhalation, would blow away his promise and my hope.

Jinying possessed a lot of good traits; unfortunately being street-smart was not one of them. He'd been sheltered too much and for too long to realize what he was up against. How could someone who had never met any challenges in real life imagine that he could get the better of his cunning and powerful gangster father?

"Jinying, why don't we just enjoy the moment? It's so beautiful out here."

He nodded, then took my hand and wrapped it in his.

As I felt the warmth from his whole being, I also felt nausea rising in my chest. A terrible thought, like a malignant ghost, crept through my mind, a thought I could not exorcise. I nodded toward an empty bench some dozen yards ahead of us. "Jinying, my feet are hurting. Can you go save that bench so it won't be taken?"

He looked at me curiously. "But I can carry you to it."

I pointed again, into the distance. "See that couple over there? Looks like they're going to sit down, so please get there first, quickly! I'll follow you. I just can't walk fast enough with these heels."

"All right," he said reluctantly, then hurried toward the bench.

When Jinying was some distance away, I immediately turned around, rushed behind a clump of shrubs to hide myself from sight, and jumped off the tall quay into the Seine.

As I fell, tears rained down my face, quickly becoming one with the expanse of water. Nineteen years of miseries, sufferings, and loneliness had hit me like a witch's broomstick. Tears stored up for nineteen years finally had their chance, their last and only one, to make their escape into eternity. Nothing would trouble me anymore, for I'd soon leave this pitiless world that, from the very beginning, had offered me little but cruelty. Of course the world wouldn't care one way or the other. It had not cared when I was alive, nor would it after I was gone. Rivers, whether in the East or the West, would continue to flow on endlessly day and night. I was a nobody, an orphan. There were no relatives to give me a proper burial, so this beautiful river in a strange country would be my final resting place. Here, no one would find me or remember that I was once a living soul. . . .

Instead of feeling sadness, when my body hit the cold water, a euphoric sensation engulfed me. I was not sure if Jinying heard the splash, but I no longer cared. There would be no good-byes. Mere minutes from now, the world that had so oppressed me would be gone.

As I was letting myself sink and feeling the cold water seeping into my eyes, ears, mouth, and bones, I heard Jinying's desperate cry ripping the air.

"What happened, Camilla? Camilla! Help! Someone fell into the river—please help!"

Soon my only sensation was the cold water, invading all my orifices. Yes, I was going to die. I was dying. . . .

But then why did I still hear a loud splash? Someone else had jumped into the river. Jinying! Why would he do that?

Fool. Please stop being a fool for once, I beg you, Young Master!

Then I felt my chilled body being held and lifted, and soon my head rose above the water, and I was face-to-face with the same world I'd just left behind. I sucked in big gulps of the life-giving air that I'd thought I'd no longer need. The world had not changed; it was still indifferent and cruel, with me or without me. Why couldn't heaven have just left me to perish so I could enter the blissful state of oblivion?

After pulling me to safety, Jinying gently laid my shivering, sopping body on the bank. Several people rushed toward us and began to ask questions in a language I didn't understand.

Jinying waved them away, speaking in English. "It's okay. She just leaned too far and fell in accidentally. Don't worry, I'll get her back to the hotel."

A young man asked in accented English, "You want me to call ambulance?"

Jinying smiled faintly. "No, it's really not necessary. She 's fine. But you can call us a taxi if you don't mind."

Jinying lifted me in his arms and carefully labored up the long steps, leaving the other people behind whispering heatedly in French.

Jinying bent his head to stare at me, his body and mine trembling in sync. "Camilla, oh, Camilla . . ."

The water dripping from our clothes left a long trail on the stairs, looking like blood in the dark.

It was a long ordeal for him to ascend the narrow steps to

ground level. When we reached the top, a taxi was waiting with the door open and the young couple standing guard. Jinying lifted me inside, then crawled in after me. He thanked the couple profusely and gave the driver the hotel's address. From the rearview mirror, the driver cast us curious glances and opened his mouth as if to ask something. But then it seemed he had second thoughts and decided against it. Inside the speeding car, the young master cradled me like a baby, probably trying to transmit his body heat to me without realizing that his body was just as soaked and cold as mine. With a trembling hand, Jinying gently smoothed aside my matted hair as he cooed soothing words into my ear.

When the car arrived at the hotel, Jinying signaled the driver to pull up at the back entrance so our bedraggled presence would not cause a stir. A few minutes later we had made our way to my room.

After Jinying put me on the sofa, I said, my voice weak and trembling from the "accident," "Jinying, please leave. Your father might come back at any time."

He shook his head. "I'm not going to leave you alone. If he finds out about us, so be it. Now stay where you are."

He dashed to turn up the heat, started running a hot bath, then came back to carry me to the bathroom. As gentle as a mother with her baby, Jinying peeled off my soaked clothes and lifted me into the tub. The contact with the steaming water began to soothe my nerves and even lift my mood.

Seeing me feeling better, Jinying began to take off his clothes and shoes, then got into the bathtub with me.

"Why?" he asked as softly as if he was talking to a newborn, taking my hands in his.

My voice came out weak and eerie-sounding. "Why what?"

He sighed heavily. "Why did you try to kill yourself?"

"I . . . I didn't. I just . . . fell, like you said."

"Don't lie to me please, Camilla. Please tell me. Tell me everything about you and why you are so sad."

I stubbornly shook my head. "Jinying, please don't make life more complicated than it is. Believe me, I fell."

He didn't respond but pulled me so my head rested on his

chest. "Camilla, if you want to disappear, let me disappear with you."

Some silence passed before I said, "Jinying, please leave. I'm fine."

"I can't. What if you do something silly again?" He said firmly. "I'll spend the night here."

"Jinying, please don't . . . what if your father . . ."

"He won't."

"How can you be so sure?"

"Because the whole gang will spend the night at Pigalle."

At first I was shocked to hear that, but I quickly realized that of course Lung was not going to miss the famous red-light district and the many exotic, French-speaking ladies of the Parisian night. As the Chinese saying goes, "Never leave a mountain of treasures empty-handed."

As relief washed over me, I closed my eyes, too tired to respond. In my semiconscious state, I felt Jinying's arms lifting me, wrapping me in a thick towel, then carrying me to the bed. In a cocoon formed by the warm blanket and the young master's arms, I soon fell into a deep, troubled sleep. . . .

❦ 21 ❧

Shopping the Champs-Élysées

The next morning when I woke up, Jinying was no longer by my side. But he had left a note:

> Dearest Camilla,
>   Sorry, I had to go back to my room, just in case my father looks for me. But I'll check on you. I wouldn't leave if I thought you were really sick. But you seemed to be fine, no fever, no shivering, and sound asleep, melting my heart.
>   Please treasure your life and your heavenly voice; many people depend on them for their happiness, including myself.
>   If you're no longer on this earth, I won't be here either.

Holding the note, I didn't know how to feel. Why would heaven use a man's love to keep me here on earth? Maybe I *was* attached to this world and didn't really want to die. Maybe my attempted suicide was a lesson sent from heaven that I shouldn't fool myself by pretending that I couldn't love. But that made things even more complicated, because there were two men who loved me, Jinying and Gao. To whom should I return my love?

Was it out of despair or sheer stupidity that I had tried to kill myself? I didn't have an answer. I only knew I was so disturbed after watching Cio-Cio San end her life that for a moment it seemed as if dying was a better way out.

Jinying saw through my lie right away; he knew my fall was not an accident. Were *suicide* and *hopelessness* inscribed on my forehead like a huge cigarette ad? Or, after years of training and practice, was I still only an amateur at lying? But fortunately or unfortunately, here I was, still breathing, sitting in a luxury hotel room, philosophizing about life. And death.

I burst out sobbing till my eyes were sore and my face soaked. Feeling some relief after the outburst, I went to sit on the sofa, ate some grapes, sipped some wine, then tried to organize my thoughts. My reason for being in Paris was to finally see Lung killed, but not only had I flubbed this mission, I'd even failed to end my own life. So what was next? I downed more wine, thinking hard.

To clear my mind and better organize my thoughts, I decided to write down the *Thirty-Six Stratagems,* which I had learned by heart, to see if I could come up with a plan. After I deleted the irrelevant ones, there were eleven left. I analyzed each, weighing it carefully against my present situation.

To kill with someone else's sword—Maybe I should seriously consider playing Jinying against his father. But I doubted that, however much he detested his old man, he'd go so far as to kill him. After all, Jinying was a man with a heart. Then what about Gao, since he also had a crush on me? But what if he refused and instead reported me to Lung?

Wait until you exhaust your enemy—But how? Lung seemed a master at absorbing energy—sexual or otherwise—from things and people around him, even the universe itself. I'd probably be exhausted before he did.

Loot a house while it's burning—This is also called "stir the water to catch the fish," meaning to take advantage of chaos. This was the strategy the fake Japanese couple and I had tried on board the ship, but it had failed.

A dagger wrapped in a smile—Unfortunately, even though I smiled a lot and was an expert in knife-throwing, I never had a chance to use this skill because I was always thoroughly searched before being allowed into Lung's bedroom.

Close the door to catch the thief—Even if I was able to lure Lung behind a closed door, how I could I later make my escape?

Feign madness, but keep your calm—This is a good one, but not something I could use now, maybe only if an opportunity arose.

Change your role of guest to that of host—My boss, Big Brother Wang, had been trying to do this for years but without success; that was why he'd sent me to do the job. Though now I was Lung's favorite woman, I was still a guest, far from being a host.

Injure yourself to get your enemy's trust—This was the inspiration for the fake robbery I had set up for Shadow. I wished I could set up something like this with Lung, to gain his trust so he wouldn't have me searched anymore.

Shed your skin like a cicada—This one means to disguise yourself or change your identity so you can sneak away from a dangerous situation. But, alas, I couldn't even do that, for my identity was already a disguise!

The last one is simply **Run away!**

To me, this was the best idea. When you run out of options, what would be better than to run for your life?

Should I escape with Jinying or by myself? What if we got caught? Unfortunately, there are consequences to any action; Buddhism calls this karma. I sighed. I must have been a whore, traitor, murderer, child molester, drug addict in my past lives to have attracted all this bad karma in my present incarnation!

As I was thus musing, the doorbell rang. I opened the door and saw neither Lung, his son, nor the head bodyguard, but instead a waiter with a cart holding a big plate covered with a silver lid.

He smiled and said in accented English, "Good Morning. Room service breakfast."

"But I didn't order—"

Ignoring me, he began to set the table. When he finished, I paid him a big tip for setting up the table elegantly, including a solitary pink rose inside a crystal vase.

Once he left, I lifted the lid and found four strips of bacons nestled by a scrambled egg and, to my surprise, a note next to the egg. I picked it up and read.

> Dearest Camilla,
> As you understand, I can't come to see you early in the morning because there are two bodyguards pacing in front of my father's room. So I tipped the waiter to bring you this note with your breakfast and to report back to me how you are doing.
> Don't forget that I'll see you, my father, and the others when they have breakfast soon.
> The rose is to show my love for you, in hope that your cheeks will always be as pink as the flower and your life beautiful and blooming.

So Lung was still alive. Since I'd been busy trying to kill myself last night, I'd completely forgotten about my suggestion for the "widower" and his nurse to kill Lung. Obviously the mission had failed again. So either they'd lost Lung on the way, or there was just no chance for them to play their poisonous hand. Next I took out the rose, inhaled its fragrance to feel its sender's love, then gently put it down. Heaven had kept me alive, so I needed to discard my melancholy and plow on with my life.

It was now six-thirty in the morning. Lung and his men were probably still sleeping. I quickly put on a simple dress and took the lift down to the hotel café—to deliver a message to the old widower.

La Terrasse Montaigne was a small haven of greenery facing a street with shops displaying elegant French fashions. Only two tables were occupied, one by a young Caucasian couple, the other by the old man and his nurse, who were absorbed in their newspapers.

When the waiter came to place my order, I said in English, "Small black coffee with no sugar, please."

Before he left, I added. "Oh, please add some milk."

I had no idea if the French staff here understood English, or my English, to be precise, but that was not my concern. I didn't care if I got my coffee right, only that I got my message through, not to the waiter but to the widower and his nurse.

"With no sugar" was a code meaning that there was not yet any other chance to kill Lung, and "add some milk" meant wait for more information. After I got my coffee, I took a few sips, meditated on the shops bathing in the early-morning Parisian light, then left to go back to my room. Just in case I was seen by Lung or his men, my excuse for being up and about would be that I couldn't sleep, since I was too excited by being in Paris.

At eight-thirty, Master Lung, Zhu, Jinying, Gao, the three other bodyguards, and I were having breakfast together at the same Terrasse Montaigne. Lung, Zhu, Jinying, and I sat at one table, while Gao and his underlings were at an adjacent one. Not too far from us, the widower with his nurse was still eating, sipping coffee, reading his morning paper, and waiting for more news from me.

Lung took a big bite of his croissant covered with a thick pat of melting butter. He gulped it down as fast as if he were getting rid of a rival. After that, he noisily sipped his coffee, sighed with satisfaction, then cast me a curious look.

"Camilla, you don't look very happy today. Something wrong?"

I tried my best to fake a genuine smile. "I'm fine, Master Lung. Nothing will go wrong as long as I am with you, am I not right?"

I dared not look in Jinying's direction to see how he was reacting. Even though I now owed him my life, I really should stop having any communication, even intangible, between us. Otherwise he would have saved me from drowning only for me to end up as bloody mincemeat on Lung's chopping board. I also avoided looking at Gao at the neighboring table. Since his loss of control inside the ocean liner's bathroom, he had looked even more distressed and had become even more taciturn. There was no possible opportunity for me to reassure him that my lips were sealed, or that I really did have feelings for him.

"You don't look fine." Lung's coarse voice woke me from my

reverie, and his eyes scrutinized me like a hawk's as his slashed eyebrow wriggled like two fidgeting lizards. "Maybe you're not used to the heavy French food or the chilly weather here." He dabbed his mouth and thought for a while. "You said you want to shop along the Champs-Élysées, so why don't we do that today so you'll cheer up, eh?"

Though after yesterday's events I was in no mood for shopping or anything else, even at the most luxurious stores in the most expensive area in Paris, I feigned enthusiasm.

I raised my voice so the widower-and-nurse duo could hear clearly my every word. "Oh, shopping at the Champs Élysées—I'd love that! Thank you, Master Lung!"

In my peripheral vision, I noticed that Jinying cast me a puzzled look, then took a meditative sip of his coffee.

Lung asked me and his son, "How was the opera last night?"

We both uttered, "It was wonderful."

"Good, because I spent a small fortune for those seats." He patted his son's shoulder. "Glad you came to Paris with us, Jinying. Otherwise, who would keep my little beauty company when I am busy?"

We both thanked Lung profusely before we immersed ourselves in eating and cautiously sipping the coffee, which was darker than my mood and as bitter as my life.

Moments passed, and I said, raising my voice again, "Master Lung, I'm so excited to go shopping at the Champs-Élysées! Can we go to the Hermès shop first? It's been my dream to own a red Hermès bag!"

Lung laughed at my childish enthusiasm. "Of course, any shop and anything you want, my little pretty."

Even the ominous Zhu looked up from his omelet and emitted a chuckle, shook his head, then resumed eating. So my acting was convincing.

I leaned to peck Lung's cheek. "I love Hermès. Thank you so much, Master Lung!" I hoped the widower and his nurse had heard everything I'd loudly announced and that they would find an opportunity to strike.

I tried to act calm, but inside my whole body was on fire. If the mission failed, I might be again sinking in the Seine, and this time not by my own choice.

The name of the Avenue des Champs-Élysées has not traveled all over the world for nothing. The huge boulevard was flanked with towering, geometrically trimmed trees like rows of green-uniformed soldiers standing guard for the rich and powerful. We started at the glorious Arc de Triomphe and set out toward the Louvre at the other end, ready to taste all the splendid wonder in between.

It was a very pleasant, sunny day, and the four of us, Lung, Zhu, Jinying, and I strolled along the tree-lined boulevard, inhaling the Parisian air as we studied the city's people and buildings. Gao and the three other bodyguards kept their distance a few steps behind us. Though they were normally undistractable, I imagined their attention would still be diverted by the beautiful French women smiling haughtily as they cast seductive glances at the tall, muscular Chinese men.

I noticed that both Jinying and Gao were watching me like a man his beloved new bride. Tears moistened my eyes as I felt a searing pain stabbing at my heart. I had done so much evil during my short life; why should I now deserve these two men's love? However, most of the evil was not by my choice, since my life belonged to others. So perhaps someday I would receive forgiveness. Thus hoping, I felt a little better.

We continued to window-shop at the many luxury stores like Ferragamo, Céline, Louis Vuitton, Chanel, until we finally approached my destination, the Hermès store. My heart began to knock hard against my chest like an inmate shaking the prison bars. It was one thing to plot a murder but quite another to actually do it or witness it being done.

The plan was that after I took Lung inside the store, I'd suggest to him that, since all men are bored by women's shopping, he could wait at the front of the store and watch the street while I looked around. Once the widower spotted him through the window, he would come in, pretend to look at the merchandise, shoot Lung, then quickly escape in the resulting confusion. However, the previous plot had failed, so what if this one failed also? Would Lung suspect me? If he was killed, would Gao and his gang suspect I'd set it up and kill me? They wouldn't worry about proof, because, without Lung alive, killing me would not be a big deal. Maybe Gao wouldn't have the heart to squeeze the trigger or plunge the knife, but his underlings would experience no such hesitation.

Of course, it was also possible that the widower, instead of killing Lung, would be spotted and killed himself. But the worst scenario would be that Lung's men would capture and torture him until he confessed. That would definitely be the end of me.

Feeling a headache coming on, I focused myself, feigning excitement now that we had arrived at Hermès. "Master Lung, here it is!"

Gao opened the door for us, while his three underlings remained outside to guard the entrance. To my relief, the store was not crowded, making for a cleaner shot for the assassin. In one corner a uniformed salesgirl was helping an elderly, elegant lady choose an evening purse. A wealthy-looking, gray-haired couple impatiently moved clothes on a rack, making unpleasant scratching sounds.

I stayed at the front, looking through piles of accessories like gloves, belts, and scarves but in fact glancing around to see if the assassin had arrived. From the corner of my eye I spotted him lurking right across the street. To me it seemed that he was being too obvious. But, fortunately, since he was disguised as an old man and acting feeble, no one seemed to be paying him any attention.

As planned, I told my patron, "Master Lung, I know this is boring for you. Why don't you smoke your cigarette by the window and look at the pretty French girls while I look around?"

Jinying moved his head as he walked away, signaling me to join him at a far corner of the store so we could talk.

But his father was already speaking. "That's what I'm about to do. Camilla, how come you always know what's on my mind?"

Lung smiled happily, gave my bottom a squeeze, then sat down on a bench against the window.

Zhu immediately sat down next to his boss. "I'll smoke with you, Master Lung."

So far, so good.

The evil duo lit their cigarettes and began to puff and gaze at the passersby outside. Just then I noticed that the widower was already in front of the store, studying some wallets in the shop window.

My heart almost jumped out of my throat. To distract Lung, I picked up a scarf and thrust it under his eyes. "Master Lung, what do you think of this?"

"Camilla, don't make me look at all this stuff. Just get whatever you want, and I'll pay for it. Make it simple for me, won't you? Men don't care what women put on, only when they take them off! Ha-ha!" He burst out laughing, then turned to Zhu. "Right?"

His right-hand man responded emphatically. "Exactly, Master Lung. That's women's heavenly duty, to please men and bear them children!"

The old French couple lifted their heads and looked at us with disgust, probably horrified by the duo's loud voices and vulgar manner. Zhu returned them a murderous look, but to my utter trepidation, the widower was now entering the store. As I watched, the assassin reached into his pocket. Just then I felt my whole being enveloped by total darkness as my legs gave out. I had no idea what happened next, but when I recovered my senses, I was being fussed over by Lung's entourage. Around us, shoppers and staff were gesticulating wildly as they shouted at one another in French.

Lung was unhurt, and the widower was nowhere to be seen.

It was obvious that because of my fainting, Wang's assassin hadn't done his job. But why hadn't he just shot Lung dead on the spot? The only reason I could think of was that he might have misinterpreted my fainting as a sign to tell him to abandon the mission.

I was helped to sit in a chair. Then I heard Lung bark to his men, "What happened to Camilla? Someone better tell me!"

The French staff and customers all stood around, gesturing wildly and jabbering intensely in a language none of us understood.

Lung shouted in his broken English, "Go away! Things good! No problem!"

Although the French might not understand Lung's English, they did get the message from his angry tone and backed away to let his men tend to me. Both the young master and Gao studied me with great concern, but only Jinying had some idea of my recent mental state, though nothing about its cause.

He said to his old man, "Father, I think it's time for us to go back to Shanghai. Camilla must be homesick."

Homesick? Go home? I wished I had a real home I could feel sick to go back to!

I overheard Lung's whisper to his son, "Poor girl. Maybe I should have her live with me so my people can take better care of her."

Then Jinying's voice, in a tone of suppressed anger, snaked into my ears. "Father, let's take her home first. Camilla must need rest."

Gao piped up out of the blue. "Master Lung, should I carry Miss Camilla back to the hotel?"

Lung's answer was "Of course, that's what I hired you for!"

Gao scooped me up like a sick kitten as Zhu opened the door for us. Amid the boisterous commotion among the shocked customers and sales assistants, Gao lowered his head and asked, his voice almost inaudible, "You all right, Camilla? If you need help, I'm all yours. I beg you, please let me know what's been bothering you."

From the corner of my eye I saw Jinying's jealous but helpless expression. But of course he couldn't possibly offer to carry me, could he?

✦22✦

Magic and
Flying Knives

The rest of our Paris stay passed uneventfully. I finally did do some shopping but felt restless because Lung's men were on full alert, and the "widower" was nowhere to be found. Lung decided to cut short our "vacation," and so after more weeks at sea I found myself back in Shanghai. Given the failure of the elaborately planned assassination, I braced myself for a severe reprimand from Big Brother Wang.

As usual, I had to speak with him on the phone, as he always feared Lung's men would spot us together and spoil his many years of planning.

"If there's another mishap, your pretty little neck will be snapped with a loud *crack*—you got that?"

"Yes, Big Brother Wang."

Even through the telephone wires I could feel my boss's anger as strongly as if his voice was pressing a sharp knife against my chest. Though I tried to keep my answers as terse as possible, lest I provoke more anger, the knife kept digging and twisting in all of the four inauspicious directions.

"Fainted? Was your training flushed down the toilet? How many times we warn you not to lose your calm under any circumstances? Even if your mother is shot right next to you and her brain splashes all over your face, you must act like you're watching a movie. You'd say, 'Isn't that wonderful?' You got that, eh?"

"Yes."

"You almost got two of my people killed. You are aware of the consequences?"

"I'm so sorry, Big Brother Wang."

"Hmm . . ." His anger seemed to abate. "I'll forgive you this time. At least you didn't lie to me."

I couldn't lie to him, of course; the assassin, having witnessed my fainting, would certainly report back to Wang. Besides, having blacked out, I didn't know what had actually happened.

But in a few seconds my boss's anger flared anew. "What's wrong with you, Camilla? You don't like living?"

"I'm sorry, it won't happen again. I swear on my parents' graves." But my parents had no graves that I knew of, so I guessed the swearing didn't count.

"It better not. Otherwise I can't guarantee if your pretty head will continue to rest on your shoulders. I'm not kidding!"

"Certainly it won't happen again, Big Brother Wang."

He was silent for a while, then said, "Since we've failed to kill Lung so many times, his lucky star must be shining really strong now. So I think we should wait for a while until his star shifts and leaves him unprotected."

"I think you're right, Big Brother Wang."

"All right, then continue to sing at Bright Moon and charm him into giving up some secrets." He paused, then added, "What about that magician, Shadow? Is she still in the news these days? Is she going to get in your way with Lung, now that you're both back in Shanghai?"

"I don't know; I was away and didn't have a chance to read the newspapers."

"I don't give a damn about a magician, but you'd better keep an eye on her if she poses a threat."

"I'll be sure to do that, Big Brother Wang."

After I hung up the phone, I felt as if a huge stone had been lifted from my chest. Now I could breathe normally for a while before Wang would ask me to strike again. But what was this about Shadow?

The next day, I picked up the *Leisure News* and saw Rainbow Chang's column.

Will the Magician Shadow Succeed in Capturing Master Lung?

Rumor goes that because of some mishaps during Master Lung's Paris vacation, he now seriously considers shifting his love interest to our other up-and-coming skeleton woman, Shadow, the magician. We heard that Shadow invited Lung and a few special guests to her private show. And since then Master Lung has been completely fascinated by this beautiful magician and her shadowy illusions.

Now our question is: What will happen to our beloved Heavenly Songbird? Will Lung leave her for Shadow?

Two ravishing skeleton women competing for the most powerful man in Shanghai! Who will capture Lung? Place your bets now!

If I were betting today, I would put my money on Camilla, because she possesses a unique secret weapon. But of course Shadow also has her tricks. Like we Chinese say "You walk your own road; I'll cross my own bridge."

What about you, my dear readers—who will get your bet?

I love Camilla's sweet voice, delicate face, and twenty-one-inch waist. Who wouldn't desire a woman like her? Magic tricks the eyes; singing tricks the heart. Especially the heart of a man with as many bills in his pocket as he has romance in his heart.

More to follow . . .
Rainbow Chang

Was this rumor about Shadow true or just made up by the gossip columnist so *Leisure News* would sell more copies? My intuition told me it was made up, for I didn't have any sense that Lung was getting tired of me. Not yet. Nor was there any sign that he was attracted to Shadow. On the contrary, he seemed more and more addicted to my contortionist sex, doubtless the "secret weapon" Rainbow had alluded to. Fortunately I still had more contortions that he had ever seen. So even if he had the energy to try out a new position every week, it would be a long time before he'd tried them all.

However, as the Chinese say about men, "No cat doesn't like the smell of fish." No matter how much a man is enamored of or even in love with a woman, he will always be tempted by another he hasn't yet tried out. To put it another way, while a man is chewing, his eyes do not stop gawking at the other dishes.

Therefore, I needed to act fast in case Shadow's charm could outdo mine. Because now I was the fish in Lung's mouth, while she was the one on the table.

For the moment I was somewhat comforted by Jinying's concern. Although I refused to see him, I did take a few of his calls; after all, he'd saved my life. I had accepted his flowers and other gifts. He asked me to promise him over and over not to do anything rash, but I still insisted that I had really just slipped and fallen into the river. He had no choice but to accept my explanation, no matter how unconvincing. As for myself, I did not have the luxury of dwelling on my mistakes or other miseries, because to stay alive, like a shark, I needed to keep moving.

Fortunately Lung had been traveling a lot lately, and his schedule only allowed us to meet about once a week, sometimes only every two weeks. I heard that recently he'd been asked to solve a problem for a banker's married son. The young man had had an affair with a dancing girl, who was demanding a huge sum of money, threatening to leak their affair to the newspapers. Worse, she was now carrying his baby. But the man adamantly refused to take responsibility and had paid Lung to intervene. Lung ended the whole sexual saga by simply having the woman dumped into the Huangpu River.

My life would have been made simpler if that woman were Shadow!

But since she was still very much alive, I needed to move fast.

I again invited the magician to my place, this time to discuss our show. After dinner, at which I again served the finest food and the most expensive wine, we went to the study to continue chatting.

Nursing a glass of wine, I asked, "Shadow, when are you going to have your next show?"

"I'm always ready. I just need a sponsor."

"What about Master Lung?" I inquired.

She didn't answer me directly but said, "Since you're my friend, Camilla, let me be honest with you. I've run out of money." She sipped her wine, then added, "In fact, my shows so far have left me in debt."

Of course, she also had to bed Ciro Nightclub's manager and the Customs House's guard to let her perform in their places.

"Shadow, maybe I can be your sponsor. . . ."

She looked stunned. I was not sure if it was by my money or by my sudden generosity.

"Actually, I mentioned that we should do a show together the last time we met, remember?"

She thought for a while. "But . . . why would you want to help me?"

"Because we're friends now." I was tacitly reminding her about having "saved" her from being robbed. "Also because I struggled and endured many hardships before I got famous. I believe in helping others, so I can continue to generate good karma for myself."

The "generate good karmas for myself" was to rid her of suspicion, because of course I was not suggesting this to be nice to her but for my own benefit.

Moments passed, and I added, "Besides, you're a magician, and I do something totally different, so we are not competing."

"But I do magic, and you sing. How can we cooperate on-stage?"

"The show would debut my knife-throwing and contortion talents to the Shanghainese. Tickets will sell out quickly when people learn they will see your incredible magic and also hear me sing, throw knives, and contort, all in the same show. So, will you do this with me?"

She answered quickly. "Of course!"

"Good. But there is one condition."

She took a big gulp of her wine. "I'm listening."

"Onstage, you'll be strapped onto a revolving board, while I throw knives to land all around you."

Wine sloshed over the edge of her glass as a cloud of suspicion crossed her face. She was now in a dilemma. If she said yes, her life would be at risk if I made a wrong move, whether intentional or not. But if she said no, she might offend me, because that meant she doubted my skill, even though she'd witnessed it with her own eyes.

Worse, this opportunity would slip through the cracks of her fingers.

I put on the sweetest smile I could muster. "Shadow, think about it, all the attention that we can get. And all the money we'll make."

She still looked puzzled as well as a little drunk.

I went on, "You must have heard the saying, 'One hand clapping fails to emit a sound.' That's why we can help each other. Remember, if this show is hugely successful—and I don't see any reason it won't be—then you'll be free to do whatever you want."

Finally a happy smile bloomed on her face. She gulped down her wine and put the glass down with a sharp click. "All right, I'll do it."

"Good, then I'll send you a contract soon."

After that, I filled her glass with more of my expensive wine. "To our cooperation and success!"

She responded by tapping her glass against mine so vehemently that I was surprised her glass didn't fall and shatter like the last time.

After she left, I realized she'd not mentioned the jade ring I had put on her pinky during our last meeting.

An encouraging sign.

Greed.

The following week I fine-tuned my plan and had a lawyer draw up a contract. Just when everything seemed to be smooth sailing, suddenly the current shifted against me. I was thrust into a situation like someone whose mother and father have fallen into the sea and who cannot decide whom to save first.

I realized I was pregnant.

The first thing that entered my mind was to get rid of the baby. But to do that would not be so simple. I would have to ask my driver, Ah Wen, to take me to see a Western doctor, or to see a Chinese doctor to get the right herbs, then ask my amah, Ah Fong, to decoct them for me. That meant at least three people would know my secret. Of course I could try to do all this by myself, but I didn't know any doctors or the right herbs. That meant I had to ask around for a doctor who did abortions, then risk my pregnancy becoming fodder for gossip in Rainbow Chang's column or any of the many other scandal sheets: *Flower Moon News, Flower Heaven Daily, Idleness News, Pleasure Talk News.*

Then I thought, maybe I *can* find a way to get rid of the baby myself. I read somewhere that taking herbs like moschus, musk, safflower, angelica rhizome, and ox knee root will do the job. Some of these, if mixed with cat's urine and rotten petals, could cause miscarriage just by the woman's inhaling the horrible odor. However, I also read that one time a girl had done this, but the herbs were so effective that she was found dead, drowned in her own blood.

Besides, I had also heard numerous horrible stories about self-induced abortions. A young maid, raped and impregnated by her master, stuck a chopstick into her vagina and pushed vigorously until the fetus flew out in a mess of bloody fluid. Yes, she got rid of the baby, but she soon died of an infected uterus. Her master, unwilling to pay for a proper burial, asked the servant to wrap her body in a thin bamboo mat, then drop it into an abandoned well. It was not until weeks later that a homeless person discovered her decaying corpse. The police tracked down her family, and her mother was only able to identify the daughter by a big, heart-shaped mole between her breasts.

Another case was of a teenage girl whose marriage had been arranged but who got pregnant by her married schoolteacher. In desperation, the girl went around to ancestral temples to collect ashes from their incense burners, mixed them in *maotai,* and swallowed it all in one big gulp. After she died, her face and body were said to be the same color as the month-old ashes.

But, apart from my fear for myself, I had no heart to kill my unborn baby.

Since I had no one on this earth, maybe it would not be so bad to have someone, especially someone whose flesh would come from mine and whose blood would flow from my arteries.

But the question was: Who was the father? Unfortunately I couldn't tell. Maybe it didn't really matter. If the baby turned out to be a boy, I'd tell Lung he was the father. Thrilled to have another heir, he'd definitely make me his untouchable number one woman, not the shadowy magician. If, unfortunately, it was a girl, I'd also announce to Lung it was his but secretly tell his son that he was in fact the real father. That way, if anything happened, the young master would protect my little girl and me against his father. Or we could escape to Hong Kong or America as he'd once suggested. Now I should just wait patiently for a few more months to find out if the baby was a boy or a girl. According to the Chinese, if the bulging belly is pointed, it will be a boy, if round, a girl.

Thus decided, I yelled toward the kitchen. "Ah Fong, from now on I'd like to have some nutritious herb soup for dinner."

Ah Fong rushed out from the kitchen. "Of course, Miss Camilla. Hmm . . . may I be so imprudent as to ask, are you not feeling well?"

I smiled. "I'm fine. Because I'm getting so busy, I need a boost to my overall energy."

After she left, suddenly another question emerged, giving me a jolt. What if the baby was neither Lung's nor his son's but Gao's?

But I had no time for conjecturing; now I needed to focus on taking care of my pregnancy and planning for my big show with Shadow. I decided to start rehearsing with her right away. If I didn't move fast, my stomach would announce to the audience what had happened to me.

I had something planned for my show that I absolutely did not want Lung or Jinying to see, but I couldn't come up with an excuse not to invite them. Fortunately, as I was thinking hard about what to do, Jinying called to tell me that he and his father would be going away soon.

He explained, "The government has just seized a large amount of opium and is secretly letting my father sell it so they'll both make a lot of money. I'll travel with him as his legal consultant—"

"But isn't the deal illegal?"

"Yes, but the legal papers will be so convoluted that no one can prove anything. I've already turned down too many of his requests, and I can't say no this time, because it is a big deal for him. If he loses his temper, he'll either force me to do it or even have me locked up. And if I can't see you anymore, who's going to look after you?"

I suppressed the urge to tell him I was pregnant and asked instead, "So how long will you be away?"

"We'll be leaving for about a month."

Perfect.

"But, Camilla, no one can know about this, because the highest levels of government are involved. So promise you'll not tell anyone."

"I promise. But where will you be?"

"I'm sorry, but I really can't tell you."

Just as well that he couldn't, because it saved me having to report it to Wang.

Two days later, I told Big Brother Wang about the show with Shadow, and, as expected, he agreed right away—because most of the profit would go into his pocket, not mine. He spoke to his underling Mr. Ho, owner of Bright Moon, who then agreed to let me use the nightclub for free. I hoped that when Lung came back, Shadow would be gone.

Thinking about and envisioning my show of the century, out of nowhere a thought emerged.

Why shouldn't I just entice Lung to marry me?

My idea was not to get a better chance to kill him, as Wang wanted, but, on the contrary, to escape from Wang's control. If I became Lung's legal wife, I could stop spying for Wang. Then I'd think of a way to escape from Shanghai. How come I'd never thought of this before? Wang wouldn't be able to touch me anymore—unless he succeeded in killing Lung first. He would completely lose his power over me. Fortunately, he couldn't threaten me by torturing or killing my parents, siblings, relatives, friends, or pets, because I didn't have any.

Thus thinking, I felt as energized as if I'd drunk several cups of coffee. I immediately plunged into work on the show, which I intended would make my shadowy rival disappear, this time for good.

A few days later, Shadow and I began to practice at Bright Moon. Though each rehearsal brought Shadow closer to her own destruction, she didn't seem to sense any danger, for she was completely blinded by the vision of the upcoming heaps of glittering gold and silver coins. How true what the Chinese say, "Humans will always die for money, birds for food."

But as the Chinese also say, "If you don't sweat and strain, you can't get the world to pay." So Shadow and I worked like coolies. Besides endless practice, we had to arrange publicity, negotiate with food vendors, hire extra security people, decide on ticket prices, design advertising signboards, give complimentary tickets to influential politicians and celebrities, and carefully arrange seating according to status.

To my relief, Shadow realized that she depended on my fame and connections to get this show, so she made things easy by doing what she was told.

However, after one of our rehearsals of knife-throwing, she asked, wiping big beads of perspiration from her forehead, "Camilla, have you ever worried that you might miss your target?"

I shook my head vehemently as my voice came out filled with confidence. "Of course not. Impossible."

"How come you're so sure?"

I stared straight into her eyes. "Shadow, I believe you never make mistakes, so why should I?"

She smiled, casting me an appreciative glance. "Maybe you're right, Camilla."

"We may be geniuses, but we also work much harder than those coolies at the Huangpu dock."

We both laughed.

"You're damn right, Camilla. I guess I just have to trust you."

My voice came out sounding as serious as I could make it. "Shadow, in all these rehearsals, have I ever made a wrong move?'

"No."

I went on. "If you trust yourself, you can trust me. We are of the same caliber. Maybe we were twin sisters in a past life, don't you think?"

Would I try to harm her if she really were my sister? I had no answer for that. History is filled with assassinations between siblings and even parents and children struggling against each other to take the throne. If they had a single moment of hesitation when their hand reached to poison, strangle, or stab, history has not recorded it. It was either win the kingdom or die. A murderer has only a scheming mind, no heart. And his eyes never distinguish relatives or friends, only power and status.

Anyway, everything depends on circumstances, and those always change. So maybe someday Shadow and I might be good friends or even sworn blood sisters—who could predict?

That's why I loved the opening line in the famous novel, *Romance of the Three Kingdoms:*

> It has always been, the kingdom once divided
> must unite, once united must divide.

Past or future sisters or not, Shadow's question about my knife-throwing showed that she was worried. I didn't want her doubts to spoil my plan. But I was confident that her financial need would win out over her fears. Like an invincible army or water rushing down a gorge, greed is unstoppable.

As expected, the show sold out in a few days.

❧ 23 ❧

Show of the Century

On the night of our show, Shadow and I arrived five hours early at the Bright Moon Nightclub's big performance hall. Signboards and flower baskets were everywhere, covered with congratulatory remarks on our about-to-be-unprecedented success. Lung's signboard, the biggest and with the most lavish assortment of flowers, greeted our eyes as we arrived. Its bright red banner read:

WHEN THE HORSE ARRIVES, SUCCESS FOLLOWS!
CONGRATULATE HEAVENLY SONGBIRD MISS CAMILLA
AND ILLUSIONIST MISS SHADOW
ON THEIR MAGICAL PERFORMANCES!

Of course it was not that Lung really cared that much about me, Shadow, or the show, but because, as the most powerful gangster head, he had to make his gift the biggest to outshine all the others.

The huge signboard was also compensation for his and his gang's absence, since Jinying, Zhu, Gao, and his other underlings wouldn't return from their opium deal in time for my show, though Jinying had said he'd try his best to come back early. If he did, he was going to witness something he was not prepared for. After that, I feared his feelings for me might change.

Having finished appreciating all the baskets of flowers, inscribed signboards, and congratulatory notes, Shadow and I went inside the performance hall to check the lighting and to be sure the snack and drinks departments were fully stocked. We verified that the red ribbons had been placed to set off the first two rows of tables that were reserved for Shanghai's dignitaries—including, of course, Rainbow Chang. Finally a hired assistant helped us check out all our equipment. When everything was as good as it could get, we went to our dressing room, put on our costumes, and then sat patiently while Old Aunt applied our makeup.

Half an hour before the show, I went to the nightclub's back door and peeked outside toward the front. Groups of people in sumptuous attire and ostentatious jewelry were lining up to get in. I spotted a few movie stars, their gloved, gold- and diamond-braceleted arms around those of their patrons. I also recognized a few businessmen, politicians, and warlords. Shiny black cars continued to snake their way to the entrance to drop off their honorable guests.

Then I spotted someone I didn't want to see—Jinying. To my shock, he was not alone but accompanied by a very pretty young woman who was leaning against him. My heart dropped an octave. Who was she: a girlfriend, mistress, or even . . . wife? But why should I care? If he was not what he'd claimed to be, what difference did it make? I was just using him, anyway. Maybe it was even better that he had someone else, because then he'd leave me alone eventually.

Then why did I feel so disturbed?

Feeling a headache coming on, I returned to the dressing room. I stared at my reflection in the mirror to see if I needed more makeup, but I couldn't concentrate.

Shadow cast me a curious look. "Are you all right?"

"Yes, why?"

"You look a bit distracted. Are you nervous about the show?"

"Not at all." I flashed her a confident smile, then picked up a brush to apply more rouge to my cheeks.

Ten minutes before the show, I went backstage, peeked through the curtain, and scanned the hall. The rich and powerful already occupied all the front tables, flanked by wives, concubines, children, relatives, maids, and bodyguards. Others were being helped by ushers to claim their seats, while more were still streaming in. Attractive young girls and boys went around with trays of cigarettes, hot towels, lidded cups of tea and snacks—watermelon seeds, sugared candies, fried peanuts, roasted sweet potatoes, and dried red dates speared with thin bamboo sticks. They navigated smoothly around the crowded hall, hoping for good sales and generous tips.

I again spotted Jinying and his lady friend up front, now both absorbed in reading the program. Before I could try to figure out their relationship and begin to sort out my feelings, something in my peripheral vision pulled my eyes away. It was Rainbow Chang and her pink-clad entourage of tall young women. I swiftly stepped back from the curtain.

Back in the dressing room, Shadow was still surveying her reflection in the mirror. Even sitting, she looked towering and gorgeous. Her flaming red dress's plunging neckline half hid, or half revealed, her swelling breasts through peek-a-boo lace. A heaven-reaching slit on the right side of her dress exposed a red-fishnet-stockinged leg, like a Greek temple's sensuously powerful Ionic column.

While Shadow presented herself as a pillar of flame, I was a reddish-gold supernatural creature. My dress, a golden *cheongsam* embroidered with a soaring red phoenix, was further enhanced by long red gloves, dangling gold earrings, and a bracelet shaped like a coiled dragon. I wanted something simple enough not to overwhelm my rather small frame, especially in comparison to Shadow's massive one. However, like Shadow's, the slits of my *cheongsam* also rose against gravity, crawling all the way up my waist. Of course I certainly did not mind that this enhanced my sex appeal,

but the most important reason was that I needed freedom of movement for my contortioning and knife-throwing. Our red and gold
color combination was Shadow's suggestion, for she believed these
two colors would bring us double luck.

But little did she know what kind of luck she'd get tonight.

I smiled at her reflection in the mirror. "You are gorgeous,
Shadow."

She smiled back, a little nervously. "You think so?"

"I'm sure you know that yourself."

"Thank you. You, too, Camilla."

A courteous, civilized exchange before a you-live-or-I-die duel.

Seconds passed, and her painted eyebrows knit slightly. "You
think we'll do a good job?"

As I was thinking about what I was going to do to her, my heart
started to pound. But I exclaimed, smiling, "Of course! After our
countless rehearsals, you still have doubts?"

She smiled back, her thick, sensuous lips trembling a little.
"You're right, Camilla. Tonight we'll take Shanghai by storm."

Just then the live orchestra played a dreamy but pleasing tune,
and we heard the master of ceremonies announce our show in a
booming voice. Shadow and I both inhaled deeply; then I took her
hand.

"Let's go out to conquer Shanghai."

Elegantly we floated out to the stage in sync with the music.
Once the audience spotted us, thunderous clapping and cheers exploded in the packed hall. Men's eyes followed us, lingering on our
faces, breasts, waists, legs. A few seemingly said, "My heart aches
for your beauty!" Women cast us admiring glances or jealous ones.
The latter group seemed to be thinking, "I'm here tonight hoping
to witness you two flop and ruin your careers!"

Shadow's hand trembled slightly in mine. Was she already
thinking of failure even before the show began? A bad omen. She
should have followed the advice in *The Art of War:* "Build up an invincible presence, and you'll win even before you begin".

I squeezed her hand a little and whispered, "Trust me, Shadow,
we will be great."

She murmured something back while smiling stunningly to the eager audience. Of course it was her life, not mine, that was at stake. Wouldn't I be equally nervous if I were to be the target of her knife-throwing?

We made a deep bow to the front, right, and left. My gaze involuntarily landed on Jinying and his lady friend. While he smiled at me, she was obviously trying to get his attention by whispering into his ear and touching his arm and shoulder with her gloved hand. But I had no time to see Jinying's reaction. Because right then Shadow turned and made a grand, sweeping gestures as her red dress swirled like a huge ball of fire. No sooner was the audience dazzled by her "flame," than, to everyone's utter shock, she vanished into thin air!

Then, before the audience even had time to gasp, she had already reappeared from behind me to greet them.

"How did she do that?" I heard the collective question from the mystified audience as I realized we were actually having a duel right under the public's scrutiny! Damn her, it was not in our plan that she would perform her famous disappearing act. And I was sure this was not something spur of the moment. Shadow had planned this to outsmart and outshine me on purpose. "To drink the first drop of the tasty soup," as the Chinese put it. She wanted to be the star tonight. She wanted to steal my show, my man, my fame.

I smiled. Maybe she had won in the beginning, but what matters is who wins in the end.

After the magician's stunning disappearance and even more stunning reappearance, it was my turn. In my famous shredded-golden-lotus steps and swaying of my willowy waist, I approached the microphone. After that, I put on my most innocently seductive smile, meditated, let my eyes wander to meet Jinying's, then began to breathe life into "The Wandering Songstress."

I had my reason for picking this song. Shadow presented her strong, imposing self to impress the audience. It would be a bad idea to try to beat her by sheer strength. She was stronger and taller than me, so the result would be like an egg dropped into a wok. So I'd adopt Laozi's two-thousand-year-old strategy of conquering the strong with softness. I would seem lost and vulnerable to arouse sympathy from the women and the protective instinct from the men. I'd win by yielding, not resisting, by being the victim, not the conqueror.

To the lively accompaniment of the small orchestra I breathed out the melody:

> At the edge of the sky and farthest corner of the sea,
> I search and search. . . .
> My love, I remember you played the fiddle as I sang
> In the days when we were of one heart and one mind.
> Now I long for my homeland, in the far north.
> Tears streak down my hollow cheeks,
> Thinking of our happier days together. . . .

As expected, after Shadow's powerful yet emotionless trick, the audience immediately warmed up to my melodious misery. A young, vulnerable woman longing for her lost love. A long-lost happiness that would probably never return. A few women dabbed their eyes with lace handkerchiefs. The men's expressions suggested that they imagined they'd die to protect me and wanted only to give me the happiness I deserved. I knew well that the women's tears didn't flow for me but for themselves. All had wealthy, powerful patrons, but how many had found true love, not just its elusive and illusive shadow?

Good, I thought, as my voice continued to squeeze out tears and sighs. Involuntarily my eyes landed on Jinying again. To my astonishment he was dabbing his eyes with his bare hand as his lady friend handed him her handkerchief. He was the son of a gangster! Had I been able to, I would have him stop this sentimentality at once, before anyone noticed.

Fearing that if I stared at him, I'd evoke more tears or other inept expression of emotion, I turned my eyes to the flowers lined up across the front of the stage. With effort I finished my song without a glitch, to enthusiastic applause.

"Wonderful!"

"We want more!"

"Camilla's the best!"

For the next act, I, as assistant to the magician, would help Shadow "steal" things from the audience. The first person she picked was an old gentleman a few seats from Jinying. Our magician politely asked the man to stand, then walked down to him.

"Sir, you're such a lucky man." She nodded toward the beautiful girl next to him, surely not his daughter. "You have everything a man desires in life: wealth, admiration, a beautiful woman, and lots of fun."

Obviously falling right into Shadow's honey trap, the old man laughed, his floppy belly shivering. "Yes, Miss Shadow, but you must know that a man's appetite is insatiable. Whenever my chopsticks pick up a bit of fish, my eyes are already eyeing the bear's paws on the next table."

The audience laughed. For Chinese, fish and bear's paws are the two most coveted gourmet dishes; thus the famous saying, "No one can get both the fish and the bear's paw."

I saw that Shadow was talking fast, making lots of little movements—twisting her hair, blinking, laughing, pointing her fingers in all directions, touching the old man intimately on his shoulders, arms, neck, back, waist.

The conversation finally ended as Shadow planted a kiss on the old man's cheek, then strode back onto the stage, flaunting her crimson goddess's legs. When she turned back to face the audience, a loud collective "Ah!!!" burst into the hall. Four items—a bulging wallet, a gold watch, a jade and diamond ring, and a thick wad of cash were displayed in her hands.

It took a few seconds before the old man gasped, realizing these were his belongings! His expression suggested he was not sure whether to laugh or cry.

A man shouted, "At least you still have your clothes on!"

Boisterous laughter exploded in the hall.

Of course Shadow returned everything to her victim, probably to her regret and the man's great relief.

After that, she went on to steal from another man—wallet, jewelry, watch, belt. Of course she returned everything. But I wondered if she'd exchanged some of the returned items with fakes. But if she was stealing what she could at the moment, how would she know in advance what fakes to prepare?

Her talents were almost as much a mystery to me as mine were to her.

Now it was my turn again. I decided to tease the audience before putting them into a frenzy with my ultimate act. A few minutes after I started to sing, the audience saw not only a songstress but a woman twisting her body into impossible, surrealistic postures. There was no clapping or cheering in the hall, only mesmerized silence interrupted by stifled gasps. Their expressions told me that they couldn't believe what they saw in front of their eyes. With Shadow, they knew she was an illusionist and that everything happening, however incredible, was a well-rehearsed trick to fool their eyes. But my performance was no trick, only the fruit of inhuman training and bitter practice. Since no one in the audience had ever seen me perform as a contortionist, the shock was all the greater.

More singing and twisting followed until suddenly I disentangled my limbs and transformed my body back to its normal shape. It took a few seconds before the audience came out from their trance and burst into thunderous applause. It was then that I noticed that Jinying and his woman's seats were empty. Had they left? *Good.* They wouldn't witness what was going to happen next. The young master must have been greatly distressed to see me twist my body into unnatural, excruciating shapes. What would he think of me if he'd been able to read my twisted mind?

The master of ceremonies went to the microphone and announced, "Ladies and gentlemen, if you think there is no more excitement in store for you tonight, then you are dead wrong! What comes next is Miss Camilla and Miss Shadow's most extravagant act, which will absolutely stun your eyeballs so much that you won't be able to sleep for many nights. And when you do, what you see tonight will haunt you in your dreams!"

Of course neither the MC nor anyone else had any idea what I was *really* going to do.

Equally oblivious of the upcoming evil, someone yelled, "Hurry up! Show us now!"

A man's voice called out, "When are you two beauties going to show some flesh?" to collective laughter vibrating in the hall.

"You'll see. Open your eyes as wide as you can so you don't miss the next shocking act. You've never seen anything like what is about to happen!" the MC said excitedly.

"Get out of the way! We want to see the girls, not you, big mouth!"

Right after the master of ceremonies stepped down, I swiftly slid a dagger from my sleeve and plunged it into Shadow's chest. Blood spurted in a crimson cascade from between her breasts. The magician, now covering her chest with her hands, looked at me with an indescribable expression. Shocked? Stunned? Tormented?

"Oh, no!" the audience cried out in alarm, but of course they had no idea what to do. I saw a few muscular men at the back spring up, ready for action. Fortunately, no one was leaving to call the police. I put on my best smile and bowed deeply.

"My apologies, ladies and gentleman. Relax. No one is going to get hurt, especially not our beloved Miss Shadow!"

At the same time, Shadow was regaining her composure. She must have realized now that she was only in shock, not in pain, and that the whole thing was, like her own magic, just a trick.

A smile materialized on her pale face as she bowed to the audience. "Ladies and gentlemen, I'm fine, really, as you can see." She patted her bloody chest where the knife had stabbed.

However, this little trick was just a warm-up for the ultimate show, a tantalizing hors d'oeuvre to whet appetites for the gourmet entrée.

I had thrust a knife into Shadow's chest, but it was not a real knife, only one whose blade was blunt and retracted into its handle. Fake blood stored inside the handle was squeezed out to create a realistic effect. So what looked like a stabbing was just an illusion. I was surprised that Shadow, as a magician, had fallen for this simple gimmick. But it is always different when the trick is on you. She needed to learn to be more shock-proof.

Shadow cast me a harsh look, whether real or feigned anger, I could not tell and didn't care.

People in the audience were asking one another what had just happened. But I was not going to explain my trick, and now was the moment for which I had planned the entire show.

Two stagehands appeared, pushing a wooden platform on which was mounted a big wheel, while Shadow and I went backstage to change. When we came back out, I took several deep breaths, silently praying that everything would go according to plan. A plan that nobody knew, not even heaven.

Shadow twirled across the stage to the big wheel and climbed onto it, her feet resting on two small projections. Next, the stagehands strapped her securely to the wheel. Then one of the men handed me a brocade bag filled with knives, while the other pushed a button on the wheel board. Slowly the huge disc began to revolve, accompanied by sinister music from the orchestra. Now a bright spotlight was shined on me, making the knife blades glint as I lifted them from the bag. Instantly the usually rowdy crowd became deathly silent.

I meditated and planted my legs firmly on the stage. Then, like a lightning flash, twenty knives flew from my hand and landed around Shadow in a perfect circle. After a moment of stunned silence, thunderous applause burst into the air.

Shadow came down from the board and walked to me, smiling gorgeously. We held hands and sauntered to the front of the stage to bow.

She whispered to me, "Good job, Camilla."

"You bet, Shadow. I never miss."

As I lifted up my head, I spotted Rainbow Chang in the front furiously scribbling on her notepad, then looking up to stare at me admiringly. But I had no time to acknowledge her or anyone else in the audience. What I had planned next would take all the concentration my years of bitter training had prepared me for.

A heroic tune streamed out from the orchestra, energizing the air. But I felt a chill, an uncanny sensation, for I was the only being between heaven and earth who knew what was going to happen next. . . .

To build up more suspense, Shadow and I went backstage to change again, she into a beaded black Western outfit and I a black tunic bordered by silver sequins at the neck and sleeves.

Holding hands, we headed back onto the stage. Again, Shadow was strapped onto the board, which began to slowly rotate, while I set the knives in a row on the floor next to my feet. Now, accompanied by a mysterious tune from the orchestra, I began to contort my body into impossible, even inhuman, postures. As I entangled and disentangled my limbs, knives flew out with lightning speed and unerring accuracy, forming different patterns—circle, square, heart—around Shadow. I was sure none had ever witnessed a woman contorting while throwing knives at the same time. The spectacle was eerie, erotic, perverse. No sound was heard except the steady thudding of the knives landing next to Shadow.

The staff pulled out the knives and handed them back to me. Next I lay belly-down on the floor, my head facing the audience, my legs crisscrossed on top of my head, and my toes holding one another above my scalp.

But something strange happened. This time the knife hesitated for a fraction of a second before, seemingly with a will of its own, flying out from my hand. I heard a sharp cry burst from Shadow's bright red lips. Her blood, this time real, sprayed onto the revolving board and splattered onto the stage.

The stunned audience remained as silent as corpses. They must have assumed that this was yet another trick. Only when the magician cried out again did the stagehands reappear.

Shadow begged plaintively, "Stop the machine!"

They quickly turned it off and helped her back down to the stage.

My secret goal had been to slice off one of Shadows' fingers, ruining her chances of success as a magician or skeleton woman in Shanghai. But right now I was no better off than she because I was "stuck" in my contortion pose. No matter how hard I tried to loosen my limbs, they stubbornly remained in their perverse—and now extremely embarrassing—position.

Staff, bodyguards, and several men from the audience rushed onstage. Amidst the resulting confusion, I saw two assistants help the pale, bleeding, and trembling Shadow off the stage. I do not know what happened next, because I lost consciousness. . . .

The next day, the gossip newspapers were in a frenzy reporting the failed show of the century. In front of the elite of Shanghai, two of its most famous and beautiful skeleton women had met with exciting mishaps: one had her finger nearly sliced off, while the other got stuck in her contortionist act and passed out.

Rainbow Chang's column read:

Show of the Century Ends in Disaster!

Last night the spectators at the Bright Moon Nightclub had their eyeballs stunned—twice. First by Camilla's singing in contorted poses, then by her even more contorted knife-tossing at her partner, the magician Shadow. Everything went fine until Camilla lobbed a knife while in a particularly weird pose. The whirling blade sliced poor Shadow's finger. In the meantime, Camilla got stuck in her pose and passed out.

So Shanghai might now have a nine-fingered skeleton woman and another skeleton woman entangled in an endless knot. Shadow lost so much blood that she now looks even more shadowy, while Camilla nearly suffocated and may never stand up straight again.

More to follow. . . .
Rainbow Chang

I felt a smile playing around the corners of my lips. I had fooled everyone. Everything had worked out according to plan and under my control—the slicing off of Shadow's finger, my being stuck in the impossible pose, and the fainting were no accidents, only strategies.

And yet as I tried to relish my impeccable plan by re-creating last night's accident, I felt a headache coming on. Something was not quite right. Why the hesitation, just for a split second, before I threw the knife? Had I felt compassion just at that moment? Were my getting stuck in the contortionist position and fainting truly a pretense, or were they real?

I racked my brain but couldn't be sure what had actually happened. Was my mind scrambling itself to prevent me from knowing the truth? Was I losing my grip on reality from my lifetime of lying, cunning, and scheming? As I brooded, my headache intensified, and fear gripped me like a tiger's paw.

Not until I awakened in the evening did I realize I'd fallen asleep. The headache was gone, so I steeled myself to analyze and plan. Maybe I should stay out of the public eye for a while to let the whole thing cool down. But first I needed to visit Shadow in the hospital. I definitely didn't want to be portrayed as both careless and heartless.

I put on a simple cotton *cheongsam* and only light makeup and was about to leave the house when the doorbell rang. To my surprise, when Ah Fong opened the door, it was none other than my ghostly rival! And I was even more surprised when she handed me a bunch of camellias and a bottle of red wine. It should be me who visited her and brought flowers and wine. Was this some new game she was playing?

I smiled nervously at the inscrutable face across from me. "Thanks for coming, Shadow, but you really shouldn't have done all this. In fact, I was about to ask Ah Wen to drive me to the hospital to see you."

I cast a quick glance at her hand. "I'm so sorry about your finger. . . . I don't know how I could have made such a horrible, horrible mistake. . . ."

She lifted her bandaged pinky while giving me a bitter glance. "The doctor said it was only slightly damaged. Fortunately the knife didn't slice into the bone, so it should heal soon."

"I'm so sorry, Shadow. I must have been so tense and exhausted by all the rehearsals and preparations that I . . ." Then I realized that I had not sliced off her finger after all, as I had intended, merely scraped her fingertip.

She said sarcastically, "Ha! And I was so naive as to believe that you never make mistakes."

I was about to respond, but she continued. "Camilla, I've eaten so much bitterness in order to be a magician, a little chip off my finger will not deter me. I'm not going to give up magic just because of this accident. In fact, I'm thankful for the valuable lesson it taught me: no one is ever safe in this life. Glory does not last forever, including mine. So I've made up my mind to ask Master Lung for long-term sponsorship."

Surely she knew that I was Lung's mistress. Did she suspect that I'd intended to get rid of her by slicing off her finger? Was this her clever strategy to retaliate? Why did this damn Shadow keep coming back to haunt me like a hungry ghost?

But I swallowed all my bitterness and smiled sweetly. "I'm sure he can't resist the request of such a beautiful woman as you."

"I certainly hope not." She looked down at her bandaged pinky.

If I had sliced off her whole middle finger I thought that she would withdraw from Shanghai's stage forever. Either she would be too embarrassed or unable to perform, or she would get my message for her to disappear. But now the damage was obviously much less serious than I'd hoped. She went on. "The doctor said the flesh might even grow back. Since you're Master Lung's favorite woman, and he once mentioned that you and I are like sisters, I decided to ask him to pay for the hospital fee. I meant to ask you to ask him, but since you don't seem to be feeling well, I'll do it myself. He is so rich—you don't think he'll turn me down, do you?"

Her statement took me by such surprise that I couldn't think of a proper response. Not only was she using this "accident" and my relationship with Lung to befriend him, she was also going to spite me by contacting Lung herself instead of asking me to do so. What nerve!

Slicing her finger had not only failed to make her disappear, it would now be a pretext for her to get closer to Lung. I was in a state of disbelief. But one thing was certain: I could not let this happen!

Although I kept my smile sweet and innocent, my heart was plunging down to the floor. I ignored her question and instead asked, "Shadow, are you angry at me?"

She answered with a sincere expression. "Yes and no. I was angry that you injured me, but then I was not angry because I know you didn't do it on purpose."

Was she dissembling or telling the truth?

"Thank you so much for understanding, Shadow. So . . . are we friends again?"

"Of course. That's why I'm here. I know you didn't do it on purpose, because you once saved my life, remember?"

She was referring to the night I'd "rescued" her from being robbed. Judging from her expression, I was pretty sure she didn't suspect anything fishy, that I had staged the robbery by having Gao disguise himself as a hooligan. Because, after all, I had "risked my life" to save hers and had even gotten a cut on my forearm.

Unless, like me, she was also an excellent actress worthy of the most prestigious award for deceiving.

"Shadow, I apologize again for my mistake, and I'm so glad that your finger is okay."

"I'm glad that you're okay, too. The police wanted to take you to the hospital for a checkup, but you resisted so vehemently, they gave up."

I was alarmed that I didn't even remember this.

I said, "Then let's not talk about unpleasant things but have some food and something to drink."

"Good." Shadow raised her glass. "To our future cooperation!" she toasted, then downed her whiskey in one big gulp.

* * *

Finally, after she'd left, to calm my nerves I opened the bottle of wine she had brought and quickly downed a full glass. I choked, surprised by its cheap, acid taste.

This dog-fucked Shadow, couldn't she get my message that it was time to leave Shanghai? Wasn't she afraid of me, of anyone? Maybe she thought I had no courage to harm her again?

PART FIVE

24

A Ghost Baby Boy

By telephone Big Brother Wang and I agreed that I would not contact him until the public frenzy around the show of the century calmed down. I couldn't let people find out that I was well and sane. But perhaps I wasn't. I stopped reading all the gossip about me, including Rainbow Chang's, afraid that I might discover that someone other than I knew the "truth," whatever it was.

For my "convalescence," I mainly stayed in my apartment and read to pass the time. I refrained from going to the Bund to practice so as not to risk being seen and to avoid Jinying, who might look for me there. When he called, I told Ah Fong to say either that I was out or that I was asleep. If he came to the apartment, Ah Fong would say that I was not home and send him away.

Finally, a few weeks after the accident, I did agree to talk to Jinying once over the phone.

His voice held love, sadness, and fear, all rolled into one. "Camilla, please, why don't you let me see you?"

"Jinying, I appreciate your concern. But I'm still not back to normal, and you don't want to see me looking sick."

Now his voice jolted up like an elevator. "That's pure nonsense! I love you, Camilla, and I don't care how you look!"

"All men care, Jinying. Don't pretend you are any different."

He was silent again, then pleaded, "Let me see you and take care of you, please, Camilla."

I didn't answer but asked instead, "How's your father? Did he hear about the accident?"

"Yes, I told him, and he sends his good wishes for your recovery. He said he'll be back soon."

I had not forgotten that Jinying had not come to my performance by himself. So I asked casually, "How did your friend like my show?"

"Who do you mean?"

Did he think I would not have noticed the pretty girl who'd leaned on him the whole time?

So I had to be more direct. "Who is she?"

"Oh, her. She's Mr. Zhu's daughter. Zhu insisted I take her to your show, since he couldn't be there."

"Anyone could tell she's very fond of you."

"I don't care about her. No other woman matters to me except you!"

"Jinying, I'm tired now and need to rest. I'll see you soon, I promise." After that, I hung up.

Jinying was not the only one who cared about me. There was also Gao. Of course he couldn't visit me and bring flowers or fruit because he was away with Lung at a meeting somewhere. But he had sent a letter.

> Dear Miss Camilla,
> I am extremely sorry to hear that you fainted
> and your partner was injured during your show. If
> only I had been there, I could have dashed
> onstage to help you.
> I am worried about you. Are you not feeling
> well? I think you are under too much strain. I
> hope you consider me a friend.
> I also hope you will allow me to visit you when

I return to Shanghai. If you need anything or any
help, just let me know. I'll do anything for you.

Take very good care of yourself, and be well
and happy.

Your loyal servant,
Gao

I didn't know why, but despite the concern of these two attractive men, I felt sad. I feared I was having more feelings toward both
than I could afford. Jinying and Gao, one a boss's son, whom so
many competed to please, the other the underling whose job was to
fend these people off. Whom should I choose? With either there
was extreme danger!

Gao's *I am worried about you. Are you not feeling well? I think
you are under too much strain,* worried me. Gao had noticed that
something was amiss with me. He had good reason to wonder if I
was pregnant, of course.

I decided to visit Madame Lewinsky to see if I could fish some
advice from her on women's matters. Although I tried to brace myself to be strong, all that had happened—and would happen—
began to weigh on me so much that I felt relieved to see her, though
I had been trained not to depend on anyone.

Lewinsky's face, familiar and affectionate, soothed me like a
cool breeze on a sultry summer day. After she led me to sit on the
sofa, she went inside the kitchen to make tea. I listened to the
pleasant metallic banging of pots and pans and had a rare feeling of
something close to happiness. Soon Lewinsky came out from the
kitchen carrying a tray. She laid it on the table and poured tea. We
began to sip the sugar-and-milk-sweetened Russian black tea and
nibbled on the sponge cakes she'd baked.

My teacher took a deep sip of the scalding liquid. "All right, tell
me everything that has happened to you lately."

I was not surprised that she didn't seem to know about the accident, because she couldn't read the Chinese gossip papers.

I said, "I'm taking a short leave from the Bright Moon. That's why I can come to see you."

"Are you not feeling well?" She placed her hand on my forehead.

I shook my head. "Oh, no, I just think I need to rest more, even my voice."

I hoped she hadn't noticed that my hand involuntarily moved to cover my stomach. I wore a somewhat loose dress, for I was now over almost four months pregnant and already had to put aside my body-hugging *cheongsams*.

"Good thought." She smiled, and her eyes studied me lovingly. A long moment passed before she spoke again, now looking serious. "I miss you, Camilla, so I want to ask you something. Since I don't have any children, and you are like a daughter to me, I would like you to come live here in my home. It's not good to live alone."

This was completely unexpected. At this point in my life I did not want to be her daughter or anyone else's!

I could not think how to answer her question right away. Then I thought of the Chinese strategy *yitui weijin,* retreat in order to advance. "Madame Lewinsky, I'm just a nightclub performer, so I don't think I am worthy to be your daughter."

She looked a little upset but seemed to recover quickly. "Camilla, you're not just a nightclub performer but a great singer, the Heavenly Songbird. Let me tell you, everyone knows that it's hard for a student to find a good teacher, but few realize it's even harder for a teacher to find good students. I'm very grateful to God for sending you to me." She took a meditative sip of her tea, then said, "I understand my request may be too sudden for you. But I hope you will go home and seriously consider it."

So as not to crush her hope, I said, smiling demurely, "I'll definitely do so."

"Please. Since we're extremely compatible, we'll take very good care of each other."

I studied her aging face and felt a tinge of pity. She must have been a gorgeous woman in her youth, sought after by men for her beauty and talent, just as I was now. But time had transformed her from a beautiful young woman to an old, lonely one. All she had now was her past glory and her students. I would end up like her unless I could escape to a life better than being a gangster's mistress and a spy.

Lewinsky's voice awakened me from my reverie. She looked at me, her face filled with concern, "Are you okay, Camilla? Don't be afraid to tell me what's on your mind."

"I'm fine, just a little tired, maybe bored." I had lost my nerve to tell her I was pregnant.

"All right, then, why don't we sing?"

We went to the piano. I just listened as her strong, round-tipped fingers began hitting the keyboard, flooding the room with music. Lewinsky began to sing in her powerful, nuanced voice. But ominously, the music was Schubert's *Death and the Maiden*.

> *The Maiden:*
> Let me be! Let me be!
> Go away, man of bones!
> I am but young! Go away,
> And lay not your hand upon me.
> And lay not your hand upon me
>
> *Death:*
> Let me take your hand, beautiful maiden!
> I come as a friend, not to punish.
> Be of good cheer! I am not unkind,
> Slumber softly in my arms!

Hearing the words, I felt a jolt of despair, similar to what I'd experienced when I'd tried to kill myself in the Seine. I didn't know why she'd picked such a depressing song. Did Lewinsky see through me and think she might exorcise my inner demons by helping me to face my fears?

Was this a premonition or just a random choice of a familiar song?

I listened to two more songs, then politely took my leave.

By the door, Lewinsky touched my cheek tenderly. "Camilla, you need someone. You really can't go on like this. If you have problems, please come to me. I'll try my best to help. If you don't want me to be your mother, at least you can trust me as a friend. I've lived what you're living now. You will learn that it's no fun getting old and see younger women steal the glory that once belonged to you."

I smiled back. "I'm fine, really, Madame Lewinsky. I just need some time to rest and think things over."

"Good, then I hope you consider my offer and come to stay with me soon."

After I left her place and headed home, I wondered if I had done the right thing by visiting my teacher. Little seemed to escape her sharp eyes. But her home was the only oasis in the perilous desert of my life.

Back at my apartment, I resolved that I would continue to carry out my plan, whatever the outcome.

My biggest concern for the moment was my soon-to-be-protruding stomach. I feared the explosion of gossip that would begin as soon as I showed. At times I still thought of trying to abort the baby. As I was soon to be a mother with no husband, others would know of my bad, lustful karma for the rest of my life. So on one dark night I took an herb I had bought from an old woman in a street market.

That night I had a dream.

A baby boy crawled to my doorstep, reached out his sticky little hands, and begged for milk from my breast.

When I tried to shoo him away, he burst out in his sharp, babyish voice, "You're my mother; you can't just get rid of me like this!"

"Little beggar!" I pushed his naked, tiny body with my foot. "I don't have a son! So get lost, right now!"

He burst out crying. "Mama, Mama! Please don't abandon me! Even though you tried to get rid of me, I managed to make my way out to this world. Aren't you now happy to see me alive and well? You wouldn't kick me away if you knew how much I suffered just to get a chance to see you!"

I spat on his face and cursed. "I don't have a beggar son like you! If you don't leave, I'll use a broom to sweep you out of my door!"

Suddenly he stood up, opened his tiny mouth, and began to sing "Looking for You" with a could-not-be-comforted, heartbreaking expression. Listening, I realized not only was he singing *my* song, but his voice was Jinying's, albeit a babyish version!

As I finally realized he was really my baby boy, tears streamed down my cheeks as I asked tenderly, "Oh, how in heaven did you find me, son?"

He spoke again in his baby voice. "You were going to abort me, so I went down to bargain with the King of Hell. Seeing that it was not my fault that I was conceived, he took pity on me. That was why he decided not to keep me in hell and sent me back up here to live."

He pointed to his right foot, which had only four toes instead of five. "Mama, this is what the abortion medicine you took did to my foot."

I felt tears burning down my cheeks. I pulled him to me and kissed him tenderly all over his face. "Son, I'm so sorry, so sorry. . . ."

With his chubby, tiny hand, he wiped the tears from my face. "Mama, you remember Auntie Shadow?"

I nodded, my whole body trembling. "Yes, what about her?"

"When I met with the King of Hell, he told me that because something you did to her and yourself, I was born with this deformed pinky." He lifted his right hand and showed me his pinky, which was too short. "Now I will never grow up to be a pianist like my father."

I didn't reply, couldn't. I just held him tightly so his warmth would keep my chilled body from trembling and my soul from plunging to freezing hell.

Finally, he detached himself from my grasp. "Mama, the King of Hell also told me that this is called karma." He stared at me curiously with his large, innocent, beautiful, long-lashed eyes. "Do you understand what that means?"

Tears kept cascading down my cheeks. "Son, I'm sorry . . . so sorry. . . ."

My baby said, kissing my cheek, "Mama, don't be sad."

This time it was I who could not be comforted.

"Mama, it's time for me to go."

"No, please stay with your mama. I beg you, son."

"No, I have to go now. But I will be back soon."

"Son, where are you going?"

"Back to your womb so I can be born into this world, this time with my all my fingers and toes so I can play the piano like my father and walk on tightrope like Auntie Shadow."

"Who's your father?"

"You know who. It's the one whose heart was broken by your callous one, remember?"

He winked mischievously, and as he scurried away on his chubby feet, I thought he looked exactly like Jinying.

The dream was so disquieting that I couldn't sleep for three whole days. But now I had no doubt about keeping the baby. Since I would soon need to keep out of sight, I decided to fake losing my voice until after the birth.

❧ 25 ❧

The Birth

Miraculously, my plan seemed to be working out. Five months into my pregnancy, when I couldn't squeeze into my loosest *cheongsam* anymore, I took another leave. I told Mr. Ho, owner of the Bright Moon Nightclub, that I was worn out and needed time off to boost my energy and nurture my voice. Then Mr. Ho made an announcement to the press and guaranteed them a spectacular comeback.

Just a few days after the announcement, one evening, after Lung and I had sex and were relaxing on his bed, he cast me a curious glance. "What's the matter, Camilla, have you been eating a lot while I was away?"

Of course he was referring to my protruding stomach.

I smiled mysteriously. "Indeed, Master Lung."

"Then stop eating so much. You know I like your slim waist."

I feigned shyness. "But, Master Lung, I *have* to eat. . . ." My voice trailed off.

"Why so much?"

I planted a kiss on his cheek. "Because I'm pregnant."

He looked at me if I'd suddenly turned into a gold pillar. "Wah!" shot out from his mouth. "Is it a boy?"

"I think so." Of course, I had no way to know, but it didn't hurt to say so. At least my status would be elevated for now.

"Hmm . . . It'd better be." He thought for a while, then said, "From now on, I'll tell my men that whatever you ask for must be granted." The he asked, seemingly without thinking, "You want to move in here so my cook can prepare better food, some baby-boy-boosting dishes for you?"

This offer took me by surprise. A dropped-from-heaven bonanza for my mission for Wang!

But I suppressed my thrill and said gratefully, "What an honor, Master Lung! Of course I'd love to. But what about the newspapers? I'm sure once they get news of my pregnancy and my moving in with you, there'll be a huge frenzy."

Lung playfully knocked my forehead. "My little pretty, just leave everything to my men. They'll make sure no one will find out."

I couldn't believe what I'd just heard. Not only would I move into his house so I could snoop around for his bank accounts and other information, I'd be served by his underlings. I was sure his chefs would cook me the most delicious and nutritious dishes, his maids would tend to me like imperial nannies to their princess, his chauffeur would drive me around in a dark-windowed, bullet-proof car so no one could see or bother me, his bodyguards would watch over me like I was a royalty. . . . But the question was, yes, I might find out what I wanted, but would there actually be a chance to have him killed in his own house? Probably not.

I thought of suggesting that he marry me, but I didn't want to risk his turning me down or, worse, getting angry. Everyone knew that Lung liked to make decisions by himself, not be given suggestions. Marrying me, or any other women, would be a big thing, and I'd better be cautious. Besides, no one—not even his son Jinying—knew the whereabouts of his original wife. She might be dead in her grave or withering away in a Buddhist nunnery somewhere as a crazy woman. I only hoped that his inviting me to move in was to show he was serious with me. Maybe that would lead to a proposal. I'd wait and see. Of course I did not really want him as my husband, but it would solve my problems for now.

"Master Lung, when should I move in?"

"Anytime. Just let me know, and I'll ask Zhu to take care of everything and Gao to pick you up."

"What about next week?"

"Sounds good."

Before the move, I also called Jinying and told him about the pregnancy. First he sounded very excited; then he asked the inevitable question, "Is it mine?"

"Yes, Jinying. But I had to tell your father that it's his. You understand?"

At the other end, there was a long silence.

Finally, his voice, sad yet filled with concern, came through the wires. "I do. But, Camilla, you won't even let me acknowledge my own flesh and blood and take care of the woman I love?"

"Jinying, please . . ."

He started to sob.

When he finished feeling sorry for himself, me, and the baby, I said, "Don't worry, sooner or later there'll be a way."

"How can you be so sure?"

Of course I was not going to tell him that I was planning to somehow get some money and run away. Maybe then Jinying and I and our child could reunite as a family. However, there was no guarantee that could happen, or if it did that Jinying would still want me, or that we would be happy together. Because as the ancient Chinese *Book of Changes* tells us, everything changes.

"Jinying, let's deal with the present situation. I'll let you know when I have a plan."

"I'll come to see you."

As I was gripped by a sudden fear, my voice turned fierce and sharp like my throwing knives. "Absolutely not, unless you want your father to find out and have us killed!"

"But, Camilla . . . you need someone to take care of you. You can't do this by yourself."

"I'm moving in with your father."

"What!?"

"So when you visit him, we can see each other," I said, then hung up.

After Jinying, the next person I called was Big Brother Wang. After I told him I was pregnant, his angry voice rolled all the way from the other side of Shanghai to assault my eardrum.

"Are you stupid or out of your mind? How come after all this training, you're so careless?"

"So sorry, Big Brother Wang." Of course it would be ridiculous to give my usual answer, "I promise this won't happen again."

"Then you'd better get rid of it."

"Of course, you are right, Big Brother Wang. But I'm already four months along, so I'm afraid it's too late now."

"Then why didn't you inform me earlier?" His tone was getting angrier.

"Because earlier I did not know."

I might be a woman well versed in lying and scheming but hiding a pregnancy was not included in my training.

Before he had a chance to respond, I added, "I already told Lung it's his baby. And he invited me to move in with him."

A few seconds passed, and then Wang said, his voice no longer angry but excited, "Hmm . . . So maybe your pregnancy is not such a bad thing after all." He paused, then asked, "You mean move into his famous mansion in Junfu Lane?"

"Yes, Big Brother Wang."

"Good, then you can look for all the things I need."

"I already planned to do so."

"But then you also won't have a chance to contact me."

"That's correct."

"That means even if there's only you and him inside the house, you can't tell me to send my people."

"I'm afraid not, Big Brother Wang."

Why did I keep repeating myself?

"Then I'm afraid you'll have to do it yourself."

"What? But, Big Brother Wang . . ."

"I've decided."

I protested, "But Lung's mansion is always filled with his people, and I'll be searched thoroughly before I move in and every time I go into his bedroom." But my boss had already hung up.

The following week, I moved in with Lung. But to my utter disappointment, I was not invited to share his master bedroom. Instead, I was allotted to one of the house's spare bedrooms at the farthest corner from his. A young maid was assigned to take care of me and run my errands. Though Lung was often away managing his empire of rickshaws, opium, firearms, and prostitution, the house was always filled with people—staff, underlings, bodyguards, servants, visitors. Even with Lung away, guests came to gamble and eat the banquet dishes, whether cooked by his chefs or ordered from famous restaurants.

When Lung was away, his bedroom and study, where I suspected he kept his valuables, were locked. And now that I'd moved in, I did not get into his bedroom at all; indeed, he never asked for sex at all. When he wanted something from me, he'd come to my room. He never said anything about it, but I knew Chinese men feared that pregnant women could contaminate them.

Life shut up in his mansion was thus tedious, especially with no possible opportunity to carry out my plans. So I told Lung I was unbearably homesick and pleaded with him to let me go back to my own place. His permission was as easy as his invitation had been. It was then that I realized that, though he was happy to have another son, I did not matter very much to him.

After I stopped singing at Bright Moon, a new singer was chosen to replace me temporarily. To my disappointment, the audience seemed to get used to her rather quickly. Of course there were still articles in the newspapers conjecturing about my sudden absence, such as this by Rainbow Chang:

Retirement at Nineteen?

It's rumored that our Heavenly Songbird is taking a long break due to some health problem. But she always looks beautiful and healthy. So what can possibly be wrong? Is it because she feels guilty about hurting Shadow at her last appearance that she decided to drop out of Shanghai's entertainment business?

Anyway, she must have made enough money for an early retirement. But at nineteen?

More to follow. . . .
Rainbow Chang

One morning, just seven months into my pregnancy, I started to have pains in my belly. I stayed in bed to rest and sent my amah, Ah Fong, with my driver, Ah Wen, to buy tonic and nutritious herbs for me and my baby. I dozed off but was awakened by even more severe pain, so severe that I couldn't think or do anything. Worse, my servants had not yet returned, so I was alone in my apartment. At first I felt a wave of panic because I had no idea what I could do. If I told Jinying, he'd rush right over, which was dangerous, and I didn't want to deal with either Wang or Lung. The only person I could think of to help me was Madame Lewinsky. I immediately hired a car to take me to her place.

When my teacher opened the door, she cried into my face, "Oh, my dear, are you all right? You're as pale as a ghost!"

She let me in, closed the door, and walked me over to sit on her sofa. Then she sat down next to me and handed me a cup of tea. "What happened, Camilla? Please tell me."

I sipped the burning liquid, my tortured nerves soothed by the hot steam and calming fragrance. "I'm pregnant."

"What? Why didn't you tell me last time you visited me?"

There was nothing to say. So I didn't say anything.

"Tell me who's the father of the baby, and I'll call him."

"I . . . don't know. . . ."

Anyway, I couldn't respond, for the pain in my abdomen came back with a vengeance.

Lewinsky said, her eyes widening in alarm, "I believe you're in labor, Camilla."

"But . . . I . . . the baby is . . . not due yet." I struggled to breathe the words out.

She thought for a while, then said, "Don't worry, I'm here, and I'll take care of you. Back in Russia, I helped my sister give birth to three healthy babies."

"Can you take me to the hospital now?"

"I'm afraid we don't have time. Stay right here. I'll go boil water."

I was breathing heavily. The cramps came and went like the revolving horse that Jinying had taken me to ride. To distract myself from the pain, I tried to focus on the noise and energy from the kitchen. Soon Lewinsky came out and half carried me to her bedroom. She put me into bed, squeezed pillows and towels under my head and body, slipped off my underpants, then spread my legs. My hands held tightly on to the edge of the mattress as moans and groans rolled out from between my trembling lips. Lewinsky quickly left and came back holding a pail of boiling water and a ceramic bowl.

Before I had a chance to ask, she said, "I'll break the bowl and use the shard to cut the umbilical cord. I don't have anything to sterilize the knife, so the inside of the bowl will have to do."

Now the pain was getting so bad that I didn't hear anything except my own screaming. Then I lost consciousness.

I didn't know how long I'd been "gone," but when I woke up, I didn't see any baby, only Lewinsky's pale, exhausted face.

"Where's my . . . baby? Is it a boy or a girl?"

She wiped a tear away with the back of her hand. "I'm so sorry . . . so sorry, Camilla. The baby didn't make it. It lived only for a few hours."

A deadly silence filled the air.

I gathered up courage to ask, "Was it a boy or a girl?'

She sobbed softly. "I'm so sorry, Camilla. It . . . was a boy."

Still too shocked to feel anything, I could only ask the obvious question. "Then where's his body? I want to see him and say goodbye."

She looked alarmed. "Trust me, Camilla, you don't want to see him." She paused to inhale deeply, then blurted out, "While you were asleep, I buried him."

"Where?"

"What's the point in your knowing now?" She picked up a towel and gently wiped my forehead. "Since you don't even know who the father was, it's better that you treat this whole thing like a bad dream and let it fade from your life. Camilla, you're very young, and there will be many chances in the future for you to have babies with someone you love. Now let me cook some soup to revive you. You need to stay right here with me for now. Tomorrow, if you feel strong enough I will call your driver and amah to bring you home."

I was so exhausted that I didn't have any energy left to argue. So I said, "Thank you, Madame Lewinsky," and I fell asleep again. I slept restlessly, sometimes even imagining I heard a baby crying faintly.

When I woke up early the next morning, I told Lewinsky that I wanted to go home. To my surprise, this time she didn't insist that I stay.

"All right, if that's what you want. I will come to visit you tomorrow and bring you some soup."

"Thank you," I replied, my voice feeble.

When my driver arrived, Lewinsky saw me off at the door, but her expression was strange. The whole atmosphere didn't feel right to me. Where was my baby? If he was dead, where was the body?

Had I really just given birth to another life—or a death? Or had this all been a dream, an illusion, a failed magic show?

Why hadn't Lewinsky let me see my baby boy, even dead?

I had never had a chance to call someone Mother, and now I had lost someone who would have called me that. My very bad karma.

❧ 26 ❧

Two Ceremonies

I told Lung by telephone the sad news that my baby was stillborn. To my surprise, instead of being furious at me or at fate, he asked nervously, "Was it a boy?"

"Unfortunately it was, Master Lung."

"Hmm . . . that's too bad."

"But, Master Lung, I promise next time I'll give you a handsome and healthy boy."

"You'd better. You know, Camilla, since Jinying is worthless, I need a real son to inherit my business. If you give me a *fengshui* boy next time, then you'll be my number one woman. You understand?"

"Yes, Master Lung."

Only toward the end of our conversation did Lung remember to ask about me. "Why didn't you tell me when you lost the baby?"

"Master Lung, it happened so suddenly, and you were away, remember?"

"Then who helped you?"

"My former singing teacher, a Russian woman."

He didn't respond to that, but said, "I'll ask Zhu to send you some money to help you out."

"Thank you very much, Master Lung."

"All right, call me again when you're fully recovered, and I'll arrange a time for us to get back together."

"I will do that, Master Lung."

After I hung up, I immediately dialed Big Brother Wang's number.

Not to my surprise, my boss's voice had no warmth nor his tone any sympathy. "I assume you're fully recovered by now?"

"Yes, Big Brother Wang."

"You realize you've already been Lung's mistress for almost a year now? So you better get your job done before he gets tired of you."

"I'm so sorry, Big Brother Wang, but everything is so airtight around him, it's really difficult—"

"I don't want excuses, only results. If you don't deliver within a month, you will no longer be needed. And you know what will happen then!" He paused, then asked, "Are you in love with this guy?"

My heart skipped a beat. At first I thought he meant Jinying, that he had found out about our relationship. When I realized he actually meant Lung, I had to bite my tongue hard so as not to burst out laughing.

I said calmly into the receiver, "Of course not."

"Good. Then I'd better read Lung's obituary soon."

"Yes, Big Brother Wang. I promise he'll be dead within a month."

"So, either him or you, you understand? And don't forget his banking documents and the lists."

"I won't, Big Brother Wang."

As soon as I set down the phone, my whole body began to shake uncontrollably. Did Wang think that killing the most powerful gangster head was the same as swatting a fly, squashing a rat, shooting a pigeon? Somehow I had also to get Lung's secret bank account numbers, his secret escape routes, and his secret list of enemies to be assassinated. How was I, a nineteen-year-old girl, to achieve all these, and in thirty days? And Wang had been pretty clear about the consequence for me if I failed.

The last person I called to reveal my baby's birth and death to was Jinying. I'd delayed telling him because I dreaded he'd be so upset, he would end up doing something drastic.

After I told him the horrible news, the young master insisted on coming to see me. Fearing that if I refused, he'd break down and tell his father, this time I agreed. However, I was not going to see him in my house or his, but in a cheap hotel room I'd book under a fake name. In addition, we'd both dress down, so the chance that we'd be recognized would be minimal.

Though Jinying was not happy about the cheap hotel, he seemed to forget about it as soon as we were alone together. I told him how Madame Lewinsky had helped me with the birth but that our baby boy had died. He listened quietly until I finished, then burst out crying, screaming and slamming his fists on the bed.

Before I could react, there were knockings on the thin wall, followed by a coarse male voice yelling from the other side, "Lower your fucking voice, won't you?! You want everybody to know that you have a big dick and are fucking her hard, eh?"

Jinying willed himself to stop, wiping his tear-streaked face with a handkerchief. Finally he calmed down, pulled me to him, and rested his head on my chest.

"Why didn't you call me that day?"

I looked down at his sad face. "You know I couldn't. I'd told your father the baby was his."

The young master didn't respond.

A long silence passed, and he said, "Let's make love."

"Here and now? Why would you even suggest it?"

"So we can have another baby."

That was the last thing I needed now, so I told him it was too soon, that I was still sore.

A week later, I went back to sing at the Bright Moon. I was glad that my fans had not forgotten me; they greeted my return with flowers and cheers. A few even brought me jewelry and, best of all, American silver dollars and gold coins.

Many newspapers quoted a Chinese proverb to describe my admirers' feelings: "A day without seeing you seems as long as three autumns."

But Rainbow Chang's article said something very different.

Camilla Came Back from Her Long Break

Finally, our beloved Heavenly Songbird Camilla has finished her vacation and begun to sing again. Though I am very glad that she has returned, I can't help but wonder, why was she gone for so long?

According to what I've heard, there are three possibilities: a private vacation with her patron, Master Lung; treatment for some horrible disease; something that lasts for nine months.

Of course the last one is just from my wildest imagination. Because, if Camilla was pregnant, where is her baby?

The songstress's absence reminds me of the other skeleton woman, the magician Shadow. What happened to her after Camilla accidentally sliced her finger? No one hears about her anymore. Will she make a big comeback like Camilla did? Or will she use her own magic to disappear into thin air, this time forever?

Well, keep your eyes and ears ready for more news soon.

More to follow. . . .
Rainbow Chang

I closed the newspaper and inhaled deeply to calm myself. If Rainbow Chang could really find out the truth, I'd be the ready-to-be-mincemeat on her chopping board. However, I couldn't think of anyone who might have leaked the news. Lung would probably tell Zhu and Gao, but they were as tight-lipped as corpses. Wang never told anybody anything, but Jinying might go whining to a friend. Then I thought of Lewinsky. Would she tell? As far as I knew, very unlikely. So it must be just Rainbow's conjecture. Thus reassuring myself, I felt a little better.

* * *

One evening when I was taking off my makeup in the Bright Moon's dressing room, to my surprise, Gao came in.

He studied my reflection in the mirror. "Miss Camilla, please get ready quickly. I am here to take you to a Flying Dragons initiation ceremony."

Of course this was an order, not a request or an invitation. I had heard of these initiation ceremonies but had never seen one, for it is something extremely secretive and esoteric. Outsiders would never be permitted even a glimpse. Women, deemed inferior with their polluted bodies, would offend the gods and so were absolutely forbidden to participate, lest the men's pure *yang* energy be put off balance by the woman's *yin*.

So I could not imagine why Lung wanted me to come to this very secret ritual. I asked Gao why he was doing so.

"Because you are his lucky star. He believes your special *qi* keeps him alive, ever since the amulet you gave him stopped the bullet."

Inside the car on the way to our destination—Gao wouldn't say where—the head bodyguard cast me a deep glance in the rearview mirror. "Miss Camilla, I'm very sorry about your baby."

"Thank you for your concern, Gao, but I've fully recovered." I paused, then asked again, "Why does Master Lung want me to attend this ceremony? I may be his lucky star, but he has never included me in something so secret before."

"It is because of your immortal boy."

I knew this was a euphemistic way to refer to my dead baby.

"How do so many people know about him?" I felt alarmed but tried to stay calm.

He shook his head. "Just us, Miss Camilla. You don't have to worry."

"But why are you taking me to this initiation ceremony now?"

"Master Lung's fortune-teller told him to hold a special ceremony for his son. A baby not given a proper burial will grow up in hell and one day come back to haunt his father."

But if this were true, did it mean that my baby would come back to haunt Jinying? I felt tears sting my eyes, but I wouldn't let them fall. "But, Gao, you still haven't answered my question. What do I have to do with the initiation ceremony?"

"During the ceremony, we make offerings to heaven, earth, the four directions, our protective gods, and our ancestors. Master Lung will put a small statue of a baby on the altar and give him a name. In that way, your son will get offerings and respect, and his soul will be appeased. Then he will be content as he waits for his next incarnation."

"I am grateful that my son is being respected like this. Thank you for letting me know."

"You're very welcome, Miss Camilla."

Some silence passed before he said, his expression very tender, "Miss Camilla, I am so sad about your baby. And I worry about you all the time now."

"I'm fine, really." It would be disastrous if I let him probe further into the dangerous zones of my life. Then I suddenly realized that he must wonder if the son I'd lost was his!

"Miss Camilla, but if you ever need anything, please let me know. You know I'll do anything for you."

"I will, Gao," I said gently, "and thank you."

The car gradually slowed to a stop, and I was surprised to see that we had stopped at the entrance of a cemetery. Gao hopped out of the car, went around to open my door, then held out his hand. I placed my small one in his much bigger, scarred one. He squeezed my fingers gently, and I could instantly feel my body being warmed by his strong, fervent love. Seconds later, he let go of my hand, then signaled me to walk with him to where the ceremony was to take place.

A bright full moon was set against a dark blue sky. Rows of graves loomed eerily in the distance, like pillows floating on a night sea. A rotten smell permeated my nostrils, and I hoped it was vegetation rather than corpses. Gao gently steered me by my elbow toward a group of people all dressed in black and moving around stiffly like ghosts. I widened my eyes to watch, in case beings from the other realm would sneak out from their resting places. Next Gao led me past two rows of people toward a makeshift altar. Tall white candles burned brightly in the gloom, rendering the ceme-

tery even more surreal and haunting. I'd heard that it was in cemeteries that the Flying Dragons held their meetings, performed ritu-
als, and even carried out tortures. They faced no risk of discovery
because at night the living Chinese would not dare pass through
the land of their ghostly countrymen. Whatever was about to happen, I suddenly thought that I did not want to see it.

I spotted Zhu and nodded to him.

He nodded back. "Miss Camilla, tonight you will see what no
other woman has ever been allowed to see. Master Lung invited
only his most trusted people for the ceremony. Now stay right here,
do not speak, and do what you are told."

Gao nodded to me, then walked to take his place with the
others.

The Flying Dragons gang members were all dressed alike in
black Western suits, black shirts, and black ties. These hard-looking
men formed two parallel rows, like a geese's outstretched wings,
flanking the makeshift altar. Lung sat in front of the altar facing
south like a king, while his subordinates faced north toward him.
The gangster head was also dressed in black except that his tie was
red, showing his position as the boss. Once he saw me, he waved
me to come to him.

Approaching him, I bowed. "Master Lung, good evening. I'm
honored to be invited here."

"Camilla, you're very privileged to witness this ceremony
tonight. Just watch and be silent." Both his expression and tone
were cold and serious, with no trace of his usual jocular manner.
"Now step back. I have something important to discuss with Mr.
Zhu."

He didn't mention "our" dead baby, but in this bloodcurdling
situation I dared not disobey his injunction to silence.

After I backed away, Lung and his right-hand man conferred in
solemn tones. I took the chance to study the different items on the
huge altar: a painting of General Guan flanked by two famous his-
torical figures, Zhang Fei and Liu Bei, sworn blood brothers with
whom he had fought and won numerous battles. Above the painting a slogan was brushed in ancient calligraphy: *Righteousness
under heaven.* On either side of this painting were numerous red

papers with Chinese sayings in ink. These were *fu,* magic talismans that are only understood by Daoist priests who possess the power to communicate with the spirits of the dead and the gods. Gangsters, like most Chinese, believe these talismans will protect them from evil forces. Ironically, they never seem to realize that they themselves are the evil forces.

Resting on the altar were sumptuous offerings: flowers, fruits, plates of dyed-red longevity buns, even a whole roasted baby pig. Then my eyes landed on the back of the altar, where, almost hidden by the piles of offerings, was a small statue of a baby boy. Pasted on it was a small piece of paper with the characters: *Lung's son Jinxiong.*

I wanted to blurt out, "It's not your son, but your son's, Jinying's!"

I bit my tongue and pressed my lips tightly together. When the shock subdued, I felt tears stinging my eyes, but I blinked them back. Then it hit me that this child I'd lost was actually the grandson of Lung, the man I was supposed to kill. Why would heaven allot me such an impossible, horrible life? My body began to tremble involuntarily. But I bit my tongue and pinched my thigh hard until the shaking stopped.

Gao sauntered toward me, leaned close, and asked softly, "Miss Camilla, are you not feeling well?"

"I'm fine. It's just chilly and scary here in the cemetery." I managed to offer a half smile as I pulled my shawl tightly around my chest. "Please tend to more important things."

"You want my jacket?"

"No, I'm really fine, thank you," I said, thinking silently, *Are you out of your mind, offering me your jacket in front of everyone?*

To distract him, I asked, "The young master is not here for the ceremony?"

Gao said, "He was not invited."

"Why not?'

"Because Master Lung won't let him see what's going to happen tonight."

"Which is what, exactly?"

He ignored my question but gestured toward the baby statue.

"Master Lung's baby is here to receive his due respect and offerings. Thus his ghost will be empowered to fight his father's enemies and protect his fortune."

So Lung was using the dead baby for his own benefit, to turn a tragedy into something beneficial!

My thoughts were interrupted by a booming voice calling out something I couldn't grasp. Suddenly, all the young initiates took off their shoes, socks, and tops, revealing bared chests tattooed with soaring dragons. Then all went onto their knees and moved as if crawling through imaginary doors. They stood back up and swore loudly in unison:

"We, members of the Flying Dragons gang, here, under the moon, swear our loyalty to the order and its sun and head, Master Lung. If we ever betray the master or this order, we step onto a path of no return. If caught, we will be beheaded and our souls forever condemned to burning hell. Even if we are able to quit the Flying Dragons with our heads on our shoulders, we will be murdered by bandits, or struck down by lightning. . . ."

After this poisonous declaration, all the initiates went up to the altar and continued to swear, voices and expressions even more vehement.

Gao explained, "They are swearing the thirty-six oaths."

"After becoming a Flying Dragons member, I will treat my sworn brothers' parents and relatives as my own. If I fail to do this, I will be struck dead by thunderbolts.

"I will never disclose secrets of the Flying Dragons, not even to my wife, children, or parents. If I fail in this, I will be impaled by ten thousand swords.

"I will never steal cash or property from my sworn brothers. If I do this, I will be crushed by ten thousand boulders.

"If I ever deny my membership and try to leave the Flying Dragons, I will be burned by ten thousand flames. . . ."

These threatening words, delivered in portentous tones, frightened me and left me drained. So my eyes wandered back to the baby's statue. But rather than feeling comforted by the ritual, I felt sorry that my son's little spirit might be witnessing this disturbing event. I closed my eyes, only to be startled by a shout, "AAAH-HHH . . . !"

I opened my eyes and saw a bloody chicken head plunge onto the ground. Zhu held up a bloodstained knife in one hand and the body of the chicken in his other. He upended the headless chicken, still seizuring, and squeezed its blood into a row of small cups. While he was busy with the unlucky chicken, another gang member began to burn a small stack of yellow talisman papers, then poured the ashes into the same cups. After that, Zhu made a signal, and all the initiates came to the front of the altar, took up a cup, and drank the ash-spiced chicken blood in a single gulp.

What happened next was even worse. One young man had picked up and drunk from a cup that was chipped. Suddenly his face turned as pale as the ashes. Zhu and another bodyguard went up to the man, took him by his arms, then dragged him out of our sight. Seconds later, a loud gunshot sliced through the deathly silence of the cemetery.

Lung's voice suddenly rang loud and clear in the suffocating air. "Brothers, now you know the fate that awaits anyone who betrays us by leaking our secrets! The chip on his cup was the mark of the traitor."

No one spoke.

The boss spoke again. "Brothers, you just witnessed how a spy meets his disgraceful end!"

At the word *spy,* my face turned pale, and my body trembled so hard, I could barely stand. Fortunately no one was paying any attention to me. How did Lung detect that this man was a spy? Did he, like me, work for Big Brother Wang? Would I end up like him? The only comforting thought was that he was granted a quick death instead of having to suffer horrible tortures. If they found out about me, would I be granted the same mercy? Or would Gao secretly let me escape? I knew he loved me, but he was a sworn member of the gang, after all.

When I saw Gao, I thought he looked a bit shaken. Or maybe that was only my wishful thinking. Then I realized why these ceremonies were held in cemeteries—so that any corpses could be conveniently dumped into waiting pits!

If any of the initiates or members were disturbed by this cruel spectacle, they did not show it.

A plump, middle-aged gangster announced, "Now please prepare for the bath of purification!"

Out of nowhere, a yellow-robed Daoist priest appeared and walked up to the altar. He meditated for a few seconds, then began to mutter some kind of esoteric mantra as he moved around in rhythmic steps. As he was dancing, his right hand wielded a sword, while his left hand performed peculiar gestures. Next he went up to the altar, picked up a willow branch, dipped it into a bowl of water, and flicked the water onto the baby's statue. After that, he continued to chant and dance, flicking more of the sacred water onto the ground in front of the altar.

Gao's voice rose, startling me. "The priest is singing the mantra not only for the baby but also for the traitor."

I was surprised to hear this. "But why the traitor?"

"The Flying Dragons respect all dead people, traitors or not."

I felt another chill. Maybe Lung would perform the same ceremony for me after he found out I was a spy and snapped my neck with his callous hands? Of course I knew full well that the real reason for the "respect" for the traitor was to appease the ghost of the murdered man so he would not come back for revenge.

Finally, everyone was given a basin to wash his face, upper body, and feet, after which they put on white robes and straw sandals.

Gao spoke again, "This is the end of the ceremony. These young men's old lives have been washed away by the sacred water; now they are reborn as triad members. "

Lung stepped close to the initiates and announced, "The initiation ceremony of the Flying Dragons is now over. Let me congratulate our new brothers!"

Thunderous applause exploded in the ghostly air. Though the members smiled, I could tell their facial muscles didn't relax; their smiles were, as the saying goes, "smiles only with the skin, not the flesh."

When the cheering and applause finally died down, Lung spoke again. "Now as brothers we will celebrate with a great banquet at the Grand Palace Restaurant!"

More cheering and applause burst out, turning the sinister cemetery into a ghastly festival.

❦ 27 ❦

A Wandering Baby

As soon as I arrived home from the frightening ceremony, I undressed and climbed into bed. Sleep came quickly but was troubled. I dreamed again of my baby boy, but this time he had a name—Jinjin, Little Handsome. This was different from the name that Lung had given him at the ritual, which was Jinxiong, meaning handsome and mighty. His living son's name, Jinying, meant handsome hero. But apparently just a handsome hero was not mighty enough for Lung, who was still hoping to spawn a handsome gangster.

In my dream, Jinjin strutted around my bed on his strong, chubby legs, like the baby Buddha who took seven steps right after he was born.

Then Jinjin stood in front of me and bowed deeply. "Mother, your son Jinjin pays you respect."

I smiled at my dark-haired little cutie as I studied his features—big, double-lidded eyes, pencil-inked, crescent-moon-shaped eyebrows, high-bridged nose, rosy cheeks. Smiling, his pink lips resembled two petals dancing in the breeze.

"Little Jinjin, come and give your mother a hug."

To my utter surprise, he stubbornly shook his round head. "No."

Did I scare him with my overly high-pitched entreaty? I lowered my Heavenly Songbird's voice. "Jinjin, be a good boy, and give your mother a hug please."

"No," he said again in his innocent yet stubborn voice, tugging at my heart.

"But why not? I'm your mother!"

"Because I am a ghost."

"Please, Jinjin, I'm your mother, and I love you still!"

"Mama, no one, ghost or spirit, has ever crossed from the *yin* world into the *yang* one. We are forever separated by death."

"But I love you," I pleaded, tears rolling down my cheeks.

"Then how come you didn't love my father? He saved your life, but you broke his heart."

I asked, "Who is your father? Do you know for certain?"

He nodded. "You know who. But it is you who is most tortured by your own bitter heartlessness. Why can't you love or show some concern for my father?"

"I love you dearly, Jinjin, but you left me alone in this dusty world! I also love your father dearly, but up here in the land of the living, fate won't let me!"

"Nah, you don't love me or my father!"

Now he began to bawl loudly. I could ignore his babyish reproaches but not his crying. "Jinjin, come let your mama hug and kiss you; then you will know how much she loves you. Please!"

"No," he said, vigorously shaking his head as he started to walk away on his chubby feet.

He looked so cute and adorable that I could feel my heart split with a wrenching *crack*.

"Jinjin, wait! Where are you going?" I reached out to his retreating back.

"To find my father who loves me and you more than anything else in the world!"

"Please don't leave your mother! Stay, please. . . ." But as I watched, he floated away from me. I screamed. "But, Jinjin, you are in the *yin* realm, and your father is here with me in the *yang* world. So how are you going to see him?"

"He loves me so much that I believe he can resurrect me from death like the scholar resurrected his beloved Liniang! You wait and see."

This referred to the opera *Peony Pavilion* that Jinying had taken me to, where the scholar used the power of love to resurrect his beloved woman from the grave.

Suddenly my baby's heart seemed to be beating within my own. Then suddenly, the beating ceased.

I cried out, "My son, are you all right?"

"Mama, my heart is broken, for you and my father!"

"Let me help you, please!"

He shook his head, turned around, and began to toddle away from me. "Mama, I have to go now." He scurried away, as if leaving a trail of broken pieces from his heart.

"Please come back, Jinjin! Please! Your heart is here!"

But Jinjin did not turn around. His body slowly faded from my eyes, but as it did, he seemed to grow into a handsome young man, looking just like his father. . . .

I awakened to find my pillow soaked with my tears, warm but hopeless.

The dream stayed in my mind for many days. I am not a superstitious person, but somehow the initiation ceremony and the dream unsettled me so much that I decided I must appease the departed soul of my baby, just in case it was Lung's, with his vindictive genes.

Lung had already carried out a ritual for him, but on the other hand, if he was not the father, the offerings might not reach Jinjin in the *yin* world. So to be sure, I decided to have a ceremony just for my baby and myself, and I would be sure to mention Jinying. If my baby's soul was appeased, I believed he'd stop entering my dreams to sadden me so. Of course I liked seeing him; I just didn't want to see him suffering.

So the next day I had a Daoist priest came to my house to perform the ceremony. Inside my bedroom, he set up a small altar surrounded by red and yellow talismans filled with esoteric characters and symbols.

The priest was a fortyish, solemn-mannered man, looking small in an oversized yellow robe embroidered with golden soaring cranes and *Yijing* trigrams.

He said in a low, sonorous voice, "Miss Camilla, let me first explain to you about babies who die. Please don't talk or ask questions until am I finished. You understand?"

I nodded respectfully. As he began, I understood the reason for his admonition, as he was quite long-winded.

"We all have two souls, the *hun* and *po*. When we die, the *hun* soul rises up to heaven and becomes a spirit, while the *po* remains with our corpse in the grave. But in the womb the child possesses only the *po,* so if he dies unborn, the soul cannot go up to heaven but is trapped here below. I must warn you that your baby's *po* soul may become a hungry ghost, wandering in misery seeking revenge. To protect yourself, you must give him a proper burial."

"But I passed out, so I never even saw him! The woman who helped me refused to even tell me where he is buried."

"Then it is imperative that you have the proper ritual for your baby. Since he lost his chance for a full life in the *yang* world, he needs to be fed and nurtured in the *yin* one. Remember, Miss Camilla, even if your baby did have a chance to experience this life for a few hours, he never experienced his mother's love."

Upon hearing this, I burst out crying.

He ignored my outburst and went on officiously, "I'm going to chant incantations and mantras to invoke and liberate your dead baby's soul. But because of what you have told me, to prevent him from becoming a wandering ghost, I will need to do a ritual in my temple every day for a year."

I cried more, even though I knew this was probably just a way for the priest to squeeze even more money out of me.

The priest adjusted the embroidered sleeves of his robe and instructed me, "Now kneel in front of the altar, put your hands together, and listen to my chanting. Even if you don't understand, concentrate on my energy and the inflection of my voice. The best is if you can also silently recite a prayer to release your child from all suffering."

He inspected the few things on the altar that he'd positioned: a small wooden baby figure, which represented my died-few-hours-after-birth baby, a small bowl of rice soup, a bottle of milk, sweets, toys, and flowers.

He spoke again, his voice turned somber. "Your baby is wandering and suffering without a mother or a father to love and care for him. When I recite the mantra, I'll summon his soul here to enjoy the food, gifts, and especially to receive the love of his mother, you. Even though your baby's body has perished, his living soul will still feel your love and warmth, and he'll be happy and greatly comforted. You understand?"

I nodded, my tears continuing to flow.

"Right after I've started the ceremony, please focus your love and *qi* on the wooden figure. During the ritual, I will summon his soul to reside in it, then activate his soul with my mantra."

Would my baby really descend onto the altar and reside in the wooden figurine? As if aware of my doubt, the Daoist master explained. "Miss Camilla, because you have never cultivated your spirituality, you may not see or feel anything now. But, unlike you, I have practiced and cultivated for thirty years to open my third eye, so I am able to see beings from the other realm."

Now memories of all that had happened rose up in my mind: my loveless childhood, my life as Big Brother Wang's spy, the cold, black water of the Seine, Jinying loving me enough to risk his life to save mine, blood spurting from Shadow's finger, my labor pains, Madame Lewinsky telling me my baby was dead, the terrible ritual in the cemetery, Wang's threats on my life, and, now that ghosts and spirits were about to be brought into my home, I felt as if my grip on reality was finally slipping. Had I really had a baby? Was he really dead? And why did I feel such love for a baby I had felt inside me but never seen? In my dream, Jinjin had blamed me for not loving his father. But since I'd never been loved, could I be blamed if I was not capable of it myself? Or was I capable of it, after all? The master had said that I'd never cultivated anything spiritual, but all I had been taught was scheming and dissembling. Was the fault with my fate or with me?

The ritual went on for almost an hour. Of course I didn't understand a word of what was said or even if this pacifying-my-baby drama was anything more than a scam. When the priest finished, I bowed and thanked him, then gave him his fee in a red envelope. I also told him that this ceremony should be strictly private between him and me. Feeling the thickness and weight of the red envelope, he promptly agreed.

Before he left, the priest gathered up the items he had placed on the altar. "I'll bring these back to my temple and place them together with all the other babies' figurines, portraits, and offerings. In that case, your boy will have company, and I will continue to look after him. You understand?"

I nodded, and then a thought hit me, and I asked, "Did you really see my baby?

He looked at me curiously. "Of course. I told you, I opened my third eye."

"Can you tell me what he looks like?"

"A very handsome boy with big, double-lidded eyes."

"Then do you know his name?"

He hesitated for a few seconds before he said, "No, since he never speaks of himself." He paused, then smiled. "Anyway, your baby will grow up to be a very handsome and intelligent boy."

"But my baby is dead!"

"Hmm. All right, I'd better go now." He began to put each item from the altar into his cloth bag. "Take very good care of yourself, Miss Camilla. Don't worry, your baby will be looked after very well in the temple. Good-bye."

"Thank you, Master, and good-bye." I bowed again, walked him to door, and saw him out.

I wasn't sure I even believed in the ritual, but now, afterward, I somehow felt my son's presence. It was a strange feeling, because it felt warm and cold, happy and sad, empty yet full at the same time.

At least I knew there was love in this cold world, and I had had the luck to taste it, even if only in a dream.

28

The Pink Skeleton Empire

Although I felt surprisingly relieved after the ritual, I felt I had no choice but to try to set aside my thoughts about my baby so as to get on with my mission. I knew Wang meant his threats. But now that I realized Lung was my baby's grandfather, how could I have him killed? Unfortunately I didn't have anyone to ask for advice, certainly not Big Brother Wang. He wouldn't care about any of this; he just wanted Lung eliminated, so he could take his place as the number one gangster.

While in this state of confusion, I unexpectedly received a letter from Rainbow Chang.

> Dear Miss Camilla,
> I am glad that you are recovered and have come back to sing at the Bright Moon. Recently I heard a lot of things about you but am not sure what is true. So please visit me at my place so we can talk. Or so I can cheer you up.
> I sincerely hope that you will grant me the pleasure and honor of accepting my invitation.
>
> Yours fondly,
> Rainbow Chang

I didn't want to go, but I didn't think I could turn down her invitation, either. In China, journalists are called "crownless kings" because they can destroy as quickly as a king. They only difference is that they remove your head with words instead of axes.

Rainbow Chang's apartment was situated in an expensive area inside the French Concession. My driver let me off in front of a majestic row of white houses facing a wide boulevard. Tall poplar trees lined the street, like sentries to protect the rich and famous, as well as to shelter them from thunder, rain, and lightning.

An amah opened the door, let me in, then led me through a foyer with a gilded mirror above a console table into the living room. Inside a spacious, Western-decorated room sat Rainbow, ambiguously dressed as usual in a stark white suit with pink tie. As always, she was attended by an entourage of young, pretty women clad in pink silk or lace dresses. In their midst, the regal-looking gossip columnist reclined on her divan, smoking a cigarette in a long holder. The girls sipped drinks and chatted languidly with one another. A few fussed over Rainbow like Gao and Zhu over their boss, Lung.

"Camilla, welcome to the Pink Skeleton Empire!"

Smiling, the gossip columnist extinguished her cigarette and got up to greet me. In an elegant gesture she lifted my hand to her lips and pressed it tenderly.

"Enchanted, Miss Camilla. Your presence brightens my humble residence."

Her manner was as gallant as a Frenchman's. One never knew what she did with her many pink-clad "mistresses." Could it be that she would ask me to become one? Although I found the idea ridiculous, I was nevertheless intrigued. Did they follow her into her bedchamber, like the concubines of the ancient emperors?

Rainbow took my hand and led me to the sofa. With a flick of her hand, she dismissed the three pink ladies who'd been sitting with her when I'd entered. She then motioned me to sit beside her as I was handed a glass of pink Champagne.

"To your beauty and fame, Miss Camilla," the gossip columnist said, then raised her glass as all the ladies raised theirs in unison.

Rainbow opened a silver cigarette box and held it out to me. "Please?"

"Thank you Rainbow." I shook my head. "But I don't smoke."

"Never tempted to try?"

"I'm afraid not."

She asked teasingly, "Why not?"

"I fear smoking will harm my voice."

But that was not exactly true. Sometimes I did smoke with Lung to please him. And I'd also smoked with Gao on the luxury cruise ship, when he'd sent me messages of love in heart-shaped smoke rings.

"You're right. And you should protect your most valuable asset. However, it is a pity, because I believe you would look very elegant smoking, especially with a long jade or ivory holder." She winked her false lashes. "Not to mention unbearably sexy." As if to emphasize the point, she took a cigarette for herself and drew deeply on it as one of the ladies held out a candle to light it for her.

She let out a chuckle. "Smoking will give you the image of a bad, wicked woman. But of course you're not wicked. You're our innocent Heavenly Songbird."

Did she really believe I was innocent, or was she hinting that she knew better? There was no way to know; everything about Rainbow was ambiguous.

Someone put on a gramophone, and Johann Strauss's *Blue Danube* filled the room. Three pairs of girls held each other and began to caress the polished floor with their feet.

Rainbow stood up and held her hand out to me in invitation to dance. "May I?"

I let her take my hand and lead me to the middle of the room. We began to swirl. It was a strange feeling for me, who spent most of my time in a house filled with tough men, to be in this pastel-colored room filled with young girls moving their slim bodies sensuously against each other.

What was this Pink Skeleton Empire about?

Holding me rather closer than I expected, Rainbow whispered tenderly into my ear, "Miss Camilla, I'm really sorry for your loss."

My heart skipped a beat. What did she mean? It could not be possible that she had found out about my baby!

As my mind was reeling, wondering what she knew, she spoke again in her insinuating tone. "Your friend Shadow, do you miss her?"

Did she guess my intent was to rid Shanghai, and myself, of the interloper magician?

"You know, Camilla, I'm very fond of beautiful girls, and that's why I write about them, especially talented ones like you and Shadow. But poor Shadow . . . what really happened to her? I meant to ask you for a long time, but then you suddenly disappeared. Why doesn't she reappear like you did?"

I smiled conspiratorially. "Rainbow, I'm sure *you* know what happened." I tilted my head toward the girls in the room. "Nothing escapes you and your pink entourage's eyes, am I not right?"

She smiled handsomely, holding me tighter to her tall, slim body that smelled of cigarettes and men's cologne. "Maybe I do, maybe not. Do you think she'll come back?"

"What do you mean by 'come back'?"

"To perform magic again, of course."

"I'm afraid it'll take a magician to find out, not a singer. Anyway, I'm sorry, I really have no idea."

Although I definitely hoped not. But I knew that even after the "accident," Shadow was determined to do another show and had been planning to ask Lung for sponsorship. Now many months had passed, and I'd not heard anything from her, nor had Lung mentioned anything about a visit from her. I would have inquired about the magician, but I'd been distracted by my pregnancy. She must be nursing her wound, if not physical then emotional, and preparing for a big comeback. It was most unlikely that she had left Shanghai. Like me, she was a person who did not give up easily. I made a mental note to call her.

The gossip columnist's voice brought my mind back to the present. "No idea?" Then abruptly she dipped me down, then lifted me up, making me dizzy and a little uneasy.

She raised one painted eyebrow. "I believe Shadow is planning a big comeback, only waiting for sponsorship. It'll be a huge disappointment if she doesn't. I really enjoy watching you two perform together, so sexy and sensational."

"But what about your girls here? Aren't they equally sexy and sensational?"

She laughed. "Ha-ha! Maybe, but they serve other purposes."

"What kind?"

"They don't entertain me like you and Shadow do. They work for me." She tilted her head to emit a laugh.

"In what way?"

"I pay them handsomely, and they get me information. Besides, I've gotten famous for being surrounded by them. Many people are willing to trade secrets in exchange for an invitation here."

A clever strategy. Honor the famous and prominent by an invitation to a luxurious and unique house filled with beautiful girls, where they can drink Champagne, gossip, and at least hope it will turn into an orgy. Rainbow had built up a mysterious empire, and everyone was dying to take a peek. Now that I had been granted this honor, it was assumed I would be grateful and therefore help her in return. But what did she want? Information or sex or both? But what could I really offer? Sex would be dangerous and information doubly so.

As if reading my mind, Rainbow smiled broadly, revealing smooth, pearly teeth. "I love to collect famous, beautiful women. Besides being a pleasure to the eyes, they help my business. Who doesn't want to be around handsome people?"

I cast glances at the dancing, chatting, drinking beauties. "They're indeed gorgeous."

She paused to look at me in a way that made me feel quite uncomfortable. "But, Camilla, no one can compete with you. No one comes close. The moon itself would be dimmed by your beauty, and the flowers would stop blooming to let you shine."

"Overpraise, Rainbow."

Finally the music stopped, and Rainbow led me back to sit on the sofa. Minutes later, one of the pink ladies came up to the gossip columnist and whispered something into her ear.

Rainbow smiled handsomely. "Excuse me, Camilla, I have to take an important phone call. So I'm afraid I will have to leave you for a while." She turned to the girl. "Nightingale, please entertain Miss Camilla until I come back. Get her anything she wants, and answer any question she asks."

Nightingale, about my age with a sweet, round face, responded with an expansive smile. "Of course I'll do that, Miss Chang."

Rainbow lifted my hand to her lips, impressed them on my hand, and walked away.

Nightingale said, a little shyly, "Miss Camilla, your name has been thundering in my ears for a long time. Welcome here."

I said to the face across from me, which was pretty but easily forgettable, "Thanks, Nightingale. So are you also working for Rainbow?"

She nodded. "Tonight you're invited to have a taste of Miss Rainbow's Pink Skeleton Empire."

I cast glances at the other party girls. "And . . . who are they?"

"Spies, informants, seductresses."

Upon hearing the word *spy,* I felt a jolt. Did Rainbow already suspect me as one and thus want to recruit me?

Nightingale flung her shoulder-length hair, smiling. "How did you think Miss Chang gets all the material to write in her column?"

"So what's the purpose of inviting me here?"

She took a small sip of her Champagne. "To be her friend— what else? Of course since you're already a famous singer, she's not going to recruit you like us—"

I interrupted. "But I don't think I can do anything to help."

"I think Miss Chang wants some juicy gossip about you and Master Lung."

"But we're already in the gossip columns."

"I know, but I think Miss Chang also wants to know more about Lung, and who knows him better than you?"

But were they so naive as to think I'd tell my patron's secrets for a glass of Champagne and a dance? Or that I even knew any of his secrets to tell?

This whole thing was getting weirder and weirder. Now I suspected that Rainbow had deliberately left Nightingale with me to feel me out, which she was doing in a not very subtle way. But judging by Rainbow's column, it was not her style to waste time beating around the bush.

Nightingale spoke. "Anyway, you'll find out soon. Tonight this party is just a getting-acquainted warm-up."

This was definitely turning out to be more complicated than I'd hoped.

The girl went on. "I'm sure you can tell that the head of our Pink Skeleton Empire is smitten with you." She looked at me, her eyes teasing.

This was definitely heading in a wrong direction. "But she already has all these girls. . . ."

"Yes, but no one is as unique, talented, and intriguing as you. You know, there are tons of pretty women in Shanghai, and they come and go, just like your friend Shadow."

Now I was wondering if they knew more about Shadow than I did, so I asked, "What has happened to her?"

"We are sure she'll come back."

"What makes you think that?"

"She's getting famous. No one is so stupid to abandon one's fame like that." She paused to see my reaction. "Besides, she has her boyfriend here."

I tried to act calm. "Oh, really? I had no idea. She never told me she had a boyfriend."

"He's Master Lung's son."

That was completely unexpected. "Where did you hear that from?"

"One of our girls saw them at the Bright Moon Nightclub during one of your performances."

It must have been that night nearly a year ago that I'd tried to match up the young master and the magician. So it was old news. Strangely, I still felt a pang of jealousy.

"I heard that she's trying to befriend Master Lung, too."

Of course, that was also my doing and also old news. I studied the round face in front of me, trying to decipher what was going on here and why I should be part of it. All my instincts told me I should handle this with extreme caution.

Finally Rainbow returned from her private phone call. She sent away all the girls and treated me to a private dinner with expensive wine and gourmet food served to us by two maids. Rainbow was seemingly casual, but somehow questions about Lung kept coming up. I replied with unimportant details such as what he'd had to eat during our visit to Paris, how he took me to Hermès to shop, and the like. I was even more uncomfortable with some of her other questions that concerned his personal habits, such as: what restaurants did he like, when was he home with me, who accompanied him when he went out, and the like. Surely she would not risk publishing such dangerous details in her column. Nor would I risk revealing anything to her about Lung's usual routines. Whenever such questions were asked, I'd change the subject to something else.

Nor did I like her rather personal questions and intimations about my life. I was sure if she sniffed something unusual, especially if it was sexual, she'd prey on me like a vulture on a corpse.

But I dared not offend her, and so I put up with her advances, even let her kiss me on the lips and squeeze my waist when we said good-bye. My strategy was to keep her curious about me so we could stay friends, and hopefully she'd keep writing good things about me. If unfortunately she did find out something about me, then I guessed I would have no choice but to pay her off or be her mistress or, more likely, both. I was sure she was not supporting her sybaritic lifestyle on her newspaper salary alone.

I had no intention of letting her turn me into a *real* skeleton, either with her pen or with what she said about me behind my back.

❧ 29 ❧

The Great Escape

My visit to Rainbow Chang's Pink Skeleton Empire unnerved me. She had an agenda that I could not figure out. Why was Nightingale so sure that Shadow would return? I knew that Rainbow and, I assumed, her assistants, never said anything without a reason. So Shadow must be planning a surprise re-entry into Shanghai, and Rainbow had decided to leak that to me through her assistant. And, while the dinner à deux might have been partly to seduce me, the questions she had asked about Lung were not simply small talk.

During the following days, besides wondering how to deal with Rainbow without getting trapped in some scheme too subtle for me to understand, I was also thinking about Shadow. The dreams about my baby had made me look at this cold world differently. Now that I felt deep love for my little Jinjin, I felt some understanding for the magician's life, which was as difficult as my own. We were rivals, but I could still have some sympathy for her.

The Chinese say, "Even flying away, a bird leaves its melodious cry; even dying, a person wants to leave a mark on the world." Doesn't everyone struggle and work hard so we will be remembered? Shadow and I did, too—but totally alone.

Everyone would prefer to be a magnificent dragon soaring in heaven than a canary in a cage. The small fish in a pond would rather roam the oceans; the hen in the farmyard would rather be a crane spreading its wings. Why had I tried so hard to prevent Shadow from succeeding?

Why had I been trying to destroy this girl who was not so different from me? Both Shadow and I were trying, against the odds, to have some happiness in the lives fate had dealt us.

Though I had been taught to sing as a means for me to lure Lung, I worked hard to improve my voice because I genuinely loved singing. But, much as I enjoyed the adulation of my audiences at the Bright Moon Nightclub, I wanted even more to escape so I could live my own life doing what I loved, out of the control of gangsters and malicious people like Rainbow Chang.

I decided to offer to do another show with Shadow if I could track her down. Perhaps that would generate some merit for myself after years of creating bad karma.

Two days later, I wrote the magician a letter. A day later, she called me.

"Camilla!" Her voice sounded excited. "What a coincidence! I was just about to call you, when I received your letter. It's been such a long time."

"How have you been doing, and how's your finger?"

"It has healed pretty well. Except for a scar, it's basically recovered."

"I'm glad to hear that. And once again, I apologize for the accident. I owe you, Shadow."

"Let's forget about it, Camilla." She paused, then asked, "How about yourself? You didn't show up at the Bright Moon for quite a while. What happened?"

Of course I was not going to tell her the truth, so I said, "I was just generally not feeling well. I guess it was the stress from our last show, my overwork, and my worry over harming you. So I decided to take a break."

"I wish I had your freedom and luxury," she sighed.

Freedom and luxury? A little while ago I would have laughed bitterly, but now I was beginning to feel something like hope and compassion, however slight. Shadow had far less than I, and was completely on her own.

She sighed. "Even if I'm dying to work, there is no money."

Because of the failed knife-throwing show, I had insisted that we refund the audience. That had been intentional, so that she would remain poor.

She went on. "Actually I tried to get sponsorship from Master Lung. . . ."

"Did you go to see him?" I was perturbed that she had done this behind my back.

"Yes. But I was turned away by his assistant, Mr. Zhu. He never even let me talk to his boss, not even over the phone, despite my reminding him that I am your friend. So one day I went straight to Master Lung's place. But when I saw all the expensive cars parked at his place and the intimidating bodyguards, I felt hopeless and lost my nerve. Moments later I forced myself to be brave and walk back to the gate, but I was stopped by his very muscular guard, Gao. It was very scary. I felt he might shoot me if I refused to leave."

"I'm sorry to hear that, Shadow."

Some silence passed before she spoke again. "Camilla, since we're friends . . ."

"Yes?"

"I wonder if you could do me a favor."

"What is it?"

"I've been thinking, since you're Master Lung's favorite woman, maybe . . . if you wouldn't mind asking him for me . . ."

I felt sorry for Shadow. She was no fool and must have realized that the "accident" with the knife-throwing was no accident. Yet she was asking for my help, anyway. That could only mean she had no one at all to turn to in her state of desperation. Suddenly it occurred to me that both of us would be better off as allies than as enemies. Fate had dropped us both into a city populated with people who would pay for their own pleasure but not to help anyone in trouble. As the proverb says, "They will add flowers to the rich's brocade but not send coals to the needy on a frigid day." They loved me singing in my brocade gown, but what if I were begging from them on the street? Then I thought of little Jinjin's plaintive cries to me in my dream. Had I been any less heartless than Wang or Lung or Zhu or Rainbow?

Shadow was even more alone than I was. But she had gone to Lung, and who knows what she would have done with him, had she had the chance? Though I felt some sympathy for her now, she might not feel the same for me. And who could blame her, considering what I had done to her? I was still in the dusty world where no one can completely relax their guard.

If Shadow, or anyone, managed to steal Lung from me, Big Brother Wang would have me eliminated sooner rather than later. I realized that it was a mistake to have introduced her to Lung in the first place. But I didn't have to compound my mistake by asking him to meet her again.

So I said, my tone serious, "Shadow, Master Lung is in a very tense business deal with some Frenchmen, so I don't think it's a good time to ask." I paused, then spoke again. "If the only problem is money, you don't have to ask Lung. I can ask Mr. Ho to let us use the hall again." I would tell Mr. Ho that Big Brother Wang wanted me to have the show. Though Ho was certainly not happy about how the last show had ended, he would not chance refusing anything Wang wanted.

There was silence on the other line for a moment, then her voice rose, this time with a suspicious tone. "But why? Since our last show turned disastrous—"

"Exactly. Because I want to make amends to you, to our audience, and to prove that no mistake would deter Camilla, the Heavenly Songbird, or Shadow, the great magician." I paused again, this time for suspense. "Anyway, our last show was a great one, and you still have all your fingers. The blood made it that much more exciting."

She replied, her tone tainted with sarcasm, "Hmm...you might be right. But maybe if you had sliced off my whole finger, the audience would have liked it even better!"

"But I didn't, and your finger is fine. I feel terrible about what I did. But, Shadow, can we set all that aside and do another show together?"

I sensed hesitation on the other end, but I knew she'd agree. After all, she did not have much choice.

"All right, then let's meet soon to make plans."

Good. The Chinese say, "If you pay enough, you can make a dead man turn a millstone." It's always easy to work with someone who desperately needs money. Indeed, what can't you do if you have enough money? If I were filthy rich, I could do filthy things, like hire an assassin to kill both Wang and Lung, then buy a first-class passage on a luxury ship to America. In a land far from China, I could boss around a slew of servants—maids, cook, drivers, bodyguards—and live like a queen. With enough money, Chinese or American wouldn't matter.

Shadow's voice woke me from my reverie. "This will be our comeback together. I'll do my best show—The Great Escape. I submerge myself in chains in a tank of water, then escape in less than the four minutes it would take for me to drown."

"Isn't it dangerous?"

"Camilla, you think letting you throw knives at me wasn't dangerous?"

I didn't like her sarcasm but couldn't blame her for it, either. "Can you really unlock yourself in time?"

"Trust me."

So, despite our unfortunate debut show together, we plunged into preparing for our next one. However, one day a complication arose. Zhu called and told me that Lung didn't want to see Shadow's face in Shanghai anymore.

Alarmed, I asked, "Mr. Zhu, why?"

"You know Master Lung does everything for a reason."

I gripped the telephone hard as he continued. "He's missing a jade dragon statue, one of his favorite *fengshui* decorations, and he knows Shadow stole it."

"Mr. Zhu, why does Lung think she took it?"

Zhu's voice was cold. "A while ago she came to Master Lung's residence. So who else besides her?"

But she never got inside. Besides, would Shadow be so stupid as to steal from Lung?

As if he was reading my mind, Zhu's tone grew even angrier. "As Master Lung said, 'It must be Shadow. Who else can appear and disappear anywhere like a ghost? If she can make a whole castle disappear, for her to steal a small statue is as easy as flipping her hand!' If you ask me, we should get rid of her. But Master Lung won't have her killed if she gets out of Shanghai. Master Lung could have someone push her down from the Customs House tower, but this time she'd become a real corpse, ha-ha!"

I waited anxiously for him to finish laughing.

"But Master Lung said that since you and Shadow are like sisters, he'd spare her life for *you*. However, she has to disappear from Shanghai for good. And Master Lung has decided that *you* must be the one to tell her. Because you caused this by allowing her to meet Master Lung."

"But, Mr. Zhu, my new show will be totally ruined! She's in it, and many tickets have been sold. If it is canceled, no one will come to my acts again. So please ask Master Lung to let me first finish my show with her."

"All right, I'll see what I can do." He grunted, then hung up.

Twenty minutes later, Zhu called back. "Master Lung said you can do the show with her but only on one condition."

"What is it?"

"That Shadow makes herself disappear after the show—forever. Ha-ha!"

After I finished talking to the gangster, I thought for a few moments, then called Shadow to deliver the bad news. There was a long silence on the other end of the line.

Then Shadow replied, "You know I'd never do anything to offend Master Lung! Besides, none of his people would let me inside his house, so how could I have the chance to steal?"

I remained composed despite her obvious alarm. "Unfortunately no one can argue with Master Lung. Everyone knows that once he makes up his mind, he'll never change it."

A long silence was followed by Shadow's sobbing.

When her sobbing subsided, she said, "Camilla, thanks for telling me. But should I just leave now without doing the show?"

"I don't think so. Because he'll think you deliberately disobeyed him to make him lose face, and he will track you down. No magic, no matter how fantastic, can save you from Lung and his men."

She cried again. So I tried to comfort her, assuring her that by doing the show, at least she could make some money for her new life outside Shanghai.

"Camilla, why are you trying to help me now?"

"We're friends, remember?" This time, I surprised myself, because I actually meant it.

If Shadow suspected that I'd made up the whole thing, she didn't show it. Of course even if I did, she still had to leave Shanghai, because the gangster head would get rid of her anyway.

When I told Wang about the show, he agreed right away. Since my boss was still waiting for his rival's protection star to shift, he was glad that I was doing something to bring in money.

For this show, Shadow would be the star and I her assistant. I would be there mostly for decoration and to attract my fans; the physical work would be done by two male assistants. There were two reasons for me to be in the show: It would bring in some money, even though Wang would take most of it. But also, though I now felt sympathy for Shadow, given Lung's animosity toward her, for both our sakes I needed to be sure that she really left afterward.

Zhu told me that Lung was not coming, since he didn't want to give Shadow face, even though he could see her disappear with his own eyes. I didn't invite Jinying, for this time it was really Shadow's show, not mine. To my great relief, Rainbow Chang declined my invitation, from what motive I had no idea. So it seemed that, for once, heaven would let me do my job without distraction.

As expected, tickets were sold out. People, especially after the disaster of our first show, were eager to see us again; they would be equally entertained by a thrilling success or an embarrassing flop.

On Sunday night, Shadow, in a black tunic outlining her shapely, muscular body, and I in my high-slit *cheongsam,* walked onto the stage to be greeted with thunderous applause. For a warm-up, I sang three of my most popular songs, and Shadow did some simple tricks. Then the orchestra struck up a rousing melody as a big glass water tank was pushed to the center of the stage. When the clapping died down, I demonstrated that the tank would be locked on top and showed them the stocks that would hold Shadow's hands and feet.

Then I made a sweeping gesture with my gloved hand. "Does anyone want to come up and check?"

Immediately two girls in pink dresses dashed up onto the stage. They put their hands into the tank to stir the water, knocked on the glass, tugged at the locks, then smiled with satisfaction.

"So you're happy with what you saw and touched?" I asked, realizing that they were pink ladies from Rainbow Chang's entourage.

They nodded.

"You can tell our audience that this is the real thing?"

They answered "Yes" simultaneously, then went back to their seats.

The music now shifted to an eerie mood as the lights dimmed and the audience grew quiet.

I locked chains onto the hands and ankles of a pale-looking Shadow. I could not tell if this was the effect of the dim lights or her fear of another disaster. Right after I finished, the two male assistants lifted her up and, with a loud *swoosh,* released her headfirst into the tank, where she could be seen wriggling like a huge fish.

I closed the lock, then, smiling mysteriously, asked the audience, "Do you all see Miss Shadow in the water?"

A collective answer burst from the crowd. "Yes!"

Someone yelled, "She is beautiful, like a mermaid!"

After making sure that everyone had a good view of the aquatic

Shadow, I draped a black cloth over it. Gasps and whispers were ejected here and there, and everyone started to count, "One, two, three, four, five, six, seven, eight . . ." with me.

Three minutes passed, and I, with another dramatic wave of my arm, lifted the cloth.

To my astonishment, Shadow had not disappeared as we'd rehearsed but was struggling spasmodically to get out of the tank! The music stopped abruptly. Her two male assistants, armed with axes, rushed onto the stage. They struck at the glass relentlessly till finally cracks formed a spidery pattern through which the water eerily oozed like colorless blood.

When the glass finally shattered, the magician's body washed out onto the stage and did not move. What the two men fussed over was now but the magician's lifeless shadow!

A huge commotion burst out in the hall.

"Is she dead?"

"Call an ambulance!"

Women covered their faces and screamed hysterically. Children cried, and teenagers giggled. People in the front, splashed by the water and hit by shards of glass, tried to push their way out toward the exit. Others pushed them back, probably eager to get nearer to the stage so they could get a closer look at the dying magician or her corpse. Shadow's two assistants swiftly carried her backstage away from the crowd.

I yelled, "Please stay calm! An ambulance is on its way!" but to deaf ears.

Unable to placate the audience, I went backstage to check on Shadow. But I received yet another shock—the magician and her staff were nowhere to be found! Had the two men taken her body away for some obscure purpose? Or was this another of Shadow's astounding illusions? Of course I knew she planned to leave Shanghai, but it was not the plan that she would drown, thus setting off a near-riot in the hall. Now that she was gone, I was left alone to face the angry audience, the sensationalizing press, my damaged reputation, and possibly severe rebukes from Ho and Wang.

* * *

The following day, all the major newspapers reported about our second disastrous show.

Rainbow Chang's column read:

A Shadow in the Shade

Last night there was a BIG surprise at the Bright Moon Nightclub.

In what was billed as The Great Escape, Camilla, the Heavenly Songbird, locked her magician friend, Shadow, hand and foot upside down inside a water tank. Shadow was supposed to disappear from the tank while it was covered with a curtain.

But the stunt went horribly wrong. When our Heavenly Songbird lifted the drape, instead of an empty tank, the audience saw a drowning Shadow. Her assistants chopped through the glass, but the magician showed no signs of life and was quickly carried offstage.

Since then, she has not been seen. Is she in the shadowy next world with the great magicians of the past? Or did she make herself disappear, just as she once did with a castle?

We wonder: Is Shadow dead or alive? If dead, where is her corpse? If alive, where is Shadow? Maybe the disaster was but another stunning magic show?

We Shanghainese are more and more mystified by this singer-magician duo. With them, whatever seems real turns out to be fake, and what seems fake may be real.

We hope that a living Shadow will come back from this fantasy. Until then, we miss her. Does our

Camilla know the truth? We hope she will let us in on the secret.

More to follow. . . .
Rainbow Chang

I had spent the night tossing sleeplessly; then reading Rainbow's column made me even more confused. Pacing restlessly in my apartment, I noticed an envelope slipped under the door. When I opened the door, there was no one to be seen, so it must have been put there during the night. I picked it up, opened it and read:

> My dear friend Camilla,
> As you might have guessed, I am alive, and I did this trick on purpose. Why not? I'm as beautiful and talented as you, so why should heaven favor you over me? Now you know what it is like to be upstaged.
> Yes, I am jealous; that's why I wrecked the show. Now we're even. You sliced my finger; I ruined your show.
> Anyway, you told me I had to disappear, and so I did. Just not in the way you expected.
> Just when I was getting famous in Shanghai, I am forced to leave. It's really not fair.
> I swore I'd never go back to my hometown in Shandong, where there is nothing but poverty. But as we Chinese say, "As long as we don't destroy the mountains, we'll always have firewood to burn."
> We will meet again in this lifetime, but I won't say when. We might need each other someday— who knows? Everything changes, as we both know well.

Something dropped from the envelope as I continued reading.

> Here's your ring. I won't need it where I am
> going. I don't know where Master Lung's jade is,
> but I did not steal it.
>
> Your Shadow

I stooped down, picked up the ring, and slipped it onto my finger, suddenly feeling a wave of loneliness. I had been planning and scheming to get rid of Shadow for such a long time, but now that she was really gone, I felt a loss. And I wondered, what was my most worthy rival up to? Would she live out her life in anonymity? Or was she plotting another spectacular comeback?

Though I had wanted to be rid of her for so long, now I realized I would miss our pretended friendship—and our feuds.

When I told Big Brother Wang that I had finally succeeded in getting rid of Shadow, I didn't get any thanks, only a severe scolding.

My boss seemed to spit out fire as he spoke. "You already spent way too much time fussing with this Shadow! You'd better hurry up and get Lung's secret bank account numbers, and then get rid of him."

"Yes, Big Brother Wang."

"You've also spent too much time with Lung's son."

"That was to get information about his old man."

"That's a good excuse. What information did you get?"

"These things take time, Big Brother Wang."

"Maybe, but you know you don't have a lot of time left, don't you?"

"Yes, I know."

"You already passed your deadline."

"I'm so sorry, Big Brother Wang, but we were waiting for his protective star to pass. I swear I'll complete my mission soon."

"All right, I'll give you one more month, but if you still can't deliver, you're no longer needed. I mean it this time."

"I will deliver, Big Brother Wang."

*   *   *

After I hung up, I had to use all my willpower to stop myself from trembling. I still had no idea how I could eliminate Lung. And he was my lost son's grandfather. I missed my little son, Jinjin, but was not ready to follow him into the *yin* world. There was no one I could turn to for advice on such a matter. The only one I could confide in at all was Madame Lewinsky. But she could only advise me on singing and how to live my romantic life. I could hardly ask her about murdering someone.

But I wondered: Why hadn't I heard from her after my tragedy? She had always seemed so concerned about me before.

❦ 30 ❧

The Secret Villa

I believed that Rainbow Chang's line, *Maybe the disaster was but another stunning magic show,* saved the event from being labeled a total failure. Heated discussions followed her article. Some newspapers said that the show failed; others argued that it was a big success because Shadow *did* make her Great Escape. To remain enigmatic, I refused to give an opinion, despite reporters' relentless urging. Gradually, the public forgot about the disappearance as I went on with my life, singing as usual at the Bright Moon.

Jinying came by himself a few times to hear me at the nightclub, when his father and his gang were away negotiating deals in Hong Kong or elsewhere. Lung's absence was a mixed blessing for me. I did not have to flirt and have sex with the old, ruthless, slash-browed gangster. However, if he didn't show his monkey face, I had no way to finish my assignment from Big Brother Wang. And now that Lung was my son's grandfather, I had even less appetite for this evil task. But given Wang's impatience, it was either Lung or me, and of course I would rather it be Lung. But time was running out, and unless I figured something out, it would be me instead of him.

*　*　*

One day, while I was still agonizing over my mortal dilemma, Jinying called, eagerly telling me, "My father's away, and he said I can use his place till he comes back. It's a beautiful mansion. Please come, Camilla."

"But there are always lots of people going in and out of there!" I was thinking of Lung's residence in Junfu Lane.

"I don't mean my father's town house but his country villa."

I'd never heard that Lung had another house, but I shouldn't have been surprised. Now Jinying naively leaked this valuable information as carelessly as someone who forgets to turn off the tap and lets the water run.

"Where is it?"

"Outside the city, but it's too hard to explain. Anyway, I'll drive."

This might be my chance to get Lung's secrets, such as his account numbers and ledgers of his illegal activities. Maybe this would satisfy Big Brother Wang for a while, while I tried to figure out the rest.

"Of course I'd love to go there with you, Jinying."

"That's wonderful, Camilla. We will have the place all to ourselves!"

"But Jinying . . . won't there be bodyguards and servants?"

"No, it'll be all ours."

"How come?"

"I've given everyone who works there some time off. Camilla, keep this top secret. Only me, Mr. Zhu, Gao, and a few close bodyguards know about his secret hiding place."

"But your father knows that you'll be there?"

"He gave me the key. He only trusts me because he figures I have no one to tell, since I've just come back from America. Promise me you won't say anything about this to anyone."

"I promise. And you trust me enough to let me know?"

Even though I was Lung's favorite woman, *he* didn't trust me enough to take me there, but his son did. Was it love or naïveté? Probably both.

But the boss's son's answer was simply, "Camilla, I love you so much."

I quickly changed the subject. "Jinying, how about you pick me up tomorrow? And we should dress down. We don't want to attract attention."

After my conversation with Jinying, I started to think that this might be a good chance to escape from both Lung and Wang. Escaping from Lung would be dangerous for me, but so would killing him. And maybe his protective star was still shining strong. After all, he'd escaped the other times I had set him up. I was starting to think that, evil as Lung was, heaven did not want him killed, at least not yet, or not by me. And whether Lung lived or died, Wang was probably just as dangerous to me. After all, in these men's eyes, women could never be trusted. So, given what I knew and that I had served my purpose, as the Chinese say, "When the rabbits are caught, the hounds are cooked."

So at this point, escaping seemed the most likely way to prolong my stay in this dusty world. After all, of the famous Chinese thirty-six stratagems, the one universally considered best was: "When you run out of schemes, just run away." Once I was gone from the Shanghai scene, everyone would quickly lose interest in me. As the saying goes, "When the birds are gone, the bows are put away."

At first I thought I would not report to Big Brother Wang the location of Lung's villa. But I realized that that would be not just be death for me but a lingering and horrible one. If I were away for more than a day, my driver and amah would report to Wang, and he'd track me down. He was probably having me followed at all times, anyway. He'd warned me many times that his men were everywhere, but I had no idea who they were.

So with great reluctance, I called Big Brother Wang to report. Needless to say, he was more than happy to grant me this "working vacation."

"Report back to me right away as soon as you find anything."

"Of course I will, Big Brother Wang."

Then, to my great disappointment, my boss said, "I'll send a few men to follow you to the villa and stake it out, in case Lung shows up there."

So the next afternoon, Jinying came and picked me up. As he was driving us across the bridge over the Huangpu river, there was a sudden downpour, so there was not much chance to talk while Jinying concentrated on finding our way. I stared out the window, my thoughts as gloomy as the weather.

I kept looking back as discreetly as I could to see if we were being followed. I was sure Wang's men must be behind us somewhere, but they did a good job, for I couldn't tell which was the gangsters' car. Or maybe there were several, acting as camouflage for each other. After a while, I dozed off, until I was awakened by a warm hand on my thigh.

"Camilla, we're almost there."

Now Jinying drove off the main road onto a narrow path half-hidden by tall poplar trees. Water was still dripping from the boughs, but the rain had stopped. After another five minutes he pulled to a stop in front of a grand white mansion.

I looked around and felt great relief that I didn't see any other car. Had Wang's men lost us in the rain? I hoped so.

The two-storied mansion peeked at us through towering trees, shrubs, luscious plants, and exotic flowers that emitted a rich fragrance after the rain. I saw at once that the front faced the sea, and the back was toward a mountain. Lung must have chosen this place through the advice of his *fengshui* master. *Beishan Mianhai,* "backed by the mountain, faced by the sea," is the best *fengshui* location. Not only because it brings good luck, but also because the mountain in back protects, and the sea in front can be an escape route.

Jinying carried our suitcases into the foyer, dropped them, and before even closing the door kissed me passionately.

I mumbled between his mouth's attacks, "Jinying . . . where's . . . everybody else?"

He smiled mischievously. "I told you there won't be anyone here, not even a ghost. We'll have this place all to ourselves."

"Good. Then I'll make you the world's happiest man tonight."

"Why not every night?" He winked as he lifted me up and gave me a twirl.

"Every morning, too, if that's what you wish. Young Master, I'm at your service." I giggled nervously, feeling dizzy from being swung—and from the possibility of finding secret lists and bank accounts.

He put me down, his brow slightly knotted. I immediately realized that, for this lawyer who had graduated from a prestigious university in America, it was the confident and independent Camilla he loved, not the submissive and obsequious one who was his father's mistress.

"Camilla, you already make me the happiest man just by being who you are."

"Sorry, Jinying."

"No need to apologize. Just be yourself."

Not so easy, since I'd been pretending to be someone else all my life. There was an awkward silence, so I took the chance to look around. By the main entrance, huge urns stood guard. I wondered if they had been used, at least on occasion, to store dead bodies. The foyer alone was bigger than the entire apartment of a poor Shanghai family. A family probably made poor because the father had lost his life's savings at Lung's gambling house, where he also smoked the opium that Lung had bought and resold for fifty times what he paid. Lung profited still more when the bankrupted father sold his daughter to Lung's prostitution house to pay off his ever-increasing gambling debts. So, if Wang succeeded, even without my help, in getting rid of Lung, it would be Lung's own bad karma, not mine. Or so I hoped.

"Let's move," Jinying said, interrupting my thoughts.

He took my hand and led me inside the living room. Here, gold and yellow were the dominant colors, accented by Chinese red. Everything was as lavish and expensive as possible: a yellow silk sofa with a gilded frame, Chinese landscape paintings mounted on gold-speckled scrolls, a red cabinet filled with celadon plates and white jade carvings . . . everywhere there were expensive curios.

In a corner behind the sofa stood a white grand piano. Of

course this had been purchased for the young master. Even though Lung disapproved of his son's love for music, he still wanted to show his love by buying him this expensive, ostentatious object. Seeing this, I felt a wave of unutterable sadness. I had grown up without parents to love me and had lost my baby before having a chance to hold him in my arms or even see him.

The young master cast me a concerned glance. "Camilla, are you all right?"

"Yes . . . I'm fine. Why do you ask?"

"Because you look distracted and . . . sad." Jinying kissed my forehead. "Camilla, you can sit on the sofa and rest while I take the luggage to the bedroom upstairs."

"I can come and help."

"I don't need help. Just relax here, and I'll be right back."

I happily agreed, because now I could snoop around.

Then he said, "If you're hungry, we can eat soon."

"So are we driving back to the city?" In case Wang's men really had lost us on the way, I did not want to give them another chance to find us.

Oblivious of my thoughts, Jinying looked completely happy. "No, we'll eat here. I'm the cook tonight."

"I didn't know that you could cook."

Jinying smiled mischievously, and I felt dangerously attracted to him.

"There are still a lot of things we need to find out about each other, aren't there?"

This last remark gave me a small jolt of anxiety. I wanted to find out more about him and his father, but definitely not the other way around.

Preoccupied with what Wang's so-far invisible men might be doing, I was in no mood to hear Jinying chatter about his cooking, but I did my best to look interested.

"I learned to cook during my years in America. My friends and I alternated cooking for one another, sometimes even gourmet dishes. It's a lot of fun. I especially love to listen to music while I cook." He smiled meaningfully. "Camilla, I may have a rich father, but I am not spoiled."

Of course, compared to myself and Shadow, he was quite spoiled, but I kept that thought to myself. Though I was curious to know more about his life in America, I wanted to avoid our talk becoming more personal.

As soon as Jinying went upstairs with our luggage, I went to the windows to look for any sign of Wang's men. As far as I could tell, there was nobody around. Next I took a quick tour of Lung's house, starting with his spacious, book-lined library. I was sure the leather-bound books that filled its shelves were only for decoration. There seemed to be plenty of places here where he could hide secret papers. My eyes scanned the room to plan what to search when I had a chance later. I paid special attention to the bookshelves, as well as the paintings and calligraphy hanging on the walls. I also peeked into vases and other receptacles but saw nothing unusual. Next was the dining room, where there was nothing unusual either.

When I walked back to the living room, I noticed an antique scholar's table against the wall. On top of it was the usual scholar's paraphernalia: a brush stand in the shape of a mountain with three hills, a roll of rice paper, a lotus-shaped ink stone, and a set of three ink sticks engraved with the scholar's "three friends"—bamboo, pine, and plum blossom.

In the corner next to the table was an imposing grandfather clock. Although I doubted that Lung would notice or care, this seemed not to fit with the rest of the décor. Yet I found it attractive in an odd, ponderous way. Still, it seemed to belong in a Western household rather than here. The reddish brown wood was finely grained and polished so it was as smooth as a young woman's skin. The polished metal pendulum shone with a mysterious luster. But what I liked most of all was its powerful and mysterious presence.

Two red scrolls beside the clock were inscribed with a couplet, *Ten thousand taels of gold; money rushing in like a river.*

To my exploring eyes, the writing table and the grandfather clock stood out, as they should have been in the library. Moreover, the perfectly arranged scholar's objects looked more like props than for use. Then why were they here?

I studied the clock and the table for long moments before I went up to inspect the timepiece more closely. I found myself fascinated by the luminous, mirrorlike pendulum. Then in it I saw Jinying's reflection behind mine, our faces dyed a metallic bronze, as if we inhabited another world even stranger than this one. For a moment, I imagined that we lived in this pendulum world, so we'd be far away from our present tribulations. Then I realized that the pendulum was not swaying and that this other world had stopped sometime in the past.

"Jinying." I turned to face him. "Do you know that this clock's not working?"

He nodded. "I told father a few times, but he has never gotten around to having it fixed."

"But now it's of no use."

"He said he bought the clock as an antique, and someday he will have it fixed, but he likes looking at it, anyway."

"It does look nice."

"Yes, I like it, too. Only after he bought it did he realize that it was broken. But because he's superstitious, he doesn't want to say so. Besides, he can't stand to think he was cheated." He paused, then suggested, "Now let me show you the library, unless you are hungry and would rather eat something first."

Indeed I was getting hungry but was more concerned to continue my survey of the villa. So I told him I would rather see the library, not mentioning that I had already looked it over by myself.

Jinying said, "I really love to come and read here; it's so calm and quiet. But I don't have much chance, because this is where my father discusses his business with Zhu."

"Does he entertain other guests here?"

"No," Jinying answered sharply. "This house is only to relax or discuss top secret business. No one can know I brought you here. If my father finds out, I don't want to imagine the consequences."

"Don't worry, Jinying, my lips are sealed as tightly as your father's safe."

Yes, he must have a safe, but where?

As we walked around, I praised the antique furniture and various curios in the spacious room, but what really occupied my mind was discovering where Lung's money and accounts were hidden.

When we had finished looking around the library, we walked back into the living room.

Jinying said, "You must be hungry, Camilla. I will fix us some quick noodles, and then I can show you the rest."

❧ 31 ❧

The Garden

Later, after we had finished our noodles and set our chopsticks down on our gold-rimmed bowls, Jinying said, "Camilla, if you're not too tired, do you want to see the garden?"

I doubted Lung would hide anything there, but you never know.

So I feigned excitement. "The garden? Of course, I can't wait!"

"Come," he said, taking my hand.

Jinying took me through a hidden passageway toward the garden. The secrecy didn't surprise me, since Lung was paranoid about assassination, and with good reason. I suspected that this must be the route to his most secret hiding place, in case his enemies found out about the villa and pursued him here.

In a few moments we had exited from the passageway into the garden, where we found ourselves beside a huge tree.

Jinying stopped and took my hand. "Camilla, let's make a pledge under this ancient tree and have it witness our love."

Maybe he was inspired by Emperor Xuanzong and his beloved concubine Yang, who had pledged their undying love under the ancient moon. But if so, this was a dreadful omen. Didn't he know that Xuanzong, the most powerful man under heaven, was later forced by his army to kill this woman he loved so immoderately?

But then Jinying began to recite from Bai Juyi's "Song of Everlasting Sorrow," a poem that recounts Emperor Xuanzong and concubine Yang's heartbreaking tragedy:

> In the sky, we are two birds flapping our wings side by side.
> On earth, we are plants whose roots are forever
> interlocked. . . .

He stopped, and I guessed that these two famous lines were all he, a Western-educated lawyer, knew. Maybe it was a good thing, for the next two lines are:

> Even heaven and earth may perish,
> But my regret knows no end.

This was the emperor's bitter remorse, because his most beloved woman had been strangled by his most trusted imperial soldiers. He spent the rest of his life trying to contact her in the other world.

"Camilla, what's on your mind? Don't you like the poem?"

Seeing that I didn't respond, the young master pulled me into his arms and kissed me.

When he let go, I asked, "Jinying, do you really believe that love can conquer all?"

"Of course, and you don't?"

"I'm a practical person."

He shook his head. "No, you're romantic."

"How are you so sure?"

"Your singing. It is filled with love and dreams."

Was it possible that he was right about me, and I was wrong? Either way, now that he had said it, I hoped it was true.

I was silent, and finally he said, "Now that we are here together, we can live together in our dream for a few days."

"But, Jinying, I worry that dreams can turn into nightmares."

Once Wang's men arrived, they would find us quickly. Or maybe they already had. I felt my spine turning into an icicle.

Of course Jinying had no idea what was on my mind. "Camilla, what's wrong with you? Why are you always so pessimistic? Even if you have some insufferable secret, I want you to share your life with me."

I swallowed my answer, *No, you would not want to share my life if you knew the truth about me.* Instead I said calmly, "Jinying, I'm fine, really."

He seemed to know that I was not going to promise anything to him, so he silently took my hand, and we continued walking.

Jinying picked a camellia and slid it into my hair. "This is for you. Camilla. You are so beautiful, I wish—"

I put a finger across his lips. "Please, let's just enjoy this magical moment."

Silence fell between us until he spoke again, now looking happier. "Camilla, a walk in this garden is an adventure, so be prepared."

He had no idea that I was always prepared, because I had to be.

As we walked farther into the garden, I was startled to see two tigers pacing in a huge cage. Worse, they looked as if they were seriously considering me as a nice dinner, or perhaps just dim sum. I involuntarily stepped back. Now I remembered the rumor that Lung had fed his enemies and troublesome ex-mistresses to tigers.

Suddenly one of the tigers dashed to the front of the cage and roared through the metal bars as it bared its pointed teeth. Were it a human, I might have bluffed, yelling back to show that I was not afraid. But it was pointless with these beasts who lived only to satisfy their appetites. We are of no interest to them unless they are hungry.

As I was feeling a chill inside, Jinying spoke. "My father keeps these as pets. He thinks they are the most beautiful animals in the world, and he tries to imitate their fierce energy."

Jinying put a protective arm around me. "You all right? Don't worry, they cannot escape from their cage."

But of course the tigers I really feared were the human ones, Lung and Wang, and neither the police nor government officials nor anyone else could confine them.

Jinying went on. "I studied in America, so I'm not superstitious. I don't believe you can borrow an animal's energy." He smiled reassuringly. "I don't agree with my father about a lot of things. Sometimes he regrets that he sent me to Harvard.' "

In the distance, under a pink-blossoming tree, I spotted the golden and turquoise body of a peacock. As if to greet us, it gradually opened its tail like a huge fan. Rather than being soothed by the sight of this beautiful and rare creature, I felt a chill, because I imagined that the countless "eyes" on his fan were spying on me. Could Lung have recruited even this bird to spy for him?

But maybe my imaginings were wrong, for Jinying said, "My father loves the haughty way it struts around like an aristocrat. To him, the 'eyes' on the tail look like gold coins, which will bring him good fortune. But, Camilla, I believe that the peacock is spreading its tail for our happy future together. "

"I thought you said you're not superstitious."

He smiled handsomely. "But I am happy that I am with you now."

He looked so pleased, I had not the heart to challenge him about our "happy" future.

We kept walking until we came to a fine mesh cage under some trees. Within it snakes glided and writhed. A dark green one hissed at me, intimidating, spitting out a crimson venomous tongue, like a hit man's blood-dripping knife. Another snake, dark yellow with long stripes, coiled its body regally on a flat rock as if it were Guan Yin meditating on a Zen cushion. I wondered, could a snake be one of the many transformations of the Goddess of Compassion reaching out to enlighten?

Did she have a message for me? Could it be the famous Buddhist saying, "Put down the knife, then become a Buddha," meaning that even a murderer can give up evil and be redeemed?

But I thought it might be too late for me. And even if I wanted to be redeemed, did I have a chance?

It was too disturbing to think about this, so I looked up at Jinying and asked instead, "Why does he keep snakes?"

Definitely these creatures were not, like the grandfather clock, here to please the eye. I wondered if, like the tigers, they might be murder weapons to be used against Lung's enemies. But I kept this thought to myself.

"They're for food. In winter my father likes to eat snake soup. He also gulps down the bitter gall, then drinks the blood mixed with his liquor. He believes these will strengthen his blood and his virility. . . ." Jinying stopped, looking upset, no doubt because this was unpleasant reminder that I was the recipient of his father's virile energy.

Just then the snake with the blood-red tongue hissed at me again, as if saying, "I know what you are, Camilla, skeleton woman!"

For the Chinese, snakes symbolize evil. Skeleton women are referred to as having "a snake's heart and intestines."

I felt a jolt and stepped back. The Guan Yin snake still seemed to meditate placidly, as if having overcome all greed and anger.

Jinying put his arm around my shoulders again. "Let's move on. I don't want them to scare you."

But what I felt was not fear but agitation, because the two snakes seemed to know just what my mind was grappling with.

Just then the sky suddenly turned dark, and Jinying suggested we return to the house. We had just made it through the door of the villa when the rain began to pour heavily, hammering at the doors and windows like hungry ghosts frantically trying to return to the world of the living.

Once inside, Jinying led me upstairs and gave me a quick tour. There were one master bedroom and two guest rooms, all elaborately decorated. I tried my best to take in everything, but nothing seemed to be out of the ordinary. However, this was Lung's hideout, so his secrets *must* be hidden here somewhere.

But where?

Finally Jinying led me back to the master bedroom. When I sat down on the king-size bed, I saw a red velvet box next to me.

"Jinying, there's a box here."

He smiled mysteriously. "It's for you. Open it."

The elongated box opened with a click of my finger to reveal a pearl necklace and a matching bracelet. All the pearls were of matching size, roundness, and luster, glistening mysteriously in the lamplight.

"Camilla, do you like them?"

I nodded, feeling an unbearable sadness. While he was feeling amorous in this gorgeous mansion with his beloved woman, I was envisioning the terrible scene that would unfold if his father arrived here. I secretly prayed that Lung would go back to his house in Junfu Lane instead of here. But if Lung did not come here and get killed, what would happen to me? I had no idea as I listened to the rain hiss as if heaven were lamenting my doom.

"Let me put them on for you."

He turned me slightly so we both faced the mirror. "Camilla, see how flawlessly beautiful you are, just like these pearls?"

"Thank you very much, Jinying," I said softly. I didn't know what more to say, for I really wanted to take them off right away. They implied that I was flawless, but I was anything but; I was bad and poisonous, a skeleton woman, period.

I wanted to scream to Jinying, "Young Master, even the snake knew who I really am! How come you can't see that?"

But of course Jinying had no idea what was going on in my mind or in my life. He looked at us in the mirror with an ingenuous smile.

He held my shoulders with both hands, then rested his chin on my head. "I love you, Camilla."

I smiled back at his reflection but said nothing.

"All right. I'm going to cook now. You look tired, Camilla, so why don't you take a nap? I'll come up to wake you for dinner."

This was the sort of opportunity I had been waiting for. "I'll nap for an hour." I said, while having no intention of doing so at all.

Once he disappeared down the stairs, I began to snoop around. Fifteen minutes later, after looking everywhere—in drawers, under the beds, inside the lamps, behind paintings, and even the water tank inside the bathroom—I still had not found a safe or anything else that looked like a secure hiding place.

When I heard Jinying calling me from downstairs, I hurried back to lie on the bed, feigning sleep. As soon as he entered the room, I pretended that I had just awakened.

"You already finished cooking?" I asked, groggily rubbing my eyes.

"Not quite. But if you're not too hungry yet, there's another interesting place for me to show you."

"Is there even more here to explore? What is this place?"

"You'll soon find out. Come on," Jinying said, pulling me off the bed.

In no time we had climbed down another flight of stairs into the basement. Jinying threw a switch, flooding the underground chamber with light and revealing its grandeur. Myriad crystals sparkled on an enormous chandelier. The densely grained floor, though covered with a light layer of dust, was polished to perfection, like a mirror reflecting its own illusions. A few paintings were scattered along the walls.

As I was wondering what was this room for, the young master went to a corner where a gramophone sat upon an antique Chinese table. Immediately the space was filled with a dreamy waltz. Jinying walked back to me, pulled me close to him, and we began to swirl.

"This is my father's private ballroom."

"Jinying, if this is a private mansion, why did your father build a ballroom—surely not to hold parties?"

"Of course not. He built this many years ago for my mother. They loved to practice their dance steps here. It was their secret paradise."

"Oh, how romantic." Did Lung really have a tender side? If so, I had never seen it.

"Then what happened? Why did he send her away?" I asked.

"I think my father just got tired of her."

But the son looked like he would never lose his romantic feelings for me, as he continued to waltz me around the polished floor that his parents had twirled across so many years ago. I felt exultant, though I tried to tell myself it was but a false happiness induced by the sumptuous music and the glittering chandelier. If only the rest of my life were but a bad dream from which I was now awakening . . .

❦32❦

The Grandfather Clock

Jinying turned out to be a good cook. He'd brought some groceries and fixed steamed fish, a simple dish but one requiring exact timing. He also stir-fried some rice with mushrooms and other dried vegetables. A plain meal but quite satisfying.

After dinner, he led me to the white grand piano I had noticed earlier. He wanted to hear me sing, but I insisted that he play first. As he stroked the keyboard, music spread through the room like honey. Judging from Jinying's entranced expression, it was in music that he found his soul. His eyes closed, and his lips trembled; he looked as if he were about to experience a sexual climax, not through a woman's mysterious gate but through the mystical interplay of musical notes.

Suddenly I saw the man's hardships, so different from mine, with greater clarity. He loved music but could not become a concert pianist because his father despised this talent and forced him to study law. He loved a woman but could not make his love public, nor even reveal it to his own father, a father who provided him with expensive luxuries but not the luxury he craved most—freedom to follow the life he wanted.

But Jinying had never been without all the luxuries he thought he despised. If one day he were stripped of them, including the Steinway concert grand on which he was now expressing himself so movingly, could he subsist by just making love with his music and me?

Jinying looked happy, seemingly pushing our difficulties into a remote chamber of his brain. After he finished his first piece, a Chopin nocturne, his elegant fingers went on to shape the same composer's ostentatious Polonaise in A-flat Major. Then he surprised me by moving on to something simple: Mozart's Sonata in C Major.

Madame Lewinsky had told me that Mozart, though living a miserable and abused life, had never expressed even a hint of his sufferings in his works. His music always seems to declare that human life is truly worth living. In his music was always happiness, never sighs nor tears.

Was there any hope that someday my life would be like Mozart's music, rather than his life?

As Mozart's sonata was reincarnated under Jinying's fingers, tears stung my eyes. The cheerful mood of the first movement evolved into the darker but mellow movement of the second, then lightened again into the third, like a bad dream dissolving in the early dawn.

Jinying stopped playing to touch my cheek. "Why are you sad, Camilla? Please stop shutting yourself off to me and to our love."

I shook my head, trying to seem tranquil. "I'm not sad. Just moved by your beautiful playing."

"Camilla, I really want to know you more. Is it about my father?"

Of course there was no way I could confess to him anything about myself..

So I said, "Jinying, I'm fine now, happy to be with you." To further distract him, I asked, "Now why don't I sing while you accompany me?"

I sang a few familiar Chinese pop songs, then told Jinying I'd try the famous aria from *La Traviata*. I felt a special connection with this opera, named for its fallen heroine. Would I, the skeleton woman, end up any better off than the protagonist, Violetta? Would I be saved by my spy training in the four "nothingnesses": no family, no feelings, no attachments, no morality? I was beginning to think not, because these had brought me nothing but loneliness and hardship.

So as the first few notes of this melancholy aria sounded, I found myself trying to charm a man I knew I shouldn't care about.

> We wait for someone we can hold,
> We pray we will never be alone.
> When you leave, a part of me leaves with you.
> But like the sun without the moon,
> It's half my life without you here. . . .

After I finished, Jinying immediately sang the lines by Alfredo, the young man who would not succumb to his father's demand that he leave Violetta.

> Love is the beating pulse of the universe,
> The torment and delight of my heart. . . .

When the last note vanished like a dream, Jinying stood up from the piano, pulled me to him, and kissed me fervently. To my surprise, I kissed him back with the same intensity.

After a long and searching meeting of tongues, the young master pulled his head back and looked into my eyes as his hand stroked my cheek.

I asked, "Is my makeup smeared?"

He looked a bit surprised. "No . . . Camilla, you're crying. . . ."

Before I could respond, my lips were again covered by Jinying's warm ones. I felt myself let go to enjoy this man's love. The sky might be about to fall, but I would still savor these stolen moments.

Jinying held me gently, stirring something inside me that I'd not known existed. Until now my world had held nothing but indifference and deceit. Stimulated by Jinying's human feelings, I felt insatiable, like a ghost in hell thirsting for water. As if drowning, I grasped him desperately and pressed my orphaned body against his cologne-fragranced one. Tenderly he lifted me up and carried me toward the stairs leading up to the bedroom.

Jinying savored my body in a way none of my other lovers had. He was like a kitten playing with its spool, or a child on Chinese New Year. I squirmed as his tongue, like a greedy lizard, crawled all over my body. His hands, freed from the restraints of the keyboard, now seemed, like those of a beggar, to be importuning my body for more and more.

As his swollen sex plunged its way inside my mysterious gate, he exclaimed, "Camilla, let me die right now a happy man. . . ."

Unwittingly he had just given voice to what I most feared. So I put a finger across his shivering lips. "Shh . . . Jinying. Please don't say inauspicious things like this."

After love, we cuddled against each other, but Jinying looked sad.

"What's the matter, Jinying?"

"I love you very much, Camilla, but . . . why do you stay with my father?"

"I told you, no woman can afford to say no to your father. I still love this life, even though it's been nothing but misery and struggling to survive." I realized that I'd just spoken from my heart, something I often thought I did not have.

"But, Camilla, don't you feel any joy being with me?"

I was afraid to say it out loud, so I said, "How can we have a future together?"

"Camilla, do you love me?"

I was even more afraid to say this, so somewhat guiltily I tried to put off this line of questioning. So I asked, "Jinying, can we not engage in a discussion about something so abstract but just enjoy our moments together?"

"Camilla, this is not a discussion of philosophy, but of feelings, *our* feelings. My love for you is *real,* not abstract. My heart is aching right now."

"Jinying, if you want me to be honest, then I'll tell you—I don't really know how I feel anymore." Again, I regretted what I'd just said. Why couldn't I *really* have been honest and poured out my heart to him?

"Do you like my father?"

"Don't be ridiculous!"

His mention of his father only served to remind me that I needed to figure a way out of my predicament as quickly as possible. My only hope to placate Big Brother Wang was to uncover Lung's secrets.

But meanwhile, there were still Jinying's feelings to deal with.

"Sorry, Camilla, I didn't mean to—"

"It's okay. I need time. . . ."

"I understand. . . ."

While he went into the bathroom, I went down to the kitchen to get him a glass of milk. When he came back, he drank the milk and soon fell asleep, having not suspected that I had added a sedative. I felt terrible deceiving him in yet another way, but I had no choice.

While he slept soundly, I took the opportunity to more fully explore the villa. I began upstairs but, finding nothing, stepped softly down the stairs to continue my search for the secret hiding place I was certain must exist. I even looked inside the radio to see if it was a safe in disguise. But still no luck.

Frustrated, I sat down on the living room sofa to think. If Lung's safe was not in this secret mansion, then I would probably never be able to find it. I got back up and paced around the room, racking my spy's brain as I scrutinized everything.

Now I was worried about the time. Maybe I should go back upstairs, in case Jinying woke up and found that I was not in bed. I looked at my wrist but saw only my pearl bracelet. My watch had been left somewhere in the tangle of clothes on the bedroom floor. I glanced up at the grandfather clock, only to be reminded that it was not working. The two hands had not budged from 10:38.

Feeling tired and frustrated, I sat back down on the sofa. Then my eyes again landed on the antique timepiece, looking forlorn in its lonely corner. It was almost six feet tall, with a reddish dark wood case and a white face that seemed to be reflecting on past glories. The pendulum was still; otherwise the gentle swinging would have generated some *qi,* as well as dreamy music when it sounded the hours.

It was a gorgeous piece of craftsmanship. But, however pleasing to the eye, a clock should still tell the time. Lung had no tolerance for failure. Why, then, would he keep something that failed to do its job? He certainly would not pay for a beautiful woman if her gorgeous legs were stuck together and refused to spread, so why pay for a clock that didn't move? So Lung must have a use for this clock; I just did not know what it was. In the luminous metal I studied my own reflection, a portrait of bewilderment and anxiety.

My eyes strayed to the nearby writing table. Again I studied the scholar's items on top—rice paper, ink stone, ink sticks, mountain-like brush stand—and again I had the sense that these were props rather than functional objects.

I went to take a closer look, and reached to lift up the brush holder. To my surprise, it refused to budge! Looking more closely, I saw that a small hole had been drilled in the wood behind the brush holder, with what looked like an electrical wire running through it. I tried pushing down hard on the middle hill. There was a whirring sound, and the front panel of the grandfather clock swung open. Inside was what I had been looking for—a safe!

But my elation subsided as quickly as it came. Yes, I'd found the safe, but not the combination to open it.

So, what to do? I had to think fast, before Jinying woke up!

But there was no way I could guess the combination. Lung had many favorite numbers that he thought were lucky for him. As I racked my brain to remember them, my eyes continued to study the clock. Then it was as if a bomb exploded in my head. The hands, pointed to ten thirty-eight—a ten, a three and an eight. The most lucky of lucky numbers.

Yes!

Again I dashed to the clock. Just then I heard Jinying's sleepy voice from upstairs. "Camilla, what are you doing? Please come back to bed. I miss you."

Obviously he had no idea what I was up to. I hoped he was too groggy from the sedative to think clearly. I exhaled deeply, then dashed upstairs to the master bedroom, where he was sitting up, rubbing his eyes.

"Jinying, go back to sleep. I'll be back in a moment. I just have to go to the bathroom." I gently eased him back down onto his pillow.

"Give me a kiss."

As soon as I did, he fell asleep again, like an obedient child.

I tiptoed back down to the living room and dashed over to the clock. Hands shaking, I twirled the handle in order to 1-0-3-8 and felt a wave of relief as I heard the sound of gears turning and saw the door swing open. I peered inside. At long last I was face-to-face with Lung's secret stash. Finally my long years of sweating and agonizing were about to be rewarded. Inside were piled bundles of documents, gold and silver coins, thick wads of American dollars, what looked like stocks and bonds, and most important, Lung's bank books and a big jade seal.

My plan had always been to photograph everything with my lipstick camera so that when Lung came back, he wouldn't suspect a thing. But now I changed my mind. Why photograph them when I could just as easily make off with them? So I made a quick detour into the kitchen, where I had seen a burlap rice bag. I dumped the rice out and sped back into the living room. Holding the bag open, I started to fill it with bundles of cash and as many gold coins as I thought I could carry. Then I took the bank books and, most important, the big jade seal. The seal was literally the key to Lung's bank accounts, but now it would be the key to my own freedom. With the seal I could go to the bank and draw out all his money. Although he must have secret accounts elsewhere, there was more in these than I would ever need. More than enough for me to seek a life outside Shanghai, even in America.

I thought I was pretty clever to have figured out that the combination to the safe was 10-3-8, the time at which the clock was stopped. The pronunciation of 10 is *shi,* which rhymes with *must,* 3 is *san,* which rhymes with *living,* and 8 is *ba,* which rhymes with *fortune.* So these numbers meant, "must bring life and wealth." I smiled to myself, because now these numbers meant my good fortune, instead of Lung's.

Now that I had what I wanted, I wished I could just sneak out of the mansion and make my escape. But it was now past midnight, and, though I knew how to drive, I had no idea where I was or how to get back to Shanghai. Nor could I bring myself to leave Jinying without saying good-bye. I knew if I did, he would go mad with worry. I did not want to be alone again, but it seemed to be my karma.

✀ 33 ✀

The Master's Return

Though I knew I needed to do something, and quickly, I allowed myself a few moments to gloat over my loot, relishing my pending life as a free woman. But then suddenly the phone rang, startling me. I couldn't possibly answer it myself; if it were Lung or Zhu, how could I explain my presence here? As I hesitated, I saw Jinying walk groggily down the stairs, then rush to the telephone and snatch up the receiver. He had not noticed the open safe, so I pushed it closed as quietly as I could, hid the burlap bag behind me, then sat still, listening carefully to the one-sided conversation.

"Yes, Father, how are you doing?"

"You are? When?" He cast me an extremely worried and disappointed look.

"All right. Yes, of course, Father."

He hung up, then turned to me, his face as pale as a ghost's. "My father is coming back now."

"He's coming here? How come?" I felt my heart stop like the grandfather clock.

"The gun deal fell through, and a few of his people were wounded, so he's coming back early, and he wants to hide out here for a while."

"When will he be here?"

"I don't know exactly; he didn't say." He went on, looking extremely upset. "Camilla, there's not a lot of time. You have to pack and leave. If he comes here and finds you, we'll both be dead!"

He collapsed onto the sofa next to me.

"Jinying," I blurted out involuntarily, "why don't we leave together?"

"Do you mean it? My father expects me to greet him when he arrives. I told him I would be here, practicing the piano."

"Let's leave Shanghai! Together! Now!" Before he had a chance to respond, I added. "Jinying, this is the best time to escape from your father's control."

"I don't have much cash. Besides, where will we go, and what will we do?"

"I have money, a lot. Why don't we leave right away?"

"Why are you carrying a lot of money?" he asked, looking puzzled.

Of course I was not going to tell him the truth. "Jinying, please, you have been asking me to go away with you. This is our chance!"

"But what about if my father chases us down?"

Of course I knew that Wang's men were also likely to arrive soon if they had not already.

"They won't find us if we go somewhere far away, like America or Europe," I said, while giving him a push. "Go pack now! I'll wait right here. Go!"

I needed a moment to think. What if I walked out of this mansion *now* and left the two gangs to confront each other? If both gangster heads got killed, then neither one would chase me down. That meant I'd be totally free. But what if they killed Jinying too?

As I tried to clear my head, I was stunned by thunder so loud, it seemed as if both the sky and my eardrums were splitting. In no time, raindrops fell like dried beans, hitting hard on the windows and hissing as if the garden's angry snake was directly outside. I looked out the window, but everything was obscured by curtains of water. Maybe Guan Yin was finally having mercy on me and was sending the rain so I could escape with the strategy, "Fool heaven and cross the sea."

Just then Jinying dashed down the stairs carrying our suitcases.

He looked as pale as a ghost. "I think I saw a car coming. You'd better hide right away!"

But it was too late. We heard fists pound at the door, echoing the murderous thunder. Jinying dashed to the door. A group of tough-looking men I did not recognize marched inside, weapons in hand. But not Master Lung.

I quickly realized that these were not Lung's underlings, but Big Brother Wang's! Had they just tracked us down? More likely they somehow knew that Lung and his entourage were coming here now.

One of the would-be murderers pointed a gun at Jinying's head, then dragged him under the piano, banging his head. The rest of the men, about ten of them, hid behind the furniture and the huge urns. Then, when no one seemed to be paying much attention to me, I dragged my burlap bag and purse and squeezed myself into a cabinet by the entrance. My contortionist training might now save my life!

In a moment we heard cars swishing through the rain and pulling to a stop. I opened the cabinet door slightly to peek and saw the door open to let in Lung, Zhu, Gao, and several of Lung's men.

For once they were taken completely off guard as a barrage of gunfire exploded from Wang's assassins. Through the smoke I thought I saw Lung collapse, followed by one of his bodyguards.

In the confusion I could hear screaming but could not tell if my patron was dead or, if wounded, how severely. Now bullets seemed to fly everywhere, resounding like the wails of hungry ghosts bent on revenge. Blood splattered on walls, mirrors, and furniture. Bodies lay on the floor, some writhing, some motionless with wide-open, sightless eyes. The floor was covered with shards of glass, wooden splinters, and blood.

There was another clap of thunder, and the lights suddenly went out. I sprang from my cabinet, grabbed my bag and purse, and found Jinying, who was lying fazed but uninjured under the piano, where he had been pushed by Wang's man. I helped him to his feet. He shook his head, as if to clear his brain, then led me through the kitchen to a back exit. Running through the soaking rain, we quickly reached his car and climbed in. In a moment he had started the engine and floored the gas pedal. The car shot out as if from a cannon into the cover of the darkness and pouring rain. Amid the thunder and confusion, it was unlikely that the fighting gangs within were even aware of our escape.

Finally, when we were a few miles away from the villa, Jinying pulled to a stop off the road. Big beads of perspiration oozed down his forehead. His hands trembled on the steering wheel, their knuckles the color of his piano's white keys.

He turned to me, a muscle in his face twitching. "Camilla, what happened? Did you tell those people about my father's villa?"

I didn't answer his question but said, "Let's go to the harbor right now and take the next ship leaving Shanghai!"

We had been lucky to escape the killing spree, but whichever gang won would be certain to come after us, once they realized that I had emptied Lung's safe. And if Wang won, Jinying would be in danger, too.

He looked at the rain pelting his window, then back at me. "Camilla, why are you so calm? Do you never feel anything? A lot of people are dead, maybe even my father!"

"But you said you hated him and wanted him dead."

"You . . . don't understand. Who are you, Camilla? Did you send for those men to kill my father? Answer me!"

Maybe this was the moment to tell him the truth about myself. I wouldn't be in any worse danger right now if I did. I suddenly hoped that if he knew all about me, he would still love me and escape with me from Shanghai. But despite his previous protestations of hating his father, it was clear that he loved him, after all. Would he choose me over his comfortable life here, or would he instead tip off his father, assuming he was alive, to my escape plan? If Lung had survived the shootout, he would stop at nothing to track me down and get his treasure back, then kill me in the most agonizing way possible. Jinying's choice would decide if I lived or died.

I desperately wanted to reveal my secrets and stop this life of lies and deceit. But I couldn't bear the thought that he'd suddenly stop loving me, maybe even shun me like a leper.

So I said, "Jinying, I don't know who I am anymore. . . ."

His tone softened. "Camilla, you are the best thing in my life. . . ."

His last sentence seemed to draw out my whole life's miseries like a magnet a needle. My tears now flooded down my cheeks, as if the dam holding back my emotions had finally collapsed.

Jinying held me. "Camilla, no matter what happens, I will never love anyone as I love you."

It was the only time I had ever felt my heart truly touched by a man. For a moment, despite our present danger, I felt a glimpse of freedom.

Jinying spoke again. "Camilla, you owe me at least to tell me what happened."

"Jinying, everyone knows I am your father's mistress. And everyone knows you are his son. Unfortunately, your father has many enemies. Any of them could have followed us there." This was the truth, but by no means all of it.

I was about to go on, but then we heard a car speeding in our direction, and Jinying called out, "Let's get out of here!"

But it was too late.

Zhu jumped from his car, dashed to ours, swung open the door, and pulled Jinying out onto the ground.

Jinying's hand moved to cover his head as he yelled to me, "Camilla, run!"

"But you're hurt! I can't leave you!"

"He's not after me, only you. Go!"

He tried to pull Zhu away from me but was knocked down again.

Now Zhu dashed around to open my door and tried to drag me out by my hair.

One hand covering his bleeding head, Jinying struggled to get up and again grabbed at Zhu. "No! No! Mr. Zhu, please don't hurt her, I beg you. I'll give you anything."

Zhu laughed sarcastically. "What can you give me, huh, Young Master? Without your father, you're a good-for-nothing dandy. Now I'm giving the orders—you understand?"

Jinying flung himself against Zhu, who stumbled for a moment and let go of my hair. I quickly pulled my door closed.

Just then another car screeched to a stop in front of us. Gao jumped out, pushed Zhu away, and jumped into the driver's seat next to me.

As Gao was reaching to close the door, Zhu lifted his gun to point at us, but Gao's gun was ready, and he shot at Zhu, who began to fire back. Without a pause Gao hit the accelerator, and our car sped away, leaving Jinying in the rain with Zhu's body.

I turned to Gao. "What are you doing?!"

He didn't reply, either because the rain had drowned out my question or because he was concentrating on driving through the storm.

Finally the car pulled to a stop. I looked out and saw a pier extending into the dark water of the harbor. A huge ship loomed in the distance.

Gao turned to me, then pointed to the ship. "Miss Camilla, that ship will sail for Hong Kong tomorrow night. As soon as it is daylight, come here to buy a ticket, and hide yourself in your stateroom. You are now a free woman."

It was then that I saw his shirt was soaked with blood.

I blurted out, "Gao, you were shot!"

He said calmly, "I know, Miss Camilla. I'll go to a doctor later. But I had to drive you to safety first."

"Why don't you take off your shirt and let me bandage you?"

He shook his head. "Heaven will decide if my time is up. "

I reached out to unbutton his shirt. "Please, Gao, let me . . ."

He took my hand and gently pulled it away. He started the car again, and in a few minutes we stopped in front of a dingy building with a sign announcing it was a hotel.

"You can stay here tonight; just stay out of sight. I need to go back now to help my wounded men and pick up Master Lung's son. I haven't seen Lung, so he might have escaped. I need to look for him too. You must leave, Camilla. I don't think we will meet again in this life."

"What about Master Lung?"

"You must leave now. Please."

"I'll go back with you."

"That would be suicide for you. I know you're worried about Master Lung's son. I am sure he's not seriously injured, just a cut on his head."

He placed his hand on my arm. "Don't worry, Miss Camilla, no one will know about you and him. I will never tell."

"You knew . . . ?" I heard the alarm in my own voice.

"I've always been watching out for you. I've seen how you two look at each other."

So Gao had known all along but still protected me. Despite his oozing wound, the bodyguard took my face in his hands and kissed me deeply.

"Good-bye, and take good care of yourself. I love you, Camilla."

I felt an urge to smooth his thick eyebrows, which seemed to be able to absorb all the wind and dust of this unsatisfactory world.

He touched my face with the tips of his big, callous fingers, then said softly, "Now leave." I was saddened that it was not this tough yet caring man but another whom I loved.

Gao used the same hand to gently help me out of the car. Then he sped away in the wet darkness before I had a chance to tell him, "I hope we will we see each other again!"

After a fitful sleep interrupted by dreams of bullets and falling bodies, the first thing I did upon awakening was go to Lung's bank. In order not to attract suspicion, I had decided to take out just enough for my future, leaving a large amount remaining. Though I was nervous, as soon as I had pressed his seal onto the forms, the teller went to the safe to begin counting out what was now my money.

However, I felt I couldn't just leave without knowing the fate of Jinying and Gao, the only two men in this world who had ever loved me. So I hired a taxi and described as best I could where Lung's mansion might be. After almost three hours' guessing and searching, the driver finally spotted the place. Policemen were everywhere.

I stuffed a small stash of cash into the driver's hand. "Can you get close to the place, so I can see what is going on?" He turned around and eyed me suspiciously. Then he shrugged and drove closer to the villa, where a gruff-voiced policeman asked what we wanted. Fortunately, since I wore large sunglasses and had tied a scarf around my head, I was unrecognizable as the Heavenly Songbird.

"Nothing's happening here. Just move on."

The driver shrugged at me again, as if to say, "What did you expect?" and I told him to take me back to Shanghai.

I wanted to ask him to drive me around a little longer so I could see for the last time the Bright Moon Nightclub, Madame Lewinsky's home, and a few other places that had been important in my life, but I thought it would be too dangerous, so I asked him to drive me to the pier.

That evening I lounged on the deck of the luxury liner, sipping a whiskey and watching Shanghai recede in the twilight like a fading dream.

Or a nightmare.

Epilogue

As the ship glided over the South China Sea, questions clung to me like hungry ghosts. What had happened to Jinying? Would Gao be all right? What about Lung? He might have escaped, or he might be dead. Though I had shared his bed, I could not summon up any tender feelings for the gangster. Nor for Big Brother Wang, who had rescued me from the orphanage but was ready to dispose of me when it suited his convenience. As far as I could tell, he had not been at the shootout. Probably he had just let his men take all the risk. The big question of course was if either of the gangsters would send people after me, or if they were too preoccupied with their own rivalry. I studied the waves, but they had no answers for me.

As all these questions were swimming through my mind, I spotted the newspaper being read by the man in the next deck chair. When I read the headline, my heart beat like the surging waves.

Massacre at Luxury Villa, Gangsters Dead

As soon as the man had finished reading, I gathered up my best smile and politely asked if I could borrow his paper.

The article read:

> Last night there was a shootout between rival gangs at a luxury villa rumored to belong to Master Lung, head of the Flying Dragons. Ten bodies were found. It is likely that some others were wounded but got away. Several of the dead were suspected members of Big Brother Wang's Red Demons gang.
>
> There is no news of Master Lung. He has disappeared, and so has his chief bodyguard, Gao. His right-hand man Zhu was found dead several miles away from the villa.
>
> Lung Jinying, the master's son, was also injured but will be released from hospital soon. Our reporter asked him about the shooting and whether he suspected that a traitor had tipped off the shooters, but he said he knew nothing about it.
>
> Police Chief Li promised a full and complete investigation into this atrocity. However, with other suspected gang shootings in Shanghai, the perpetrators have never been arrested.
>
> Last night, the police searched for Camilla, known as the Heavenly Songbird, to inquire about her patron's whereabouts. But she also was nowhere to be found. Police Chief Li is investigating the possibility that she had something to do with this gangster war and expects that she will be found soon.

To my great relief, the buildings of Shanghai were now dots in the distance as the ship rose and fell on the swells of the open sea. If the police had guessed that I was on this ship, they would have come after it by now. Anyway, we would soon be in international waters. By the time they figured it out, if they ever did, I would be in the British Crown Colony of Hong Kong.

I continued to flip the pages until my eyes landed on Rainbow Chang's column:

The Disappeared Shadow

Since the disastrous Great Escape show, we haven't heard from the magician Shadow. Rumors fly. Some say she took her own life out of humiliation; others say that she went back to where she came from, which is who knows where. Anyway, we miss her and hope one day she'll reappear as dramatically as she disappeared.

As for Camilla, we haven't heard from her, either. Maybe she's also hiding out somewhere to restore her energy. But we think she may never show up in Shanghai again. Some doctors say that during her contortion show, when she couldn't disentangle her body, she might have suffered from too little oxygen, her brain is a little fogged. Maybe that's why she was willing to be Shadow's assistant at the Great Escape show and let her rival be the star.

Will our beloved, legendary Heavenly Songbird ever fly back to her nest in Shanghai and massage our eardrums again?

I definitely hope so. For we all want to know the secrets behind that mysterious face.

More to follow. . . .
Rainbow Chang

So I was leaving with another sly dig from Rainbow, this time that my brain was damaged. But what did it matter? In a few days I would be in Hong Kong, no longer the Heavenly Songbird but also no longer Lung's mistress or Big Brother Wang's spy. And Rainbow could write whatever she wanted about me; I would never even read it.

Maybe someday I would travel to the Gold Mountain—America. Wherever I ended up, I would place an altar for my parents and make offerings to them to appease their souls. But I would not make offerings to my baby boy, Jinjin. Because he had come to me so often in my dreams, I hoped that he was alive somewhere. After all, Madame Lewinsky would not show me his little body, so I wondered if she was hiding him somewhere to raise as her own. I wanted to think so, because then he was being cared for, even though, like me, he would never know his own mother.

As I looked out over the sea stretching endlessly away from me, I felt a tremendous sadness. Yes, I'd soon have many things in life—except the man I loved and who loved me even more. But at least I had been loved, and by two men, not just one.

I also found myself wondering about my two skeleton sisters, Shadow and Rainbow. Would we cross paths again someday? If so, would we be friends or enemies or both?

But for me there would be no going back. Even if Lung was dead, whoever succeeded him as boss would need to regain face for the gang by finding the woman who had taken their treasure. And even if little Jinjin were living there, would I be able to recognize him?

But we do not decide these things; heaven does, never telling us her plans in advance.

SKELETON WOMEN

Mingmei Yip

ABOUT THIS GUIDE

The questions and discussion topics that
follow are intended to enhance your
group's reading of this book.

Discussion Questions

1. How does Camilla's training to have no emotion affect her life as a singer and as a spy?

2. What strategies does Camilla employ to survive, despite being a pawn in the struggle between the two most powerful gangster heads in Shanghai?

3. The biggest change in Camilla's life is from an emotionless woman to someone who can finally love. Which of her experiences result in this change and how?

4. What is the relationship between Camilla and Madame Lewinsky? What happens when Camilla goes into labor and turns to Lewinsky for help? What happens to Camilla's baby and why? How does this experience affect Camilla?

5. Why does Master Lung proclaim Camilla his lucky star? What do you think about being a lucky star in someone else's life?

6. What kind of person is Master Lung's son, Jinying? How has being the son of a gangster affected his character?

7. The feud between Camilla and the magician, Shadow, is both physical and mental. Why are they enemies, and who do you think emerges as the winner?

8. What is the role of the gossip columnist Rainbow Chang in Shanghai's gangster world, and what does she want from Camilla?

9. Why does Camilla attempt suicide, and how does this change her?

10. Camilla cares for both Gao and Jinying. How would you characterize her feelings for each of them?

11. What meaning does the scene from the opera *Peony Pavilion* have for Camilla?

12. What do you think about the ancient Chinese strategies in the *Art of War* and the *Thirty-Six Stratagems,* and how do they apply in real life?

13. What is the outcome of Camilla's plan to kill Master Lung?